BALCONIES,
BALLROOMS,
BURNING DESIRES

New Orleans, splendid and spoiled, had salons to rival the grandest in France and plantations more vast than Europe might dream of. There, for a price, one could buy treasures from every corner of the Earth.

But there was not enough money in all the world to buy Leah's heart. Though they said she was born to be kept as mistress by some fine Louisiana gentleman, she refused to be humbled—

Not by Charles Anderson, whose savage lust was just the beginning of his villainy. Not by General Benjamin Butler, whose Yankee troops were now an Occupation Army. And not by Baptiste Fontaine, though his very touch was fire to Leah's soul.

Avon Books are available at special quantity discounts for bulk purchases for sales promotions, premiums, fund raising or educational use. Special books, or book excerpts, can also be created to fit specific needs.

For details write or telephone the office of the Director of Special Markets, Avon Books, 959 8th Avenue, New York, New York 10019, 212-262-3361.

BARBARA FERRY JOHNSON

DELTA BLOOD

AVON
PUBLISHERS OF BARD, CAMELOT, DISCUS AND FLARE BOOKS

DELTA BLOOD is an original publication of Avon Books.
This work has never before appeared in book form.

AVON BOOKS
A division of
The Hearst Corporation
959 Eighth Avenue
New York, New York 10019

First Avon Printing, April, 1977

AVON TRADEMARK REG. U.S. PAT. OFF. AND IN
OTHER COUNTRIES, MARCA REGISTARDA,
HECHO EN U.S.A.

Printed in the U.S.A.

WFH   21   20   19   18   17   16   15

For my children: William Green, Anna Starr, and Charlotte Lee;

For Ward, who has become a son;

For little Anna "Blue Shoes" . . .

And for all who believe

Acknowledgments

My gratitude to:

Bill Mitchell, for so generously allowing me to borrow from his valuable library of Civil War literature;

Helen Jordan and Margaret Sites, for always finding the very book I needed; and

Lucy Turney-High and Dr. Harry Turney-High, for sharing their vast knowledge of and love for New Orleans.

PART I

The *Vieux Carré*

Chapter One

WALKING OUT ONTO THE BALCONY, I turned my back
on the blazing lights of ornate chandeliers and heavy
silver candelabra in the adjacent ballroom. My face
was flushed, and my heart pounded like the warning
drum of an advancing enemy. For a minute I thought
I was going to faint, until a freshening breeze from
Lake Ponchartrain blew across my face and I felt my
cheeks begin to cool. Leaning against the wrought-iron
railing, I looked into the courtyard, one flight below,
where flowering trees colored the soft spring evening
with their fragile blooms and perfumed the air with an
almost imperceptible fragrance. Under their shadowy
branches, couples sat around a number of small tables,
some joking and laughing, others deeply absorbed in
more intimate conversations. All were sipping cordials
or eating fruit ices.

I ran my tongue over my parched lips and fingered
the gold locket hanging from a narrow neck ribbon. My
mouth was dry, partially from the exertion of dancing
in the overheated ballroom, but more from fear and
loathing. A tangy-sweet lemon *glacé* would be refreshing, but I did not want to sit alone at a table. My only
refuge at the moment was this far corner of the balcony,
shielded from anyone in the courtyard by the branches
of a large magnolia and from the ballroom by the
curve of the balcony itself.

How long could I remain undiscovered, I wondered.

3

How long before a pair of lovers would seek the privacy this corner of the balcony afforded?

It was not a tryst I sought this night; it was freedom and solitude.

For the moment I was alone, and I found myself looking out over the city. In the immediate distance, the St. Louis Cathedral loomed up in the darkness against the city lights like a protective guardian. Beyond the cathedral was Jackson Square, not as busy now as in the daytime when it was the hub of all activity in the *Vieux Carré*. But if the park was more quiet, the rest of the city was not. From Royale and Bourbon streets rose the voices and laughter of people leaving Antoine's or the Paris Opera after an evening of dining or the theatre. Farther away, along the levees of the Mississippi, Negro workers labored far into the night and sang as they loaded goods on ships preparing to sail as far upriver as St. Louis or out into the Gulf, bound for East Coast ports, Europe, and Asia. Underneath these sounds, I seemed to hear in the far distance the more muted drumbeats and stomping of bare feet in Congo Square, where slaves were enjoying the revelry of a night off. New Orleans, the busiest port on the Gulf in 1858, was a city that never slept. In the Crescent City, a buyer with enough money could purchase any product, legal or illegal, from any part of the world.

The intrusion of two male voices brought me back to my situation on the balcony. Perhaps I should go down into the courtyard and mingle with the others rather than run the risk of being discovered. I would be safer in the company of many. I looked down again at the men in their expensively tailored dress suits and immaculately starched linen. Their severe black and white evening wear set off to perfection the full-skirted, décolleté gowns of the women. The dresses were flounced and draped in the latest Parisian style. In the women's elaborate coiffures were entwined flowers, ribbons, or real gems matching those at their throats and around their wrists. I looked at them with mingled feelings of loathing and pity for their shame. Such gifts of jewels could be mine also, but it was from just such offers I hoped to flee.

Before I could descend to the courtyard, from whoever was approaching the balcony from the ballroom, my way was blocked by a laughing couple, their arms entwined about each other's waists, coming up the stairway. I retreated into my niche.

The wide, multipaned glass doors leading onto the balcony had heavy, full-length draperies that could be pulled across them. Now, however, the curtains had been drawn aside by ornate silk ropes to allow the doors to be opened to the cool night air. If the two men I'd heard came through the doors, or I tried to pass the doors to the stairway, they would see me. I huddled against the outside wall, hidden for the moment by the heavy curtains.

The men paused at the open doors, and to my relief they came no farther. When they spoke loud enough for me to understand their words, I became more frightened. I recognized one of the voices.

"Are you enjoying your visit to New Orleans, Lord Cheshire?"

"Very much, sir, very much."

The first man spoke in well-modulated French, but he was answered by one with an English accent.

"Good! We have much in the way of entertainment to offer a visitor. Not as much, perhaps, as London, but a number of amusements quite unlike any you are familiar with. I hope you are also enjoying tonight's ball. It's something quite unique. I doubt you'll find another like it anywhere in the world."

"Extraordinary!" Lord Cheshire exclaimed. "Most extraordinary. You are quite right. I've never attended one like it. Quite brilliant of you Creoles to think of it. Typically French, I should say. Doubt that its like would be accepted in London. The ladies, bless their hearts, would never allow it."

I listened impatiently while the Creole explained the custom of quadroon balls.

"They've been a tradition in New Orleans for quite some time now, Lord Cheshire. They give free women of color—mulattoes and quadroons—an opportunity to introduce their daughters to wealthy white men. The younger women hope, of course, that these white men will ask them to become their mistresses in a system called *plaçage*. The men come by invitation only, so they're restricted pretty much to the old Creole families of the French Quarter, descendants of the early French and Spanish settlers."

"And the young women prefer this to marriage?" the English guest asked.

"Women of color cannot marry a white man, and most prefer not to marry one of their own. They're much better off as mistresses to men who will provide a home and the assurance of security for life. No gentleman would deny his *placée* either of these, and if there are children, it is expected they will be provided for as well."

"And the wives? They don't object?"

"We follow the Continental custom of marriage for convenience, M'sieu. Some wives object, of course, but they have no say in their husbands' private lives. Many are actually pleased. It frees them from being burdened with having a child every year. You might find it hard to believe, but it is not unusual for a Creole to leave a will dividing his property equally between his two households, and many of the *plaçage* children are sent abroad to be educated. Having a quadroon mistress is as much a mark of prestige and distinction in our part of New Orleans as owning fine horses and carriages."

I closed my ears to the rest of the conversation. Anger and humiliation and frustration welled up inside me until I thought I would choke. The voice of the Creole was all too familiar, and the sound of it made me blush with shame.

I had come to this ball, as I had so many others, at

my mother's insistence. As I well knew, these dances were my one opportunity to meet wealthy young men from the fine Creole families, and my whole future depended on attracting the right one. It was the custom. My whole life had been ruled by those four words. Whenever I tried to rebel or follow my own desires, my mother quietly brought me to my senses. "It is the custom, Leah."

For seventeen years I had bowed to tradition, sustained all the while by the belief that my mother was wrong and someday I would be able to escape the tyranny of that tradition. Now the time had come to flee from a situation I could no longer endure. Tonight I had suffered the ultimate insult to my dignity, and it was just the impetus I needed to force the decision.

In the past I had maintained a stoic indifference to the men with whom I danced. Young or old, it made no difference. With cool dignity and poised demeanor, I had usually been successful in giving the impression I would welcome no further overtures or suggestions of a more intimate nature.

Until tonight.

I had danced first with a man I'd long known as a friend of my father. Monsieur Lebeau loved to dance and came to the balls for that one reason, so I felt comfortable and relaxed with him. Unfortunately, he introduced me to a young man who had just moved to New Orleans from the North and was living in the American section of the city. Americans were seldom invited to these balls, and immediately I felt uncomfortable with him. Charles Anderson spoke no French, and although I understood English, I'd never tried to speak it.

That immediately struck Anderson as very, very funny. He began making caustic remarks about people who lived in the United States but couldn't speak the national language. I reddened with shame and humiliation, but since I couldn't respond to his insults, he continued taunting me. Thoroughly enjoying my discomfort, Anderson started whispering vulgar and obscene suggestions into my ear.

I felt like a helpless animal, trapped in his tight grasp and forced to listen to foul words that made me feel naked and unclean. In spite of my full skirts and numerous petticoats, I felt the hard pressure of his thigh against mine and his hand moving inside the back of my low-cut gown. He held me much too close, and I shriveled under the eyes of the other dancers; but when I shuddered involuntarily, he grasped me so tightly I could not breathe. Everything about Charles Anderson revolted me; he reminded me of a lizard with his sickly, greenish white pallor and his damp hands, his long, pointed nose and narrow lips. I felt his hot breath on my neck, and I wanted to scream.

Before I realized what was happening, he circled to the edge of the dance floor and forced me into one of the small rooms adjoining it. With a single determined push, he shut the door.

"Now we'll get down to the real business of the evening, shall we?" he sneered.

"I don't know what you mean," I said as coldly as I could in French.

Understanding the tone if not the exact words, Charles laughed. "I didn't come here just to dance, so let's not play games."

He had both arms around me now, but I did my best to resist when he brought his mouth down hard on mine. I was unable to move my hands, but in my fury I began kicking his legs and biting his lips.

"That's it," he whispered hoarsely. "Fight me. I like it better that way."

With one swift movement he pulled my dress down over my shoulders, exposing my breasts and pinning my arms against my sides. His mouth was all over me now, covering my face, my neck, and my shoulders with wet, slobbering kisses. When he cupped his hand over one breast and began squeezing it, I moaned in pain.

He panted harder and rubbed against me with greater urgency. "Moan, my beautiful tiger cat," he urged, "but don't scream, or I'll break your neck."

He twisted his fingers through the ribbon around my throat, pressing the gold locket against my windpipe. Weak with fear, I knew he was obsessed enough to carry out the threat.

Over and over his mouth came down on mine, forcing my lips apart until I thought I would gag, while his hands explored every part of my body he could reach. He forced me back against a wall, and while he bit me on the neck with his sharp teeth, he lifted my full skirts and ran his hand up and down my legs.

How soon, I wondered desperately, would he force me over onto the couch. One hand still held the ribbon around my throat, like a man holding his prey on a leash, loosening it a bit, then drawing it tighter. He started unfastening the back of my dress while he looked suggestively toward the couch.

"Now, let's have a taste of that sweet, dark honey I've been hearing so much about. I know why you're here, and you know why I'm here, so let's just relax and enjoy ourselves."

Though he was pulling the ribbon even tighter, I began fighting in dead earnest. Up to now the whole situation had been disgusting and revolting, but if I were finally forced to submit, it would not be without a struggle. In my desperation I knew I would rather die than be raped by this man. Unfastening some of the hooks on my dress, he had loosened it just enough to free my arms, and I began clawing and scratching at his face.

Shocked at being attacked in that way, Charles Anderson moved back a single step, and this gave me the leverage I needed. With one swift kick I tripped him up, and the two of us went sprawling onto the floor. Now I could really fight—and fight I did, kicking and pummeling him with fists and feet.

Suddenly the door opened and Anderson looked up

startled. I tried to use the opportunity to get up and run out of the room; but when my legs gave way under me, I collapsed, crying, against one of the chairs.

"What the hell do you think you're doing, Anderson?" The intruder spoke in French-accented English.

"Just enjoying myself like you said I would. And what do you mean by coming in here?" Anderson snarled. "I thought there was an unwritten rule about not opening these doors."

"There's also an unwritten rule about behaving like a gentleman at these dances. Get the hell out of here, and don't ever come back."

"Don't act so haughty, Fontaine. You can't keep me out, and you know it."

"I can have you barred for attempted rape."

"Rape? On a nigra!" Anderson tried to laugh, but his quivering voice indicated he was more frightened at the threat than he wanted anyone to know.

"Leah is not a Negro. She is an octoroon, the daughter of a free woman of color. Nor is she a prostitute. She has been as well educated, and as gently and strictly brought up, as the white daughters of the finest Creole families. Now, are you leaving or do I need to call the club president to have you thrown out?"

"I'm going, but this isn't the end of it, Fontaine." Anderson turned to me and menaced, "Nor is this the last you'll see of me, Miss Leah," grinning leeringly as he stressed the word "miss."

Still sitting on the floor, I turned around to look at my rescuer. I'd seen him at other balls, and I recognized the name Fontaine. Baptiste Fontaine. He was tall, well over six feet, with a slim, muscular physique accentuated by a well-cut evening suit. Short, black curly hair framed a strong, square face, highlighted with sparkling blue-black eyes, a disarming smile, and a pair of deep dimples. Except for a full, neat mustache, he was clean shaven.

Baptiste reached down to help me to my feet, and I was grateful for his strong arms. Suddenly I realized my dress was still pulled down, and he was staring openly and unabashedly at my breasts. Blushing under his intent gaze, I tried to cover myself, but the dress kept slipping when I reached around back to fasten it. Without a word, he stepped forward and put his hands on the lace-trimmed bodice.

"What do you think you are doing?" I sputtered.

"Only trying to help. You seemed to be having the devil's own time doing it on your own."

"I can manage quite well, thank you," and I stepped back from him.

"As you wish." Baptiste let go of the dress and it immediately fell down, once again exposing my breasts.

"Oh, bother!" I cried and started sobbing again.

"There, there," Baptiste said soothingly. "Turn around. You hold the dress up, and I'll fasten the hooks. That will solve the problem."

I did as I was bid, wondering all the while why my heart started beating more rapidly when this man looked at me or touched me.

"Thank you, M'sieu Fontaine. I can manage now. And thank you for coming in when you did. But why did you? I know that unwritten rule, too."

"That rule, Leah—it is Leah, isn't it?—is so people who wish a quiet game of cards or a private conversation will not be disturbed. It's true these rooms are also used for more intimate *tête-à-têtes*. But I'd overheard Mr. Anderson talking. I knew he was scoffing at the traditional intent of these dances and did not intend to honor the customs. I saw how he was dancing with you. I was disturbed when I returned from the bar and saw neither of you on the dance floor. I started to go down to the courtyard, but then I saw this closed door. I guess I would have been the one thrown out, if it had been anyone but you in here. I just didn't stop to think."

"Thank you again, M'sieu Fontaine. I—I think I'll go out for some fresh air."

"Don't you think you could call me Baptiste now?

And how about a reward for saving you from that horrible fate worse than death?"

Baptiste tilted my chin up with one finger and bent down to kiss me. Without a second thought, I slapped him hard across the cheek.

"You—you, man, you! You're all alike. You humiliate me, you stare at me, and then try to take advantage of me."

"And we rescue you. You *are* a regular tiger cat. Go now and get a breath of air. But you won't forget Baptiste. I won't let you."

I continued to stare down into the courtyard. Tradition had brought me to an impasse, but the same tradition had also saved me from the pain and horror of being raped. The twin customs of *plaçage* and the quadroon ball. How they had determined and ruled my life. Up to now. Tonight I would flee from both and begin a totally new life. As a completely different person.

Chapter Two

MY NAME IS LEAH and I am an octoroon.

My mother, Clotilde, was a quadroon. My grandmother Rachael had been a mulatto slave and my grandfather, a white plantation owner. Rachael was very beautiful, a personal servant to the plantation owner's wife. The coming of summer around New Orleans brought with it the dreaded yellow and malarial fevers, blown over the city by winds from the surrounding bayous. It was traditional for those white people who could afford it to spend the hot months away from the city. During one such summer, Rachael remained behind on the plantation when the family left. The owner, however, made frequent trips back home, ostensibly to check on business affairs, but actually to see my grandmother.

As the months passed, the casual liaison begun during the summer developed into a relationship that neither tried to hide. As a child, I heard my grandmother speak with genuine adoration and love for her devoted Henri. She felt no shame at being the illicit lover of her white master.

Because of the slavery system—the buying and selling of slaves according to whim or necessity—parents and children, mothers and fathers were separated, often being sent miles away from each other. As a result there were few formal, legal marriages among them. Rachael had been separated from her own mother when she was only ten years old, given as a wedding present to her white mistress, and moved to New Orleans, over a hundred miles from her former home. After this experience, she considered it an honor to be chosen by her white lover; but more important, the arrangement gave her a much-needed sense of security that she would not be sold away from the plantation.

With the birth of my mother, Clotilde, in 1812, however, the relations between the white master and his wife became so strained, Rachael was sent from the house to become a field slave, a demotion more degrading than just going from easy, pleasant work indoors to the more rigorous, backbreaking drudgery in the fields. House servants held themselves above and apart from the other slaves and were considered by all as an elite group with special privileges. Rachael had been born a house servant and had never soiled her hands by grubbing in the dirt of the fields. She had never had more onerous duties than caring for her mistress's wardrobe, helping her dress, and arranging her hair.

Feeling deeply hurt and rejected, Rachael found no solace among her own race. Instead, she was jeered and taunted because she had become an outcast, forced to do the hardest work, and given no succor when she fainted or became ill from the unfamiliar toil in the sugarcane fields. To add to her problems, she feared for her daughter's life. Clotilde was a sickly child, but Rachael had to take the baby with her to the fields, carrying her in a sling across her back because none of the other women would care for her during the day. There were no trees to shelter the child from the unremitting rays of the sun. When it came time to nurse Clotilde, Rachael could only bring the baby around to her breast and hold her there while trying to cut cane at the same time.

After two months of this arduous life, Rachael ran away to the bayou in hopes of finding refuge with other runaways who had set up their own villages deep in the swamps. If she had been alone, Rachael might have made a successful escape, but she had Clotilde. After days of wading knee-deep in the morass, nearly drowning when her feet became entangled in trailing vines, and narrowly escaping several deadly water moccasins, she discovered she had been traveling in a circle. She thought seriously of drowning herself, but she could not let her baby die. After dragging herself back to her cabin and being discovered by the overseer, she was whipped across her back until her skin hung in shreds and it seemed she would bleed to death. The punishment would have been more severe if she had not returned voluntarily.

Out of consideration for his wife, Rachael's lover had to permit the whipping, but he remitted any further punishment. She was neither branded on the cheek as a malcontent nor had her heel tendons cut to keep her from running away again. In spite of all this, Rachael never stopped loving my grandfather, and he went to her cabin whenever he could escape the vigilance of his wife.

Ultimately, in 1815, he showed his love in the way every slave dreams about. He presented her with manumission papers that guaranteed her freedom and that of Clotilde and any other children she might have for the rest of their lives. In addition, he bought her a house on the Ramparts in New Orleans and set up a trust fund that assured she would always live in comfort and security. And so my mother grew up in pleasant, happy surroundings as a free woman of color. However, after the age of three, she never saw her father again, nor did Rachael see her lover, although she remained faithful to him until her death in spite of many suggestions from both white and free men of color to do otherwise.

My father was Jean-Paul Bonvivier. He had an unusual history because he, too, was the child of an unusual misalliance. His father, Claud, was a French sea captain, skipper of a trading ship that plied a route among the South Sea islands. Becoming enamored of the carefree, idyllic life enjoyed by the natives, he established a second home on one of the more isolated islands. From the beginning he was accepted and made welcome by the aborigines, even to the extent of being adopted by the chief as his son.

One of the prerogatives of Claud's new status was the right to participate in the traditional mating rituals of the young people who had reached marriageable age, although there, too, the relationships were seldom permanent. Often they lasted no longer than a few days, occasionally until after a child was born. There could be no promiscuous coupling until after the ritual ceremony, but from then on both men and women were free to select new mates whenever they chose. As a result, the children were children of the whole tribe, with more than enough mothers and fathers to keep them both happy and well behaved.

Prior to his adoption, Claud had invited a number of compliant beauties to share his bed. He liked it that way: no entanglements, no nagging wife. There was a fiancée, selected by his parents, waiting back in Paris, but not even the most authoritative letters from his father sent him sailing for France.

Then something unexpected happened to Claud when he joined the ritual dance. He fell in love. Lei-lei was fifteen to his thirty-two, but like most Polynesian females of her age she was no longer a child. Fidelity was not unknown on the island; but no one, least of all Lei-lei, expected it of a white man. However, Claud wanted even more than that; he wanted a marriage, legal in the eyes of his country and blessed by the church. To that end he set the bowsprit of his schooner toward France, for the first time in six years, to introduce his bride to the elder Bonviviers.

On board ship, Claud gave up his richly furnished cabin to Lei-lei so that she would be comfortable during the long voyage from the Pacific, across the Indian Ocean, around the tip of South Africa, and north to France. Although they had lived together as man and wife on the island, once Claud knew he wanted to marry her, he stayed away from her. Lei-lei was puzzled when her lover tried to explain. As long as they were with her people, his conscience allowed him to live according to their mores. However, with his decision to formalize their relationship, he chose not to sleep with her again until she was his wife. He found it almost as difficult to explain to himself as he did to Lei-lei. His decision stemmed not from a sense of guilt or a feeling of having sinned or even a need to prove he was strong enough to endure several weeks of abstinence. It went far deeper than that. It was to show Lei-lei how very much he loved and respected her as a person, that she was more to him than a warm, desirable body or someone to cook his food.

At first Lei-lei thought marriage to Claud—a strange custom to her way of thinking—was going to mean he would never be her lover again. If he loved her as much as he said he did, he would want to spend every night with her. Her greatest fear was that he now thought her ugly and no longer desirable. Over and over he reassured her that he was just as eager as she to resume their lovemaking; and as soon as they arrived in France, they would spend every hour together. Lei-lei finally decided that among the white sailors' taboos was one forbidding them to sleep with a woman while at sea.

At night Claud stood watch and slept fitfully on deck, his mind filled with images of Lei-lei's beautiful body and long, glossy black hair, which he loved to twine around himself when they lay close together. Her smooth skin emitted the tantalizing aroma of coconut oil and jessamine, which he could smell even in her absence as he guided his ship by the stars. During the day she joined him at the helm, standing within the curve of his two arms while he held the wheel. When her nearness became more than he could stand, he sent her below and wished with all his heart that a storm or some emergency would demand his full attention.

Claud had sent word to his parents by a faster ship that he was bringing home a bride, and he wished them to make all preparations for a wedding. But when he introduced Lei-lei, the horrified look on their faces told him all he needed to know. If his wife would not be welcome in their home, he would not remain there. In spite of her simple, crystalline beauty which made her elegant Parisian dress look tawdry, Lei-lei was and always would be a savage to them. When Claud was told by his father that marriage to Lei-lei would mean being disinherited, Claud did not waver in his decision. He and Lei-lei were married in a small chapel, after which he immediately set sail for the Caribbean island of Martinique, vowing never to return to France. He never did.

In Martinique, Claud established a successful trading company and became a settled landowner. Over the years Lei-lei presented him with seven sloe-eyed children; the girls all as beautiful as she, and the boys as handsome and stalwart as their father. Eventually he expanded his import-export business and opened an office in the natural trading center of the South—New Orleans. To this city he sent his oldest son, Jean-Paul, as resident manager. As the business continued to flourish, Jean-Paul became a very wealthy merchant.

In New Orleans, Jean-Paul married Claudine de Poitiers, the daughter of minor nobility, emigrés who fled France to avoid persecution and possible death during the revolution. The marriage of convenience brought to both partners what they desired. Claudine acquired the money she needed to live according to the style she thought due one with her royal connections. She claimed to be a descendant of Diane de Poitiers, mistress to two kings: Francis I and his son Henri II. Jean-Paul became an accepted member of the city's aristocratic Creole colony. Aside from that, the marriage was something less than felicitous, Claudine allowing Jean-Paul in her bed scarcely more than the number of times required to sire six children. After the birth of the last, she locked her door, but he was hardly aware of it. Long before this he had met my mother at a quadroon ball and established her in a small house two blocks from the four-story mansion over which Claudine presided. Jean-Paul was proud of his children by Claudine, but I knew his real love was for me because of his deep adoration for my mother.

Jean-Paul never tired of telling me about his handsome, adventurous father, who stood well over six feet tall and had a zest for living never daunted by hardship or grief. And about his beautiful, almond-eyed mother, whose long, delicate fingers held a magic touch that cured fevers and eased the pain of childhood's bruises. My mother listened just as eagerly as I to these stories about her white protector's family because she felt it was important that I know who I was and who my forebears had been. While she herself did not remember slave conditions, she had learned from her own mother how easy it was for slaves to lose touch with their families and know nothing of their heritage. They lived in a tragic limbo, surrounded by a cloud of ignorance, deprived of the comforting knowledge that they belonged to someone.

From my Polynesian grandmother, I inherited my straight black hair and almond-shaped eyes, but my pale fawn skin, narrow lips, and slim nose were those of my white ancestors. The gift bestowed by my mother—the art of pleasing a white lover—came to me gradually through the years.

And so I grew up loved and protected until it was time for me to be presented to Creole men, until the night I was insulted by one man and rescued by another.

Chapter Three

I LOOKED OVER THE RAILING of the balcony and into the courtyard, which was gradually becoming deserted as the evening grew more chilly. As soon as I was sure I would not be observed, I hurried down the steps and though the courtyard. Once outside the wall, I made my way across Royale Street to the garden behind the St. Louis Cathedral and a large tree where I had, earlier in the day, hidden a few items. I reached inside the depression where a large limb joined the trunk. My cache was still there.

I unwrapped the shawl containing the few items I planned to take with me. I had some trouble fitting the simple dark blue bonnet over the thick curls and poufs of my elaborate coiffure, but I didn't want any of my hair to show. Once my hat was securely in place, I checked the coins in the small mesh bag and then slipped that over my wrist. Later I would fasten it under my dress for safe keeping. The dress. I had to do something to make it look less obviously a ball gown. Quickly, but careful not to rip the dress itself, I tore off the flowers and bows decorating the skirt. It was still a silk gown, but being a subdued shade of teal blue with deeper blue velvet binding, it could pass as a traveling dress. I threw the heavy, dark blue shawl around my shoulders. The bonnet was covered with a thick veiling which could be pulled down over my face, but for the time being I could keep it up. It was not unusual in New Orleans for free women of color to be out this time of night, and I felt I was in no danger of being stopped.

Walking out onto Royale, I hailed a hansom cab and asked to be taken through the American section, to the edge of the city near the river. As I lay back against the leather cushions, for the first time I seriously considered what I was doing. My mother would worry, even after finding the note, but I could not let that stop me. Clotilde had been content with the life she built around Jean-Paul and me, but I had chosen a different path for myself. Deep inside I burned with a passion just waiting to be released, but it was not a desire a man could satisfy. It was something far more elemental and primeval—the need to be free.

By the time I was twelve years old and learned what it meant to be a woman, I knew just what I wanted from life. At that time I began plotting my future carefully, step by step. Not usually as emotional as my mother nor as sensual as my Polynesian forebears. I found it easy to first adopt and then inculcate within myself a stoic attitude. Nothing, I decided, would ever move me to tears or to a show of emotion of any kind. I developed a stately carriage, elegant manners, and haughty demeanor to give men the impression I was cold and untouchable.

When my father brought me gifts, I kissed him dutifully and thanked him kindly, but I would never let him see how much I loved him. I knew he adored both my mother and me, but I was determined to deny him the satisfaction of knowing that adoration was returned by me. He was considered a white man in spite of his Polynesian blood, but I was colored, even if my skin was paler than his. He could come and go as he pleased, moving from a prestigious white world in which he was an accepted member of the "pure" society to my mother's world—four rooms of a secret house in which I was imprisoned.

I must never leave that world, never cross over into my father's other life. Nor could my mother. Night after night I covered my ears to keep out the sounds of my mother crying because Jean-Paul had not come as promised. It was true we never wanted for any material thing. But when I crept furtively away from the small, enclosed yard and ventured out into the *Vieux Carré*, I often saw my father driving with his white wife and children, laughing and talking to them or proudly showing them off to his friends. I knew then what my birth denied me; but though I ached with the knowledge of it, I did not shed a tear.

If my mother had tried to tell me she was content with her life as Jean-Paul's mistress, I would not have believed her. However, Clotilde never knew I was not happy in our small but beautifully furnished house. To her, I presented as serene a countenance as I would always show to the world, though damning them both all the while.

When Clotilde began preparing me for my particular place in Creole society, I was an apt and willing student. The arts of dancing, gourmet cooking, conversation, and later the vast variety of ways to arouse and satisfy a man would all be useful to me in my plans for the future. Not as mistress to a Louisiana gentleman who could use me as he pleased and then ignore or discard me whenever he chose, but as wife to a white man away from the fetid South and its abominable traditions. When the right time came, I would flee north and "pass." Dutifully I attended the balls, ignoring my mother's request—and later demands—that I be more pleasant to the men and amenable to their wishes. I, and I alone, would decide when I would give myself to a man, and that would not be until I was accepted as a white woman and legally married. Casual liaisons played no part in my plans.

I had not been certain when I hid the shawl and bonnet and money that I would really leave that night. If I hadn't left, I would have destroyed the note to Clotilde. In a way I was testing myself to see just how far I would go. But the decision had been made for me. I could not take the chance of being trapped again. In addition, my mother was pressuring me to relent and select one of the young men who had approached her for permission to establish me as his mistress. In spite of my cold, aloof manner, I had attracted admirers.

No, there was no turning back now. The cab would take me to the edge of the city and from there I would make my way to a levee farther upriver. Once there, I could board a paddle-wheeler for the trip up the Mississippi to the Ohio River and one of the Northern states. My father's generous cash birthday gift was more than enough to pay for the steamboat, which was why I decided to take the cab rather than make my way through the city on foot. I would have enough walking after he dropped me off and before I reached a boat landing. I wished now I'd thought to include a heavier, sturdier pair of shoes in my cache. My dancing slippers were hardly suitable for making my way along riverbanks and across rugged sugarcane fields.

"This where you wanted to go?" the driver asked, pulling up under a large oak near the edge of the river.

"*Oui,* this is fine."

"Mighty lonesome place out here for a young lady alone."

"Thank you. But I'm meeting a friend."

The cab driver winked knowingly when I paid the fare. "If you like, I'll stay around 'til he gets here."

"No, thank you. I'll be fine."

I waited under the tree until the driver turned around and headed back toward the center of the city. I took a small packet out of my purse and tucked it deep into my bodice. Then I fastened the purse to a narrow belt I had earlier tied around my waist under my skirt. Now I was ready to set off on my great adventure.

In many ways I was ill prepared for the trip, but I had enough confidence in myself and enough hatred for what I was leaving behind to sustain me until I could get settled in a new life. I sewed beautifully, and I knew there was always need for good seamstresses in a small town. A small, rural town was what I wanted, a place where I could settle down and feel a part of things. If I met someone I could love and marry, fine. If not, I would be content to live as a spinster. I was a solitary person, and being alone held no fears for me. Better that than the life I had learned to despise.

Although barely seventeen, I looked several years older, and I knew I could easily pass as a woman of twenty or twenty-two. I had earlier purchased a plain gold band which I would later wear as a wedding band. It was not safe for a young, single woman to travel alone. I would introduce myself as a widow when necessary.

Cautiously I followed the course of the river. In its constant twisting and turning, the Mississippi was forever eating into the banks and forming new points on one side and undercuts on the other. If I were not careful I could step on what seemed like solid ground, only to fall into the water because the river had eroded away the bank underneath. Yet I dared not wander too far inland or I would lose my way in the dark.

There was a narrow, solid-packed highway which paralleled the river, sometimes close to the bank, elsewhere several hundred yards away. This was part of the notorious Natchez Trace, connecting Natchez and New Orleans. Well traveled during daylight hours, at night it was the haunt of the worst scourges of Mississippi and Louisiana: vagrants, murderers, prostitutes, marauders, and renegades of all kinds. I had to be wary of all sounds if I didn't want to fall into one of their traps or become the victim of a sneak attack from behind. But I must also make haste and get far enough upriver to reach a landing within a few days. Once my mother found the note, I knew she would contact my father, and Jean-Paul would be sure to send someone looking for me. To avoid detection, I had to travel at night and find shelter to sleep in during the day.

My one concern at the moment was keeping my clothes clean and as little mussed as possible because I wanted to appear a lady, and having no valise of any kind would arouse enough suspicion. To this end, I finally took off my stockings and slippers to keep them from being worn to shreds. Barefoot, I had to be even more cautious with each step I took, and my progress was slowed. I was afforded some relief, however, when my path took me across freshly plowed fields where the earth was still soft and there were fewer stones and stalks to bruise my feet.

Fortunately there was just enough moonlight for me to make out large obstacles like trees, clumps of shrubbery, and occasional buildings. Crossing a part of one plantation where the lawn sloped from the house to the river, I took time to rest in a white latticed gazebo near the bank. The spring breeze was cool and fragrant with nearby bay blossoms, and I was tempted to stretch out on a cushioned bench and sleep until morning. But I did not dare. After a few minutes I got up and plodded on, wishing desperately I knew how far I'd traveled since leaving New Orleans.

Twice, as I walked along, feeling ahead with each footstep to keep from twisting my ankle in a chuck hole, I jerked my head up, realizing I'd almost fallen asleep while plodding steadily along. The first time I was roused by the barking of dogs in the distance. But the second time all was silent. Suddenly I knew what had startled me—the sound of hoofbeats coming up fast behind me, the very thing I dreaded. No one on a casual ride would be out this time of night, or very early morning. I scrambled away from the bank and lay down in some tall weeds to the right of the approaching rider. For a moment I thought he'd seen me when the horse slowed to a walk. I was sure he could see the bent grasses leading right to my hiding place. Whoever it was sat tall and slim in the saddle as he paused to look first out over the river and then toward the place where I lay.

A large-brimmed, flat-crowned hat hid the man's face, but from what I could see, he appeared well dressed, much like the gamblers who frequented the Trace and the riverboats. I caught my breath when he reached into his pocket. He had seen me, and whatever his plans were, he was going to enforce them with a gun. Then I almost laughed aloud from relief when he brought out a long cigar, and after lighting it, kicked his mount once more into a canter.

More weary now than I realized, I began stumbling over small rocks or ruts in the ground. Once, where my path dipped nearer the river, I tripped over the exposed root of a large water oak and rolled down the bank. I was able to slow my fall by clutching more roots, but I could not keep from going into the water. Now my dress and petticoats were soaked to my waist. There would be no going on until I got them dried. Not only would their weight hold me back, but I would be in danger of catching cold. I collapsed on the ground in tears. Whatever happened, I was not going back. Somehow I would manage to rest and get my clothes dry. Out of desperation I found the strength to get up and go on. It took me several minutes to maneuver another hundred yards, having to call on much of my energy to hold up the wet, dripping skirts and keep from falling. In the distance I saw a shed, open on one side and with part of the roof missing. It did not offer the comforts of the fancy gazebo, but it was a shelter.

There were no seats of any kind inside and only a scattering of grain and straw on the dirt floor. It looked as though it might have been used to feed or house small animals, but had been deserted. Although at least two hours remained until daylight, two hours I could have used to get farther along on my journey, I knew I had to stop.

I didn't much like the thought of disrobing, but I must remove my dress and petticoats if they were to dry out. Carefully I hung the petticoats from loose boards in the roof, fluffing them out as I did so. Taking more care with the dress, I smoothed out the wrinkles as best I could. I hung it to cover part of the open wall of the shed. There was no place to lie except the dirt floor, so I whisked away most of the debris, wrapped the shawl around me, and lay down.

As tired as I was, fear and excitement prevented me from going immediately to sleep. I heard the bass tones of frogs "nee-deeping" in the rushes and the sound of water lapping against the riverbank. Far in the distance, side-wheelers and stern-wheelers churned up the Mississippi while their deep horns warned flatboats and small barges of their approach. It would be good to get on board a steamboat in a day or two.

Then another sound shattered the night—the wail of a screech owl. I shuddered, remembering a night many years earlier when I was nine years old and lying in bed listening to an evil screech owl in a nearby tree.

Chapter Four

THE NIGHT I HEARD THE SCREECH OWL as a little girl,
I remember shivering, then sliding deeper under the
patchwork quilt. The sound of the bird was an omen of
death, and I had to know if he were perched near the
house. I'd been too frightened to move, yet I knew
what would happen if I didn't scare him away before
midnight. Just hearing him meant there would be a
death before morning, but if he were in one of our
trees, he would be warning of a death in the house.
And there were just two of us: my mother and myself.

I hoped my mother would hear him and chase him
away, but there was no sound from the other bedroom.
I had to go out in the dark all by myself. Quickly saying a "Hail Mary" for protection, I reached for my robe
and then had to feel around under the bed for my slippers. I shuddered at the thought of putting my hand on
some creepy thing, like a woolly caterpillar or jeweled
lizard, hiding under the dust ruffle. I caught my breath
as I remembered the time a green snake had crawled in
from the ivy around the window and slithered away
when I discovered its hiding place.

Once dressed, I tiptoed from my room into the
kitchen, grateful for the faint light from the fireplace
where my mother had banked the coals for morning.
There was still no sign that she had heard the owl.

If I were lucky, I might have to go no farther than
the back stoop. From there, at least I could make out
where the hideous bird was perched. In my room, his

eerie call had sounded quite close, but once I was outside it seemed to come from more than one direction. I
would have to go out into the yard where the tall grass
was tangled and wet from an early-evening shower. As
I felt my way down the steps, I pulled the skirts of my
gown and robe above my ankles. This left me without
a free hand to feel my way through the lantana, oleander, and azalea bushes, and a large cloud completely
obscured the moon. The house itself blocked any light
from the gaslit street lamp in front.

I stood close to the back gallery and listened. For a
moment I thought the owl had flown away, and with a
sigh of relief turned to go back in. Then suddenly a
long, spine-chilling *whooo-ooo-oo* came from the catal-
pa tree in the far corner of the garden. There was
nothing to do but scare him away. Letting my gown
drag across the grass, I worked my way through the
shrubbery until I stood right under the low branch
where the owl perched. If I could reach the limb, I
might be able to shake him off, but even jumping failed
to bring me high enough.

Picking up a dead branch, I tried poking at him, but
he only moved nearer to the trunk, screeching and
flapping his wings the whole time, as though threatening to fly down and attack me. I wanted nothing so
much as to turn and scamper back to the house and the
security of my room, but the threat of death to me or
my mother endowed me with new courage.

I remembered shivering from the clammy touch of
wet cotton around my ankles. I took off both slippers. I
had no idea I would hit my target, but maybe just
seeing something flying through the air would make the
owl decide to move. Taking careful aim, I threw the
slippers as hard as I could, one right after the other.
He squawked as the first one bounced off the branch,
and he only screeched louder and flapped more furi-
ously when the second hit him on the shoulder. But he
stayed on the branch, his unblinking eyes staring right
through me.

I was ready to cry. "Go away, you ugly old bird," I screamed. "Go 'way and don't come back. Go screech at someone else."

Suddenly, as though bored by the whole business, he flew straight up off the branch. I stood startled for a minute, amazed that he had actually gone. I'd saved my mother and myself from certain death.

Now to get back to the house. There was no point in looking for the slippers in the dark, so I simply ran as fast as I could toward the kitchen, closing my mind to all the dreadful things I might be stepping on. Quietly, so as not to disturb my mother, I tiptoed back across the kitchen to my room and changed into a dry gown. The door between the two bedrooms was cracked open a couple of inches, and I peeked in to see if my mother had remained asleep. I fully expected to hear her call out, "Where have you been, Leah, this time of night?"

She wasn't there. Nor had her bed been slept in. Now I was more frightened than ever. I had been alone in the house all the time. When I went to bed, she had been sitting before the fire in the parlor, sewing on my winter school ensemble. There had been the first feeling of frost in the air that day, and she was hurrying to finish a red merino wool dress and cloak. Most of the girls at the convent school wore dark blue or gray or brown, but Clotilde never dressed me in anything but bright or pastel colors. She had kissed me goodnight, reminded me—as she did every evening—to say my prayers, and returned to sewing in the dim light.

I always fell asleep long before my mother retired to her room, so the shock that went through me at seeing the empty bed left me rigid with fear. The screech owl had been trying to warn me. Something had come and carried my mother off. Not someone, but some horrible, ghoulish thing that flew or crept about in the shadows of darkness.

Somehow I found my way back to bed, but there was no sleep for the rest of that night. I had no idea what time it was when the owl awakened me nor how long I'd been up, but I lay for hours waiting for the sun to rise. I had seen the first gray fingers lighting up the sky, heard the mockingbird greet the morning, and listened for the first stirrings of activity along the levees. Once it was daylight I could go to the cathedral and seek out Father Leclerc. He would know what to do. I clutched my rosary in one hand and my faithful rag doll Binkie in the other. They had always been my security against the secret horrors of the night.

Much to my relief, I finally heard the "squeak, squeak" of Clotilde's old leather shoes on the back gallery. If I had not seen the empty bed in the middle of the night, I might have believed I had dreamed most of what happened and that my mother was merely returning from an early trip to the market. I kept my eyes closed while she walked through my room to hers. When she settled on the feather down mattress, I heard the woven rope support squeak against the wood and the dropping of her shoes, one at a time, to the floor. The next sound was the slap of her carpet slippers on the bare wooden floor as she approached my bed.

"Wake up, *ma petite*. Hot, fresh croissants for breakfast."

When I didn't answer, she coaxed, "We'll open a crock of strawberry preserves, shall we? And your cup of piping hot *café au lait* is waiting on the table."

Maybe I had been dreaming. Maybe the screech owl and the empty bed had been just a nightmare. But when I checked the laundry basket, I found my nightdress stuffed down inside, the hem still wet. And my slippers were not under the bed.

All through breakfast my mother chatted about how busy the market had been for so early in the morning and what a beautiful day it was going to be.

"Not a bit of chill this morning, Leah. Almost like a spring day. I can finish your dress and cloak in plenty of time for cold weather."

No word about where she'd been all night or why

she'd left me alone. How often, I wondered, had it happened before. I had been afraid to go out into the dark and chase away the owl, but I had done it. Now I would have to get up my courage to follow my mother the next time she left the house at night. It would mean staying awake and listening to her every movement, but I had to do it if I were to have any peace of mind.

I had been interrupted in my musings by my mother's gentle reminder that it was time to leave for school. The reminder became an urgent prodding when a neighbor hurried in to say she had something terrible to report. I lingered as long as I could, hoping to hear what the "something terrible" was, but my mother hurried me out into the side courtyard. Before I reached the front gate, I looked back once and saw my mother pouring a second cup of coffee and listening with a horrified expression to what the neighbor had begun to tell her.

It was all I could do to get through the long day at school, beginning with the celebration of High Mass for All Souls' Day in memory of the saints and those who had died during the past year. That was it! Someone had died the night before. The screech owl had been warning me. If I hadn't chased him away from our yard, it might have been my mother or I who was dead today.

I started to run home after school. I knew it was not like my mother to tell me anything that might upset me, but I had to find out what news the neighbor had brought. Something terrible had happened to someone we knew, of that I was sure. After running two blocks, I changed my mind. I knew where I could find out. There was one place where everyone knew the latest news and where they would be talking about it loud enough to be heard by a little girl wandering around quietly. I headed toward the Market. In my pocket was a gold piece my father had given me on his last visit, and while I ate a *crème glacée* I could listen.

The Market was crowded for the middle of the afternoon. Usually shoppers made their purchases for the kitchen in the morning when everything was fresh, but that day there were crowds around the stalls selling coffee, hot doughnuts, flowers, pralines, small rice cakes, and ice cream. All of the buyers—men and women—were chattering as fast as they ate or drank. I purchased my *crème glacée* and found a seat on one of the benches.

"He's dead, all right," said one man as he tipped his tall hat unceremoniously to the woman who seemed to be doubting him, and then he swung his cane as if to emphasize his point.

A voice from another direction caught my attention, and I turned to listen to a Negro woman, obviously a house slave, wearing a stiffly starched dress, wide white apron, and white tignon.

"I don't believe it," she said to a Negro driver standing by his master's carriage. "He was the devil hisself, and the devil can't be killed. He just fooling everyone. You see."

"No, Rebecca, he dead," the driver said. "I seen him when they cut him down. There warn't a bit of life in him. He ain't gonna hurt nobody no more."

The devil himself! I shivered and crossed myself. No wonder the neighbor was so excited and my mother hurried me out the door. I finished my ice cream and walked slowly from one stall to another. From bits of conversation at each one I finally pieced together what had happened. François Dubonnet, a free man of color who lent money to desperate Negroes and other *gens du couleur* in the *Vieux Carré*, had been found strangled with a cord of braided red string and hanging from a fig tree in his courtyard. His mouth was stuffed with chicken feathers. All that was horrible enough, but even worse was the one word I kept hearing in all of the conversations: Voodoo.

"Voodoo, that what it was. Ole Damballa finally got him. François should've known someone would put a

Voodoo curse on him someday. But he wouldn't listen. He given the *gris-gris*."

"That warn't Voodoo," another insisted. "Dr. John can make up a *gris-gris* to put a curse on someone, but it warn't Voodoo. It don't kill like that. But someone wanted it to look like it did."

I had heard the word all my life, and I knew about charms. My mother kept a love charm she'd purchased from Marie Laveau, a Voodoo queen, under her pillow. But I didn't think it was working very well. Jean-Paul had not been to the house for several weeks.

My head had been in a spin. Voodoo, the screech owl, the dead François to whom so many people owed money. Did my mother's disappearance the night before have something to do with any one of them, or with all of them? Clotilde was a Christian who followed faithfully the tenets of the Catholic church, but so were many others who did not hesitate to admit they also practiced Voodoo. I was more determined than ever to follow my mother the next time she left the house at night. I said nothing about the death of François Dubonnet to her, nor did she enlighten me as to what it was the neighbor had been so anxious to talk about. But that did not surprise me. My mother was a woman who kept many things to herself.

Chapter Five

IN THE SHED ON THE TRACE, I finally drifted off to
sleep. I awoke once to see it was not yet noon,
straightened the shawl around me, and went back to
sleep.

When I woke up again, the sun was bright in my
eyes and flooding the interior of the shed. For a minute
I was confused. Then I knew why. My dress was no
longer hanging over part of the open wall. It had been
stolen! Damn, why hadn't I thought of that. I looked
up. The petticoats were still there, but I couldn't get
very far—in fact, I couldn't go anyplace at all—without a dress. Maybe it had blown down.

Cautiously I got up and crawled to the opening. I
was not on a plantation but on one of the small farms
that clung precariously to the edge of the river and
gave just enough crops to provide a living for the
owners. An unpainted, dirt-brown house hugged the
ground several yards away; and near it a second out-
building leaned to one side, waiting for the next good
wind to blow it down. So far no sign of my dress.

I moved farther out of my shelter, still staying low to
the ground to avoid being seen. The dress was lying
across a fallen tree trunk, as smoothly spread out as if
it had been carefully placed there. No wind had blown
it down like that. I shuddered. Someone knew I had
been sleeping in the shed, yet there was no one in
sight. Maybe I could retrieve the dress and make my
escape before whoever had taken it down returned.

Still crawling on my hands and knees, I moved as

fast as I dared through the dry stubble, ignoring the cuts on my hands and feet from the sharp tips of the stalks. The farm must be deserted, or the owners would have plowed the remains of the fall harvest under in preparation for planting. Only when I was gathering up the dress from the log did I realize I was not alone.

"Looky what we got, boys."

I looked up into three filthy, unshaven faces. Tobacco juice dribbled out of each uncouth mouth. The men—one gray-haired and two young enough to be his sons—all wore sweat-stained shirts and rough, work-worn trousers. I lost all hope when one of the younger ones leered down at me.

"You baited the trap right fine, Paw."

That's why the dress had been so carefully displayed. To draw me out of the shed.

The older man read my thoughts. "Just playing a little game with you, girlie. No matter, we would've come in and got ya anyway."

"We was watchin'," the second young man snickered. "We watched through the boards and seen ya crawl out."

I remembered how carefully I had looked all around before leaving the shed, and they had seen every move I made. How they must have been laughing at me.

Suddenly I realized I was half lying, half sitting in front of them wearing only a sheer chemise and fine cambric pantalettes. There was no way to reach my petticoats, but I could put my dress on. As I started to slip it over my head, the older man reached out and grabbed it from me.

"We think you're prettier without this, don't we, boys? 'Fayette, come help the young lady to her feet. 'Poleon, fold up the dress real careful-like. We might want it later."

I tried to rise by myself, but the one named 'Fayette grabbed my arm and jerked me roughly to my feet. "My paw says I'm to help ya." Still holding my slim arm in his big fist, he stared at my breasts, more enhanced than concealed by the sheer material of my chemise. Then his gaze slid down my body, past my waist, to my pantalettes and the bit of lace decorating the hems of the garment. With the back of his left hand he wiped the saliva drooling down his chin.

Meanwhile 'Poleon held my dress up to his face, inhaling the perfume that clung there and contorting his face into all sorts of odd grimaces while leering over at me. I wished I had gone ahead and fallen into the river. Drowning could not be any worse than what I was experiencing now.

All this time the old man stared quietly at me, as though I were a cow or horse being appraised for market. I had long since stopped blushing, but I grew more uncomfortable under his steady gaze than when the younger men had looked at me. I followed his eyes as he looked at my hair, now relieved of all its pins and cascading over my shoulders, my full breasts straining against the chemise, my slim waist, and my well-fleshed hips. For the second time in less than twenty-four hours I was facing the possibility of rape. But this time was far more dangerous. There was no handsome Creole to come along and rescue me. I was just about to faint from fear and despair when the old man spoke.

Having been free all my life, I was unprepared for what I heard. I'd known I was in danger of being attacked along the Trace by robbers or murderers, or even such evil men as these. But I'd forgotten about a group that scoured the countryside with their packs of dogs every night.

"Well, boys, I think we got us a runaway slave."

From somewhere deep inside myself, I found my voice. "No, no, you're wrong. I'm not a slave. I'm free."

"Come, come, girlie, who's gonna believe that? You're light enough to be one of them mulattoes or quadroons, but you're a slave. If I know one thing, it's the skin and hair of a nigra. Ain't that so, boys?"

"Yes, Paw."

"Sure thing, Paw."

I swallowed hard. They spoke a rough kind of Cajun French, the imprecise dialect of the bayous, but I had no trouble understanding the words.

"My father is a wealthy Creole merchant in New Orleans," I said, desperately hoping they would believe me. "He'll pay you well to see me returned safely."

"Oh, we'll get paid, all right, but not by no high-class city man. You think we're dumb enough to take you into New Orleans and get arrested for kidnapping? No siree. Now if you'd said you were owned by a white man—well, that'd be a different story. But even a ransom for a runaway don't pay as good as what we're gonna get."

In spite of myself, I couldn't restrain the sobs that rose in my throat. I had run away from what I thought were the horrors of *plaçage*, and here I was faced with the worse terror of being sold as a slave. My one hope was that I would be sold to a kindly person who might believe my story and contact Jean-Paul. I knew he would refund the purchase price to get me back safely. Clinging to that thought, for a minute my spirits perked up.

"Yesiree, I know just the woman who's been looking for a beauty like you for some of her special customers. Light-skinned and thin-lipped but with the hot blood of Africa still in your veins. You'll do just fine, and she'll pay plenty when she sees you."

For a minute the meaning of the old man's words didn't penetrate my mind. When I finally became aware of what he was saying, I sank to the ground in spite of 'Fayette's strong grasp on my arm. A prostitute! I was to be sold into prostitution. I knew it happened all the time. I'd heard many stories about it, but I always thought that being free I was safe from such dangers. What a fool I'd been!

'Fayette jerked me roughly back into an upright position. "She sure is pretty, Paw. Kinda hate to let her go."

"Yeah," 'Poleon said. "Why don't we keep her for ourselves. We could use a good slave around the house, 'specially in the bedroom."

"Shut your mouth, boy. Free or slave, someone's gonna be looking for her. If we don't get her up to Baton Rouge and sell her quick, we could be in a heap o' trouble. And I don't aim to have that kind of trouble on my hands. I'll give you your share of the money, and you kin spend it on something just as good."

"*Bon Dieu*," 'Fayette mumbled, "I sure would like a taste of this sweet-smelling thing before we let her go."

"Well now, boys, we might be able to arrange that. We really oughta check out the merchandise so we can set a fair price on her. Don't wanta cheat the good madam up in Baton Rouge."

"Ya mean it, Paw?" 'Fayette chuckled, moving in close and rubbing his hands along my arms. "She sure feels good."

"Take her back in the shed. Always had a hankering for something luscious like her myself. You know, she musta just been wishing for us to come along. All undressed and waiting like she was."

'Fayette started running, dragging me along. All my attempts to pull away from his strong grip were useless.

"Hold on there, boy. Remember, I'm your papa and I go first. Gotta break her in gently or we'll be shortchanged for selling damaged goods. Now just watch me, and I'll show you how to get her hot blood boiling."

The two boys shoved me none too gently down onto the shawl, and together they held me immobile on the ground. Too paralyzed with fright to move even if I'd been able, I closed my eyes against the sight of the filthy old man approaching me. I could hear heavy breathing from all three of them and feel the sweat in the hands holding me down. 'Poleon began to giggle and 'Fayette kept urging his father to hurry up.

I felt rough, grubby hands lifting my chemise and rubbing along my thighs. I held my breath waiting for the heavy body to bear down on top of me. I thought I was going to be sick from the stench of dirty bodies and tobacco-juice breath.

Surprisingly, without warning, the old man screamed and leaped up. Almost immediately the boys freed my arms and legs, but I still lay there, afraid to open my eyes or sit up.

"What is it, Paw?"

"What's the matter?"

"Why ya quit?"

"Looky there." The old man's voice sounded as scared as I was. Was it a snake? Was I lying beside a rattler or a moccasin? I couldn't think of anything else that would so frighten a man.

"I'm lookin', I'm lookin'," 'Fayette said, "but I don't see anything but the prettiest piece of—"

"Shut up, boy, and look at that thing tied around her waist."

"A money pouch! Hell, Paw, we coulda got that after we're through. That wouldn't stop me. You're gettin' too old."

"Not the money, boy; next to it."

"That little wad of cloth?" 'Poleon sneered.

"Not just a wad of cloth. That's Voodoo. She's a Voodoo witch. She wears that to protect her."

"God damn, Paw. That's just superstition."

"No, it ain't. It's serious. I ain't touching her and neither are you."

"So what do we do?"

"We'll still sell her up to Baton Rouge, but we ain't gonna touch her. I don't want my cows dying and my corn shriveling up. And I won't wanna be dead neither."

I tried not to show my relief too clearly. If my

Voodoo charm had saved me from these three men, it might do the same later on.

" 'Fayette, go get the wagon. 'Poleon, get some rope. We'll truss her up in that to take her up the Trace."

The old man reached for my dress, but in his fear at seeing the charm, he had leaped back on it, grinding it down into the dirt and tearing it beyond repair.

"Well, here," he said, "put on one of these." He threw down a petticoat.

"May I have the other one, too?" I hoped to drape it around in such a way as to cover myself from the waist up.

"Ya don't need it. The boys'll enjoy looking at you while we ride. But they won't touch ya. I'll see to that."

Leaving bonnet, shoes, and shawl behind, I was carried to the wagon and tied down with ropes drawn through the floorboards. The cords were so tight I couldn't turn, and soon the rough wood was tearing the chemise and rubbing my back raw.

"You'll never be able to sell me," I said quietly, "if my back and legs are bruised. Whoever it is you're taking me to will think you've been abusing and mistreating me. If you want full value, you'd better treat me more gently."

"Boys," the old man said gruffly, "take off your jackets and put them under her. Loosen them ropes, too. She won't get away."

We jogged along for hours, and lulled by the steady movement of the wagon, I fell asleep. It was well after dark when 'Poleon awoke me with an offer of cornbread and a cup of water. They had stopped in a grove of hickory trees, and the mules were unharnessed. One after another I saw the men step some distance into the wood and then return. The old man came over and untied my bonds.

"Thought you might want to stretch your legs a bit," he said. "But don't be gone too long or I'll come after ya."

Wondering at his change of tone but grateful for the chance to be alone for a few minutes, I walked toward the trees. When I returned, the old man tied me back in the wagon again. The two boys were sprawled under a tree, apparently asleep. For a long time I forced myself to remain awake, afraid 'Fayette and 'Poleon would get into the wagon with me once they were certain their father was asleep. No Voodoo charm would scare them away, but it seemed they were very much afraid of the old man. Once I'd convinced myself of this, I clutched the charm in my hand, got as comfortable as I could, and dozed off.

My introduction to Voodoo had occurred a few nights after my experience with the screech owl. Determined to learn where my mother went almost every night after dark, I feigned sleep until I heard her footsteps on the gravel path behind the house. In less than a minute I was out of the nightgown I'd slipped over my dress, and I had put on a pair of sturdy shoes.

Keeping my mother in sight but never allowing myself to be seen, I had followed Clotilde along several familiar streets of the *Vieux Carré* and to the edge of the bayou. Here she slowed down, feeling her way more carefully from hummock to hummock, avoiding the treacherous morass, and pulling aside entangled snakelike vines. In the darkness, I was afraid I would lose sight of her or become mired in the deadly swamp, so I shifted my eyes steadily from the shadowy figure gliding among the trees to the path beneath my feet.

Once deep enough into the bayou to be completely lost, I began to hear voices coming from all directions. They seemed to be converging on a spot just ahead, near where my mother had stopped. After another few steps, I saw a dark shape, low and oblong, looming up in the night. It wasn't exactly a building because I could discern the vague silhouettes of trees through it. Coming closer, I saw I was approaching a structure consisting of a low, flat roof supported by four sturdy poles at the corners. After a few more steps, I squatted down. The people on the near side of the structure were chanting something in a high, eerie tone. At first it was just a jumble of sound, but then as the group sang in unison, I could begin to make out some of the words.

"Papa Legba, guardian of the gates, let your children in. Papa Legba, most benevolent, we would enter the house of mystery."

Over and over, while they marched and swayed toward the enclosure, the worshipers sang these two lines. I recognized many of them as slaves and free *gens du couleur* I had seen my mother talking to in the Market.

The problem now, I thought, was to see without being seen. All my life I'd overheard people talk about Voodoo in hushed tones, often stopping in the middle of a sentence when they saw I was listening. I had come this far, and I would not be denied the chance to see what a Voodoo ritual was like. I need not have worried. All eyes were focused on one end of the mystery house, and I was able to join those seated on the ground near a rickety bench at the farther end.

In spite of the thick cluster of people, I was able to see the front of the house, where several blankets had been hung from the roof. Against this backdrop was a low, oblong table or altar of rough boards. On it were a number of incongruous objects: a crudely carved wooden serpent symbol, a crucifix, a bowl into which the celebrants dropped offerings of food as they entered, another hollowed-out stone bowl with a tiny floating flame, and two bags of some coarse material surmounted by feathers which I later learned were Ouanga packets. On one end of the altar was a stuffed black cat; on the other, a white. Both animals had their backs humped and their mouths open, as though hissing.

Towering above all this was a huge black doll in a dress covered with variegated cabalistic signs and emblems. Around its neck was a long necklace of snake vertebrae from which hung the fang of an alligator. On the ground at either end of the altar were built-up square pillars of bricks, and on each a bright charcoal fire glowed, casting a lurid red light over the whole scene.

In the smoky haze from these fires, I looked at the people around me. All the men and women had white kerchiefs tied across their foreheads. In addition, the women wore the traditional bandana, draped and tied turban fashion, that was the badge of their African ancestry. After a governor in the 1700s passed a law forbidding them to wear bonnets, no Negro or woman of color, whether slave or free, could appear in public in New Orleans without such headgear. He had been urged into it by the Creole women who said the fancy bonnets of those with darker skin were so much more beautiful and elaborate that they outshone theirs. Later I learned the bandanas worn in Voodoo ceremonies were tied symbolically in seven points, all upturned to heaven.

The voices of the celebrants were now joined by other sounds, strange harmonies of music from men sitting on the ground near the altar and playing drums, sheep-shank bones, turkey-leg bones, and a gourd filled with pebbles and wound around with snake vertebrae. Like the others, I was beginning to sway under the spell of the weird, hypnotic music.

I looked around for my mother, but couldn't see her in the half-light of the flames from the altar and the torches tied to the four posts. A pale moon, waning from full to half, seemed imprisoned within the skeletal branches of the trees brushing against the roof of the structure.

As though orchestrated by an unseen director, the chanting and music ceased, but into the ensuing silence came a new sound—the bleating of goats. I didn't realize it at the time, but I was witnessing a blood sacrifice ceremony, held at the request of one of the worshipers either to avert a danger or to bring about some desired event. Since most of the participants were devout Roman Catholics, that person would likely also light candles in the St. Louis Cathedral or offer a special mass to the same end. But of the three forms of request, the Voodoo ceremony was the most important, appealing to some deep-seated, primitive memory inherited from ancestors who worshiped the fearful gods deep in the jungles of ancient Africa from whence these rituals had come to America.

The music and chanting began again, slowly at first and then becoming more frenzied. With a shock I opened my eyes wider. I saw my mother now, garbed in a scarlet robe and feathered headdress, revolving and swaying in a sinuous dance. She was a Mamaloi, or priestess of the voodoo cult. I swallowed hard. I was both awed and frightened. Preceding her was a young man whose upstretched palms supported a sword, and following her was a group of women robed in white. Immediately behind them was a young man leading two bleating, reluctant goats garlanded with flowers.

The ritual had begun. While the music grew louder and the chanting voices more fervent, my mother whirled and danced in front of the altar until she finally fell prostrate on the ground, remaining there for several minutes. I was more and more terrified, smothered by the sounds and the bodies around me. I remembered the stories I'd heard about the tortures of hell and the horrible acts committed by the souls of the dead who came back as ghouls to haunt those who had wronged them in life. Were these real people around me or spirits come to whisk me away?

The beat of the three drums, the rattle of the bones, the shaking of the gourd, the wail of the chants, and above all, the bleating of the goats. I cowered under the bench when I heard the worshipers call on Damballa, the great serpent god, most powerful god of Voodoo.

Suddenly a great shout went up, accompanied by the stamping of feet and clapping. "He has come!" they screamed. "He has come among us to bless our worship of him. Oh, great Damballa, we thank you."

I watched the mass of people separate into two groups, as though to make a path for someone to walk between them. But no one did. Then I saw their eyes as they followed the movement of something on the ground. I looked down to see a huge black snake gliding sinuously along the narrow, open space near my feet. I dared not scream, so I squeezed my eyes as tightly shut as possible and drew my feet in under my skirt. From what I heard, I gathered that the snake was not a part of the ritual, but had merely slithered in of its own accord, and was now considered a good omen by the gathering.

The chanting began again, and Clotilde as Mamaloi was once more on her feet, dancing in front of the altar and leaping straight up in the air.

"Oh, great Damballa, now we know you approve. You will accept our sacrifice of goats in place of a human sacrifice."

Still dazed and a little sick, I watched as first one goat and then the other had its throat slit and the blood of both was allowed to drain into a wooden trough. I held my hand over my mouth when I saw my mother dip a wooden bowl into the trough and drink some of the blood, then scrambled out between the last row of worshipers and into a cluster of trees. In a cold sweat, and doubled over with pain and nausea, I retched and gagged until I finally collapsed in exhaustion. Behind me the frenzied worshipers were begging to be sprinkled with the blood of the sacrifice and blessed by the great Damballa.

I'll never know how I did it, but I waited until my mother left the gathering and retraced her twisting path through the bayou and into the city. Once in the *Vieux Carré*, I took a different route, running as fast as my ebbing strength would allow to reach home before my mother did. Fortunately, she was exhausted, too, worn out by the exertions of the dance and the passions of the ritual. I was in bed and seemingly asleep when she tiptoed through my room.

When I was thirteen, I was initiated into the Voodoo cult and given my own Ouanga packet. By this time I had attended many ceremonies with my mother, and I became familiar with the ritual. I was finally able to control the queasy feelings that unsettled me whenever there was a blood sacrifice; but I still could not overcome my terror of snakes, and I cringed each time they were a necessary part of a service. As long as I didn't have to touch them.

On the night of my initiation, I was robed in white and with the other initiates formed a crescent before the Mamaloi. Garbed again in her scarlet robes and feathered headdress, my mother looked sternly at us and hissed like a snake through her teeth. I looked for her kindly, familiar face beneath the red and black plumes and dreadful visage. Her cheeks were drawn in tightly around the bones, giving her head the appearance of a skull over which skin had been glued.

The chanting and the weird instrumental music were the same as during all previous rituals. Along with the usual articles on the altar was a mounded pyramid of cornmeal on which rested an egg. My mother whirled three times in front of it, her arms reaching out in supplication.

For over two hours I stood swaying on my feet while the ceremony continued. How my mother could keep on dancing, twirling, and jumping without falling from exhaustion, I didn't know. By concentrating on her movements, I hypnotized away the cramps in my legs and the ache in my back. It was all a swirling montage of fluttering white roosters which finally had their necks wrung by the Mamaloi, a goat decorated with flowers and painted designs which was first offered the blood from the cocks and then had its own throat slit. The Mamaloi dipped her fingers into the bowl filled with the goat's blood, made cabalistic signs over those of us being initiated, and sprinkled us with blood.

I had tried to prepare for what was coming next by putting myself in a kind of trance, shutting out all sights and sounds, until I was surrounded by a protective cloak of courage. Yet I still froze with terror. The Papaloi, or priest, came in carrying a long, writhing snake which he sang and whispered to. This was Damballa incarnate, who must approve of the new members of his cult. Paralyzed, I watched the undulating body and whipping tongue. Slowly the Papaloi walked among the initiates, passing the snake over the shoulders of each of us. Finally he retired, and I began to breathe again.

To end the ritual, my mother took the egg from the mound of cornmeal, traced with it a cross on the head of each girl, and then dashed it to earth. As the blood had symbolized mortality, sacrifice, and death, so the egg symbolized rebirth, fertility, and re-creation. The Mamaloi now put her arms around each of the initiates, crying out as she did so, "Legba, Papa Legba, open wide the gates for this my little one."

When my mother approached me, the last initiate, I opened my hands to receive the Ouanga packet which had been prepared for me while the ceremony was taking place. It would be my special charm to ward off danger throughout my lifetime as well as a sign to all familiar with Voodoo that I was a worshiper of Damballa.

In a square red cloth were mingled roots and leaves charred in the stone brazier and pounded into fragments, a tuft of hair from the crown of my head, a thumbnail paring, small pieces of gold, silver, and lead, and a small scrap of material from a garment I had worn next to my skin.

From that moment on, I kept the packet near me at all times, wearing it on a string around my waist or hung from my bedstead.

Chapter Six

I TURNED OVER IN THE WAGON to find a more comfortable position. In the distance I heard the occasional sound of travelers along the Trace. I prayed that one of them would make a detour into the trees and find me in the wagon. But even if that happened, who would disbelieve the old man's story that I was a runaway slave being returned to my master?

Lying tied on the floor of the wagon, I could only listen to the sounds of the night around me and stare up into the darkness of the trees by which the wagon was sheltered, well away from the road. Suddenly I heard a horse approaching, then slowing down. It was almost a repetition of the night before when I crawled through the tall grass, but this time I prayed I'd be discovered. The horse was walking now, and it seemed to have turned in the direction of the grove of trees. In another minute I heard its snorting and heavy breathing, and I saw the figure of the rider loom up beside the wagon.

The man was in shadow, but I sensed he was looking down at me. With one finger he tilted back his broad-brimmed hat, and I found myself looking up into the solemn face of Baptiste Fontaine.

"What the hell's going on here, Leah?" he whispered.

My eyes filled with tears, and my body shook with sobs I could not control.

"K-k-kidnapped. I've been kidnapped."

Baptiste looked over at the three men still asleep on the ground.

"Have they hurt you?" he asked gently.

"No, but they are going to—to sell me in Baton Rouge."

"Oh my God. The bastards!"

Baptiste unbuttoned his coat and, placing one hand on each hip, brought out two guns.

"Can you shoot?" he asked.

"No, I never have."

"Well, surely you can hold one of them. They won't know you can't."

Baptiste quickly untied me; while he waited, I rubbed my wrists to restore the circulation. Then he assisted me up into the saddle of his horse and handed me a gun.

"Hold it steady with both hands," he cautioned as he showed me how to aim it. "I'll wake them up with this one, but we need to keep them covered while I scare off the mules."

"Couldn't we just leave them and go off?" I said anxiously.

"No, they might wake up any minute. I want to scare them so thoroughly they won't try to follow us."

Baptiste untied the animals but waited until he had the men well covered before he sent them running.

"Wake up, damn you!" He kicked first one and then another.

First 'Fayette, then the old man, and lastly 'Poleon roused up, still too sleep-dazed to know what was happening.

"Eh, what? What's going on? Whatcha doing with that gun?" 'Fayette's voice was shaking.

"Who are you?" The old man was more defiant. "What're you doing with that slave?"

"She's no slave, and I'm taking her back to New Orleans."

"No, you ain't!" The old man jumped up and only

then saw the gun aimed at his belly. "She's mine. I found her. I claim the *re*-ward."

"She is no slave." Baptiste spoke slowly and clearly. "One move and you're dead. Now I'm going to release the mules, and you're going to stay right where you are. Hear?"

"Yes, sir, we hear." The old man was suddenly cowed. "We ain't done nothing to her, ain't touched her. Just wanted the reward."

"You lying old bastard, I ought to shoot right where I'm aimed."

"No, no! Leave us be. We won't cause no trouble."

"You're damn right you won't. Leah, keep the gun aimed over this way."

If the old man or the boys had any idea of attacking Baptiste when his back was turned, they changed their minds when they saw the gun in my hands and the hatred on my face.

Baptiste slapped the flanks of the mules and they took off, ambling back toward the farm. Then he swung up on the saddle behind me and urged the horse into a fast canter. With one hand he guided the reins; with the other he held me close to his chest.

I could feel his firm arm muscles and hard chest through my sheer chemise. Surrounded by his strength, I felt secure and safe for the first time in over twenty-four hours. I didn't realize until we had traveled several hundred yards just how frightened and alone I'd been from the time I'd left New Orleans. After being captured by the three men, I'd been too terrified to react physically. Now I began shaking and crying uncontrollably.

At first Baptiste misunderstood the reason for my tears. "Are you uncomfortable, Leah?"

"Just—just a little bit," I sobbed. "It's hard riding astride with—with just this petticoat on."

"I'm sorry." He pulled the horse to a stop and helped me shift to a sidesaddle position.

With both arms around me now, he held me closer

to his chest, and once more the sobs shook my body as
the power of his strength made me realize anew how
close I had come to being sold into prostitution. His
cheek lay against my hair, long since freed of pins and
falling around my shoulders, and I could feel his warm
breath on my neck. Gently he moved one hand up
from my waist until it rested on the underside of my
breasts. The desire to have it remain there surged
through my body, but without a word I moved it down
again. If he was disturbed or chagrined by the action,
he gave no sign. I needed his strength, but I was unable to cope with any emotional upheavals.

"Want to tell me what happened?" Baptiste asked.

"No, but I guess you deserve to know," I said,
amazed at how calm my voice was. "I was running
away."

"Because of what happened with Charles Anderson
at the ball?"

"Partly. But I'd already planned to leave New Orleans. From the time I was a little girl I knew I'd do it
someday."

"Going north? To pass?"

"I thought I could do it."

"You could, but not that way."

"Oh, Baptiste, what if you hadn't come along?"
Without thinking I'd called him by his first name, and I
wondered if he'd noticed.

"Getting tired?" he asked. "I think we could stop
and rest for a few minutes."

"Yes, please."

Baptiste helped me down, then took off the saddle
and spread the saddle blanket on the ground. "I'll lean
back against this tree," he suggested, "and you put
your head in my lap."

I was like a puppet, with Baptiste pulling the strings.
With my head in his lap, I lay quiet while he massaged
the ache from my arms and legs where the ropes had
been drawn tight. I began crying again as the cramps
were eased away.

When Baptiste cradled me in his arms, I snuggled contentedly against his warm body.

"This is the second time I've rescued you, Leah. Don't you think I deserve a reward now?"

As he spoke, he began caressing one breast and bringing my mouth up to his. His kiss was gentle, while under the touch of his hand my breasts swelled and my loins ached with desire for this virile man. My heart urged me to respond to the demanding pressure of his body and the urgency of his mouth. Without a word, just a simple movement of hand or body, I could indicate my willingness to let him make love to me. But moved as I was by strong passions, I knew this was not what I wanted. I had not fled from New Orleans and been rescued from prostitution to fall under the sway of a handsome Creole to whom I meant nothing more than a brief moment of pleasure.

"Please, Baptiste," I begged, "I've no energy to fight you. If you want to take me when I can't resist, go ahead. But I'd rather you weren't one of the things I was running away from."

"No, Leah, I don't want you that way. But this is the second time, so just remember—the third time's the charm. I'm not going to let you get very far away. Someday you'll turn to me, I promise. Now let's go."

We rode quietly the rest of the way, neither of us able to find anything to say. I don't know what Baptiste was thinking as we trotted easily along, but I was searching my soul. I was strongly attracted to this man who held me as gently as a baby now and who, once I'd indicated my feelings, did not persist with his attentions. He was just as obviously attracted to me, and he'd said he would be waiting for me to need him again. But whether he was truly enamored or just desirous of a brief affair, I had no way of knowing. Either way, I must not let myself get involved if I meant to carry out my intentions of never becoming a *placée*. It might be months before I could start north again, but nothing would alter my determination to leave the

Vieux Carré and its imprisoning walls of custom that degraded the human spirit.

I was a human being, and according to what I'd learned at the convent school, I had unlimited potential. There was nothing I could not do if I were willing to discipline myself and make the necessary sacrifices. The easy way would be to compromise my ideals and accept an offer from one of the men who wanted to set me up in *plaçage*. I would lack nothing in the way of comfort or fine possessions if I chose one of the wealthier men who'd approached my mother. Or I could encourage an affair with Baptiste for however long it might last and then hope to find another protector or lover. I would merely be following the path walked by my mother and grandmother. It was considered no disgrace among many *gens du couleur* for a woman to go from lover to lover if she did not find a lifelong protector. But I would not succumb, either to the emotions of the moment or the desire for security. My feelings for Baptiste were strong, but even stronger must be my willpower if I were to live out the life I had determined for myself. Baptiste was just a man, no different from the many others I'd scorned. With these thoughts, I once more assumed the stoic attitude and cool demeanor of the past.

The sun was just lighting up the horizon when we rode into New Orleans. Baptiste had wrapped the saddle blanket around me to cover my near nudity.

"Are you going to take me home, Baptiste?"

"No, I'm taking you to my apartment."

"After what I said before?" I asked, tensing in his arms.

"Relax, Leah. I don't plan to dishonor you. My mother keeps some of her clothes there for when she's in the city. I think we can find something to fit."

"I'm sorry, Baptiste. It's just that I—I—"

"I know. I told you; next time you'll turn to me. There will be a third time, and I'll be waiting."

Chapter Seven

"You were very foolish, Leah."

"I know, Mama."

"Did he violate you?"

"Who? Baptiste? No, Mama, he never touched me."

"And the other men?"

"They were afraid of my Ouanga packet."

"You must learn to be content with this life, Leah. Find a rich young man and learn to be content."

"Like you, Mama? Crying yourself to sleep when Papa doesn't come here?"

"I'm silly sometimes."

"Oh, no," I said vehemently. "I have too many memories. Remember when I was six years old and we went to the Jackson Day parade? You made me a new pink dress and a bonnet with pink ribbons. You even dared to wear a bonnet yourself, in spite of the law."

"The police were too busy with the parade to enforce that law," she said quietly.

I responded as though I hadn't heard her. "How I waited to see Papa leading the local militia. 'But don't call out to him,' you said. 'Don't let anyone know he is your father.' I stood on the edge of the banquette and waited. And when he came, all splendid in red and gold, I couldn't help myself. 'Papa,' I cried, 'I'm here.' Then you snatched me away and dragged me home. But you didn't see him wink at me before we left. Papa didn't care. Only you cared. And that night you cried yourself to sleep again. You cried while I ate pralines

and cried, too. I didn't know then what I'd done
wrong."

"But you understand now."

"I understand that when I won the awards for leading my class at school, you weren't there because you
were afraid you'd embarrass Papa. Only he wasn't
there, either. His son—his legitimate son—was having
a birthday party. So I was alone. Among all those
people I was alone."

"But you received an education," my mother said,
"a real education. That's more than I did. You know
how my mother learned to read and write? From the
newspapers the fish were wrapped in at the Market.
And how did she teach me? By scrimping with the
little money my father gave her, in order to buy me
cheap secondhand books. They are still my proudest
possessions."

"I know, Mama. I'm sorry. I treasure them, too.
Haven't I read every one of them over and over? But
what good does that education do me here?"

"You can be a good *placée*, a real companion to a
white lover. One who can talk about important things,
not just—not just—"

"Not just sleep with him, you mean? And cook
meals he doesn't bother to show up for? No, thank
you. I mean to get more out of life than that."

"Leah, you are colored and you can't forget that.
You are neither Negro nor white. You are colored. But
you are free. No one can ever take that away from
you. That is a gift from your grandfather."

"My great white grandfather I've never seen," I
stormed. "Nor you. What else did your father ever give
you besides your freedom?"

"It was enough."

"It's not enough for me. I'm colored, but seven-
eighths of me is white. I could pass for white and you
know it."

"Not here, Leah. Your feet have already been set in
the path you must follow. Your father has been good

to me, Leah. I've not been unhappy, nor have I lacked for things I needed. You, too, can know contentment with the right man."

Even before I graduated from the convent school at sixteen, my mother had begun preparing me to become the mistress of a white man. Practical lessons included shrewd buying at the Market—how to select the crispest vegetables, the freshest sea food, and breads hot from the oven. In the afternoons we prepared meals, which involved a great deal more than just cooking the provisions we brought home.

"Food is the second most important thing to a man, Leah, sometimes the first. A tasty meal will soothe even the most temperamental. When he comes home after a busy day, he wants to relax with a cigar or pipe and then sit down to a well-set table and satisfying meal."

I learned to add the special touches, the seasonings and colorful embellishments that turned a simple stew or roast into a gourmet's delight. Bouillabaisse, turtle soup with sherry and topped with grated boiled turtle eggs, crawfish bisque, shrimp and lobster gumbos, crisp fried shrimp, crab-stuffed flounder: all these became part of my repertoire. My proudest moment came when I served a complete meal from delicate onion soup to pecan pralines and iced *gâteaux* to my father and received his highest accolade: a kiss on each cheek followed by a smart slap on the rump.

Then it was time to concentrate on sewing; real sewing, not just embroidering cross-stitch samplers. My mother started me on mending my father's ruffled shirts, with minute, invisible stitches, and slowly I progressed to hemming dresses. I sucked many a sore or pricked finger before I was allowed to cut out and put together a complete outfit. My mother seldom gave compliments, but I knew I had passed her most severe test when she suggested I make my white graduation dress.

Somehow I had learned that simplicity became me more than the ruffled and beribboned gowns, inset with lace and embroidery, that were the latest fashion from Paris, and I selected the least elaborate pattern. The softly gathered skirt of moonstone silk was attached to a tight-fitting bodice with an off-the-shoulder, deep bertha collar of fragile lace, a gift from my father.

On many occasions between my fourteenth and sixteenth birthdays, I seriously considered taking the vows and becoming a nun. The Catholic church was the one institution in New Orleans free from segregation and discrimination of any kind. For that reason most free people of color and many slaves were Catholic. It is true, of course, that Southern Louisiana was settled by French and Spanish Catholics who indoctrinated their slaves with the tenets of their church. Masses were held regularly on plantations, and slaves accompanied masters and mistresses to the St. Louis Cathedral in New Orleans. However, once free, a man or woman of color could make his own choice. A few formed their own churches, but many preferred to remain Catholic, especially in the *Vieux Carré*, and I'm sure it was because in the cathedral and the eyes of the Catholic God all men were equal.

Yes, I gave much thought to entering the novitiate, for the nuns at the convent school had always been very kind to me, and one of them was a free woman of color who had taken vows for much the same reasons that compelled me to think about it. She preferred belonging to the Church rather than to a white lover like her mother before her.

Sister Angelique was several years older than I, almost of my mother's generation. I longed to talk with her, to pour out my frustrations to an understanding heart, and receive the balm of encouragement. As sweet and gentle as she was, I hesitated to approach her because of her shy, reticent manner. In the classroom there was no question she would not answer, and she encouraged our inquisitive minds by assuring us there was no such thing as a stupid question if we sincerely wanted to know the answer. She was the ideal teacher for adolescent girls fearful at each tentative step they took toward maturity. I wanted to be just like her.

Once outside the classroom, however, she withdrew into her own silent world, and all communication with others ceased. I hesitated to penetrate her world, yet something impelled me to search for a way to approach her. I wanted her to reach out toward me, but I knew she never would. In the afternoons, as soon as classes were dismissed, she joined other nuns in the parlor for tea. I often saw her there as I passed through the hall on the way out, sitting quietly in one corner while the rest of the sisters chatted or shook their heads over some shocking new student misdemeanor. I knew her isolation was self-imposed, for the others often turned and tried to include her in their conversation.

One afternoon I remained later than usual; why, I don't remember, unless it was to make up some work I'd missed because of illness. I was almost fifteen then, and I was experiencing, much to my disgust, one or two painfully sick days every month. If that was what it meant to be a woman, I thought, I would prefer to remain a child. Still acutely ignorant after listening to my mother's tentative, awkward hints about bodily functions and babies, I had somehow come to the absurd conclusion that if I became a nun rather than a *placée*, there would be no babies and my monthly problems would cease. Undoubtedly that was one—if not the main—reason for considering the novitiate.

On that late afternoon, I passed the parlor door as usual and saw Sister Angelique sitting alone. The others were busy rehearsing some of the younger students who were preparing a pre-Lenten fête. Sister Angelique had finished her tea and had her head bent close to her breviary. It was the first time I realized she was very nearsighted, almost blind in fact. And then I remembered she never used a book in the classroom, but always relied on what must have been a fantastic memory. It was against all polite custom to disturb her at her devotions, but I might never again have the opportunity to see her alone and undisturbed. Or more importantly, not hurrying away from contact with anyone.

"Sister Angelique," I whispered, dreading to disturb the silence of the room. "May—may I see you for a minute?"

She looked at me and gave me a smile such as only the blessed and the serene possess. She then held out her hand and spoke as though I were the one person in the world she wanted to see.

"Come in, my child, come in." She pointed to the chair beside her. "Would you like some tea? I'm sure there's some left in the pot. Or a cake?"

I shook my head, too full of wonder and gladness to speak.

"Are you feeling better?" she asked.

"Yes, thank you, Sister, much better."

"Good. Such a pity you have problems, but it is the curse of Eve that we must suffer for our sins." The "we" startled me for a minute, and I wondered if I'd erred in my ideas of the physical life of a nun. She looked me straight in the eye. Her expression told me she was ready to talk about whatever was on my mind, but I must not dissemble or procrastinate. I must come directly to the point.

"I want to be a nun," I said.

"Why?" No smile of approval, no guiding questions.

I wanted to say, *Because I want to be like you,* but I was afraid. "I want to teach."

"What do you know about teaching?" she asked sternly. Did she know I was avoiding the truth?

"Nothing," I stuttered, "but I can learn."

"Then that is no reason for thinking you want to be a nun. Is there another?"

I knew I blushed as I forced myself to answer! "I—I don't want to be a *placée*."

Sister Angelique's face softened, and her tone became more conciliatory. "Leah, one does not enter the church to escape from something, even something she finds distasteful and abhorrent. It should be thought of as a true vocation, one a girl is called to. It must be a movement forward to a new life, not a retreat from an old one. Do you understand what I'm saying?"

"Yes, Sister." There was something I had to say, and I prayed she, in turn, would understand. "I truly want to be a nun, but you are asking questions I cannot answer. I don't think that's fair."

Sister Angelique leaned back in her chair, and I saw faint hints of laughter dancing around her mouth.

"You are right, Leah. I am the one who needs to practice understanding. I sympathize with your wish not to be a *placée*, but we need to consider what other paths you could follow, such as marriage to a free man of color, governess with a fine family, or a small business of your own, like dressmaker or milliner. The church is a strict and demanding disciplinarian. Think well before you take the veil."

I swallowed hard. There was one question I had long wanted to ask. I knew she would either give me an honest answer or ask me quietly to leave.

"Please, Sister Angelique, why did you become a nun?"

I was afraid for a moment she was going to cry. Her eyes filled with tears, and she turned her face away so I could not see her wiping them with a square of fine cambric. I waited agonizing minutes before she spoke.

"Leah, you have asked an honest question, one I know has long troubled you or you would not have presumed on my privacy. I am going to entrust you with a secret I have never revealed to anyone else except my confessor."

Slowly and painfully Sister Angelique began to tell me her story. Her mother was a mulatto from Jamaica who fled from a cruel master and sought refuge with a kindly ship captain headed for the Gulf Coast. Once in

Biloxi, he set her up as an apprentice to a dressmaker. There Sister Angelique's father, a cotton planter, first saw her when he went to pick up gowns for his wife. From then on, she was his mistress. Having fled from slavery in Jamaica, she was considered a free woman under the protection of her lover. Sister Angelique was one of five children, but unlike me, she and her two sisters were not reared to please white men. Instead, they were expected to become seamstresses or milliners.

Sister Angelique had never questioned her future nor given much thought to whether she would marry. Nor did she think about receiving a formal education, for her mother could neither read nor write. When her father left behind a book of French fables which he originally had bought as a gift for the child of a friend in New Orleans, Sister Angelique looked at the pictures and cried because she could not understand the words written under them. The next time her father came to see her, she pleaded to be taught to read, and he said he would see. On his return from New Orleans— whence he'd taken her precious book—he said he'd made arrangements for her to be a boarding student at a convent.

Her happiness was so great, she thought she would explode. For thirteen years she had spoken English and been reared in complete ignorance of any religion. Within a month, her father told her, she would be part of a small world in which only French was spoken and where one attended mass every day and lived according to the regimen of the Catholic Church. As alien as that world sounded to her, it held no fears if she would be taught to read and write.

During the next two weeks, while she was preparing to leave her family, Sister Angelique learned that attending the convent would be not just an exciting experience but could be the means of saving her sanity. Completely innocent about life and naive about the ways of men, she was tragically unprepared to cope with what happened one afternoon. She was alone in the house, packing newly sewn undergarments in her trunk, when she heard someone approaching the bedroom she shared with her sisters. She was alerted to the fact it wasn't one of the family by the stealthy, cautious footsteps, so different from the rambunctious running of her brothers and sisters.

Her father's youngest brother was standing in the doorway. Without saying a word, and before she realized what was happening, he forced her down on the bed. While holding one hand over her mouth so she could not scream for help, he raped her, and she fainted from the pain. When she regained consciousness, he fell on her again and raped her twice more before leaving her crying from the agonies of pain and humiliation. Somehow she was able to look ahead into the future and realize what life in the white world held for her: a constant fending off of men who considered her easy prey for all their passions. She had thought learning to read would merely give her pleasure; now she knew it would prove to be the key to a safe, secure refuge within a hostile world.

Never telling anyone what had happened, she left for the convent, and once there, studied with such intensity she was soon the top student. Within a year, she asked to become a postulant, and she devoted all her hours to becoming a worthy bride of Christ. With a passion that would never be enjoyed by a lover, she prayed to be purged of the sin that tortured her constantly. Somehow, some way she must have tempted her uncle into attacking her, and only by devoting all her energies to the work of the Church could she atone. But once she became a teacher, her experience was of great value to her. It gave her a great compassion for the girls in her charge who sincerely looked to her to free them from the shackles of ignorance.

"You see, Leah, I speak from experience when I say you cannot use the Church as an escape from a desperate situation. I did, and it took many years for me to accustom myself to the stringent discipline. I spent a most unhappy novitiate rebelling inwardly against the training while outwardly presenting a subservient mien to those around me. I found my only peace during the solitary hours in my cell when I could release my frustrations in tears and reading. Not prayers. Not at that time. Gradually I learned to adjust, and before too long I discovered how much I loved teaching."

She paused, and I knew I had to reveal one more truth. "Sister Angelique, I want to be just like you."

"No, Leah, you want to be yourself. You are a child of God, and each of his children is a unique person. Think about it for a year. If you still feel you have a true vocation, I will happily guide you through your novitiate. Now, it's time for you to go home. Please remember me in your prayers tonight."

Before the year was over, I had envisioned a future for myself that included neither the church nor the *Vieux Carré*, for neither altered my birth or place in New Orleans.

Once I graduated from the convent, the more serious instructions for becoming a well-placed mistress began. These were more difficult for my mother to teach and harder for me to comprehend. Not just the simple facts of life, but how to please a man during more intimate moments; how to arouse one who is tired or sated with the pleasures of the flesh. I cringed with revulsion at some of the details she imparted to me, but she assured me I would accept them when the proper moment came. Dressing and undressing were no longer routine matters but became artistic accomplishments, done seductively and with finesse. Undergarments were taken off and put on slowly; dresses were unfastened with graceful movements.

In addition, I learned which herbs could be concocted into elixirs to cure impotence or increase desire. Ancient Voodoo recipes contained ingredients that would induce abortions when desired, and others included charms to assure a lover's complete devotion or make a disinterested man fall in love.

To all of this, I listened attentively, but not for the reason my mother intended. The arts which would entice a Creole lover would also attract a Northern husband.

At seventeen I attended my first quadroon ball, and I had to admit I was impressed. When I entered, the ballroom was already crowded with men attired in immaculate black and white evening dress. Negro waiters moved quietly and obsequiously among them with trays holding hollow-stemmed crystal glasses of champagne. On long tables covered in fine white linen were large trays of sliced turkey, ham, and beef as well as silver goblets of wine. A small orchestra began tuning up.

I was frightened. Among the other girls being presented for the first time there were some I had known at the convent school, and they all seemed so much more poised than I. Although I despised the existence of the affair and my reason for being there, I was feminine enough to hope one of the handsome young men would ask me to dance. I knew the gaily informal quadroon balls were far more popular in the French Quarter than those sponsored by the leaders of the élite white society, from which the men often excused themselves after a polite dance or two. For a while, at least, I wanted to be part of the fun without bearing any of the more serious consequences of the affair.

For days my mother had worked to create just the right gown to reveal my charms. Being tall, I could carry the full hoops gracefully. I had learned to walk in the peculiar fashion which made me look as though I were gliding effortlessly across the floor. I can still remember the long, back-breaking hours I spent standing inside the hoops while my mother draped yards and yards of pale pink gauze over deeper pink silk. Additional fabric was draped in deep swaths like a softly folded shawl around the off-the-shoulder neckline.

There were no ruffles, but here and there the skirt and shoulder drapery was caught up with minute bouquets of pink silk roses. I would have preferred something less elaborate, but my mother insisted that, for my debut, I wear the newest style.

To make me even more uncomfortable, she piled my long hair in a pyramid of poufs and dips with a single cluster of curls brushing my right shoulder. Like the dress, this artificial coiffure was embellished with pink silk roses. To keep every hair in place, I walked with my head high, increasing the hauteur I had already learned to affect. Although I was not aware of it at the time, my cold, proud mien intrigued the men more than the smiling faces and flirtatious actions of the other girls. However, I received no proposals, for which I was grateful, though my mother was upset.

"Leah, dancing with the men is not enough. You must also carry on a spritely conversation so they can learn something about you and you can reveal more of your charms."

"I'm sorry, but I find such idle talk boring. I'm not there to entertain them. If they want me to talk to them, let them find something interesting to talk about."

"You are there to find more than a dancing partner, Leah."

"Not yet, Mama, please. I'm not ready to belong to someone I don't know."

"You can't wait too long. You are at the age when your charms are coming to full bloom, which makes you attractive and challenging to any man. Young men will not be afraid you are too worldly and experienced. Older men will be attracted to your fresh, virginal beauty."

"You make me sound like something for sale in the Market!" I cried in anguish. "Smell it to make sure it's fresh! Break it to make sure it's crisp, or pinch it to see if it's still tender. Am I ripe? Am I overripe? I'm not a vegetable or a crayfish to be bought or tossed aside."

"No, Leah, you are not a piece of merchandise, but you are selling yourself to a potential lover and protector."

"Selling! Protector! I might as well be a slave instead of a free woman." I wanted to cry out at the unfairness of it all.

"A free woman of color, Leah, whose only hope for a secure future is as mistress of a wealthy Creole. You can marry a man of our own kind, but I fear you will be quickly disillusioned with the life he will provide for you."

"And I must do one or the other?"

"There is no acceptable third choice. I cannot continue to support you, nor will your father. I will be provided for, but not enough to include you. You may inherit from him, but that, I pray, will be many years away."

"I can provide for myself," I insisted. "There must be something I can do."

"And what would that be?" my mother asked. "Go into a household as a servant? As a hairdresser? There are slaves for that."

"I can do fine sewing. You've taught me that."

"Yes, you could, if you think you can live on a mere pittance. I will not let my home be turned into a mercantile establishment."

I was forced to acquiesce. For a time, until I could find a way to leave for the North, I had to seem to follow her lead.

"Will I be free to make my own choice?"

"I'll not force you to enter into a *plaçage* you vehemently oppose. But, remember, you can never really know a man until you live wtih him for some time. Let me know when you receive a proposal you wish to accept and I'll talk to the young man. If I receive the proposal, I will consult with you before I approve."

"But what if I don't like him after I've known him for a while? What if he is a different person in the—in the bedroom from on the dance floor?"

"You will learn to accept him, to be the person he wants. Your future happiness does not depend on loving or even liking him. But it does depend on his providing you a secure future with a house and a generous allowance. Those are the things I will handle. You need never fear being left in poverty even if he should tire of you and seek another mistress or marry and be unable to see you again."

My mother saw only the practical side of the arrangement while I longed to be loved and cherished. No, more than that, to love and respect the man I lived with—and I couldn't do that unless I were married to him. How I might meet such a man, I did not yet know, but the quadroon balls would give me the experience I needed to feel more at ease with men and to learn what most appealed to them.

After the incident with Charles Anderson, I begged off going to a ball for nearly two weeks. I think I would have died if I'd seen him. In spite of Baptiste's assurances that my attacker would never be allowed to attend a ball again, I couldn't be sure he wasn't just saying that to console me. Finally, to placate my mother and dissipate the chilling atmosphere from the house, I agreed to go back.

During the next three balls I received two honorable proposals which I declined and which I did not reveal to my mother. She in turn had been approached by three or four young men, and I promised to consider their offers. This eased the situation at home for a while.

It was not until my fourth ball that I saw Baptiste again. With a cool air of disdain, as though he were asking his hostess for a duty dance, he led me onto the floor.

"I'm hearing some very disturbing news about you, Leah."

"Oh. Interesting news, I hope," I said just as coolly.

"I hear you're playing hard to get. There are several young men getting impatient for your answer."

"I didn't ask them to make the proposals."

"Your being here does the asking for you. Why do you come if you're so opposed to *plaçage*?"

"Do you really want to know? Well, I'll tell you. To keep peace with my mother and because I like to dance."

"And that's why you smiled at me? Because you like to dance? I thought you were glad to see me."

"I was. You're the best dancer I know. But don't make any offers I'd have to refuse," I said haughtily.

"Don't worry, Leah, that's one refusal you won't have to concern yourself with. I have no intention of asking for you. I like my freedom."

I stiffened in his arms, hurt and insulted by his attitude.

In silence he swung me around to one of Strauss's fast-stepping waltzes and then returned me to my mother's side. With a crooked, knowing grin he bowed stiffly and bade me goodnight.

Chapter Eight

THE MARKET WAS MORE CROWDED than usual for a weekday morning, and I was jostled at every stall I tried to approach. Along with Negro cooks in aprons and bandanas, mulatto and quadroon *placées* in fashionable day dresses and tignons, and various male servants, I stood back to allow white women customers to make their selections first. This meant the choicest fruits and vegetables would be all picked over.

On most days everyone mingled and chatted, comparing prices and quality, exchanging recipes, and whispering about the latest gossip. The Market—like the cathedral—was ordinarily a place where all humanity met on equal ground. Rarely was I made aware of my status in the *Vieux Carré*, but when it occurred, I wanted to turn and run away, furious at the society that had created the situation. I wanted to pull off my tignon and scream out, "Look at me, everybody! I have arms and legs just like yours. My eyes see the same boats on the river and my ears listen for the same bird songs in the morning. I'm not a freak. I'm a human being just like you."

But I didn't. I completed my purchases as fast as I could, forgetting the special seasonings my mother wanted for dinner, and started home.

Suddenly a shout went up from near one of the carriages. "Stop thief!"

My mistake was in proceeding on my way as though what was happening was none of my concern. Several ahead of me had turned around and were pushing toward the carriage to see what the excitement was all about. Tired of being shoved first one way and then another, I moved ahead faster to escape the confusion. I was getting a headache from the strain of coping with the crowd as well as my own personal upheaval. All I wanted was to get home and lie down in the peaceful calm of my own room.

It was not to be.

I heard a man scream, "There she is," and I felt a hand tugging at my market basket. Two more strong hands grabbed me brutally by the shoulders, and I was spun around until I stared into the ugly face of the huge man who held me immobile. I don't know whether he was the man who'd screamed or just a bystander caught up in the frenzy of the moment.

"Let me go," I snarled. "Take your filthy hands off me. Who do you think you are that you can grab me like that?" I forgot for a minute that one did not talk to a white man like that, even an ugly, vulgar example of the poor white trash scorned even by Negro slaves.

"More to the point," he said roughly, "is who you are. You're a thief." And he glanced down into my basket.

There among the vegetables and fish I'd purchased for dinner nestled a lady's small mesh bag, embroidered with ornate jet beads. Amidst all the confusion the thief they were screaming for had found an opportunity to drop the purse into my basket. He might even be the very man who now held me.

In a panic, knowing I would be arrested and couldn't possibly prove my innocence, I tried to wrest myself free from my captor; but his hold was too strong. Acting out of desperation, I brought one knee up with all the force I could muster, and I struck him right where I'd aimed. Doubled over with pain, he let go of my shoulders; and while the others stood dazed at what had happened, I started to run.

Unfortunately my way was blocked by a policeman who'd heard the shouting and came to investigate.

Racial tension was much less severe in New Orleans, especially in the French Quarter, than in many other parts of the South; but it did exist under a seemingly placid surface, and occasionally it erupted when least expected. At those times curfews for Negroes and colored were more strictly enforced, while police were put on the alert for any action that might start a real outbreak of trouble. We'd just been through such an uneasy period following the killing of two men of color who claimed to be free but whom a planter said were his runaway slaves. This was one of the reasons for the hostile atmosphere at the Market. It had also meant being sure I was off the streets and behind the walls of our courtyard within half an hour after sunset. Never did I feel such a prisoner of my dark heritage as when forced to submit to a lockstep life controlled by the whims of a white government.

Until I was seventeen I had lived a fairly sheltered life, moving without too much restraint between home, Market, the cathedral, and the convent school. Accustomed from birth to a particular way of life, I had only rebelled inwardly at the differences between my father's world and mine. However, since my experience with Charles Anderson and my brief, aborted excursion along the river, I had come to feel that only by openly defying what I thought was unjust could I preserve my identity.

The policeman was merely one more obstacle between me and the ultimate freedom my soul craved. I did not see him as a symbol of authority. He was merely a man I had to get away from. In my ever-increasing panic, I failed to keep my head, failed to realize I could, with my father's help, prove my innocence. Without thinking, I swung at him with my basket, knocking him to the ground. I noted that he was unconscious before I lifted my skirts and fled as fast as I could along the nearest street.

Once it dawned on me what I'd done, I realized I was in serious trouble. Badly hurt or merely stunned, the man was an officer, and the penalty for a nonwhite, slave or free, who struck a law officer, was years of imprisonment. And if he died? I refused to let that thought take root in my mind. Execution would be no worse than a life behind real prison walls. I had lived behind imaginary ones, and the threat of incarceration sped me along faster than I had thought I could move.

I didn't know what streets I ran along as I turned one corner and then another, trying to outwit my pursuers. People called to me. I lost my small purse of money. My tignon caught in the low branch of a tree and was pulled off, releasing my long hair to fall around my shoulders. I was gasping for breath, yet dared not stop. Not until a sudden, painful stitch in my side doubled me over did I slow down.

Clutching the cramped area with my free hand—I had steadfastly refused to let go of the basket—I hobbled into the first opening I saw, an arched entrance into a spacious courtyard. There were fragrant lemon and orange trees and numerous flowering shrubs, but no place to hide. Then I saw the curved wrought-iron staircase leading to apartments above the shops on the street. Maybe, just maybe, there was a place I could conceal myself until the hue and cry died down. Then I could think logically about what my next step should be.

After my first flight I might have asked my father to appeal to the authorities, but not after hitting an officer. No, I had to find a way to flee the city, and this time successfully. There must be no mistakes, no danger of being discovered by either the authorities or kidnappers.

Engrossed in my thoughts, and stumbling blindly up the stairs, I didn't see a man walk out of his apartment, then turn and lock the door behind him. Almost at the top of the stairs I ran into him, knocking him against the railing and falling down onto the step at his feet.

Strong arms helped me up, and a friendly voice made me feel that perhaps all was not lost.

"Here, here, what's wrong? Let me help you." Only when I looked up did he see my tear-streaked face.

"Oh, Baptiste, hide me quick. Please, get me inside. Is this your place?"

"Yes, yes. Come along." With one arm supporting me, he unlocked the door he'd just exited, and led me inside.

"Sit here. I'll get some wine. Then you can tell me what in God's name this is all about."

Sitting stiffly on the edge of the sofa, still too tense to relax, I stared straight ahead, unseeing and unthinking.

"Here, drink it down. But slowly. It's the best France sends over, so don't guzzle it."

Once again I was doing exactly as he ordered. In my confusion, I hadn't recognized either the street or the court where Baptiste lived, but some inner sense must have led me there. I sipped the aromatic wine slowly, letting its warmth suffuse through me until I felt each of my muscles relax and my nerves cease quivering. I even allowed myself to slide back on the couch, but I still sat up straight, alert to any sound outside the door.

"All right, Leah, what mess have you gotten yourself into this time?"

Without answering I reached into the basket, pulled out the beaded purse, and handed it to him.

"So?" His eyebrows went up. "You want me to play guessing games?"

"I'm sorry. I just don't know how to tell you."

"How about starting at the beginning. I've plenty of time."

"Are you sure? You were going out."

"Just for a ride. So settle back and start talking." Baptiste lit a cigar, put his feet up on an ottoman, and followed his own advice about relaxing.

It wasn't as hard as I thought it would be. Baptiste had the goodness not to interrupt while I detailed the events from first hearing the words "Stop thief!" to my hitting the policeman. He allowed a faint grin to cross his face when I related what I did to the first man, but then became serious again.

"This is the purse?" he asked, fingering the mesh bag.

"Yes."

"Of course someone dropped it in your basket when he thought he would be caught. I can see why you panicked, but that was your first mistake."

"I know. But—but who would believe me?"

Baptiste didn't answer my question, just continued talking. "How hard did you hit the officer?"

"He was unconscious."

"But you don't know how badly he's hurt."

"It's enough that I hit him, isn't it?"

"I'm afraid it is," he nodded sternly.

"So what do I do?"

"That, Cherie, is what we have to figure out. Where did I put the purse?"

"Here." I picked it up off the floor where it had fallen from his chair during my recital.

"Let's start with the easy problem. Maybe if we can return it, there won't be any trouble there." He opened it and peered inside. *"Mon Dieu!"* he exclaimed. Pulling up a small table, he turned the purse upside down and emptied the contents.

Spread out in magnificent disarray on the highly polished wood surface were an emerald and diamond ring, matching diamond necklace and bracelet, and a pair of emerald and diamond earrings. I had never seen such beauty amassed in one place before, but it was a beauty that could mean my death.

"My God," I blanched, "what have I done?"

"Intentionally or otherwise you have committed grand larceny if I'm any judge of gems."

"Then I'm lost." I collapsed among the pillows on the couch.

"Never, Cherie! Not while you have Baptiste on your side."

He strode up and down the oriental rug, his thumbs

tucked in his vest pockets. "Here's what we're going to do. I'll go out into the streets and see if I can find out who lost the jewels. Once I learn that, I'll know better how to proceed about returning them. Let's hope the owner just wants them back. Then I'll ask some judicious questions about the officer. There'll be plenty of rumors, I'm sure, so it may take a while to learn the truth about his condition. If he's dead——" Baptiste paused for a long moment, smoothed his mustache. "If he's dead, we'll find out soon enough."

"And me? What do I do?"

"You stay right here."

"No!" I got determinedly off the couch and started toward the door.

"Leah, come back here! Stop thinking what I know you're thinking. I'm in no mood to try to seduce you. I like my women compliant and alluring."

"And I'm not alluring, I suppose," I retorted heatedly.

"No. Don't be so vain. You look like a long-lost waif. When we settle all these little problems you've so generously dumped in my lap, you might appear more attractive. Right now you're just a pesky irritant."

"Well, thank you, M'sieu Fontaine. If I'm such a burden to you, I'll leave right now. I'm sure I wouldn't want to impose on your magnanimous sympathy."

"No, you aren't. You're staying here. I don't want you on my conscience, either. You can sleep in there." He pointed to the same small bedroom where I'd put on one of his mother's——or so he said——dresses the night he'd rescued me from the kidnappers.

"You'll need some clothes. You may be here a few days."

"My mother will give you what I need."

"No, I can't chance going there. No one must know where you are. I'll get a few things."

"I'll make a list of what I'll need."

"Not necessary. I——I've shopped before."

I'm sure you have, M'sieu Baptiste, I said to myself. I'm sure you know just what a young lady wears.

As soon as Baptiste left, I heated water for a bath, feeling a desperate need to cleanse myself of all the vileness I'd been through. The water was hot, and Baptiste had a plentiful supply of imported lavender soap and fragrant lotions. Either he was more of a dandy than I realized, or I was not the first woman to luxuriate in the large brass tub in his room. Over and over I soaped and rinsed, having no inclination to leave the seductive warmth of the tub. Only when the water began to cool did I step out and wrap myself in one of his huge, soft towels. The way I felt I might have been Cleopatra stepping from a flower-filled pool or Venus rising out of the sea.

With the towel draped loosely around me like a cloak, I gazed at myself in the long pier glass in the bedroom. We had no such mirror at home, and I'd never looked at myself full-length before. I stared as though studying the body of a stranger, and I was not disappointed in what I saw. My legs were long and slim with well-formed thighs. My hips were well fleshed, but not too broad, and my stomach was firm and flat. I was proudest of my perfectly formed breasts, neither too large nor too small. Yes, I thought, I do have a beautiful body, one to be saved for the right man, not to be used on a whim and then discarded or sold in exchange for material comforts. Lost in my dreams of going north and marrying, all thoughts of present troubles forgotten for the time, I was still wrapped in the towel when I heard the outer door open. I trembled lest Baptiste think I was in the other bedroom and walk into his own without knocking.

"Leah?"

I sighed with relief.

"You haven't run off, have you?" I caught an undercurrent of anxiety in his voice.

"I—I'm bathing in here. I didn't think you'd mind. I'll be right out."

"Don't dress," he called back. "Slip on one of my robes. I've brought you something more attractive than that awful skirt you had on."

Feminine curiosity being what it is, I quickly donned a long, heavy satin robe that almost wrapped around me twice and tripped me up when I walked. Fascinated to learn what he'd bought, I didn't take time to brush my hair, but hurried right out.

"No, on second thought," he leered, "I might just make you keep that on. You're far more desirable looking than when you came in."

"Now, Baptiste," I backed away. "Remember what you said."

"Calm down. I'm just giving you a compliment. I've no intentions of raping you. Here, try these on," and he handed me an immense box.

Carrying the box and having to hold up the robe at the same time, it was impossible to move as fast as I wanted. I must have cut a grotesque figure, for Baptieste began chuckling as soon as I started walking toward what would be my room for far longer than I first expected.

The box contained everything I needed from the skin out, but never before had I felt such delicate lingerie against my body or pulled on silk stockings of such gossamer sheerness. The pale yellow dress was a simple delight, exactly to my taste and beautifully made. Everything—chemise, petticoat, even the shoes —fitted perfectly. Either Baptiste was an astute observer or he'd made purchases for many another young woman.

When I turned around for his scrutiny, he applauded in approval.

"Now you look the way you should," he said. "You're too beautiful to wear those drab things I think you refer to as market dresses. Speaking of Market, I'm hungry. I went by there and bought a few things. Do you think you could fix some dinner for us?"

Startled as I was by his assumption I would willingly

cook for him, I was glad for something to do. He had bought things that could be cooked quickly, so within half an hour we were seated together at an intimately small tea table near glass doors leading to a balcony and overlooking a garden. Baptiste had opened a bottle of fine rosé wine, and we might have been dining at an elegant restaurant with no more pressing concern than whether to go to the opera or the theatre that night. But there were more serious problems, and they could not be put aside for later consideration.

"What—what did you find out while you were gone?"

"Oh," Baptiste smiled, "here you are going to have to admire my ingenuity. The word of the theft has, of course, spread all through the *Vieux Carré*. But what had been stolen and who had been robbed depended on who was telling the story. The thief—you—was accused of filching everything from an empty purse to one filled with a king's ransom in gold pieces. Interestingly enough, no one mentioned jewels. So, thought I, either the jewels were already stolen property or they belong to someone who felt exposure to publicity was the last thing she desired. I say *she* because you said it was a woman who screamed. You didn't describe her, but as it turns out, it wouldn't have helped. You'll see why in a minute. Anyway, the secrecy surrounding the theft made my task somewhat easier. Certainly it eliminated a number of people among my acquaintances wealthy enough to own the gems and who would have gone immediately to the police. And I say, without pride, I know all the Creole families in the quarter. She called out in French, so it was highly unlikely the victim was from the American quarter. Anyway, they seldom shop at the Market."

Baptiste paused to light one of his long, fragrant, imported cigars.

"So, my mind then moved to the *demi-monde*. Now, I'm not quite as familiar with thieves and fences, so I discarded the notion of investigating that route, at least for the time being, and decided to explore another area. Sipping a liqueur at the Absinthe House, I kept my ears open. All information filters into there eventually, and I was in no hurry. But fortunately I didn't have long to wait. A maid, very flustered and agitated, came in and also purchased a glass of absinthe. From a word here and there, I surmised she had run from her mistress who was threatening to kill her for being careless. Given time, she said, the woman would calm down—she had a brutal temper that flared up quickly but just as quickly subsided—and she could return. Her mistress adored her. Anyway, she had plenty more of what the maid had lost. Eventually the girl left, and with the persuasion of gold, I was apprised by the publican of the mistress's name. She owns a house just a few blocks from here and runs an establishment that is legal but which she would prefer not to have given the wrong kind of publicity. Let us just say she is rather shy about having her name in the paper. So, it was no problem for me to see Giselle and persuade her not to press charges if the jewels were returned."

"You know her?" I asked.

"Let's just say we have a number of mutual friends."

So Baptiste had good friends among the *demimonde*. His statement about Giselle's reluctance for publicity and her concern that a certain man would learn she had lost his gifts of jewelry did not convince me. Other considerations, such as a close relationship, had surely influenced her not to press charges. After all, it was no concern of mine whom he numbered among his acquaintances, or how familiar he was with a woman like Giselle. The important thing was that one of the problems had been solved.

"What about the officer?" I asked tentatively.

"Whoa, slow down. How much do you think I can do in less than two hours?"

"I—I just thought you might have heard something," I said, feeling thoroughly chastised.

"Well, actually I did. But remember—again it's only

rumor. He's either unharmed but humiliated by his fall in the line of duty, suffering from a varied assortment of bruises, or dead. And this time the truth will be harder to learn. I can't just go around asking questions, or another truth we want to keep hidden will be revealed—namely the fact you're here. I'll proceed as cautiously, but as quickly, as I can."

Baptiste could have been speaking to the wind after the word *dead*. I felt myself go white, and I thought I was going to faint. I drank the rest of the wine and steeled myself to keep from passing out.

"The man is dead?"

"Good Lord, Leah, haven't you been listening? I said it's rumor and nothing more. He could just as well have gotten up and walked away. It's just going to take a few days to find out. Meanwhile, I might take a chance on seeing your father. Jean-Paul and I have worked on various projects before."

"You know my father?"

"Quite well, although usually as an adversary. But this time our interest is mutual. I'll see. I don't want to involve him if I don't have to."

"And my mother? She's going to worry."

"She'll just have to for a while. We simply can't risk revealing your whereabouts."

The few days lengthened into two weeks, and then three. Baptiste brought me two more dresses and changes of underclothing the day after our conversation. He attended to his business at the cotton brokerage he owned, independent of his share in the family's sugarcane plantation. I learned that Baptiste Fontaine was a very wealthy man. He also kept all of his evening engagements, so I was alone much of the time. He kept his word about not touching me, and soon I felt as much at home in his apartment as in my own house. Strangely, he never referred to what he'd said that night on the Trace about the third time being the charm. I was both piqued and relieved by the fact he'd forgotten. Feminine pride made me wonder if I'd lost all my ability to charm a man, but worry over my present problems made me grateful I didn't have a seducer to cope with, too.

Baptiste loved to tease, tilting up my chin until my face was close to his, then asking if I'd been a good girl all day and smacking me on the rump. One evening he suggested I look in a certain closet to see if there were anything I wanted to wear. He doubled over with laughter at the expression on my face when I pulled down two sheer black gowns and a lavender negligee.

"No doubt they are precious mementoes of past conquests," I fumed.

"Oh, no doubt," he laughed in response.

He delighted in calling me his white virgin or South Sea goddess, but there was never a suggestion that he was pleading with me to submit or a hint that he could force me if he wished. I was as helpless as a rabbit in a snare and he knew it; but never did I feel the need to bite off my leg to avoid the hunter. Baptiste was an enigma I could not riddle. Passionate by nature, I knew, yet gentle and sympathetic.

During the day I opened the long doors onto the rear balcony and sat there reading or sewing after I'd straightened the apartment. In the evenings Baptiste was away, I was content to sit in the candlelit salon and just enjoy the beauty of the room.

Pale apricot brocade draperies covered the floor-to-ceiling glass doors that opened onto the front and rear balconies. Flowered satin in a deeper shade of apricot covered a pair of matching sofas. A white marble fireplace was flanked by Italian gilded chairs upholstered in cut velvet. A Chinese rug in shades of blue and gold covered most of the parquet floor.

In its own way his bedroom was as rich as the salon; but where the latter was exquisite, the former was heavy and masculine, all dark woods and heavy maroon draperies. The room I slept in was simply furnished and without much apparent thought, as though anything were preferable to leaving it empty. I suspected I was the first young lady to sleep there rather than in his huge walnut four-poster.

By the end of the second week, all this luxury began to pall. Baptiste had learned that the officer had suffered some cuts and bruises from his fall, but was recovering. The problem for Baptiste was to contact the man without revealing his connection with me. Again he counted on the Quarter's propensity for gossiping about every casual or shocking event that took place within its confines. Small though it was compared to the rest of New Orleans, as a microcosm of the world it contained all aspects of humanity. One had only to discover the gathering place of each element— aristocrats, merchants, *gens du couleur*, or *demi-mondaines*—and one could learn all the news considered too unsavory or unimportant to be printed in the dailies. Antoine's, the Market, ill-lit bars on the Ramparts, the Absinthe House—each was the social center of a particular stratum of society, and those who frequented them felt perfectly free to discuss the news of their own milieu. Fortunately Baptiste had entrée to all of them, and he moved from one to the other with ease.

The Market was the best place for picking up rumors, but these Baptiste did not need. He doubted the policeman, as a symbol of the law, was inclined to patronize the poorest bars, centers for every kind of illicit traffic. His life wouldn't be worth a picayune. Baptiste decided to concentrate on such places as the Absinthe House and Le Coq d'Or, where aristocrats and workmen mingled casually. Yet, listen as he would, he came upon no clue as to how he might prevent me from being prosecuted for assault when I emerged from my hiding place. Baptiste was about ready to give up and confer with my father and a lawyer on my behalf.

By a stroke of good luck, at the beginning of the third week Baptiste attended a dinner party at Antoine's. Among the guests was a prominent physician who'd been in the hospital when the officer was brought in. He was familiar with the case, and by appearing casually curious, Baptiste was able to learn the man had been released a few days earlier. The patient had received no disabling injuries, but his family had had a number of setbacks and were going through a difficult time. Baptiste assumed they were in financial straits, and he decided to act on that hunch.

"If my plan works, Cherie," he said after barging enthusiastically into the apartment sometime after midnight and waking me up, "you'll have no worries in a few days."

I'd slipped into a robe, and Baptiste insisted I join him in a nightcap to celebrate. He sprawled his length along one couch, tie off and shirt open, while I sat forward on the other, listening eagerly to all he told me. Between us, on the low table, was the decanter of wine and a plate of fruit and cheese. With each word, I found myself relaxing more and more. I hadn't realized how tense and fearful I'd been during the previous weeks, and I felt I could breathe more naturally now there was hope I would be free.

"I'll see your father tomorrow. I can ask him for help now that we know which way to move."

Baptiste stood up and strode back and forth across the rug. Then he sat down beside me and bit hungrily into the slice of apple I'd pared for him. For the first time since dashing blindly up the curved stairway I felt uneasy at being so close to him. I watched his long, strong fingers as he cut another slice of fruit. Under his open shirt I saw the faint flexing of his muscles each time he moved, and I thrilled with an inexplicable desire to touch the tightly curled black hair on his chest. Drinking wine right after being awakened had given me a heady feeling. When he reached over to pour another glass for himself, his leg touched mine, and I began to quiver beneath my robe. I hoped he wouldn't notice.

"To you, Cherie," he said, raising his glass. "To you and freedom."

"Thank you, Baptiste. Thank you for all you've done."

"Think nothing of it. It's been an exciting challenge playing detective." He winked at me. "Especially since I think I've solved the case."

"I know I've been a burden, and I'm—I'm sorry if you've had to change any plans because of my being here in the evenings."

"Not a burden, Cherie, a pleasure." He threw back his head and laughed. "You must think my whole life revolves around one amour after another. Don't believe all you hear."

"I only meant—"

"I know what you meant, Leah, and I appreciate it. Now, I'm tired. So kiss me goodnight and off to bed." He tipped up my chin and planted a gentle kiss on my lips. No passion, no invitation. Just a friendly goodnight kiss.

As Baptiste had predicted, my father agreed to the plan he proposed. Together they visited the officer I'd injured, and in return for a generous sum of money he agreed to change his original statement—given while semiconscious in the hospital—to assure the authorities I had run into him accidentally. It didn't take long for him to realize that in addition to receiving money much needed by his family, he would no longer suffer the humiliation of having been thwarted in his duty by the shopping basket of a mere woman. No longer would he be the butt of fellow officers' jibes.

"So, now you're free to leave this prison," Baptiste said, looking around the apartment.

"It's been a lovely prison. A little lonely sometimes, but I haven't minded."

"What do you plan to do now, Leah?"

"Go home, of course. I know Mama has been frantic all this time. I'm glad you finally went to see her."

"I'd hoped you'd want to stay, Cherie."

"No, Baptiste, you know how I feel. I'm surprised to

hear you say that. You—you've given no indication you wanted me to."

"I didn't want to pressure you when you were already under such stress. I was afraid you'd think I was taking advantage of the situation and would hesitate to refuse."

"Thank you, Baptiste."

"You've already given your answer, so I won't ask the question. I don't like to be refused a second time. Just remember, I'm here if you need me. I'm fond of you, Cherie, and I don't want to see you hurt."

Sadly I walked toward my room to pack. I should have been happier then than at any time in my life, but I couldn't shake off the feeling I was turning my back on a real friend and a life I could eventually find much to my liking. But, I convinced myself, it was *not* what I wanted. I would still be chattel, the property and not the wife of a white man. I was too young to compromise my ideals.

Baptiste insisted I take home everything he had bought me. Carrying his gifts in a small bag, I walked hurriedly down the wrought-iron stairway and through the streets to my house. Mama was not at home, so I unpacked and fitted my new clothes among the old in the wardrobe.

Chapter Nine

WHEN I HEARD MAMA open the door, I ran to throw my arms around her.

"Why have you come home?" she greeted me tersely.

"I'm safe now. The jewels have been returned, and the authorities convinced I did not steal them."

"But you have disgraced me. You have been living with a man named—named—"

"Baptiste Fontaine. You know it as well as I do. But I haven't lived with him in the sense you mean. Didn't Papa explain it to you?"

"Yes, he told me what happened. It makes no difference. You have lived in a man's apartment for over two weeks. I can never take you to another ball. No man will want you for his *placée* now. Lovers, yes— there will be plenty swarming around—but no real protectors."

"But he never touched me, Mama! I'm as innocent as the last time you saw me."

"*Bon Dieu!* Who will believe that? No one. Not of a man like Baptiste Fontaine who has bedded Creole as well as colored wenches."

"Mama, I was never in his bed nor he in mine. Can't you believe me?"

"And if I believed you? If I, as a respected midwife, examined you and found your maidenhead unbroken, should you then expect me to shout it to all the world? Or put a sign around your neck? No, Leah, you have been violated. If not physically, at least by being compromised."

"But he saved me, Mama, from prosecution and from prison. Does that count for nothing?"

"Then return to him. Or find another, if he will not have you. You have disgraced me in the eyes of our society."

"Am I so different from you, Mama? What have I done—or not done—that you did not do?"

"Quiet! I have lived in *plaçage*, an honorable institution. I was properly introduced to your father, and I have been as faithful to him as any wife to a husband."

"And I was properly introduced to Baptiste."

"But he did not ask me for permission to set you up. He flouted custom, as have you. I shall be ashamed to show my face among our own kind."

"And my grandmother?" I was treading on dangerous ground to bring her into the discussion and seem to hold her up to scorn. "You consider her a disgrace?"

"Your grandmother was a slave and of a different generation. White people think we have no morals, but we are striving to establish moral codes of our own in the best way we know to improve ourselves. I could have married a free man of color and perhaps lived in near poverty. I chose the life I thought best for myself and my children. But I have lived a moral, decent life with a man I love. I have lived by our code. You have not. I'm sorry, Leah, but you are no longer welcome here."

"I'm sorry too, Mama. Sorry I ever thought you would understand. I'll send for my things."

I ran through the yard and out the gate as quickly as I could so she would not see my tears. I had been denied by the one person I was sure would understand. I fought back a rising panic. Logically and unemotionally I had to figure out what I could do, where I could go. My father? He would give me money, perhaps, but not refuge. With the money, however, I could once more leave New Orleans and head north. Certainly the city held no future for me now, and this time I wouldn't make the mistakes I had before. No more walking at night and falling among slave traders. This time I'd let my father make arrangements for me to board a riverboat in New Orleans and I'd travel incognito. He would do that much for me, I knew. Once he'd learned of my mother's actions. If only I'd packed my clothes before retreating. I shouldn't have weakened so quickly.

Although I had never been in his export office, I'd passed it often. I'd need money for the trip, for emergencies, and—oh, yes—new clothes. I couldn't shop in the *Vieux Carré*. There were only a few ready-to-wear stores, for Creoles and wealthy colored frequented couturiers, and others, like my mother and myself, made their own dresses. My sudden purchase of a complete wardrobe would arouse suspicions I preferred not to stir up. I'd never been across Canal Street, but I would simply have to swallow my distaste for the American foreigners and then do my best to make my clothing needs known.

All these thoughts raced through my mind as I made my way to the export office and warehouse. Who would I see first? And would he then let me see my father? I had a natural timidity—born of humiliation and years of being relegated to the back of public conveyances and the top balcony at the opera houses—about dealing with white strangers. Should I merely ask for him as though I had some business to transact with him? Yes, that would be best. But what if they asked what business it was? I—I wanted to see about imported materials. That was it. I would pretend to be a dressmaker inquiring about laces from Belgium.

Now that I had walked several blocks, I was much calmer and more in control of myself than when I'd run out of the house. I could already visualize myself boarding a side-wheeler as a young New Orleans lady traveling north to Ohio or Pennsylvania. I straightened my shoulders and carried my head proudly when I entered the front office and reception room of my father's establishment. I felt somewhat uncomfortable without a

bonnet, but more comfortable than if I'd worn a tignon. I had pulled my hair back into a neat bun with a
few tendrils falling loosely around my face.

A young man, no doubt still an apprentice clerk,
stood behind a counter. There were two uncomfortable
chairs and a spitoon between it and the door, but in
the distance I could see a larger reception room with
several cushioned chairs, tables, and ornate lamps.
That must be where most of the business was conduct-
ed.

"May I help you?" Was his voice cold and supercili-
ous, or was I only imagining he knew my status?

"I would like to speak with M'sieu Bonvivier—on
import business, of course." Now why had I added
that? Why else would I be there?

"I'm sorry, but M'sieu Bonvivier is not here."

Having counted on his being there, that information
unsettled me for a moment, but I recovered my poise
almost immediately.

"May—may I ask when he will return? It's rather
important. A shipment I'm expecting."

"Not for at least three weeks. He has just left for
Martinique to see his mother who is ill. Perhaps I
could help you, if you'll tell me what you are waiting
for."

Now I was shaken, bereft of the one hope I had of
solving my dilemma. There was no way I could wait
three weeks, or four or five if my father decided to remain away longer. My mother had made it perfectly
clear I could not return home, nor would I even if she
relented. I had been alone before, and I knew that if I
put my mind to it, I could come up with something. If
only I weren't pressed for time. And why did I have to
mention a shipment? The young man was looking at
me curiously, waiting for me to speak.

"Are you all right?" he asked. "You look ill."

"I'm fine. Just disappointed."

"Perhaps I can find the imports you were expecting."

"No—no, thank you. I needed to see M'sieu Bonvivier personally. A matter of credit."

"Ah, yes, I see." Once more his tone was cold and unfriendly, but at least I'd solved one problem. The word "credit" had backed him off from being too inquisitive about my order.

"Shall I tell M'sieu Bonvivier you called?"

"No—no, thank you," I repeated. "I prefer to see him myself."

"As you wish." A sneer told me all I wished to know about his opinion of me.

I stood on the banquette in front of the export office for only a minute and then walked to the levee where crowds of excited, gaily dressed travelers were boarding a steamboat. Because many Spanish and French Creoles had swarthy complexions, many quadroons and octoroons passed for white in Louisiana. However, I steered away from such a course of action, afraid that so close to home, I would give myself away. Laws in most Southern states gave token white status to those who could prove three or four generations of white blood, but I knew they were still stigmatized and denied many prerogatives of the pure white society. No, I would have to travel many miles away to feel completely free, and so I thought briefly of going aboard and stowing away; but the idea was too absurd.

With twin stacks pouring forth energetic streams of smoke, horns tooting, whistles blowing, the great stern-wheeler slowly pulled away from the levee. It was like a fiesta and bon voyage party rolled into one. Some of those on board were going upriver to St. Louis, thence west to make their fortunes; many more were returning home after visits with relatives; but a majority were flatboatmen who had sold their produce in New Orleans for a good profit and were going back to their Ohio, Kentucky, or Illinois farms with heavy pockets and light hearts. Men waved their hats and women fluttered handkerchiefs, while small children raced around and around the deck, oblivious to parental warnings that they would slide right through the railings if they didn't slow down.

Those left behind on the levee waved in answer and shouted across the water final words of farewell and good luck or a reminder to say hello to Uncle Jim. They kept on smiling until the *Louisiana Belle* moved out of sight around one of the innumerable bends in the Mississippi. Among those left behind, a dozen or so small Negro boys jiggled to the rhythm of tambourine and drum, waiting for the pennies they hoped would soon fall at their feet. A Negro seller of rice cakes, her tray still half full, walked away toward the Market.

As the boat moved farther upriver, I watched the sun set into the bayous beyond the Mississippi. I looked into the dark, muddy depths of the river and wondered if that would be my only solution. For some, death was the easy way out, but not for me to whom life meant so much. No matter what lay ahead, I would be the master, not the slave, of any situation. No, the swirling waters held no temptation for me.

Once more I squared my shoulders and walked confidently back toward the center of town. I had to have a place to stay until I could come up with new plans. Could I maintain my dignity and still relinquish enough of my pride to ask for help? That was the enigma I faced. But did pride need to be bartered for self-preservation? I thought not, and if I followed the inspiration that occurred to me, I would soon learn if I were right or wrong.

Fortunately I was not disappointed at the next place I went. Baptiste was home.

"Leah, what are you doing here?"

"May I come in? Are you alone?"

"Certainly, come in. Yes, I'm alone."

I walked over to a couch and, as soon as I sat down, began crying in spite of my resolve to remain in control. Baptiste asked no questions, but brought me a strong cup of coffee and a glass of brandy.

"Drink these. We'll talk later."

I almost choked over the potent liqueur, but I finished the glass before drinking the coffee. Baptiste sat on the couch opposite, watching me closely but with no apparent curiosity about my reappearance. In fact, it was almost as though he'd expected me to return.

Only when I'd put the cup down on an end table did he raise his eyebrows inquisitively, waiting for me to speak. But I couldn't without starting to cry again.

"Are you all right now?" he asked.

"Yes—no. I mean I didn't know who else to turn to."

"Oh?" It was obvious he was not going to say anything to help me.

"My mother won't let me return home." There, it was out. "And my father—to whom I went for money to go north—left this afternoon for Martinique for several weeks. I'm all alone with no place to go."

"So you came to Baptiste," he chuckled. "I warned you, didn't I? I said you'd come to me at last."

I didn't answer, but I walked to the long window overlooking the street and looked down at the people busy with their own concerns. How quickly, I thought, the *Vieux Carré* had changed from my home to an alien, unfriendly land where I was a pariah.

"What did you mean," Baptiste asked more gently, "when you said you can't return home?"

"My mother said I was compromised by staying with you."

"I don't understand." He was genuinely puzzled. "She takes you to the quadroon balls just to meet a Creole lover. Why her concern over two weeks with me?"

"I'm damaged goods. I'm no longer of any value on the market. My people's moral standards may be different from yours, but they are standards that have allowed us to maintain a certain pride while finding a way to live decent, comfortable lives, and my mother has adhered strictly to them. *Plaçage* is one thing; a promiscuous affair is something not to be condoned. More to the point, men want a virgin for a *placée*, so I have no secure future."

"But—but I never touched you!" Baptiste shouted.

"I know that and you know it. But, tell me, what man will believe we spent two weeks together and didn't even hold hands? You know a *placée* must be as chaste as a bride. Oh, I can pick up lovers, but there is also a name for that."

"What do you want from me, Leah?"

"I don't know. A place to stay until I can sort out my feelings. Right now I'm too confused to decide which way to turn."

Baptiste walked over to the window and stood behind me. Gradually his arms encircled me, and he turned me around so my head rested on his shoulder and he smoothed my hair with his hand.

"What if I suggested planning your future for you?"

"What do you mean?" I looked up into his eyes.

"Let me set you up in a house as my *placée*."

I pulled away and stepped through the window onto the balcony.

"Don't look down, Cherie," he said. "Don't ever look down. 'Come live with me and be my love.' Do you know that poem, Leah?"

I shook my head.

" 'And we will all the pleasures prove.' I can show you pleasures you've never dreamed of. You have only to ask, and I'll give you whatever you want."

I looked over the balcony to the city and the river in the distance. "You've been here when I needed you, and you've been kind, Baptiste, but I don't love you."

"I know."

"The first chance I get I'll try again to go north."

"Leah, I'll take you north if that's what you want. I'll show you how you would live and be treated. It's not the land of milk and honey you visualize. Discrimination is just as vicious there as it is here."

"But I'd be white! I wouldn't be colored or be called 'nigger.' "

"Leah, look at me." He tipped up my chin. "You are the most beautiful woman I've ever known." He looked deep into my eyes. "When you're excited, your eyes are like deep purple amethysts, and your skin is as smooth and delicate as fine old ivory. I want your beauty to belong to me. But——" and here he turned me around to face a mirror "——there is no denying your mother's blood or your father's Polynesian heritage. And the latter is just as suspect as the former.

"Oh," he continued, "you might pass for a while, but soon there will be whispers, started by women who are jealous. No, Leah, look for your happiness here; don't go seeking tragedy among strangers."

I needed time. Everything was closing in on me too fast. Baptiste offered comfort and security, but could I live with myself if I acceded to his wishes? To be seduced by a man was merely a giving of one's body and easy to do, but to be seduced by comfort and security was to relinquish all the standards I lived by. And there was no compromise. I could not do the one and deny I was doing the other.

"Leah!" Baptiste's imperious tone startled me out of my reverie. "Come here!"

I walked toward him and he pulled me roughly into his arms. His kiss was urgent and demanding, and I knew I didn't want him to stop.

"Cherie," he whispered, "I'm going to tell you something I've never told anyone else. I love you. Do you have any idea what it's been like for me these past weeks with you? Why do you think I spent so much time away from here? Because I couldn't bear to be so near and not be able to touch you. Night after night I spent long hours awake, visualizing you in the next room, wearing the modest gowns I'd bought for you. When I kissed you goodnight that one time, it took all my self-control to keep from holding you in my arms. I'm a patient man, Leah, but I'm not inhuman."

"And will gratitude rather than love suffice in return?" I asked.

A faint smile tilted the corners of his generous, passionate mouth. "It will do for a start. I'll teach you to love me."

"But you won't force me to say it?"

"Leah, have I ever forced you to do anything?"

"No, Baptiste."

He seemed to sense that I had acquiesced, and he assumed a new stance. It was gentle but commanding, admitting no argument.

"Go into your room and put on what you see there. I bought it when I thought you might stay. Take your time. I'll see you back here when you are ready to come out." He reminded me of a parent telling a child, "You may come out of your room when you are ready to obey me." As much as I resented the paternal attitude, I somehow welcomed it at the same time. In fighting to escape the prison of custom and color, I had inadvertently built a wall of independence around myself. I had shut out one world, but as a result I was alone in a world of my own creation, and I was suddenly tired of having to make my own decisions. I needed someone to tell me what to do.

I gasped when I saw what was spread on the bed—a sheer white gown and matching negligee. With trembling fingers, I undressed slowly and then slipped the gown over my head. The material was as fine as gossamer, but its several layers revealed only hints of my body's contours. The negligee was edged round the neck with delicate lace, as fragile as a spider web, and more of the lace fell over my hands from the cuffs. It was beautiful but scarcely more concealing than the gown. And yet, I realized, I was wearing even less when Baptiste rescued me from the kidnappers.

The sound of a cork popping reminded me that Baptiste was waiting. I had only to walk out into the salon to become his *placée*, or I could change back into my clothes and walk out of his life forever. The decision was mine and mine alone, and once made it would be irrevocable. I remembered Sister Angelique telling me not to try to be like anyone else, but to remain the unique individual I was. And it didn't matter what my surroundings were; it was what I felt myself to be that was important. If I felt free, then I was free. Perhaps, I thought, I could be Baptiste's *placée* and still not be enslaved. Whatever my life was to be from this point on—once I had committed myself—it would be entirely up to me to make of it something worthwhile.

When I walked from the bedroom, Baptiste had lighted candles in the deepening twilight and was pouring champagne into two goblets. He looked up.

"Just stand there a minute, Leah. I was right. You make more beautiful even the most exquisite garments. I shall delight in seeing you in all the gowns I plan to buy for you."

He handed me a goblet.

"To us," he said. "Last night, I drank to you, but you're alone no longer. From now on it's the two of us."

I'd drunk scarcely half the glass when he took it from me and gathered me into his arms. The pressure of his body against mine and the insistent touch of his mouth aroused a need in me long kept sequestered by the fear of admitting what I really wanted. There would be no holding back now, and I could freely release all the pent-up emotion I had tried to deny.

I knew Baptiste was both surprised and pleased when I responded so eagerly. And yet I think he knew that once I came to him by choice, not force, I would give of myself as completely as I could.

Cradling me in his arms, he carried me to his bed, and with tongue and fingers introduced me to all the delights of love. I found myself responding passionately to each new sensation, and when I cried out with the first painful thrust, he hushed my cries with a gentle but definitely proprietary kiss. I was his, and I was never to forget it.

Chapter Ten

BY BECOMING BAPTISTE'S *placée*, I entered a world more luxurious than any I'd envisioned in my most extravagant dreams. There were gifts every day: clothes, jewels, furs. But the most precious gift of all was my own house.

When we drove up to it, I was overwhelmed. It was not an old "shotgun" shanty on the Ramparts or an apartment in one of the poorer sections of the Quarter. It was a small but beautiful home on an exclusive street, once the bridal house of the larger one beside it. There was a luxuriant side garden surrounded by a low stone wall topped with intricate wrought-iron grillwork.

Baptiste had furnished it with exquisite antiques. These were not hard to find. Many of the French emigrés had been forced to sell their more valuable belongings in order to stay alive. Late in the evenings these destitute but proud people—who had escaped death by fleeing the revolution in France—discreetly carried into the shops the items they'd selected to dispose of. During the day, happier and more affluent shoppers arrived at the shops, eager to buy and able to name their own prices.

Baptiste knew I would not be comfortable in his apartment where I would be constantly reminded of the part of his world in which I had no place. I knew, of course, there were other women, but as long as I did not love him, they could not hurt me.

There was a wife, Marie Louise, to whom he'd been betrothed at the age of fifteen and married at twenty-two. Their marriage had been the usual Creole arrangement, the merging of two families whose lands adjoined in France and who had continued their friendship through three generations on nearby plantations in Louisiana. Neither young person objected to the marriage, as long as Baptiste could retain his apartment and freedom in New Orleans and Marie Louise could spend most of each year in Munich with the baron who'd become her lover during the traditional European tour the year before her wedding.

Baptiste had a unique way of presenting me with gifts. We frequently attended the opera or theatre. Now that I belonged to him, I was no longer relegated to the next-to-upper balcony for free persons of color, just under the one for Negroes. Now, I could sit with him in his curtained loge. Before each outing to the opera or theater, he would bring home an exquisite piece of jewelry—an emerald necklace, a diamond bracelet, diamond earrings, a rare old sapphire brooch—then casually say, "Let's go somewhere and show it off."

To celebrate our six-month anniversary of *plaçage*, Baptiste gave me a triple strand of pearls with a diamond clasp. I had just finished bathing and stood wrapped in one of his huge towels I loved so much. He removed it carefully, and as he wound the strands of pearls around my throat, he let them fall over and between my breasts, where they lay glowing alive against my skin.

"Don't move," he said huskily. "That's the way you should always be, dressed in jewels and nothing else."

"A bit chilly, don't you think, for going to the theatre," I laughed, "and perhaps a trifle immodest?"

"Who said anything about going to the theatre? I'm talking about when you're alone with me."

He reached up and pulled me down on the bed. "Now my bejeweled princess, I have you in my clutches at last."

"But Baptiste, you promised to take me to see *Julius*

Caesar. The Booths won't be back for another year, and I want—"

Baptiste stopped all my arguments with his mouth, and I surrendered to his ardent entreaties as I always did. There was never a time when his lovemaking didn't force all other thoughts from my mind.

"There, you see," he said, as he brushed my hair back and gently wiped the beads of perspiration from my forehead, "we've plenty of time to make the first act. But how much more delightful to have had this overture first. Don't you agree?"

I could only reach up with both arms and bring his face down to mine. "I shall never argue with you again."

"And that's as it should be," he said, beginning to don the evening clothes I'd laid out for him. "I'll even fasten all the hooks and eyes for you while you put up your hair. Or better yet, wear it long. Then I can run my hands through it while we watch the play and look forward to getting back home again."

One afternoon, at the beginning of autumn, Baptiste came home early and suggested we go for a drive.

"Where're we going?" I asked, once the carriage had started down Chartres toward Canal Street.

"It's a surprise. A place I very much want you to see."

"Out in the country?"

"You'll see, my inquisitive one. Just sit back and enjoy the ride. It's a beautiful day for one."

We went slowly through the city and then took a road that led along the river, much the same road I had taken when I fled from New Orleans. This time the day was serene and bright, not too hot, with a blue, cloudless sky overhead and the familiar busy sounds of the river to keep us company.

After some time I realized we were slowing down. I looked around and saw we had come to a plantation and Baptiste was turning into a long, oak-lined driveway. The horses were now moving at a gentle walk.

"Is this it? The surprise?" I sat up and looked around.

"This is it, the Fontaine plantation. The family's away, gone to the mountains of North Carolina, so the house is closed up. But we can get out and walk around."

"You wanted me to see this?"

"I want you to know all about me, Leah, and this is where I started. I'm not out here much, but I guess my roots are here."

He led me through the gardens and toward the back of the house where the lawn sloped down toward the river. We walked along paths bordered with low, well-trimmed azalea bushes; past beds of camellias and gardenias, and toward a large weeping willow whose graceful, swaying branches swept the ground.

Startled by what I saw next, I suddenly grabbed Baptiste's arm. In one corner of the lawn was a small but beautiful white-latticed gazebo.

"What is it, Leah? You look so shocked."

"The gazebo. It's the one I lay down in to rest the night I ran away. I should have stayed in it and then turned around and gone home."

"But then I wouldn't have rescued you. Perhaps it was better you didn't."

"No, never that." I shook my head. "Not after what I went through."

"I forgot. I'm sorry," Baptiste said. "It was a brutal experience."

"Let's not talk about it. This has been a wonderful afternoon, and I don't want to spoil it. I've enjoyed seeing your home. I really have. Thank you for bringing me out." I wondered if the same thoughts were going through Baptiste's mind as were going through mine. I could see the house from the outside, walk through the gardens when none of the family was there, but the inside was forbidden to me. My place in

Baptiste's life was tacitly accepted, as long as I remained invisible, but my presence must remain an intangible; a name, nothing more.

On the way home, we stopped at the Market and ate supper by walking from stall to stall, munching on succulent boiled shrimp handed to us on squares of hot bread, drinking steaming cups of thick, black coffee, and sucking roasted pecans covered with brown sugar.

Gradually, almost imperceptibly, fall followed summer, and before I knew it, we were lighting the Advent candles. Christmas brought a gift I'd long thought I would never receive. The lack of it had been my one sorrow in an otherwise nearly perfect world. That Baptiste would spend the holidays with his family came as no surprise. All the plantation homes would be lighted from roof to cellar to welcome friends, neighbors, and guests with a continuous round of open houses. Every family hosted a holiday ball, and the gala period lasted from the traditional breakfast following midnight mass on Christmas Eve to the feast of lights on January 5. In reality, it ushered in the entire festive season of Mardi Gras that ended on Ash Wednesday.

So Baptiste would be away from New Orleans for at least two weeks, and I had tried to gather around me enough projects to keep me occupied until his return. It was easy to ignore the fact that his wife would be in attendance at all the affairs. It was not so easy to dismiss the other Creole belles that would be vying for his attention. There was nothing binding us together but fragile words, and yet I found myself missing him even before he left.

The morning of Christmas Eve, Baptiste dashed into the house exclaiming I had to come outside immediately. The night before had been one of tender goodbyes and ardent lovemaking; no mention of the time he'd be gone but plans for when he returned.

"Come on," he called, "you don't need a wrap."

I saw he had driven up in a new landau carriage, all

black lacquer and gold trim with a matched pair of black geldings, and I smiled at his extravagant taste. Perhaps, I thought with a chill cold enough to make me wish I'd brought a wrap, it's a gift for his wife, who had indicated she might remain in Louisiana for the winter season.

"How do you like it, Cherie?"

"It's very handsome," I acknowledged.

"Then why aren't you more excited? I bought it just so you'd be able to get out more over the holidays."

"You mean—you mean," I stammered, "it's mine?"

"Of course it's yours. Merry Christmas!"

"Oh, Baptiste, and all I gave you was an embroidered smoking jacket."

"And months of happiness," he whispered, gathering me into his arms.

"But who's going to drive it?" I asked, looking up at Pierre, Baptiste's coachman, sitting on the high seat.

"Pierre. I've had an apartment fixed for him over the carriage house. He can run errands for you, and help you in other ways. Also, he'll provide protection when I'm away."

I was a little uneasy about the thought of having a slave to command. Many free colored, particularly those who owned their own plantations, had slaves; but I had never considered the prospect of one in my home. Yet I didn't want to hurt Baptiste's feelings. Perhaps if I remembered that Pierre belonged to Baptiste, not me, I could accept the situation without feeling guilty.

"Can we go for a ride right now, or do you have to leave for the plantation?"

"No to the first and yes to the second. There's someone waiting inside to see you, and I have to be off. But I'll be back in about two weeks, and I don't think you'll be lonely."

I watched him ride away on the horse that had been tethered behind the carriage, and I told Pierre he could put the horses up and go to his apartment until I needed him. I would probably want to go for a ride after I saw whoever was in the house, but I didn't know how long my visitor would stay. Or, for that matter, how he or she had gotten in without my noticing.

I began to cry the minute I saw her standing in the middle of the room. Her arms hung stiffly at her sides, but I saw there were tears in her eyes, too. She suddenly seemed very tiny and helpless.

"Mama! Mama!" I cried, hugging her close. "Oh, Mama, I'm so glad to see you. I never thought to see you again."

"I'm sorry, Leah. I was wrong, but I was too ashamed to ask forgiveness."

"Come in the kitchen," I urged. "There's coffee on the stove and cakes fresh from the oven. We'll talk in there."

I sensed she was uncomfortable in the parlor, no larger than the one at home but far more richly furnished.

"Now, Mama," I said, spooning cream into her cup, "tell me what finally brought you here."

"Baptiste. A fine young man. The kind I'd always hoped you'd settle down with. He's been to see me several times, and he finally persuaded me how wrong I'd been about—about those two weeks last summer. And since you're living with him as his *placée* there is no more gossip."

"Mama, we'll have a wonderful Christmas. We'll shop all day today. Then we'll go to Mass tonight and have our own festive breakfast right here afterward. We'll go to the Market first and then to the shops. Baptiste left me plenty of money, so I'm going to buy you a whole new outfit."

"But I make my own, Leah."

"Not this time. We're going to the dressmaker where Baptiste orders all of mine."

"You're happy here, then?"

I hesitated. "For the moment, Mama, I'll say I'm content. You used to say I would be. But happy? I don't know. I still want to leave, to find out what it would be like as someone else."

"Leah, my dear, you will never be anyone else. Do you think it matters how others see you? It's how you see yourself that's important. Not in a mirror, but when you look deep inside. Do you think that would change just by moving to a new place? No. You will always be who you are. But what you are—proud or subservient, strong or weak—you determine for yourself, and place plays no part."

"Why, Mama, I've never heard you talk like this before."

"I've never felt as close to you before. You've always been proud, and now I think you are getting stronger as well. Just remember, within your own society, you make your own place. No one else can do it for you."

We had a wonderful Christmas: shopping, going for long rides in the beautiful carriage, and just getting to know each other all over again. To Mama, I was a woman now, and we began a whole new relationship.

All my life I'd wanted to join the gaiety of Mardi Gras—or Fat Tuesday—the eve of Ash Wednesday and last night before Lent. The *Vieux Carré* was separated from the American section of New Orleans by Canal Street, where Mardi Gras festivities were centered, but I'd never been allowed to attend. To all entreaties to be allowed to go, my mother had said a firm "No!" It had not occurred to me then to disobey.

Now I was going with Baptiste. I stood in front of my own long mirror adjusting the headdress of a Voodoo priestess. Multicolored feathers of brilliant red, purple, and green from the tail of a fighting cock fell in wild profusion around my face. A scarlet satin cloak enveloped me from shoulder to ankle.

Baptiste handed me a black domino to slip over my eyes.

"You make a fascinating mystery woman," he said.

"I'll have to watch you closely, or every man in New Orleans will be flirting with you."

"And if I flirt back?"

"I'll cut off their heads!" Baptiste brandished his pirate's cutlass.

"You're quite a swashbuckler yourself," I said. "You make a very handsome pirate. Jean Lafitte would be quite jealous of you."

We joined the celebrants thronging Royale and Chartres on their way to Canal to watch the parade put on by the Mystic Krewe of Comus. Laughing and cheering as each moving tableau came by, we found it impossible to stand still. Souvenir trinkets and foil-wrapped sweetmeats rained down on us in a shower of gold. Like children at Christmas, we ran alongside and scrambled on the ground for the treasures.

"Having fun, Cherie?"

"Oh, yes, Baptiste. It's like a dozen parties rolled into one."

Attendants danced by holding flambeaux, and acrobats leaped from wagon to wagon, turned cartwheels the length of the parade route, and entertained with tumbling acts. One mountebank, with a perpetual grin on his face, stopped in front of us and proceeded to juggle more than a dozen apples, oranges, and bananas. Concluding his act, he bowed and handed us each a piece of fruit.

Caught up in the festive, carnival atmosphere of the gala night, we linked arms with complete strangers and joined the dancing in the street. I found myself being passed from one partner to another and soon lost sight of Baptiste in the mêlée. From the arms of a would-be Napoleon I was twirled into those of a fat, jolly clown. If this is Mardi Gras, I thought, as I laughed and teased with my jovial Pierrot, let it go on forever.

All too soon I found myself grabbed by a tall, macabre skeleton draped with moldy cerements, so hauntingly real as to be frightening. I shuddered. Nonsense, I thought, this is all make-believe, and I looked up and laughed at him. His grim mouth did not laugh back. Instead he stared unblinking as though to pierce through my disguise, and rather than twirling me around in a frolicsome street dance like the others, he gripped me tightly around the waist and remained standing in one spot.

"I saw you looking at me," he whispered hoarsely, "and I knew you wanted to leave here with me." He spoke in English, so I assumed he must be from the American section or from out of town.

"I—I'm sorry, sir, you must be mistaken." I was a little frightened, although I knew there was no real danger with so many people around us. "I've never seen you before."

"Don't tease," he said. "I know an invitation when I see one, and I know what you want." He was drunk, and he began pulling me along. "So let's go."

"Take your hands off me," I said in a voice steadier than I felt, "or you'll be sorry you ever touched me." I hoped it wouldn't prove an idle threat.

The man stared at me and then laughed, "That Voodoo getup doesn't scare me."

"It should," I said in as menacing a tone as I could command.

"Listen, honey, let me tell you something," he said, gripping me tighter. "Nothing frightens Charles Anderson—"

I froze. If he knew who he was holding, he might try to avenge the treatment he'd received at the ball the night I ran away. But if I hadn't recognized him, maybe he wouldn't recognize me.

"—and I always get what I want."

"Not this time you don't," I mumbled under my breath and began struggling in earnest.

"So let's go where we can really have some fun."

I tripped over something and realized he was pushing me off the street and up onto a banquette. Next I was being shoved roughly along a wall.

"Let go!" I said between gritted teeth, "you're hurting me. Can't you see I don't want to go with you?"

"Just another block, and you'll be glad you came." He was panting now.

I stumbled on purpose to see if I could throw him off balance, but he just jerked me up and pushed me back into a doorway. In the carefree spirit of the gala, many couples were embracing, and Anderson took advantage of this to take me in his arms and begin slobbering kisses all over my face. Oh, Lord, I prayed, if only someone would come along who lived in the building, or someone open the door from inside.

Suddenly his hands were under my robe, trying to remove the single petticoat I had on beneath it, and his body was pressing harder against mine.

Where was Baptiste? Why hadn't he stayed near me? I began clawing at the man's face, but I couldn't get at it through his mask. He grabbed my hand and forced it behind my back.

Now he was biting my lips. His movements became more urgent. My God, I thought, he's going to try to rape me right here on the street. With all the laughing and screaming around us, no one would pay any attention if I shouted for help.

The dancing crowd continued to swirl by us, oblivious to my terror. Suddenly from out of nowhere a huge, grotesque figure in the costume of a dragon came lurching drunkenly across the street and lunged at Anderson. His grip was loosened for just the brief instant I needed to slide away from the wall and dash into the throng.

I had escaped Anderson, but where was Baptiste? We might be blocks apart by now. Dozens of men had chosen to dress as pirates, and even if Baptiste had been the only one, I couldn't begin to find him among the milling masses. Where would a pirate most likely be found? I wondered, remembering a game my mother used to play with me when I'd misplaced something. "Now, Leah," she would say, "where do you think you would go if you were a book or a shoe?" So I'd pretend to be the lost object, think hard about where I might go, and sure enough, I'd usually find it there. So, where would a pirate go?

To the Absinthe House! Where the most famous of all New Orleans pirates, Jean Lafitte, was said to have plotted with General Jackson to save New Orleans from the British during the War of 1812. Quickly I sped along Chartres to Iberville, then up one block to Exchange Alley, which took me through to Bienville. Two more blocks brought me to Bourbon Street and the Absinthe House. Anderson had either not attempted to follow me, or I had lost him when I turned a corner.

The place was jammed with those who wanted to celebrate as much as possible before midnight. With Ash Wednesday and the beginning of Lent, life would settle—at least for a week or two—into a more somber and rigid regimen of fasting and general sobriety. There would be no elaborate fêtes or balls and very little entertaining of any kind in the French Quarter until Easter; and lovers must curb their impatience until the high holy day arrived, for no marriages were performed during the season of atonement.

But midnight was still a good two hours away, and one could manage a great deal of celebrating in that time.

"There you are, Cherie," I heard Baptiste call from a table in the corner. "I was waiting for you."

"Oh, you were," I said, after I'd managed to make my way through a press of revelers. "And how did you know I'd come here?"

"Because this is where I said I'd meet you when that foppish Pierrot grabbed you away from me. Don't you remember?"

No, I didn't remember, but something deep in my mind must have heard him, because there I was.

"I ordered a brandy for you. All right?" he asked.

"Yes, fine." It was just what I needed, and by sipping it slowly, I didn't have to talk for a few minutes, time enough to regain control over my shaking nerves.

"Now," Baptiste announced, "we're going to one of the balls. You can see how the élite celebrate. Not nearly as much fun, but colorful."

I thought of the "fun" I'd been through and knew even a dull ball would be an improvement. Then I hesitated.

"But they're private," I said.

"I'm a member."

"I'm not. I don't belong. I—I'll be out of place."

"You're my guest, Cherie. Anywhere I go, you can go." Baptiste was more than a little under the influence.

"No, you're wrong." But I said it to myself. There'd be no harm if we stayed for just a little while and I didn't have to unmask.

Baptiste led me to one of the boxes reserved for patrons of the ball. "Be back in a minute, Cherie. I'll get us some champagne."

"Don't be long. I don't feel very comfortable sitting here."

"Nonsense!" And he strode off.

Two young women, daringly dressed in sheer, clinging gowns of the Napoleonic period, sat down in the box next to mine, separated from me only by velvet curtains.

"Did you see who came as a pirate?" I heard one ask.

"Which one? There must be a dozen pirates here, all trying to look like Jean Lafitte."

"Over there, Caroline. The one who really does look like Lafitte."

"Oh, it's Baptiste Fontaine, isn't it? Who in the world do you suppose he's brought with him this time? Another guttersnipe pulled in off the street, or one of Giselle's girls like last year."

"God only knows!" the as-yet-unnamed one answered.

"He does it just to shock, Hélène, just to see what everyone will do when they discover he's playing a joke on them. I think he hopes the girls will do something really daring."

"Well, this one looks like a horror in that costume," Hélène said. "What's she supposed to be?"

"Oh, come on," Caroline said, "you're not that naive. She's trying to look like a Voodoo priestess, a mama something-or-other. But I think she's overdone it with that heavy satin robe. No nigra could afford material like that."

I dug my nails into my hands to keep from screaming. It took all my willpower to keep from pulling back the curtain and scratching their eyes out. Instead I sat perfectly still and forced myself to listen to the rest of their conversation.

"Well," Hélène said, "I'm glad you're sure she's masquerading. I wouldn't want to be this close to real, live Voodoo magic."

"No, she can't be real. I don't think they allow white women to belong to a Voodoo cult." There it was, they thought I was white. Only that compensated for the rest of what I was hearing.

"I wouldn't want a spell put on me," Hélène said. "They say Voodoo can kill with just a glance."

I fingered my robe and wished I could do what she claimed. Not real, indeed! How I would love to show her just what I could do if I wanted to. Wouldn't she be shocked if I began calling on Damballa or Papa Legba, bringing their curse on everyone at the ball. What if I should start leaping up and down while I chanted or twirled around until I fell down in a trance?

"One look at her is enough to turn anyone to stone," Caroline said. "I don't think anyone should come to a party looking like that."

"I have a feeling she shouldn't be here at all. After all, this is a private ball."

"We'll find out at midnight. If I know Baptiste, he'll

rip off her mask and then start laughing like mad at the joke he's pulled on everyone."

"If the mask is all he rips off, we'll be lucky," Hélène said. "I wonder what she has on under the robe?"

"Oh, she wouldn't dare have nothing on."

"I don't know. You know Baptiste's taste in women."

"Speak for yourself, dear," Caroline said. "I didn't get caught by a storm and have to spend the night in the carriage mired in a mud puddle."

"And who disappeared during a Christmas dance and was seen returning from the gazebo with mussed skirts?"

"So," Caroline said, "we both know Baptiste for what he is. Go find the men. I want them to be here when we discover who she is."

Please, Baptiste, I screamed inside, please hurry back. I want to get out of here. I'd thought I would enjoy looking at the costumes, but now they were just a whirling blur of color that was making my head ache. Never before had I crossed so completely over into the exclusive world of the whites, the world to which I so desperately wanted to belong. I knew now how an outcast, a pariah, felt amidst those who avoided the contamination of his touch. At the cathedral or in the Market, I was but part of the milling throng, but here I was a lone representative of that limbo whose occupants were neither slave nor completely free. Is this what it would be like if I went north and tried to pass? No one here had identified me as a *femme du couleur*, yet I could not forget what I was. Is this what my mother meant when she said it didn't matter what I saw in the mirror, but only what I saw with my inner eye?

"Here, Cherie," Baptiste handed me a glass of champagne. "I'm sorry I took so long."

"May we go home, Baptiste? I—I'm not feeling very well."

"I'm sorry, Leah. Certainly we can go, but we'll miss the unmasking."

Is that what you want, Baptiste, I wondered, to shock the assembly by daring to bring your *placée* here? I shuddered. If I felt smothered by a simple black domino and feared to have it removed, what would it be like to surround myself with a mask of lies and live in dread of being stripped naked by whispers and innuendo?

"Will that be such a disappointment?" I said coolly. "Surely you know everyone here, and they all know one another. I'm the only stranger here, the only one who is not a member. Are you so anxious to see their faces when they discover who the Voodoo priestess really is?"

I saw Baptiste's expression change from bewilderment to sorrow. "Forgive me, Cherie, I wasn't thinking. Of course we'll leave right now. Believe me, I would never intentionally do anything to hurt you."

With our arms around each other's waist, we walked back through the Quarter, amid low-burning torches and late revelers, to our own house. I had been to my first Mardi Gras celebration, and I was ready to resume the rational life.

Chapter Eleven

WITHIN THE YEAR our son René was born. I had not particularly looked forward to motherhood, knowing it would be one more cord binding me inextricably to *plaçage*. If, during the first months of my association with Baptiste, I still had dreams of fleeing north, I put them carefully aside when I knew I was pregnant, accepting for the time being the fact I was a prisoner of the Quarter. However, I was more determined than ever that my child would not suffer the humiliations I had endured. Some way would be found for him to live free. Many children of *plaçage* were sent to France to be educated. Some remained, becoming French citizens; others returned to America, having shed the stigma of their color, and took up residence miles away from those who knew their heritage.

I looked down at the baby in my arms and smiled at the rosy mouth pulling hungrily at my breast. Tendrils of soft black hair curled close to the scalp, and long black lashes fringed the glowing cheeks. On each side of the baby's mouth was a tiny dimple. René was a miniature image of his father.

While one tiny hand clutched my gown, the baby tugged harder at my breast, demanding every drop I had for him; I felt the pull of love spread through my whole body and reach deep inside my heart. I held René close. Such a helpless little creature, completely dependent on me for his life and sustenance. He released the love I'd held within myself for all these years, in thrall to the fears that it would be crushed by indifference or shattered by rejection.

How, I wondered, could anything so tiny bring forth the depths of love I felt? At the first sight of him, he became the center of my world: nay, he was my whole world. From the moment I sensed movement, I felt that love spring to life and grow, nurtured by a need I could not define. Tenderly I removed the blanket from around him and gazed at his perfectly formed body and his slim legs tucked froglike under his tiny buttocks. It was a position he assumed when ready to sleep. In fact, he had fallen asleep while still nursing. I kissed the top of his head where one dark lock of hair curled in the opposite direction from the others. We'll have trouble with that one, I thought with a smile.

If René was my joy, Baptiste's pride in his son was unbelievable. There was champagne for all his employees the day after the baby was born, and he insisted on carrying René to the cathedral to be baptized. My father, much to my surprise, acknowledged the birth of his grandson with the gift of a handsome wicker carriage. Even before I was up and around, Baptiste took René for a stroll through Jackson Square every afternoon, oblivious to the gossip of Creole society for his blatant flouting of convention. *Plaçage* might be a quietly accepted custom, but a man was expected to be circumspect about his side-street liaison, not ask everyone to admire an offspring of it.

Less than two weeks after René was born, Baptiste and I had our first serious disagreement.

"What's that ragged thing hanging on the bed?" he asked, pointing to the headboard.

I looked at the small red bag hanging next to my rosary and remembered the day I'd received it.

"That's my Ouanga packet, a charm to ward off evil."

"You mean it's Voodoo witchcraft! Well, take the damn thing down. It's filthy," Baptiste ordered.

"It's Voodoo, yes, but not witchcraft. Voodoo is a

religion. Mama was horrified when she saw I didn't have my Ouanga on the bed. She just knew the baby was in danger."

"You're a Christian, Leah. How can you rationalize that Voodoo is a religion, too? You're not a member, are you? I mean, the costume you wore at Mardi Gras was just a joke, wasn't it?"

"No, Baptiste, it was no joke. I was initiated when I was thirteen, and soon after began my training as a neophyte priestess. Most of us belong. It's a very ancient religion, much older than Christianity."

"But you can't believe in both, Cherie."

"Why not?"

Baptiste had been sitting on the edge of the bed, watching while I nursed René. Now he got up and began pacing the floor. "It means you're a heretic, that's why," he argued.

"How can I be a heretic when I attend Mass every Sunday?" I asked. There had never been any thought in my mind that the two were mutually exclusive. There were areas that God controlled, and other areas under the influence of Voodoo power.

"Because you also worship a pagan god—whatever his name is."

"Damballa, a very powerful god," I said. "Didn't he save me from being harmed by those three men the night you found me?"

"How can you say it was Damballa?"

"The old man saw my Ouanga packet and wouldn't touch me. Wouldn't let his sons, either. It stays on the bed. I want a healthy baby."

"Leah, listen to me. You cannot be a Christian and worship two different gods."

"Baptiste," I insisted, "did or did not God create everything in the universe?"

"He did," Baptiste nodded.

"Then He must have also created Damballa and all the other Voodoo gods. Therefore, he must also have expected that there would be people who would worship them."

"I give up. When you start in with your peculiar logic . . ." Baptiste threw his hands up in surrender. "But can you drop it over the back of the headboard so I don't have to look at it?"

When I began living with Baptiste, I'd put the packet away in the wardrobe. I hadn't counted on my mother's reaction.

"How is René doing?" she asked one afternoon. "He looks puny to me."

"He's fine, Mama, and seems to be putting on weight."

"You're doing everything you can to have plenty of milk? He's getting enough?"

"Look at me, Mama. I'm as healthy as you could wish, and René sucks like a little pig. Don't worry."

My mother hastily crossed herself. "Don't bring on bad luck. You must be careful of everything you say and do. You haven't lost your Ouanga packet, have you? I don't see it here in your room."

"It's someplace around. I—I just didn't want Baptiste to see it."

"Baptiste, bah! He doesn't count now. Anyway, he's Creole. He was brought up to know the power of Voodoo. Get out the packet immediately and hang it on your bed. It should have been there since you knew you were pregnant. We can only hope Damballa has not already put a curse on the baby."

"I don't think Baptiste will like it." I shook my head.

"It's your duty to take all care," my mother said. "You must not displease Damballa now. No telling what he might do to you."

And so the Ouanga stayed on the bed in spite of Baptiste's protests that the filthy thing was probably more dangerous than any harm it might ward off.

When I was strong enough to begin keeping house

again, and my mother had returned home, Baptiste and I had our second disagreement; only this time I was the one to give in.

He came home early one afternoon while I was fixing supper and announced he had brought someone he would like me to meet. I turned around and was startled to see a pathetically thin little Negro girl peering out from behind Baptiste's back, her head almost smothered under a new red bandana. Her face seemed to be not much more than two big eyes, staring in wonderment at me. One tiny hand clutched Baptiste's coat, and the rest of her wasn't visible at all.

"Come on, Tom, don't be frightened," Baptiste said gently. "Miss Leah isn't going to hurt you."

"Who is she, Baptiste? And why is she here?"

"This is Tom, and I bought her for you. You shouldn't be doing all the housework now. It's too much for you, so I bought you a slave."

A slave. I had accepted Pierre, the coachman, because he really belonged to Baptiste. I knew many free *gens du couleur* had slaves; it was a common practice, but I had never thought about having one myself.

"But she's just a child, Baptiste! Where is her family? She should be with her mother. I just don't know."

"She has no family, Leah. That's why I thought you would accept her. She came from a plantation somewhere up near Natchez where her mother died in childbirth. Her owner sold her downriver, and I knew you wouldn't want her to be bought by someone who'd mistreat her. I really had been thinking about getting you a servant to help out around here, and when I saw Tom on the auction block, I couldn't turn away. You should have seen the looks on the faces of the men who were appraising her."

"Thank you, Baptiste," I said. "But from the looks of her, I don't know who's going to be taking care of whom. She's not any bigger than a cotton stalk."

During all this, Tom didn't move or show any

change of expression except to blink her big black eyes as she stared at me.

"How old is she?" I asked. "Does she speak French?"

"Yes, ma'am." The little girl answered that question herself, and she stepped out a little farther from behind her protector.

"The auctioneer said she was fifteen," Baptiste said.

"Well, if she is, she's been half starved to death. Come here, Tom, and let me see you."

I looked at the pinched face and tiny arms. Small, but well-formed breasts, pushing against the too small blouse, indicated she was probably the age the man had claimed, even though she stood less than five feet tall.

"Tom. That seems like a strange name for such a pretty little girl," I said, kneeling down and putting my arms around her. "Is that really your name?"

"Tomasina, ma'am. But they calls me Tom."

"Well, Tomasina it shall be from now on. Have you learned to do anything around the house?"

"Yes, ma'am," Tomasina nodded. "I can cook and clean and take care of babies. My mama was cook at the big house afore she died."

"That's very good. I need someone like you. But first things first. And that's a bath and some better clothes."

I turned to Baptiste, who grinned as he leaned against the doorway. In another minute, however, his expression changed and he began to protest.

"No arguments, Baptiste," I said sternly. "You brought her here, so you're responsible for her, too. While I give her a bath, you ride over to Mama's and tell her you want some of the clothes I wore when I was about eleven or twelve. I know she's saved them all."

"You want me to go over to Clotilde's and ask for some of your clothes?" Baptiste looked stunned. "She's going to think I'm crazy."

"Just tell her I want them, not what for. I'll have to break Tomasina's place here to her diplomatically. I'm not sure she'll approve of my having a slave. As a matter of fact, I'm not sure I do either. You say she's really mine? I mean, she's not yours and you're just having her stay here?"

"She's all yours," Baptiste assured me. "The papers are in your name."

"Then I can set her free if I want to?"

"And what would she do then? Where would she go?" Baptiste turned to the little girl. "Tomasina, do you want to be free?"

"No, sir, I wants to stay here." Her lips began to quiver.

"You see, Leah, she's scared to death she's going to be turned loose again, maybe sold to one of those men she saw looking at her."

"I didn't mean let her go," I insisted. "I want to keep her here, but as a free servant."

"Let that wait awhile, Leah. Believe me, this is the best way for her right now. Pretend you've adopted her if that will make you feel better."

"All right. Now, go get the clothes. Supper will just have to wait until I can get her out of these rags and into something decent."

Never having had a full bath before, except maybe for a swim in the creek, Tomasina looked so awed by the big tub and soapy water I prepared for her she stood absolutely motionless while I stripped off her few clothes. Once in the water, however, she began to giggle when I sluiced the suds over her head and down her back. Like a child, she popped bubbles between her hands and slid deeper into the water when I said it was time to get out. Finished long before Baptiste returned, I wrapped her in a big towel and told her to stand in front of the fire in the bedroom.

"Now, Tomasina, you will have your own tub in your bedroom, and I expect you to bathe like this at least once a week. Hear?"

"Yes, ma'am."

Still draped in the towel, she followed me to the nursery, her eyes getting bigger with each new detail they took in. I wondered just how much of the "big house" the child had really seen if she was so over-whelmed by this small one.

"This will be your bed, Tomasina. Now, come over here." I walked to the crib and picked up René, who had begun to whimper. "Do you like babies?"

"Oh, ma'am, he's beautiful."

"René is almost four months old, and if you promise to do just as I say, I'll let you help me care for him. Would you like that?"

Tomasina nodded, too excited to speak for a minute. "I promises. I be a good nurse, Miss Leah, and I walk him every afternoon."

So I acquired not a slave but an adoring shadow, and René, a second mother. Her greatest delights were bathing the baby in the morning and taking him out in Jackson Square in the afternoon. I was not allowed to turn my hand to a thing around the house, except in the kitchen where Tomasina dutifully watched and listened while I taught her to cook.

Within a week after her arrival, we shortened her name to Seena. Baptiste said that by the time he got the word "Tomasina" out, he'd forgotten what it was he wanted her to do.

Chapter Twelve

ONE MONTH FLOWED EASILY into the next, the days measured not by the dates on a calendar but by René's new accomplishments: his first cooing sounds of pleasure, his finally rolling from front to back without any help, his learning how to get up on his knees. The day he sat by himself we went for a long ride in the country, and when he began to crawl, we celebrated with champagne. If he seldom cried, it was because his needs never went unfulfilled. He was fed when hungry, held when fretful, and played with when he demanded attention.

"You're spoiling him, Cherie," Baptiste teased when I put down my sewing and picked René up the minute he began to whimper.

"Love never spoiled anyone," I insisted. "Could any baby be happier or more healthy than he is?"

So completely was René the center of my life, I scarcely missed Baptiste when he had to spend several days at a time working with his father on the plantation. Yet I was always ready to welcome him back when he returned. "You will learn to be content," my mother had said, and now I could honestly say that I had found contentment. If life still lacked certain satisfactions I needed to be really happy, at least I had subdued the restless spirit that had once driven me to run away from New Orleans.

Easter came early in April, and it proved to be the harbinger of a long, hot summer. Before the end of the month, the plants in the garden flourished as dampness and heat made New Orleans a natural hothouse. Now sitting in the garden was like being trapped in the middle of a sweltering jungle and even the slightest movement of air was considered a luxury.

I lay back on the chaise longue fanning René, who lay asleep in my lap. I had discarded all my petticoats and unbuttoned the light cotton dress as far down as I dared; Baptiste had his shirt completely open; but both of us were drenched with sweat. René's black curls clung to his head in tight, moist ringlets, and I kept wiping his face and body with a cloth I constantly dipped in a basin of tepid water.

Baptiste lit up and immediately threw away his third cigar of the evening.

"Leah, I received some disturbing news today," he said. "I have to go to Europe."

I held my breath. Europe could mean one of two things: problems with his brokerage firm or trouble with his wife.

"You aren't going to ask why I'm going, Cherie?"

"I knew you'd tell me if you wanted me to know."

"It's Marie Louise." He shook his head. "She had a fight with her baron, and he kicked her out of his castle. She tried to commit suicide, and he did have the goodness to put her in a private hospital. I know her. She'll recover, and probably have a new lover by the time I get there; but as her husband, I do feel some responsibility for her."

"I—I understand," I said shakily. I refused to admit even to myself that I would be lonely without him. But his absence would give me time to loosen the dependency on him I'd begun to feel. I must never forget that, in spite of his declarations of love, my future depended on the whims of a white man. Mistress. *Placée.* They were but polite terms for what I really was—a white man's prostitute. That was what hurt the most.

"How long will you be gone?" I asked.

"I should be back early in the fall." Baptiste leaned

forward, taking René from me and sitting the boy on his knee. "Oh, Cherie, I'm going to be miserable every day I'm away. I hate the thought of missing René's first step. How soon do you think that'll be?"

"Any time now," I said. "He's almost a year old. He's trying. One of these days he's just going to take right off and head for his papa."

I looked at the two of them. I never ceased to be amazed at how perfect an image René was of his father. I might have had nothing to do with his creation except for birthing him. Baptiste was bouncing the boy on his knee, and René threw his head back, laughing the same way Baptiste did when he'd gotten his way. The twin dimples deepened and the delighted laughter came pouring out, uninhibited and boundless.

Baptiste pulled René into his arms, holding him close and burying his face in his son's curls.

"Whose little boy are you?"

"Papa," he cooed.

"That's right," Baptiste nodded. "You hear that, Cherie? He's Papa's boy."

"I'll remember that when he won't eat or needs a spanking."

"Never! I'll never lay a finger on him." And he said *I* spoiled my son.

"Or when he needs changing," I grinned, watching the damp stain spread from René's diapered bottom to Baptiste's trousers.

"Oh, no, not that," Baptiste frowned. "Here, take him."

"Ah-ha, backing down already. Here, baby, Mama'll take care of you." I stood him on the grass next to my chair. "Hold on tight while I get up."

René clung for a moment to the chair arm with his chubby little hands. He turned around, smiled at Baptiste, and cooed, "Papa." Then he broke into baby laughter and, toddling unsteadily but not falling, walked the few feet into his father's arms.

"Look, Leah, he did it! Has there ever been a smarter little boy?"

"Certainly not. He's your son, isn't he?"

The days grew hotter and René more active now that he was trying to walk all the time. Seena was inclined to grow lazy in the unrelenting heat, and much as I hated to do it, I was forced to get cross with her. After a day of running after René and staying right behind Seena to keep her working, I crawled into bed exhausted but unable to sleep. In the still, humid nights, the fragile netting draped around the bed hung absolutely limp and motionless.

In May, as in most of the previous months, the levees were crowded with emigrants from Europe who were being imported to work on such municipal improvements as widened sewer lines, new gas mains, and street paving projects. Mingling with them was the normal montage of sailors from ports all over the world. Tired, frightened, and weakened from many days without sufficient food, the immigrants stayed on the ships, which at least offered them the security of familiarity, until housing could be found for them. Once or twice a day they emerged to seek a breath of air on the levee, and their children ran up and down, jostling the sailors and begging coins from New Orleans citizens who had business on the wharves.

Amid this crush of humanity, one of the newcomers became sick, and before the illness was diagnosed, it spread from ship to ship and along the levees with the speed of a malicious rumor. Within a few days, the reported deaths from cholera, the dread plague of seaports, reached well over a hundred. How many more were kept secret by weighting dead bodies and throwing them in the river would never be known.

Meanwhile, outside the city, another health threat was being regenerated in the hot, stagnant water of the bayous. Soon the miasmas arising from the dark green depths would be blown into the city, carrying with them the annual scourge of New Orleans: yellow fever. Some years there were relatively few deaths; in others, the city was decimated by epidemics.

In a routine way, I'd made preparations to protect René and myself. For some as yet undiscovered reason, the Negroes had an almost natural immunity to yellow fever and the milder summer threat, malaria. Their African inheritance or the years on the islands in the Caribbean had developed through the generations a strong resistance to the diseases. So Seena was entrusted with all the shopping and other errands while I kept René within the walls of the garden. Thus, I was unaware that both yellow fever and cholera were threatening to reach epidemic proportions.

Baptiste had had to spend the two weeks prior to his sailing for Europe on the plantation. But on the morning he was to leave, he found time to come by the house for a few hours. He talked about how serious the situation really was.

"Take care, Leah, it's going to be a bad summer."

"What more can I do than stay right at home? I haven't been outside the gate in days. I don't even know how Mama is."

"Would you feel better if I brought her over here to stay with you?"

"Oh, yes, please. At least we'd be company for each other, and she'd enjoy being with René."

"I'll get her now," he said, "and finish lunch when I return."

"I hope she won't refuse. You know how stubborn she can be."

"She won't have time. And if she does, I'll just pick her up and carry her off."

I smiled. He would do it, too.

"Do you have time before the ship sails?"

"Set out the dessert plates and start the coffee. I'll be back before it's ready."

Baptiste didn't move quite that fast, but he did return with a breathless Clotilde soon after I set out the cups in the parlor.

"*Bon Dieu!*" my mother exclaimed. "I haven't been swept off my feet like that since Jean-Paul made his proposal during our first dance. Really, Leah, you should have sent some warning."

"How could I, Mama? I didn't have time."

"You could have sent Seena. Baptiste didn't even give me time to do a proper packing."

"Nor was there time to send her. Seena can go over tomorrow and get what you need. More coffee, Baptiste?"

"Wish I could, but I'd better go. C'mere, monkey," he called to René, busy toddling from chair to chair begging sips of sweetened *café au lait* and broken pieces of pralines. "Take care," he said, "and do just what your mama tells you, hear?" René nodded seriously, and I had to laugh because I saw the mischievous glint in his eyes that belied his promise.

I followed Baptiste into the garden.

"Be good, Cherie," he said, taking me into his arms.

"I don't want you to go, but I know you must hurry."

"I'll be back as soon as I can, I promise." He drew me closer. "Be sure to pull all the shutters to every night and lock them tight. And check all the netting."

"Yes, yes, I'll remember." I clung to Baptiste a minute more and then watched him mount up and ride away toward the ship.

The first of July ushered in daily rains. Now the midsummer heat was intensified by the unbearable humidity and constant dampness. Clothes mildewed overnight and food spoiled within a few hours. Open sewers, between banquettes and streets in the *Vieux Carré*, overflowed from the excess of water. Canals were being widened and sewer pipes laid in the American section of the city, but in our older French Quarter, the streets ran foul with dirty, stagnant water and the overflow from unsanitary outdoor privies which became flooded.

By the middle of July, there were over two hundred deaths a week from yellow fever, and thousands were fleeing the city. Some places of business closed when both owners and employees ran before the onslaught of the disease. Ships coming up- or downriver learned of the epidemic and turned around before ever reaching the port or sailed on past for safer destinations.

Mama, René, and I remained in the house or garden. Every morning Seena went to the Market, and each day she returned with the news that fewer and fewer of the stalls were open. Fear and the macabre horrors of a city ravaged by disease increased the numbers who refused to bring their produce to town. I feared that famine would soon follow in the footsteps of plague.

When the stench from sewers and the dead being transported in carts and hearses along the street drove me inside, I watched, from the window, a New Orleans slowly succumbing to its most dreaded enemy. No invasion by English, French, or Spanish during her past history had ever taken the toll of lives now being lost to the fevers. But few were dying without putting up a fight first.

Superstition was rampant. Those who had to go out in the streets wore boots of yellow paper covered with tallow. Snuff and mustard were soon unavailable in what shops were open when people, willing now to believe anything they were told, heard that these substances would protect them from the disease. On every corner, great pots of tar and pitch were set afire at night and cannon were fired constantly, hour after hour, in the belief that smoky discharges would purify the air. In actuality, the first beclouded and heated up a city already suffocating from constant rain and heat. The perpetual reverberations from the cannon drove the inhabitants nearly insane.

July became August. Now it was no longer two

hundred a week dying, but one hundred a day. I sat at the window. The area was almost empty of pedestrians at a time of day when it was usually busy with shoppers. But the stores were closed, and people who did not have to be out were secluded behind tightly locked blinds and drawn draperies.

If the banquettes were empty, the streets were not. I watched the parade of carriages, drays, carts, and wheelbarrows transporting the dead to the cemeteries and the sick to the hospitals. The most obscene sights—dead bodies found in the streets in the morning and people fighting over the use of a cart—became routine occurrences.

I had to get some relief from the oppressing atmosphere of the closed-up house. The rain had lightened to a steady drizzle. The garden was flourishing, and I walked around examining the freshly washed, shining gardenia leaves, the new growth on the azaleas, and the buds on the fall-blooming sasanquas. Would Baptiste return in time to see them?

Chapter Thirteen

SEENA CONTINUED GOING TO MARKET every day. There was no fresh meat or seafood available, and the bakery stalls remained locked. A few who had gardens within the city ventured out for an hour or two, and Seena seldom came home empty-handed. Meals now consisted of small helpings of vegetables and a few squares of cornbread. After each trip, I put something in the storage bin against the time when there would be nothing to buy. From root vegetables and wilted greens I would be able to concoct a meatless stew.

On August 15, everyone in the house seemed more restless than usual. The epidemic had raged for nearly three months, and we felt we had been doomed to suffer in an inferno from which, like sinners in hell, there was no hope of salvation. René had stopped walking; he had resumed crawling on the floor and demanding to be picked up when he wanted to go to another room. Clotilde was fussing over the arrangement of the nursery, and insisted I help her move the furniture around. No, Seena would not do. She wanted me.

Long before the usual hour, I picked up René to give him his bath and get him ready for bed. He screamed at having his clothes removed, at being put into the small tub, and again when it was time to get out. His face fiery red from the temper tantrums, he refused his supper.

"I don't blame you, honey," I sympathized. "It isn't very appetizing. But I do have a surprise. Seena got it on her way home from the Market." I handed him a

130

fresh pear, plucked that very morning by a neighbor and given to the maid for René.

René watched while I peeled it and cut it into small slices. After one taste, he put all the pieces on his plate and devoured them one by one.

"Good for you, honey," I said. "Now, time for bed. Hot as it is, you don't really need anything more to eat."

Before putting René in the crib, I enjoyed my favorite part of the day, rocking him and singing old lullabys brought over from the islands by the early slaves. I held him close, brushing the damp curls off his face and seeing in it more than ever the face of Baptiste. Suddenly René jerked violently and vomited the pear he'd had for supper.

I shouldn't have urged him to eat even that, I thought. It's too hot for anyone to eat. I wiped off his face and started to put him in the crib. He needed quiet more than rocking. Once down, however, he began retching again, vomiting up first bile and then blood while his little body shook with sobs.

I ripped off his gown. His body was hot and wet with perspiration. I bathed him, forcing back the fear I refused to acknowledge. He did *not* have the fever. He was only ill from the heat. His eyes glistening with tears, René stared vacantly at me, silently begging me to help him.

"There, there, baby, it's all over. Mama will stay right here. Here's Binkie." I handed him the rag doll I'd had as a child and without which he never went to sleep. He let me lay it in his arms, but he didn't clutch it the way he usually did just before dozing off.

René quieted down, and I waited for him to close his eyes. Instead, they seemed to glaze and become more protuberant, and he stared with an unseeing look. The exertion of vomiting had left his face pink and mottled with dusky orange splotches.

Not until I saw drops of blood beneath his nose and

inside his ears did I panic. Only then did I force myself to admit what I'd known all along.

Calling to Seena, who was cleaning up the kitchen, I told her to watch René while I went out for a few minutes.

"Just keep bathing him. Miss Clotilde is in the parlor if you need her. But don't leave him alone, hear?"

Seena took one look at René, started screaming, and ran out the back door as fast as she could go. She didn't stop at the carriage house, but headed for the street beyond.

"Damn her sorry hide," I said. "I hope she runs straight into the bayou and drowns." No, that wasn't fair. Seena was only a child, more like an adopted charge than a slave. Maybe she'd return once she found it more frightening to be alone than to be among the sick.

"Mama," I called. "René is ill. Come sit by him while I go for the doctor." She said nothing but looked up, studying my face.

"Yes, Mama, it's the fever. Just sit by him."

"I know, Leah, I've nursed cases of fever. They do not all die."

For over a year I had thought how fortunate René was to have inherited all the characteristics of his white forebears on both sides. Now I prayed that in that one-sixteenth of him which was Negro he carried whatever his body needed to fight the fever. It was the one way I and my heritage could aid him now.

Ignoring the mournful wails of the bereaved in the streets and the clacking of carts on the pavement, I hurried the four blocks to the doctor's house. When no one answered my first timid knock, I banged on the door.

"What do you want?" A woman's face appeared at a small, grilled window.

"Mrs. Jourdin? You don't know me, but I need the doctor. My baby—"

"Go to the hospital." Immediately the face disappeared and the window was slammed shut.

I lifted up my skirts and ran, across Jackson Square and down two more blocks. The distance seemed endless. Once at the hospital, I was frustrated again when I couldn't open the double doors. Thinking they were locked, I began pounding on them with both fists just as I'd done at the doctor's, and I felt them give way under the pressure. I kept pushing, finally getting one open wide enough for me to step through. Then I saw what had blocked my way—a man had fallen to the floor in front of the doors, and dying there had been left until someone found time to move him. Covering my mouth with my hand, I carefully stepped over him and looked around for the doctor.

What I saw next almost dissuaded me from my errand. There were two rows of cots, all filled, some with two occupants. Between the beds and covering every bit of floor space were pallets of old mattresses, blankets, or rags on which lay more sick and dying. No one could walk two feet without stepping over patients. The stench of black vomit, unwashed bodies, unchanged linens, and diseased blood fouled the air like putrid swamp gas. The moaning never ceased, but seemed to rise and fall in an eerie, hypnotic rhythm. The monotony of sound was broken sporadically by a high-pitched series of wails or a long, drawn-out scream.

I no longer felt sick. Only helpless. As helpless as anyone faced with the inexorable fact of death. The sudden awareness that one is mortal. These people were dying.

Brought up short by the thought of René suffering at home, I looked again for the doctor. At least René was in a clean bed and would be given constant care. My mother had nursed many to recovery; René *would* get well.

Dr. Jourdin appeared suddenly at my side. Although I'd never seen him before, I recognized him from Baptiste's description.

"Something I can do for you?" The doctor's voice was weak, and his face as pale and drawn as those of many of his patients.

"Please, sir—my son. You don't know me, but my son is ill. He's—he's Baptiste Fontaine's son. You are their family doctor, I believe. Can you come with me?"

"The fever?"

Too close to tears to speak, I could only nod.

"Look around you, m'amselle. It's impossible for me to leave."

"But what can I do?" Now I did break down and cry.

Dr. Jourdin put his arms around me. "How old is the boy?"

"Fourteen—no, fifteen months. Just a baby."

"Babies are strong," he assured me. "You don't want to bring him here."

I shook my head violently.

"I'll give you something mild to ease his pain and quiet the vomiting. You try to lower the fever with bathing and keep him—and everything around him—clean. That's what's wrong here. We can't keep them bathed."

Dr. Jourdin disappeared into a small room and, returning, handed me a bottle. "Half a teaspoon every two hours, oftener if he can't keep it down at first or he seems to be in pain. It can't hurt him."

"Thank you, Doctor."

The body in front of the door had been moved by some unseen attendant, and I left immediately. Once more I ran across the square and through the streets, darting among wagons and carriages, oblivious to the woman who reeled ahead of me and then fell in the doorway of a closed shop.

My mother had put René on my bed and then lain down beside him. Both seemed to be asleep, but when I touched René, he opened his eyes.

I heard someone scream out in anguish, then recognized the voice as my own. With his first effort to

move, René began bleeding from the eyes and hemorrhaging profusely from nose and ears.

Remembering the doctor's comforting reminder that
babies are strong, I stripped off René's soiled gown
and wrapped him in a clean crib sheet. Putting the
bottle of medicine to his mouth, I forced him to drink
what I thought was half a teaspoon. It immediately
came back up. Over and over I made him swallow until he was able to keep some of the medicine down. I
bathed him constantly, wiping away each drop of blood
the second it appeared. If care and cleanliness could
save him, he would not die.

The bleeding stopped, at least temporarily, and I
woke my mother. After repeating the doctor's instructions to her, I said I had to go on one more errand.

"I'll be back in less than an hour."

This time I ran in the opposite direction. There was
another way I could save René. I'd prayed, I'd tried
medicine, and now I would seek a third great power.

In a few minutes I found the house I sought and was
relieved to see a light inside and sounds of normal activity.

"Leah, is that you?"

"Yes, I need your help. My son. He has the fever. I
think he's dying."

"And?"

"Maîtresse Ézilée. Can we have a special ceremony
to her? Do you have charms?"

"Yes to both. Come in." Marie Laveau, New Orleans' most renowned Voodoo priestess, held the door
open for me.

The ceremony was brief. I cut my wrist, sacrificing
my blood to save my son's life. Marie Laveau offered
the blood to Maîtresse Ézilée, special Voodoo goddess
and protector of women and mothers, then she mixed
it with a number of ingredients to make the charm.

It was night when I started back, the darkness intensified by the ever-present smoke, hovering like a pall

over the city, from the burning pitch on every streetcorner.

I heard René crying as soon as I entered the back garden. But more frightening than that were the sounds of moans and retching I knew had to come from my mother. Now burning with fever, she was already hemorrhaging from every orifice. Within an hour the fever had attacked her in its most virulent form. To some, death came quickly: to others, it waited in abeyance for a short time; few recovered.

There was no time for resting. I put René back in the crib while I changed the bed and bathed my mother. Back and forth between the two I moved—bathing, changing, dispensing medicine. There were moments of calm when both slept. Times when one slept while I tended to the other. More often both demanded my attention at once.

Was there no letup to the bleeding and vomiting?

When René became restless I held him in my arms and rocked until the motion almost put me to sleep. Soon after sunrise of the second day I did sleep, still holding René in my arms.

It was the silence that woke me. Everything was very still. Not a sound from the streets where for weeks rolling wheels and steady hoofbeats had echoed ceaselessly. Too soon the lull ended.

René had loosened his hold on my shoulder as he often did when finally sound asleep, and his arm dangled across mine. With his eyes closed, the long black lashes fringed his cheeks where two tears lay just above his dimples. The bleeding had stopped for good.

Rocking and crying, I held my son tight against the breasts which had nurtured him for so many months, as though somehow, some way, I could nurse life back into him as I had once given him sustenance. I could not let him go, though I knew I had to. Once more I looked at his beautiful body, just as I'd done the day he was born. The sturdy legs that would never again run to greet his Papa when he came home. The delicate mouth that could change in an instant from a winsome smile to a mischievous grin. The slimming baby hands that held my heart as tightly as they gripped any toy. And I knew my heart would be going with him. He had loosed his hold on life, but he would not make the dark journey alone. A part of me would always be with him.

In the same quiet way, while I slept for a few hours, my mother, too, had died. The pain was over for them, but mine had just begun.

There were things that had to be done. I knew that. And done quickly. Once those tasks were over there would be time to mourn.

Slowly and deliberately I went about the business of readying my son and my mother for burial. I dressed René in a new white suit, whose collars and cuffs were edged in lace I had just finished tatting. For my mother I chose a pale blue gown of silk. Carefully I brushed their hair, twining each of René's curls around my finger for the last time. He was the most beautiful child I'd ever seen, and he had been mine for fifteen wonderful months.

Taking time to change into fresh clothing, I went first to the cathedral. It was empty: no one praying; no priests. I would find one later, perhaps at the cemetery, perhaps coming from a bereaved home. I walked to the cabinetmaker to see about coffins. His door was locked, the windows boarded up.

"He been gone for days." An old Negro lounged against a lamppost. "You has to go right to the graveyard."

Now I really became frantic. I was all alone. I had to find someone to help me. The old man was right. I would go to the cemetery. Maybe I would find a priest and he'd tell me what to do.

The cemetery gates were open, but I had to hold on to them to keep from fainting when I saw the pile of dead bodies just inside the wall. Most of the dead in New Orleans were buried above ground in rows and tiers of vaults. But now I saw men, dressed in the garb of convicts, digging shallow trenches. A guard stood nearby.

"What are they doing?" I gasped.

"Getting ready to bury the dead. No time to build vaults or dig private graves."

"Convicts?"

"No one else left to do it. Have to watch 'em close, too. One fell in the other day soon as we finished, and before anyone knew he was there, they'd piled the bodies on top of him. Heard him screaming and we got him out. Another man wasn't so lucky. He'd brought his brother here. Couldn't stand what he saw and passed out right by the trench. We figured he was dead, too, until he screamed. Tried digging him out from under the bodies, but we were too late. Died of fright, I guess."

Now that he had an audience, the guard seemed ready to go on and on with grisly stories, but I had seen the priest, and hurried over to him.

"Father, I need your help." Once more, in spite of all my efforts to remain calm, I began to cry. "My son—my mother. At my house. Can you come?"

The priest was a young man, to judge from the looks of his still dark hair and uncreased face. But grief and exhaustion showed in his eyes which were circled by dark shadows.

"No, my child. My work is here. You see it all around you. There is no letup. Bring them here, and I'll give them burial."

"The last rites. The anointing and the sacraments?"

"I'll do what I can here."

"And they'll be saved?"

"God in His infinite mercy will not condemn them at this time of sorrow. I'll be waiting for you."

I was forced to do some serious thinking on the way home. I had to complete the preparations for burial and then find a means of conveying the bodies to the cemetery. They were corpses now. Only by reminding myself that the essence of life which had been René and Clotilde no longer inhabited the physical bodies could I touch them and do what had to be done. The essence—or the souls—would remain with me in memory and amidst the objects they had loved. I would never lose that.

I managed to find two more clean sheets. I wrapped Clotilde first, folding her arms across her chest and tucking the material closely around her. I took longer with René, putting off covering my son's face as long as I could. Twice I removed the linen, once just to look at him again and kiss his Cupid's-bow lips and then to tuck Binkie, the rag doll, into his arms. He wouldn't sleep well without it.

Now for transportation. Baptiste had had Pierre take the carriage out to the plantation for some repairs, and either because of fear or the patrols set up to keep people from leaving and entering the city, he had not returned. I stood on the banquette, seeing for the first time things my eyes had refused to register in my previous trips outside the house. Several dead dogs, poisoned by the authorities in an attempt to keep the epidemic from spreading, lay putrefying in the street. Near the corner, a coffin, probably fallen from an overloaded wagon, had broken open, and the body was sprawled grotesquely, half in and half out, the swollen face covered with engorged blue flies.

A cart came rattling up, driven by a lean man in a motley assortment of rags and a mildewed top hat tilted over one eye. One of his fingers boasted the largest diamond I had ever seen.

I stepped back in horror. There was something repulsive about the man.

"Bodies, ma'am? You got someone needs burying? I take 'em to the cemetery for ya."

Revolted as I was, I knew he might be the only one who could help me.

Seeing me hesitate, the man spoke again. "Won't cost much. I don't charge much. Got three others in the cart; going there now."

I walked to the cart and peered over the sides. I began choking and gasping. "They're naked!"

"I told ya. I don't charge much," he grinned, "but I take everything they got on."

"No, no! Go on. I don't need you." I ran back inside.

Scavenger, I thought. An unscrupulous scavenger who preyed on the frightened and bereaved. I'd manage somehow, even if I had to carry them in my arms. I had to rest and think. I started to move a chair away from the window when I saw the old Negro man who sometimes delivered fruit and vegetables to the house. He was driving his rickety wagon. Knocking on the window to get his attention, I waved for him to stop.

Could I use his wagon? Yes, he wouldn't need it for a while. No, he wouldn't help carry anyone out.

I picked up my mother. She was heavy, but I managed to carry her to the wagon and lay her down. René was lighter, but I found the burden of carrying him greater. I was preparing to bury the one person I loved with every fiber of my being. I had given him life, and in the normal passage of years, I should have died first. He should be the one to weep, not I.

When I reached the wagon the second time, the old fruit peddler was gone. He'd hobbled off and left me to drive. Well, so be it. I found a place for the wagon in the cortège of other conveyances headed for the cemetery. There I held back, watching, as bodies were carefully laid or unceremoniously dumped into waiting trenches. Even as the priest sprinkled a few drops of holy water on the remains, men were heaving in spadesful of dirt. So that was the burial ceremony. No last rites, no anointing, no final prayers of absolution. A few drops of water must suffice for Extreme Unction.

Seeing me waiting, the priest walked over.

"Follow me," he said quietly. "There's a smaller grave farther back, prepared earlier. The man's wife then decided to open the family vault—and make room for him."

Had she merely pushed aside the bones of the previous occupant, I wondered, or had she perhaps strewn them in one of the common graves?

The wagon creaked over the rutty path as the priest led the mule to a spot near the rear wall of the cemetery. Dug large enough to contain a casket, the grave could easily accommodate Clotilde and René. While sprinkling the holy water, the priest took time for a few prayers before beckoning to someone to fill the hole in.

"Thank you, Father," I said. "I appreciate it."

"Would you believe me if I said I, too, needed the time for a quiet moment of prayer? Up until last night I'd been here for forty-eight hours straight, burying the dead and consoling the bereaved who were able to accompany them. I went home for a few hours' sleep. When I arrived at six this morning, there were more than a hundred bodies piled against the locked gate."

"Will it never end, Father?"

"It will. Now go rest." He didn't need to add, "Or I'll be burying you."

Too exhausted to sleep, and suddenly overcome by my loss, I wandered through the house. In the kitchen, I realized I hadn't eaten for over two days. I prepared coffee, spread some cornbread with jelly my mother had brought from her house, and found a dried-up apple in the cupboard. Numbly I ate and drank, unaware of what I was tasting.

Then it all struck at once: my loss, my grief, the futility of it all, and the overwhelming desperation of being alone. Resting my arms on the table for support, I cried until there was not a tear left. My mind and body revolted against all the tragedy and horror I'd been forced to endure. Feeling dizzy and sick, I managed to get to my room and fall across the bed before I fainted.

I slept for over eighteen hours, from sometime late

in the afternoon until noon of the next day. My throat was parched, and I felt hot, but not from fever. Once more I made coffee, and taking it into the garden stretched out on the chaise longue.

René and my mother were gone. There had been no word from Baptiste, and I had the strange feeling I should begin planning for a life alone. I could stay in the house and mourn my dead, or I could do something to give life meaning again.

Where was I needed? Being needed had always seemed to me more important than being loved, and from now on this would become the credo of my life. Suddenly I knew where I could be of help. I could work and mourn at the same time, for René would never be out of my thoughts while I was awake. I had no intention of becoming hard and inured to sorrow; instead I would derive greater strength from it.

Finishing the coffee, I changed into a simple, cool cotton dress. Into a small bag I put a few supplies I might need, and I wound a white bandana around my head. Not to observe local custom, or Voodoo tradition, but simply for cleanliness. Slowly I walked the distance to the hospital.

The situation there was much as it was on my previous visit: crowded wards, filthy beds, sickening stench, acrid smoke from burning pyres of refuse outside, and the ever-present moaning. I waited for Dr. Jourdin to finish examining a patient.

"You wished to see me?" In less than a week the doctor had aged several years, and it seemed to me his hair was much grayer.

"I was here the other day, but I doubt you remember. My son was ill. I've since lost him and my mother. Now I would like to help here."

"Doing what?" His tone indicated his disbelief that any woman, let alone one so neatly dressed, would volunteer to do any real work. I was sure he was thinking that bereavement did strange things to people, and I'd probably run out at the first real crisis.

"Anything you tell me to do," I said. "I can bathe, change linens, give medicine, try to ease those in pain. I'm not afraid nor do I faint easily. I have been through three days of hell, and now I need to work. Will you let me help you?"

"Young lady, if you can do even one of the things you mentioned, I'll bless you for the rest of my life. There's water over there; some linens—we need more—in that room. Just start cleaning up."

"I'll bring some sheets as soon as I wash them out."

"Good, I'll see you in a few hours."

"You'll what!"

"I have to go to another hospital," Dr. Jourdin said as he turned to wash his hands in a basin of scum-covered water. "Three of the doctors died, and the rest of the staff took off. There's one attendant out back boiling what sheets we can use again, and another doctor should be here soon—if he's still alive." With that and with no further instructions, Dr. Jourdin left.

From then on, I spent ten to twelve hours a day at the hospital, and one week flowed into the next. The work was hard, and there was no pay, but I was well rewarded by the assurance that many walked out of the hospital who would have been carried out except for my ministrations.

Sometime in mid-October, I noticed we no longer needed pallets on the floor and some beds were empty. At the end of the month, three days went by with no deaths from yellow fever. However, the epidemic had been one of the worst in New Orleans' history. Over forty thousand had been stricken with the disease, and there had been more than eleven thousand reported deaths. Many more were probably buried secretly in private gardens or weighted with bricks and thrown into the river. Whole families died in their homes and went undiscovered for days. Near the end of October, the pitch pots were extinguished and the cannon silenced.

I walked home late one afternoon, looking forward

to three days of rest which Dr. Jourdin insisted I take.
I was tired, more tired than I'd allowed myself to admit during all the past weeks. I paused for a minute in
the garden to admire the sasanquas, every bush covered with a prodigal array of pale pink or deep rose
blossoms.

I pulled off the turban, shook out my hair, and went
straight through the parlor to the bedroom. I'd nap
first and then think about some supper. The Market
was finally open again, and I'd been able to purchase
some fresh food. Within two minutes I was asleep.

At first I thought I was dreaming. Someone was
touching my arm, and I could smell the faint bouquet
of fine wine.

"Here, Leah, drink this."

I opened my eyes slowly but had no strength left to
take the glass.

"Baptiste! Oh, my God, is it really you?"

"There, there, Cherie." He sat on the bed and took
me in his arms. "Take it easy. I'm here now."

I clutched at his chest, unable to speak.

"René's gone, isn't he?" Baptiste held me close, as
though trying to comfort me and himself at the same
time.

I had not cried for many weeks, not since the funeral, but feeling Baptiste's arms around me and held
tightly against his strong body, I broke down once
more.

"There, there, Cherie. Cry all you want to." He
brushed the hair away from my face, and reached for
his handkerchief to dry my cheeks. Gradually my tears
ceased, but I still shook with sobs.

"Was it bad, Cherie?"

"Very bad. How did you know?"

"I knew the minute I walked in. And Clotilde?"

"The same day."

"I loved him, Leah. René was someone special. He
was my son. He was a part of me, and now something
deep inside me has been destroyed."

"I know." I tilted my head and kissed him gently on the lips. Baptiste seldom let his emotions show, and I was unsure how to respond to them.

"I sat in the kitchen and cried for two hours after I got here," he said slowly. "I didn't think I was going to be able to stop. If I'd had any idea—" Baptiste struck the bed with his fist "—I'd have been home much sooner."

"It's been terribly lonely. That's the worst of it, being all alone. Oh, Baptiste, he was so sick, so terribly, terribly sick, and there was nothing I could do. So helpless. Everyone dying."

"I'm with you now," he comforted me, "and I won't have to leave again. You're the one who needs to be taken care of. Look, I've filled the tub with hot water. Drink this while I help you."

I sipped the wine while Baptiste unfastened my dress and slipped it over my shoulders. Once he had me completely undressed, he carried me to the tub and insisted on bathing me as though I were a child. Sliding into the water, fragrant with lavender, I relaxed under his soothing hands. Then he wrapped me in a big towel and carried me back to the bed.

"Here's a gown. Now get into bed. I've supper all prepared, and I'm bringing it in on a tray. You're not to stir from this spot."

"And you?"

"I'll put my tray on this table and we'll eat by candlelight. Leah, our life isn't over. We've years ahead, haven't we?"

"I—I hope so."

Once we finished and I'd told him all about my decision to work at the hospital after the agony of the two deaths, Baptiste reached for a cigar.

"I'll go outside to smoke. You go to sleep. I'll try not to disturb you when I come in."

Dear, considerate Baptiste, I thought, as grieved as I over the loss of our son, but doing everything to console me. Now it was the two of us again, almost like starting anew. René would remain a precious memory, but I would not let his death cast a shadow over my life.

I was asleep when Baptiste returned, but sometime during the night I woke up. He was lying on his side with his hand just barely touching my back. Gently, so as not to wake him, I lifted it enough to put it around my waist, and then I curled up in the arc of his body.

"You all right, Cherie?" Baptiste mumbled.

"Um."

"I love you, Leah." Baptiste reached over and turned me so I faced him. His hands sought the soft curves of my body and I welcomed his mouth hard against mine. Now we were really together again. Once I felt his love flooding through me, filling the long-empty void, all the loneliness I had endured began to vanish.

PART II

The War

Chapter Fourteen

IN THAT AUTUMN OF 1860, our own personal tragedy was soon overshadowed by the greater tragedy of the nation.

All New Orleans reverberated with the question uppermost in the mind of every American: Would the Southern states secede from the Union?

With a large French-speaking population and a mixed Spanish and French Creole culture, the Crescent City had always considered itself different from any other in the United States. New Orleans was an entity unto itself, separate not only from other sections of the country, but, along with the French-speaking parishes in the Southern section of Louisiana, also from other areas of the state.

The *Vieux Carré*, or French Quarter, of New Orleans was more Continental than American. Its capital was Paris, not Washington, and children of wealthy Creole parents received their formal education in Europe, not at American colleges. There was an American section across Canal Street, to be sure, and though it was larger than the *Vieux Carré*, it counted for nothing within the French Quarter. For many it did not even exist. They lived their entire lives without ever entering it.

There were few ideas the two disparate sections agreed about; but on the subject of secession, they spoke with one voice: *"Vive la liberté!"*

The hope of most Louisianans was for all the Southern states to secede, but some went so far as to express the opinion it was the South which should remain as the United States while the Northern states should be expelled from the Union. A few lonely voices argued that such schismatic thinking would lead only to tragedy, but their opinions carried no weight after thirty thousand copies of Bishop Palmer's sermon of November 29 were printed and distributed.

Bishop Palmer averred that the South had a trust to defend. "Not 'til the last man has fallen behind the last rampart," he said, "shall it drop from our hands; and then only in surrender to the God who gave it." First his congregation and then all of New Orleans and Louisiana were ready to take up the banner, whether as part of a Southern confederation of states or as a single, independent government.

In the market, the women no longer gossiped about the latest Paris fashions or the most recent scandal, but speculated on how soon Louisiana would be free to pursue its own path of self-determination, no longer shackled by the laws of a Northern-dominated Congress. Sometimes I joined in the talk; more often I just listened. Remember, my mother had said, I was neither Negro nor white; I was colored. In this volatile autumn of 1860, I realized this could also mean I was neither slave nor free white. Politics and national affairs occupied a far less important place in my life than human relationships and my sense of belonging to the *Vieux Carré* as a free person of color. Although having no strong feelings about secession, it never occurred to me to doubt the wisdom of whatever choice the state leaders made.

Like so many others, I knew that many disparate factors were moving the South toward secession, but I sensed that slavery was the most insidious because it was the most inflammatory. I heard Negroes, although unsure of what was causing all the furor, speak openly on the possibility of being free. On the other hand, white citizens vacillated between two fears: a gradual attrition of Southern values if they did not secede; a Negro rebellion if they did.

More than at any other time in my life, I found myself in a limbo of ambivalence, unable to identify with either group. I was a slave owner, yet I had never ceased to loathe the white traditions that circumscribed every aspect of my life. Although not a slave, my heritage endowed me with a natural antipathy toward the institution. Therefore, I walked alone, unmoved by the arguments of either group, because I knew that no matter what the outcome of the conflict, I myself would never be free from the chains of custom.

Weeping piteously and begging my forgiveness, Seena returned to the house soon after the yellow fever epidemic ended. My fury had long since been dissipated by tragedy; and when I saw how frightened she was, I gathered the half-starved little girl into my arms and welcomed her back. I forebore asking her about where she'd been, but I eventually learned she'd found her way to Marie Laveau's, and the Mamaloi had encouraged her to return home. Any thoughts I had of freeing Seena were postponed until the girl reached maturity and could take care of herself. But I knew, too, that the decision might be made for me.

I did not return to work at the hospital, but I frequently sent anonymous gifts of linens, clothing for indigent patients, and other items I knew were needed. Occasionally I saw Dr. Jourdin on the street, and he always stopped for a friendly chat. Aside from that, the past tragedy seldom intruded into the present. In memory, René remained the beautiful blue-eyed baby I'd adored.

As long as I could remember, I had faithfully accompanied my mother to St. Louis Cathedral. However, until after the deaths of René and Clotilde, I had practiced my religion by rote, experiencing no deep sense of satisfaction from either the public ritual of the mass or private prayer. At my moment of greatest despair, when I envisioned the future as a dark meaningless void, a weary priest who took time to say a few prayers showed me that, though lonely, I was not alone.

While the epidemic continued and I was busy in the hospital, I had not gone to the cathedral; but once Baptiste returned, I began to drop in more and more often. Gradually, I found the quiet of the sanctuary filling a need I had never sensed before, and finally hardly a day went by that I didn't spend a few minutes in silent prayer or contemplating the altar painting of St. Louis proclaiming the Seventh Crusade. By December, I wondered if New Orleans and the South were about to embark on a crusade of their own.

I seldom spoke about what my religion had come to mean to me, but my faith created a reservoir of strength that was to support me during several crises which would have been unendurable earlier.

During the last quarter of 1860, Baptiste, along with other brokers and planters, was debating whether to sell immediately at a good profit or hold cotton and sugarcane for the higher prices they would surely command a few months or a year hence. Both broker and planter, he was among the wealthy of the city who exerted a strong influence on the state legislature. Few doubted that the question of secession would soon come up for formal debate. Therefore, he listened intently to the opinions I gleaned from overheard conversations at the Market.

Still, New Orleans was in a gay, exuberant mood. The theatre and opera seasons promised to be especially spectacular; and while the women ordered new gowns, the men made the money to pay for them. No one thought of secession in terms of war or, if it came to that, war in terms of death. Like the night before Napoleon's defeat at Waterloo, or the days preceding Armageddon, New Orleans played.

Rumors became reality when the Secession Convention of Louisiana was called to order on January 23. 1861, and former Governor Mouton was elected president of the body. Governor Moore announced he had seized Forts Jackson and St. Philip below New Orleans, the United States Arsenal at Baton Rouge, a Federal revenue cutter, and other government property. South Carolina had been the first to issue a proclamation declaring itself a separate, free, and sovereign state on December 24. On January 9, Mississippi became the second state to secede, and in Charleston Harbor, shots were fired from a shore battery toward the *Star of the West*, which was attempting to resupply Fort Sumter. On the two succeeding days, Florida and Alabama became the third and fourth states to pass ordinances of secession. More and more pressure was being exerted on the remaining Southern states. Then Georgia responded to the challenge on January 19 by voting 208 to 89 in favor of secession.

During the ensuing week, all Louisiana seemed to be holding its breath. Caught up in the manic mood of anticipation, like a child waiting for Christmas morning, no one could remain indoors for long. Mornings, the Market was a center of harried activity, accompanied by a constant repetition of the all-important question: Will Louisiana be next? In the afternoon, businessmen congregated in small groups on the banquettes, and women discussed the latest rumors while selecting shoes and bonnets in the shops or sipping tea in the privacy of their parlors.

Once the Secession Convention began in Baton Rouge on January 23, the populace began to converge on the various newspaper offices to await the latest word from the capital, which was posted periodically in the windows. Finally, on Saturday, January 26, their vigil was rewarded. Louisiana was the sixth Southern state to declare itself independent of the Union and a great cheer went up from those standing closest to the windows.

"Turn up the gas!" Baptiste called, opening the door and running into the kitchen where my hands were deep in biscuit dough.

"Why? It's scarcely first dark yet."

But Baptiste had already disappeared into the bedroom, lighting every lamp he passed.

"What—what's going on?" I asked breathlessly when I finally caught up with him.

"Get out all the candles we have, Cherie, and see if you can find those oil lanterns we put in the storage shed. We can put them along the top of the wall and hang them from the trees in the courtyard."

"Baptiste Fontaine, I'm not moving a step until you tell me what this is all about."

"Secession, Cherie. Louisiana has seceded from the Union. The whole town is celebrating. Mayor Monroe has asked everyone to light up their homes and shops."

In the distance I could hear the thunder of guns along the levee at the foot of Canal Street and the carnival merriment of people in the streets.

"If it's a celebration," I said, "then what are we doing in here?"

"Right you are," Baptiste shouted, grabbing me around the waist. "Get a wrap. Supper can wait."

We lighted candles in all the windows and set more than half a dozen lanterns on the wall.

"There," I said, "we've done our part."

The whole quarter was lit up like a reflection from a gigantic bonfire—homes, store windows, the Cabildo, the cathedral. Many celebrants had made pine knot torches and were parading around Jackson Square. The deep notes of cannons echoed and reechoed across the river and the bayous while cathedral and church bells added a harmonious descant. It was wild like Mardi Gras, joyous like Christmas, and suffused with a newly gained sense of freedom like the Fourth of July. There were no strangers, no color lines, no social distinctions. All celebrated together the new birth of Louisiana as a free and independent sovereign state.

Some groups linked arms and marched along the streets laughing; others stood on steps above the crowd and entertained with ribald songs; now and then a long cheer went up: "Down with the Union; up with Louisiana!"

Someone had unearthed an old state flag and, climbing up a lamppost, was madly waving it over the heads of the crowd. This encouraged more cheers. Baptiste and I walked as far as Canal Street to watch the crowds milling around the Pelican and Boston Clubs, then back to St. Charles where the Pickwick Club and Kittridge's store outshone all the others in brilliance.

Exhausted but too excited to sleep, Baptiste and I stayed up half the night, eating a late supper and toasting everything we could think of in champagne.

"To Louisiana," Baptiste raised his glass.

"To Louisiana," I repeated.

"To us!"

"To New Orleans!"

"To General Jackson!"

"But he's dead," I giggled.

"I don't care," Baptiste said; "he's worth a good toast and this is good champagne."

"To the future!"

"To you," Baptiste said solemnly.

"To me," I said, in a slightly blurred voice.

"You don't toast yourself," Baptiste said. "That's not ladylike."

"But I'm not a lady," I giggled again. "Because ladies don't get drunk, and I think I'm quite soused."

"Who else do we drink to?" Baptiste asked. "There's half a bottle left."

"To Napoleon!" I stood up and began singing "The Marseillaise," slightly off-key.

"He's dead, too," Baptiste said. "You said we couldn't toast a dead man.

"Oh," I said, missing the edge of the couch and sitting down suddenly on the floor, "I didn't know. That's too bad." I started giggling again. "To the ghosts of Napoleon and Jackson, may they rest in peace." With that I slid farther down on the rug and fell asleep.

On the following days readers devoured every word in the local papers. The *Picayune* said: "The deed has been done . . . the Union is dead. . . . To the lone star of the state we transfer the duty, affection, and allegiance we owed to the congregation of light which spangled the banner of the Old Confederacy." The *Crescent* echoed the same thought: ". . . with a calm dignity and firm purpose, Louisiana resumes her delegated powers, and escapes from a Union in which she could no longer remain with honor. . . ."

Only the *True Delta* was opposed to secession: "Everything in this city appears to be in rapid progress toward a war establishment." It wasn't long before most people realized the paper spoke with the prophetic voice of a Cassandra. It issued a warning that no one would believe during the first exhilarating days of independence.

By the middle of February all United States property had been secured by the state. On February 12, the convention adopted a new flag with thirteen stripes of red, blue, and white representing the tricolor of France. A yellow star on a red ground in the upper left-hand corner honored the red and yellow colors of Spain. Louisiana remained an independent state until it joined the Confederate States of America on March 21.

Within a few weeks after Louisiana seceded, the state began mobilizing her military strength, and New Orleans took on all the aspects of a military camp. Walls of buildings were covered with recruiting placards urging volunteers to join various companies. Many gave themselves very romantic or distinctly Louisiana names: the Lafayette Rifles, Beauregard Guards, Knights of the Border, Catahoula Guerillas, Caddo Lake Boys, Mounted Wild Cats, Yankee Pelters, Louisiana Tigers. Each company was formed of a motley assortment of Irish, German, Italian, Spanish, and native Louisianans. For the first time within recorded history, these nationalities melded into a single, unified force, forged together by one desire—to remain free. There were accountants and small farmers, shopkeepers and boatmen, teachers and laborers, and a few Cajuns from the bayous. Those Cajuns who did not volunteer for formal fighting ultimately proved their prowess in the swamp when they harassed the enemy or helped Confederate families escape ravaging Union forces.

Some men were organizing cooperative regiments in which costs would be shared until the Confederate government could assume the expenses. However, Baptiste was offering to shoulder all the responsibilities of his. He had posted his own placard, urging volunteers for the Crescent Cavaliers. He offered to provide a full uniform, a strong mount, and a generous stipend to each man joining his company. Some other recruiters offered uniforms and pay—in order to ease the financial burden on the state—but few were providing horses, expecting each man to ride his own. So Baptiste had little difficulty getting volunteers to sign up. Men were far more willing to leave home if they did not have to deprive their families of a much needed horse for working the farm or pulling the carriage.

"Baptiste, do you think you should?" I asked, when he told me what he was doing.

"Yes, I can afford it, and it's my way of assuring that any skirmish will end soon. As long as I provide everything the men will have no excuse for leaving and going home. With money in the bank, they won't be worried about their families. The bank will automatically transfer the funds to their accounts each month."

"Can't you just provide the men? Do you have to go yourself?"

"Leah, I couldn't live with myself if I didn't. We've got to prove to the North that states have the right to secede if they so choose."

"I've got 'em, Leah. I've got my full complement of men!"

"So you've got the men," I said. "What do you plan to do with them?"

"Train them, of course. We'll start drilling in Jackson Square just as soon as I find a place to put them up. Most are from town; I think the others can put down bedrolls on the second floor of the warehouse. It won't be long before I'll be given a bivouac area on the outskirts of town. We've each put in a bid for a preferred location."

"Why drill? I thought yours was a cavalry unit?"

"They still have to learn how to march in formation. There'll be times we can't use horses, or—or we might find ourselves without them."

"Why? Why would you leave them behind?"

"Because they might be dead."

"Please, Baptiste, I don't like to hear you talking this way. You make it sound as though war is inevitable."

"It is, Cherie. It's coming closer every day."

"Maybe not," I insisted, "maybe the Union will just agree we have the right to secede."

"Never. Don't fool yourself into thinking that."

"But why not? What's wrong with there being separate sovereign states, or a confederacy of Southern states?"

"Because it weakens the power of the Union. We have things, especially cotton, they need."

"Pooh, they can get along without us, or we can trade with them, the way England and France do. We don't want to fight them to make them do as we say. Why should they want to fight us?"

"Because we've taken over things the Federal government says belong to them—forts and supply depots and Federal buildings."

"But they're in our states, aren't they? Why shouldn't Fort Jackson and Fort St. Philip belong to Louisiana? Or Fort Sumter to South Carolina? Or Ship Island to Mississippi?"

"They're in our states, yes, but they're manned by Federal troops."

"Well—tell the troops to get out. We'll man them ourselves."

"Oh, Cherie, your logic sounds so simple. I wish things were that simple, but they aren't. The government leaders in Washington just aren't going to let the nation be divided. I'm convinced they will go to war to keep us united. They feel it's America's destiny and her strength. They argue that if we split up, we can be invaded and conquered by a strong European power. But that's just one reason. There are so many others that make sense to them if not to us. They're emotional ones, but it's emotion that moves most men."

"Like slavery?"

"Yes, Cherie, like slavery."

By early spring, New Orleans took on more and more aspects of a garrison, and the streets were full of Turcos, Zouaves, and Chasseurs in garish scarlet, blue, and gold uniforms. Infantry and cavalry in gray and homespun drilled in Jackson Square, and local militia paraded before the Cabildo, the former United States Mint, and the Customs House.

Tailors refused all orders for civilian clothes in order to concentrate on uniforms, and seamstresses turned out dozens of the new Louisiana and—after March 21—Confederate flags of all sizes—large enough to fly over official buildings, small enough to be waved by children.

As each company was formed, there was an elaborate ceremony. Little girls in fancy party dresses carried bouquets; wives and sweethearts presented flags made from their own silk gowns; politicians stirred the crowd with patriotic orations, and young women representing each of the Confederate states recited heart-moving poems.

They're all playing at war, I thought, like a lot of little boys with a new Christmas set of tin soldiers. All pretending to be officers, they'll move their soldiers around in formation until they get tired of the game. One by one the little tin soldiers will all fall down, and the boys will run away to play at something else.

Encampments were established around the outer perimeter of the city, and they soon took on the ambivalent air of martial splendor and holiday festivities. Every day a parade of expensive carriages, filled with gaily dressed, chattering young women, started out from the city just before noon. They arrived in time to admire husbands, brothers, and sweethearts drill their troops. Once the men were dismissed, cloths were spread on the earth, hampers unpacked, and the area became one huge picnic ground. But the baskets contained no simple picnic food. Out of them came tureens of hot, spicy gumbos; rich game braised to a turn; the freshest fruits the market had to offer; and the most expensive wines.

Throughout the afternoon, the women strolled beneath the trees and flirted with handsome officers in meticulously tailored uniforms. Before departing for the city at sunset, wives and sweethearts presented the gifts—practical or impractical—which they hoped would ease the privations of camp life. Many were foolish, handmade tokens of love but all were received gratefully by the men. Like the knights of old who wore their lady's favor on their arms or tied around a lance, they would carry these gifts wherever the conflict took them.

Carpets were cut up to cover the floors of tents; slippers, smoking caps, tobacco pouches, cigar cases, and portfolios for writing materials were made from shimmering satin, softly crushed velvet, brightly colored ribbons, and silk braid.

At least one day a week Baptiste came into town to reorder supplies for his company, and he was usually able to stay overnight.

"When are you coming out to the camp, Cherie?" he asked while he held me close in a hungry embrace.

"I—I don't think I ought. I'd be too conspicuous, out of place."

"Oh, no, Cherie."

"Oh, yes. For one thing I'd be riding out alone."

"There are others, Leah, who prefer to come alone."

"But I'd be recognized as—as a *placée*."

"Wear a veil. Please, Leah, I've looked forward to showing off my men and our fine camp."

"I'm sorry, Baptiste, I'm not the mystery woman type. I'll see them when you parade in town. Surely you'll come to town soon."

Baptiste impulsively pulled me into his arms again, took the pins from my hair, and ran his fingers through it as it fell around my shoulders.

"Ah, it will be good to stretch out on the couch and watch you set the table. You're a lot prettier than Pierre, though I swear I don't know what I'd do without him."

"Thank you, kind sir. Now, get comfortable and I'll bring some wine."

I watched him unwind the heavily fringed yellow sash and toss it into the corner of the couch. Then he carefully folded and laid his coat across the back of a chair. He noticed me looking at the sash.

"Marie Louise made it. Her family ordered her to return and play the dutiful wife. Her acting when she put the sash on would have put the great Rachel to shame. She couldn't stand it for long, though. The effort was too much. It wasn't long before she was flirting with the handsomest young officers, and I've no doubt she is now sharing the tent of the most obliging."

"You sound bitter, Baptiste."

"Not bitter, Cherie, just disgusted. I don't like being played for a fool in front of my men."

"I didn't make a sash," I said, handing him a large bundle, "but I have been busy with these."

About a month earlier I thought I'd surprise Baptiste with a half dozen gray broadcloth shirts. Since he began spending most of his days and nights at the en-

campment, I found myself with much time on my
hands. The sewing would keep me occupied. But what
was to be a pleasant diversion turned out to be a real
chore. I'd forgotten how many women would be making shirts for their men. It took five days of searching
the stores, including those in the American section, to
find enough smooth but serviceable cotton for three
shirts. But I'd made up my mind that Baptiste was going to have six new shirts. Finally I decided that they
would have to be of a material other than broadcloth,
and I waited breathlessly for Baptiste's reaction.

"These are handsome, Cherie, but—"

"But what, Baptiste?"

"Silk! When will I wear silk shirts?"

"When the others get dirty?" I suggested hesitantly.
"Or for parades?"

"Oh, Leah, you're wonderful! For parades, it is.
And they'll feel very good next to my skin. I'll save the
others for battles. But I'm not sure how Pierre will
take to laundering silk shirts in camp."

I'd heard only one word—*battles*. "There won't really be any fighting, will there?"

"It's headed that way. Just depends on who pulls the
trigger first."

That trigger was pulled on the morning of Friday,
April 12, from Fort Johnson and the Battery of
Charleston, South Carolina. The Confederate bombardment on Union-held Fort Sumter was heavy and
constant all day. Word came to us that crowds of
people thronged the Battery or climbed up on roofs to
cheer the volunteers and The Citadel cadets who
manned the cannon for thirty-four hours until Fort
Sumter surrendered.

I had had the feeling New Orleans was playing at
war. I was wrong. The first months of 1861 were not a
game. They were a preparation for unspeakable car-
nage, rapine, destruction, and death.

Baptiste was still as excited as a little boy with his

set of toy soldiers. He'd come into town to check on supplies and pack a few personal items.

"Now that you've trained the men, Baptiste, can't you turn them over to another officer and remain here?"

"Hardly, Leah, not after working this long under me. And we've lots more work to do to get ready for real fighting. The men don't know anything about what they'll be up against in the field."

"And you do?" I didn't mean to sound as sarcastic as I did, and bit my lip.

"Not about fighting maybe, but in handling men, organizing, and issuing orders. I won't be on my own, remember; I'll be following orders, too, and I'll just pass them on to my men."

"And if you do find yourself on your own?"

"If I can predict the price and harvest of cotton, I can sure figure out what a bunch of Yankee soldiers will do."

"You sound pretty confident, Baptiste."

"More than that, I'm excited. I'm an adventurer at heart, Leah, and I can do one thing for just so long. Then I have to break away. That's why I started the brokerage. I could have stayed on the plantation—but I wanted to do something new, on my own. Just to see if I could. If I'd lived two hundred years ago, I'd have been an explorer or a privateer."

"And do you also find it difficult to stay with one woman for too long a time?" I had not forgotten the reputation he enjoyed in the *Vieux Carré* when I first met him. Nor had I—night after night—been able to ignore the scar on his upper thigh, inflicted during a duel over one of New Orleans's most popular belles. "Two inches higher, my love," he explained laughingly, "and you would never have had to fear I'd try to seduce you." But somehow I was unable to laugh with him.

Baptiste didn't answer my question.

"You're hesitating, Baptiste. Did I ask the wrong question? Is there no answer for that one?"

"I'm looking for the right words, Leah."

"To tell me you're tired of me, too? To say that's why you're looking forward to going to war?"

"No, to convince you that my love for you is the one steady thing in my life. I may wander. I may get restless for adventure, but I'll always return."

"Are you so sure I'll always be here?"

"No, Cherie, and perhaps that's why I find you so fascinating. I can't take you for granted. But I—I hope you'll be here waiting when I do get furlough time."

"Don't worry," I smiled. "I'll be here. How soon will you be leaving?"

"Just as soon as our orders come through."

"Any idea where you'll be going?"

"Not far. We'll stay right in Louisiana, I imagine, to patrol the river. We'll probably bivouac somewhere between here and Natchez, then spread out to cover as much territory as possible. The delta is well protected by Fort Jackson and Fort St. Philip, so the real danger will be from ships coming down the Ohio to the Mississippi. Temporary posts will be set up every few miles. Once the Yankees realize they can't come south via that route, they'll turn back and we'll have no further trouble from them here. New Orleans will never be in danger from any real attack."

Chapter Fifteen

As HE'D HOPED, Baptiste's company was positioned near Baton Rouge. New Orleans was more active than ever with parades, more intensive recruiting, the construction of small industrial plants to produce goods normally imported, as well as munitions and such military supplies as tents. Boats roved the rivers and bayous to collect scrap iron while collection points were set up within the city for old pots and pans. Gunboats were fitted out for river patrol, and more were ordered to protect New Orleans.

During the spring and early summer of 1861, the war still seemed very far away in spite of the preparations going on all around us. True, men like Baptiste were leaving every day to protect Louisiana's boundaries, and the streets of New Orleans swarmed with more and more soldiers. But the atmosphere was rather more like that of a never-ending Mardi Gras celebration than the prologue to a tragic war.

Other than adjusting to living without Baptiste, my life went on much the same. In truth, I delighted at first in being alone and feeling the independence I had so long yearned for. I had a house, plenty of money, and a well-trained servant in Seena. I was free to do exactly what I wanted. So then I was faced with the question of just what it was I wanted to do. The lists of those invited to the balls and bazaars held almost daily to raise money for hospitals and the men in the field did not include my name, nor that of any other person of color. After years of skirting the edge of the white world but never being able to penetrate it, I had a sudden desire to delve more deeply into the world of my mother and grandmother. Now that it no longer threatened me, and I no longer felt intimidated by it, I yearned inexplicably for knowledge of my colored heritage which I had earlier turned a deaf ear to whenever my mother tried to speak of it.

So began a new and interesting regimen for me, a commingling of two strangely disparate ways of life. Excitedly I approached two women who would never under any circumstances meet, but whose opposite ideologies had in the past sustained me during moments of extreme despair. But they had touched me only superficially, and now I meant to immerse myself completely in their ways of life.

Although I had not seen Marie Laveau since shortly before René's death, she welcomed me with open arms and agreed enthusiastically to fulfill my request. After an early supper every evening, I ran the path to Marie's house, my cheeks brushed by Spanish moss draped from live oaks and my dress skirting the low palmetto shrubs, the lair of the deadly rattler. Before arriving at my destination, I passed the bayou, the domain of the even more deadly moccasin which gave no warning before striking.

I was to continue my training—interrupted by my meeting with Baptiste—to become a Voodoo priestess. In no time at all, I relearned the chants and rituals for the various ceremonies. In addition, Marie taught me how to concoct the various charms, potions, *gris-gris*, and Ouanga bags. She took me through her garden where she cultivated many of the herbs used in Voodoo as well as those for curing numerous illnesses and pains. Not all of the Voodoo mysteries involved love potions, supplications to Damballa, charms to ward off danger, or curses placed on enemies. Voodoo also concerned itself with the good health and comfort of its adherents. More than that, it offered peace of mind and an outlet for the frustrations of those relegated to the lowest level of society by the chains of slavery or custom. Standing at the altar, intoning the ancient chants of Africa, I tried to become one of the practitioners, feeling their fears and sharing their hopes. The outward observances were easy to learn and put into practice; absorbing the philosophy was more difficult, but I had to try. I had to know for sure who and what I was.

Sister Angelique greeted me just as warmly as had Marie Laveau, but she was more reluctant to accede to my request.

"Please, Sister," I pleaded, "I finished with honors. Surely there is some way I can be of assistance in the classrooms. I told you once I wanted to teach, but you discouraged me then."

"No, Leah, I discouraged you in your desire to be like me, and I urged you to think seriously before deciding to be a nun. Don't confuse that with my merely asking you what you knew about teaching."

"I'm sorry, Sister. You remember better than I."

"Why do you come here now?" Once more Sister Angelique was coming directly to the point and demanding I do the same.

"I'm not really sure. That is, there's really more than one reason. It's not just that I have time on my hands or that I merely want something to do. Would you understand if I said I needed to find out who I am?"

"Perhaps," Sister Angelique said softly. She waited for me to continue.

Where should I start? How far back need I go? The placid serenity of her face assured me of her willingness to listen to whatever I had to say; and as she relaxed in the chair, I knew she was ready to give me all the time I required. Over the years, I had gone irregularly to confession, and always as a duty; the priests had been professionally impersonal. But now, with Sister Angelique, for the first time in my life I felt I was confiding in someone who was genuinely concerned about the person who was me—Leah, the daughter of Clotilde, not just one nameless member of the flock.

"When I graduated," I began, "I knew one thing about myself. I was a woman of color. According to the laws of the state, I was legally free; but according to custom, my life was rigidly circumscribed by unwritten laws of prejudice and tradition. I was free to do what? Meekly accept the lowly position accorded to those of my color.

"This I refused to do, having planned for a long time to flee a situation I found intolerable." Omitting few details, I told Sister Angelique about my experiences at the quadroon balls, my aborted attempt to run away, my rescue by Baptiste, and my ultimately becoming his *placée*. I found it most difficult to speak of René and his death, but her sympathetic attitude enabled me to speak of the loneliness and despair I had felt.

"For almost three years," I continued, "I knew who I was—a *placée*, mistress to a white man—and I learned to accept it, nay, to enjoy real contentment living with a man who loved me and ultimately to know exquisite joy as the mother of our son. Through all the happiness and sorrow, I had a sense of being, of knowing who I was. Now—once again—I'm lost."

"Because Baptiste is gone?" she asked.

"No—no. It's the war itself, the real reason it's being fought. I said I didn't come here just to have something to do. I could easily fill my hours with sewing, making bandages, and doing other things for the war effort. But where do I belong? Which side is my side? I'm not one of the white women who attend balls and bazaars; neither am I a slave waiting to see if I'm going to be freed. I was born and bred a Southerner. New Orleans is my home. But—oh, Sister Angelique, who am I?"

The cry came right from my heart, and before I realized what I was doing, I'd laid my head in her lap as

I had done when a little girl. She smoothed my hair with her hand just as she might have comforted a child who had fallen and needed to be assured the hurt would soon disappear.

"You are a child of God, Leah."

"I know," I sobbed. "You told me that before. But what do others see when they look at me?"

"Externals are not important, Leah. It's what you see when you look inside yourself. That's the person you are."

"You're wrong!" I lifted my head and looked at her hard. "My skin—my hair, these are what make me who I am. Don't you think they dictate what I can and can't be? They are the stigmata of my heritage. Maybe my blood doesn't show, but they do."

"Nor can you change who you were born."

"I know that. But you say to look inside myself, to see who I really am. That's what I can't do. When I try, I see nothing but turmoil. It's the war that's done it."

"No, Leah, it's not the war. That's taking the easy way out—to lay the blame on something outside yourself."

"So, we're back to me again and no closer to a solution."

"Perhaps we are, Leah. You say you want to teach. Do you have any idea what moved you in this direction after all these years?"

"If I'm honest, I know what I should say. To run away and hide, to find sanctuary from thinking about the war and what its implications are for me; to escape from having to make a decision of some kind as far as my loyalties are concerned."

"Yes, that's a frank and honest answer. But do you think I am not troubled by the same thoughts you have?"

"I—I didn't think of that."

"No matter, we'll talk of that another time. If I say yes to your request, what would you like to do here?"

"I want to work with the children of *plaçage*. Our world is a very isolated one, not only from the rest of the community, but we are often isolated from one another. We keep pretty much to ourselves within our own homes. You may think it ironic after all I've said, but I think it will be among my own people that I'll find out finally who I am—and learn not only to accept it but to be proud of it."

"And the children?" Sister Angelique said.

"What do you mean?"

"I must think of the children. You speak as though they are here for your benefit. I can't let you upset them in any way."

"Oh, please. I won't do anything like that. Surely I could help with the teaching, or supervise them at play."

"Yes, I think you could. There are times when the classes need to be divided into smaller sections for more personal tutoring. Both Sister Theresa and Sister Maria could use your assistance with the groups not being taught at the moment. Come tomorrow at eight. I will talk to the other sisters tonight. Now go. I need time for my prayers before supper."

"Thank you, Sister Angelique. I'll not disappoint you. Please include me in your prayers."

So my days took on a new dimension—two new dimensions, I should say. Every morning Seena brought me coffee at seven which I drank while I dressed in simple cotton gowns that could take the smudges from chalk and sticky fingers. Promptly at seven-thirty I breakfasted on croissants, a hard-boiled egg, and my second cup of coffee. By ten to eight I was walking the few blocks to the convent school.

There the delightful children waited. Sister Angelique had denied my request to work exclusively with children of *plaçage*. "You will only become more provincial in your outlook. To really know yourself you must break free of all shackles. You call white people prejudiced, but you are far more narrow-minded and predisposed to judge by externals. You will work with all the children."

As usual, Sister Angelique was right. While Sister Theresa, Maria, or one of the others was giving special instruction to one small group, I helped the others with their reading or supervised written work. The most pleasurable times were those spent in the play yard or reading to the little ones.

At first I learned to identify them by the color of their skin: deep brown Sophia, dusky Suzette, pale fawn Lizette, and Rachael of the *café au lait* complexion. Then there were the pink and white Carolines, Maybelles, Lauries, and Mary Annes. Within two weeks, if anyone asked which was the quadroon—Suzette or Caroline—I would have responded with shocked amazement. They had become children, my children, each an individual in her own right; and I began to see what it was Sister Angelique wanted me to learn. Time is not only a great healer, but also a patient teacher.

At three in the afternoon, after tea with the sisters and a planning session for the next day, I left the school and hurried home for a quick supper and change of clothing. Before five I was on my way to Marie Laveau's. By early July, I was assisting her in many of the rituals. A new group of girls was being readied for initiation, and I was deeply involved in their training: teaching them the chants, the meaning and uses of various charms, and their secret responsibilities once they were welcomed into the cult. When the important evening arrived, I went early to the Mystery House to prepare the altar and assist Marie Laveau in robing herself. Through all this I recalled the dreadful wonder that overpowered me when I witnessed the first blood sacrifice and the awe and fear at the initiation procedure.

I learned much about the dark side of my nature during these weeks—the fears and superstitions which

had evolved in Africa through centuries of struggle
for existence amid such enemies as the powerful
forces of an often malevolent nature: storms, floods,
droughts, and the animals of the plains and jungles they
must compete with for food as well as do battle for life.

So the ancient Africans created gods as powerful and
fearsome. Damballa Oueddo was the mightiest of all;
the huge serpent that terrified them was his avatar and
the lightning that snaked through the sky his sign. He
wielded the power of life and death over his worshipers, and to him must be given blood sacrifices to
appease his voracious hunger. At his side stood always
Ogoun Badagris, the bloody dreadful one whose voice
was the thunder. Loco, god of the forest, and Agoué,
god of the sea, were dual-natured beings. They provided the necessities of life, but they could also destroy
in mysterious ways.

There must be benevolent gods, too, and thus were
created Papa Legba, keeper of the gate, and Maîtresse
Ézilée, the blessed protector of women. To her the adherents of Voodoo prayed for ripening wombs and
guardianship of their children.

Sometimes at night, when I was preparing the altar
alone, I heard a lone woman singing her mournful
plaint in the patois unique to Southern Louisiana, "*Pas
'joudhui moins gagnin chemin; Damballa, moins bien
prête, moins pas 'river.*" "It is not today that I will find
the path, Damballa. I am ready but the road is
barred." Or another, perhaps a young woman, who
feared she was barren, would cry out, "*Maîtresse
Ézilée, vini 'gider moi,*" pleading with the goddess to
come to her aid.

Wrenched from their homes and forced to cross the
treacherous sea of Agoué en route to the terrors of the
unknown, the Africans brought their gods and beliefs
with them. Enslaved by masters whose language, religion, and ways were abhorrent to them, they clung in
bewilderment to what was familiar. They found sur-
cease from their travail and the new fears born of slav-

ery in worshiping the old gods. Nor did they see any incongruity in adding the symbols and tenets of the Christian faith to those of Voodoo. If both God and Damballa were omnipotent, they were merely two aspects of the same power.

I did not become a Mamaloi, or Voodoo priestess. When I assisted Marie at the altar, I saw the worshipers as a part of my shadowy past, as one source from which I'd emerged, but as less than one half of my whole being. I respected that past and I appreciated the worshipers' need for what Voodoo could do for them, but it was not my present need; and once learning this, I did not return to the House of Mystery. When I thought of Voodoo in terms of "they" instead of "we," I knew my roots were the same as the adherents', but there were too many generations separating us.

Busy as I was, days went by without my being reminded there were battles being fought in such faraways places as Virginia and Missouri, or that the people of New Orleans were deeply involved in intensive preparations for the defense of the city. I left the house before eight, remained secluded in the convent school until midafternoon, and was often busy with Marie or the Voodoo ceremonies until nearly midnight. I was not so completely isolated by my own concerns, however, that I was not aware of the Union blockade of the Gulf and East coasts, the seizure of Confederate vessels, or the threat of Union ships coming downriver. Rumors were rampant about the number of foreign ships carrying goods to the South that turned back rather than risk running the blockade; but so far, necessities and even some luxuries were still available.

On May 3 had come the official declaration of war and word that Arkansas and Tennessee had also seceded. This was followed by the welcome news that the Confederate privateer *Calhoun* had captured the bark *Ocean Eagle* from Maine, not far from New Orleans. With others I cheered when the C.S.S. *Sumter* ran the blockade, opening the way for more ships to follow with supplies. On July 5, a Federal setback in Missouri relaxed the fears that the Union would get control of the upper Mississippi.

All was not peace and calm in New Orleans, however. There were rumblings of discontent and muttered threats of revolt by various groups of slaves, especially those volunteered by their masters to work on fortifications. Some objected and ran away. Others took the opportunity to flee north in the belief this was their one chance for freedom. Many, like Pierre, followed their masters into the field.

On the other hand, many free Negroes and *gens du couleur* were, like myself, pro-Confederate at the beginning of the war. Although this was especially true of those who owned slaves themselves, many nonslave owners also contributed to the defense fund of New Orleans. In April, Jordan Noble, the drummer boy at the Battle of New Orleans in 1815, was the moving force behind the free Negroes who offered their services to the Confederacy. Even when, as a child, I'd seen him gaily lead the annual Jackson Day parade, he'd seemed like an old man. Now once again he was offering to defend his beloved city. In May, Governor Thomas Moore authorized the formation of a free Negro regiment to guard New Orleans.

By midsummer I had not yet found what I was looking for. The key to the enigma of who I was remained just beyond my reach, but I was happier than I had been in a long time. If Voodoo had not provided the clue, the children at the convent school proved my life had gained meaning by being needed.

Twice in June Baptiste came downriver seeking supplies, and though our moments together eased some longing in us, they were too brief to recapture the easy, familiar relationship we'd had before he became the soldier and I the woman waiting at home. The war was not only separating us by miles but also by time.

In early July his company was ordered to Virginia to

help protect Richmond, the new capital of the Confederacy. As a parting gift, I made him heavy cotton sheets or blanket liners which could be taped on the blankets and removed for washing. They would be more comfortable against his skin as well as more sanitary. As an afterthought, I worked pockets along the lower hem to hold such personal items as soap, razor, shaving mug, and other necessities.

Baptiste reported to New Orleans for his orders, and we had one day together. He arrived unexpectedly just before eight one morning, before I left for the school, and I sent word by Seena that I could not make it that day. He shared my breakfast of coffee and croissants. We walked in the garden and then to the Market for a second breakfast of coffee and doughnuts at the *Café du Monde*. All the while we talked—of his work and mine—as though we feared the silence that separates, and yet each knew what was on the other's mind. Baptiste was leaving the next day for Virginia, where there had been a number of skirmishes in areas he would have to pass through as well as an announced determination by the Union to capture Richmond as soon as possible. He was headed away from the comparative security of patrolling the Mississippi to a section already scarred by bloody battles.

Once back in the house, we sat in the parlor on separate chairs, our eyes avoiding the bedroom door, as if the thought of making love in the daytime were somehow indecent. Seena spread a table on the gallery and fixed us a light lunch which neither of us could eat.

"I have a gift for you," I finally said, and walked without thinking into the bedroom to get the blanket liners I had made for him.

I didn't know Baptiste was following me until I felt his arms go around me and his lips on the back of my neck. In another minute I was pressed against his chest, my tears wetting his neatly starched shirt, and his hands smoothing my now loosened hair.

"Oh, Baptiste, I'm frightened for you."

"Please, Cherie, there'll be no real danger at Richmond. We're just going to patrol the outskirts."

"But—but between here and there."

"We're going by train, by a well-guarded troop train."

"And if there's a battle? What if the train is stopped?"

"And what if the war ends before we get there?"

"You think it will?" I brightened up.

"No, but there's as much chance of that happening as there is of my getting hurt."

I drew his head down with both my hands and kissed him desperately while he began unfastening the back of my gown. Without saying a word, he carried me over to the bed, and I welcomed his embrace with a hunger born of loneliness and fear. For the first time, as our bodies were joined, I experienced the sensation of being one half of a perfect whole. I found the answer; I knew who I was—Baptiste's beloved—and that was all that mattered. There was no North or South, no war between Union and Confederate, no slavery and antislavery causes. There was just the two of us, the perfect union of two imperfect souls.

"I have to go, Cherie," Baptiste whispered.

"What time is it?"

"Almost five. I have to meet my men at the depot in less than an hour."

"I don't want you to go. Can't you get your orders changed?"

"No, Cherie, and you wouldn't want me to."

"Yes, I would," I mumbled into the pillow. "I want you here in Louisiana, where you'll be safe." When I rolled back over, Baptiste had begun dressing.

"Don't get up, Leah. I can't think of a nicer way to remember you than lying in bed, your hair all tousled and your cheeks flushed."

I lay back, trying to look as alluring as possible, but Baptiste only laughed and I began to cry.

"There, there, Cherie. No tears. I'll write as soon as I can."

"Um."

Baptiste leaned over and tenderly kissed me good-bye. "I love you, Leah."

"I—I—take care of yourself, Baptiste."

I buried my head in the pillow again until I heard the door slam, and then I began crying harder. Not because Baptiste was gone, but because I still couldn't say, "I love you." The words were in my heart, but I couldn't release them. Not yet. And I cried for what I had received but could not give.

Although I continued working with the children at the school, there still remained too many empty hours in which I worried about Baptiste. I knitted socks and scarves, sewed shirts and hospital gowns, and ripped up old sheets for bandages. At first my days focused on news of the war, highlighted by a rare letter from Baptiste. He had very much wanted to remain stationed near Baton Rouge, or at least go upriver to Kentucky or Tennessee to prevent Federals from capturing the river ports and proceeding downstream to attack Vicksburg and New Orleans. However, Generals Jackson and Beauregard had sent out pleas for as many men as possible to join them, perhaps convinced as were so many that a resounding defeat of the Union in Virginia would bring a quick end to the war.

Hopes rose in New Orleans that this would happen after word came of the successful rout of Federal troops at Manassas, Virginia, on Sunday, July 21. All New Orleans celebrated, lighting up the city and drinking toasts to General Beauregard, their gallant son and hero. It was some time before I learned that Baptiste had been in that battle. I had thought him at the Shenandoah with the troops under command of Joseph Johnson, but Johnson had been ordered to join Jackson at Manassas to strengthen Beauregard's forces. As news slowly filtered down to us about the battle and the tremendous number of casualties, I realized I would have been frantic had I not thought Baptiste many miles away in the Shenandoah. By the time I learned he had been a part of what would later be known as the Battle of First Bull Run, he was back in the valley and writing me about his part in defeating the Federal troops. But with the realization that he might have been one of the almost two thousand casualties, the war suddenly became very real to me.

Blockade runners were still managing to sail into port about once a week, and when one was sighted we all crowded the levees to see what had been smuggled in. Even though the prices were exorbitant, they were worth paying for a new pair of soft leather slippers from France and several yards of silk for a dress. These were luxuries, to be sure, but much needed by the women to keep up their morale. Other necessities we eagerly waited for were such vastly different items as coffee and pins. There was as yet no shortage of food.

However, letters from Baptiste urged me to save plenty of seed from my garden and buy more chickens. Before he left, he had purchased a small plot of land from the man whose back lot adjoined my side yard. I fenced off the small kitchen garden near my carriage house and had a chicken coop built. I hired a man to plow the new plot. With only part-time help for planting and hoeing, Seena and I cultivated a garden that provided us with a variety of vegetables all summer and fall, plus a good surplus to store for winter.

I had my first experience of deprivation when I tried to purchase glass canning jars. The supplies from Northern factories had been cut off, and none were being manufactured in the South. It came as a real shock to realize that certain common items could no longer be taken for granted. From now on nothing could be wasted or thrown away.

My chickens laid well, and once a week I took a

basket of eggs to the Market to trade for butter and milk.

In September, while sewing hospital gowns, I was reminded of the days I'd helped at the hospital during the yellow fever epidemic, and I wondered if there would be a place there for me again.

There was a place, but not what I'd hoped for, based on my previous experience. The routine was strictly regimented, and the various tasks clearly assigned. Only white women were allowed to nurse, assist the doctors, feed the patients, and change the bed linens. Only white volunteers were considered well bred enough to write or read letters, or chat with the patients. At first there were plenty of such volunteers for these tasks. Yes, there was work for me—if I were willing to scrub floors, empty slop jars, and carry out pails of filthy, bloody, pus-covered bandages. I swallowed hard. Not my pride. I was never too proud to do work that needed doing. I swallowed the bile that rose at the smells emanating from the wards and the foul conditions in what passed for an operating room.

I wrapped around me the apron I'd brought from home, straightened my tignon, picked up a bucket, and began to scrub. If I had my way, I would make this the cleanest hospital in the South. I dreaded many things, but hard, physical work was not one of them. From three to eleven every night I scrubbed, carried slop jars, and held the pail the doctors threw the soiled bandages into.

With no real fighting near New Orleans, few of the wounded we received were emergency cases; most were soldiers who had been treated elsewhere and then sent home on medical furloughs. There were relapses, flare-ups of infections, and changes of bandages. There were enough cases who needed additional surgery or continued bed care, however, to keep the hospital full and everyone busy. The saddest cases were those who had lost limbs or been blinded and who could not get proper care at home.

In February, Baptiste wrote that his company, at the request of Governor Moore of Louisiana, was being transferred to strengthen the forces at Fort St. Philip, below New Orleans at the mouth of the Mississippi. Federal troops had taken command of Ship Island, off the coast of Biloxi, Mississippi, and had already launched one attack on that city. There was fear now that Union troops would try to take control of the river from the Gulf end since their attempts to move south along the waterway had not yet succeeded. If both Fort St. Philip and Fort Jackson, located across the river from each other, were made invulnerable, there would be no way for Federal ships to get past them and occupy New Orleans. Fort St. Philip had been repaired and strengthened by the great General Pierre Beauregard himself when he was a mere lieutenant right out of West Point, and again after his brilliant campaign in Mexico.

By this time I had given up my work at the school in order to spend more time at the hospital. I was sorry to leave the children. The days with them had brought me a peace of mind I thought I would never enjoy again. The decision was a hard one to make, but by the winter of 1862, more and more wounded were being brought into the hospital, and I knew the need there was greater.

Baptiste's letter, mailed early in February, said he was traveling overland to Natchez, then south on the new gunboats being readied for the defense of the Delta. By the time the letter reached me, Baptiste had already sailed past the city, and I had missed my chance to stand on the levee and wave to him. I was sorrowful at first, knowing he must wonder where I was, then realized it would have been harder to see him and not be able to talk to him or touch him. His letter ended with the assurance he would get leave as soon as possible.

Chapter Sixteen

BAPTISTE HAD ARRIVED at Fort St. Philip little more than a week before the Federal mortar fleet sailed up to Ship Island on March 11. People who were there said that as far as one could see, from shore to horizon, there was a continuous line of white sails. With the island as a secure base from which to work, the Union forces could begin their attempt to penetrate the Delta and secure the entrance to the Mississippi.

Since the seizure of the island by the Union Navy in September of 1861, the Federal blockade had been drawn tighter and tighter around the Gulf ports. From the first days of the war, the North knew it had to gain control of the few Southern ports that connected with the interior by railroad or navigable rivers. New Orleans, the "doorway to the Confederacy," was the most important of those ports against which the blockading squadrons began immediately to concentrate their efforts. The Crescent City also presented the greatest challenge in the Gulf because of its numerous outlets through the passes of the Mississippi and Lakes Pontchartrain and Borgne.

At the same time, the Confederacy recognized how vital the port—indeed the entire length of the Mississippi—was to the South. Loss of control at either the northern or southern end would not only cut off a flow of goods and communication between various sections, it would also provide an open channel for invading armies, fleets of transports, and convoys of gunboats.

Because the Confederacy had a small navy, letters of

marque were issued to owners of private ships to harass Northern shipping and run the blockade, in spite of the fact that one of Lincoln's first acts of war was to declare them pirates and make the crews liable to punishment as such. During the summer of 1861, there had been feverish activity along the levees as seagoing tugs, powerful side-wheelers, and swift sailboats of all sizes were designated privateers and sent out under letters of marque. They earned their way by seizing Yankee commercial ships and bringing the goods through the blockade. This activity slowed down considerably after the Union capture of Ship Island, and by the spring of 1862, the relentless pressure of the blockade was felt in all ports, including New Orleans. For the first time since they were constructed, the levees were almost deserted.

Coincident with the February arrival of David Farragut, commander of the *Hartford,* at Ship Island, Baptiste had received his orders to report to Fort St. Philip, which, with Fort Jackson on the opposite side of the river, guarded the entrance to New Orleans twenty-two-and-a-half miles above the Head of the Passes. Fort Jackson had seventy-five guns, and Fort St. Philip, the better built of the two, had fifty-two. By the time the Federal mortar fleet arrived at Ship Island on March 11, there were about seven hundred men stationed at each of the forts.

In spite of rumors that Farragut's mortar ships were too heavy to get over the bar at the mouth of the river, the Mississippi was being lined with explosives, each charge capable of blowing up the largest steamer. An additional line of defense was created when, just below the forts, a chain was stretched across the river by resting it in a line over the bows of six schooners.

The great mouth of the Mississippi now seemed impregnable.

My work at the hospital had continued very much the same throughout the winter months, the duties clear-cut and firmly impressed on me. Such menial tasks as emptying jars and basins, mopping the bare wooden floor every day and scrubbing it on hands and knees once a week with harsh lye soap no longer seemed so degrading once I realized how badly I was needed. Unlike the nurses, the jars didn't yell orders at me or ignore me except when there was some particularly loathsome task to be done. What kept me going were the few nursing sisters and the patients themselves, who always thanked me and seemed grateful for the work I did. Sister Angelique had given up her teaching position to work with the desperately ill and dying, and in her very quiet way eased their pain more effectively than our small supply of drugs. Drugs—not coffee or silks—were the one item we prayed was on board each time a ship did get through the blockade. As our prayers were answered less and less often, Sister Angelique's ministrations became more and more desperately needed. Her gentle hands soothed away pain, and her calm, quiet voice stilled the screams of the men in the fiercest throes of agony. She and I seldom spoke, but she always had a serene smile for me, as if to acknowledge that each of us had at last found an answer as to what our place was in the war.

When the doctors changed dressings, I stood by with a pail to take bandages soiled with blood and pus. The more considerate doctors aimed for the pail; others just dropped them on the floor, forcing me to bend down and retrieve them. Occasionally when the hospital was exceptionally busy or a patient required extra care, I was called into the operating room to gather up dressings used to stanch blood and suppurating wounds as well as parts of uniforms torn from maimed bodies. Silently I stood by, carrying out orders either yelled at me or delivered in a quiet, requesting tone. But, above all, I must never do anything that could be construed as a nursing function.

More and more often, Dr. Honoré, one of the quiet, considerate ones, called for me in the operating room. I anticipated his movements, standing nearby when he needed me and moving back when he required more room. My calm, unemotional mien seemed to soothe him during the most harried operations, and my presence steadied his hand after long hours of trying to save young men who should be plowing fields or going on picnics instead of playing at war.

The first indication of my elevation in status came when Dr. Honoré ordered me to stay with a patient who'd had lower back surgery and needed to have his sheets changed often to keep the bed dry and clean. No human waste must be allowed to soil or seep through the bandage. My gentle way of handling the task without disturbing the patient impressed Dr. Honoré. Anyone could scrub floors, he said, but few were gifted with the touch that eased pain or kept it to a minimum. From that day on I took over the care of the linens and the changing of the beds. I no longer had to scrub floors, but continued to empty the jars when others refused to do so. It was a job that had to be done, and that was that.

"Leah!" Dr. Honoré's voice reached me just outside the rear door of the hospital when I was engaged in my daily task of emptying jars into the trough leading to a partially covered cesspool. My stomach still churned from the nauseating odors, but habit has a way of taking over and getting one through even the vilest experiences.

"Leah!" Dr. Honoré called again. There was no time for me to rinse the jars under the pump and return them to the ward. Someone else could do that. Washing my hands hastily in a basin by the door, I hurried to the operating room.

An officer in a dirt-streaked blouse lay on the table. One attendant was slowly dripping chloroform into the paper cone over the lower half of his face; both eyes were covered by a bloodied bandage. A second attendant was ripping away the ragged remains of his trouser legs. Almost at the same time, Dr. Honoré was hurriedly cutting off the makeshift bandages around the legs. I stood by, taking the torn pieces of uniform and stained bandages as fast as they were removed. Three pairs of hands moved in perfect unison until the legs were uncovered from the knees down.

I gasped involuntarily, and Dr. Honoré looked around, startled at the first expression of emotion he'd ever seen from me.

"He was standing next to an ammunition shed when a shell hit it," Dr. Honoré said tersely, and turned back to his patient.

The man's legs were completely shattered, the flesh mangled, with pieces of bone sticking out at macabre angles. One foot dangled loosely, still clinging to the leg by a few tendons. The kneecap was crushed into so many pieces it looked like a jigsaw puzzle someone had tried unsuccessfully to put together. The officer had bled profusely, and it was a miracle he was still alive. Looking at his chest, barely rising and falling, I expected to see it stop altogether at any moment.

The attendant stopped dripping chloroform and looked at Dr. Honoré. "What do you plan to do, sir?"

"If you'll get back to work with that anesthetic, I plan to operate. What else would I do?"

"I only thought, sir—well, there's no hope for him, is there?"

"Don't think; that's my job. As long as he's still alive, I'll do my damndest to save him. That's my job, too."

"How, sir?"

"By amputating! What else?" He turned to a second attendant. "Get the cauterizing irons ready. Leah, get all the bandages and pads you can hold and stand by me."

Stunned at his request, which would ordinarily be addressed to one of the male attendants, I instinctively chose the right materials. Hours of standing by to take the soiled linen had taught me which ones Dr. Honoré preferred and when he needed them. As he turned to the nearby worktable, I lifted the piece of clean linen

covering the already sterilized instruments. Sterile surgery was a new idea, and scoffed at by many as an unnecessary and useless precaution, but Dr. Honoré had
studied medicine at the University of Pennsylvania. No
matter how much time it took, he carefully followed the
procedures he'd learned about, boiling his instruments
between operations whenever possible. The knives and
scalpels were honed beforehand to a sharp, blue edge,
so that his incisions were always sure and fine.

Dr. Honoré selected a long scalpel and began cutting away the diseased flesh just above the knee of the
more damaged leg. With no time to undress the patient
completely, he ordered a clean sheet placed over the
parts of the uniform the man still wore.

Now I really went to work, handing over clean linen
pads and taking away those quickly soaked with blood.
The wounds had already begun to putrefy, and the
stench was overpowering, but I swallowed hard and
concentrated on keeping my hands moving. At one
point, when Dr. Honoré was trying to cut and stanch
blood at the same time, I unconsciously reached over
and held a piece of cotton against the spurting blood
vessel. Dr. Honoré looked amazed and then nodded
approval. I moved in closer, and the operation continued with the two of us working side by side. Now I
was the one replacing bloodied pads and trying to aim
for the waste pail under the table.

I was all right as long as Dr. Honoré was cutting
through the flesh above the man's knee. I'd seen
enough bullets removed and mortified flesh cut away to
inure me to such a sight. But when he reached for the
saw and I heard the sound of steel cutting through
bone, I had to hold onto the table for a minute. While
the doctor didn't need my hands, I used them to support myself as the room started spinning around, the
people focusing and unfocusing. I would not faint! It
was my will against my body, and I determined the will
to be stronger. I forced myself to look at the leg which
was slowly being severed from the thigh. Dr. Honoré

was working with precise but swift movements to decrease the danger of shock.

Sensing my response to the surgery, Dr. Honoré gave the one order he knew would restore my strength. "Hold the leg tight, Leah, right there below the knee. It must be absolutely immobile to keep it from jarring when I make the final cut, or the bone end will be jagged."

Gently, as though the man could feel my touch, I placed my hands firmly on the mangled flesh. I felt a shudder through my entire body as the leg dropped soundlessly the inch's distance to the table. Aware of my distress, Dr. Honoré turned away from me when he removed the now useless limb and deposited it on another table. With more swift, sure movements, the attendant cauterized the open wound, filling the room with the noxious odor of burning flesh and bone. Immediately Dr. Honoré folded over and skillfully joined the flaps of skin he had carefully preserved, alternately sewing and cutting with the instruments I handed him.

I was prepared for the amputation of the second leg. Less damaged, there was a chance the patient could eventually have an artificial limb fitted to this one if he survived. To this end, Dr. Honoré worked a little more slowly to ensure a well-shaped stump just below the knee, padding the bone end with loose flesh and making certain the skin was pulled taut with no raw edges.

Before the end of this operation, the patient stirred and began moaning.

"More chloroform!" Dr. Honoré shouted. "What the hell are you doing, letting him wake up?"

The attendant himself was almost asleep, overcome by the fumes of the anesthetic he'd been steadily dripping into the cone for well over an hour. The doctor's voice startled him back to alertness, and in another second, the patient was once more unconscious and relieved of pain.

"All right," Dr. Honoré said, "as soon as I check his

eyes, we'll put him in the last bed in the large ward and pull a screen in front of him."

I wondered at his decision. Most of the men in that ward were recovering from much less severe wounds. Then I realized with a deep sense of satisfaction what Dr. Honoré was doing. It was my ward, and he wanted me to take over the nursing of this patient we had worked together to try to save. It was his way of saying I was no longer assigned to the onerous duties of a scullery maid. I would not disappoint him. His trust in me would not be misplaced.

Dr. Honoré was cutting away the rest of the soldier's uniform to assure no further danger to the wounds. I leaned over to take the trousers after he cut along the two sides. In my other hand I held a sheet to cover the patient immediately. There would be no attempt to put any kind of gown on him until he was showing definite signs of recovery and could stand the movement.

Then I saw the familiar scar on his upper thigh. First disbelieving and then like one waiting for a nightmare to end, I looked at the face from which the attendant was removing the cone. There were twin dimples on either side of the taut mouth. I reached up to touch his face where the skin was as deathly white and as cold to the touch as alabaster. Baptiste had gone into deep shock from which I knew it was doubtful he could recover.

Dr. Honoré called for blankets, which he immediately warmed over the coals in the brazier where the cauterizing irons had been heated. I understood this procedure, but not the next. Ordering the attendant to raise Baptiste to a partial sitting position, a move I thought would surely kill him, Dr. Honoré instructed the assistant to get as much water down the patient's throat as he could without choking him. He counted on the body's natural reflex actions which would force the throat to start swallowing. It was a desperate chance he was taking. Baptiste could either choke or begin to regurgitate as a result of all the chloroform he'd inhaled.

I knew now I'd reached the end of my endurance. I stayed long enough to help wrap Baptiste in warm blankets and watch while Dr. Honoré removed the bandages from his face. One eye had been permanently damaged by pieces of shrapnel. There was no way yet of determining the condition of the other eye, which fortunately contained no foreign matter and did not bleed. Dr. Honoré rebound the head with clean bandages.

Once again the doctor seemed to perceive my emotional fatigue, although he was not aware of what had brought it on.

"Leah, please see that the bed is ready. I think he's responding, and the attendants will bring him in in a few minutes."

On unsteady legs, I walked to the door and then turned around once. I saw Baptiste's legs, piled amidst the other refuse on a side table. Legs that had danced, walked proudly along the banquettes of the city, and ridden with such pleasure on a fast-stepping horse.

I began shaking with chills. I felt frozen to the bone, and I broke out in a nauseating cold sweat. I had to find some relief from the awful cold that was numbing my body but not my emotions. I couldn't stop shaking. The threat of being sick passed, but I had to get warm or I would die.

Moving toward a large storage room where the doctors had installed a cot for brief rests between operations, I lay down and pulled a blanket around myself. If I could just get warm. If I could just forget it was Baptiste lying in there dying.

I was barely aware of Dr. Honoré's entrance, of his covering me with another blanket and then rubbing my wrists and ankles to stimulate circulation.

"Leah, can you sit up?"

I tried, but fell back, too fatigued to remain upright. Dr. Honoré pulled me toward him, now rubbing my arms and shoulders with the stiff blankets.

"Wake up, Leah! Don't fall asleep. I don't think I can handle two patients in shock."

"Why did you operate on him?" I cried out. "Why didn't you just let him die?" Now that I was recovering from the first stages of shock, I began sobbing. "Will he live?"

"I don't know. The chance is slight, but I couldn't just let him die without trying."

"The legs couldn't have been mended, could they?"

"No, Leah. You saw them. Amputation was his only chance. Now if you feel better, I want you to take over his care."

"I can't, not now." I wanted to tell him why but couldn't get the words out.

"I won't insist." Dr. Honoré stood up and started to leave the small room. "Maybe you'd better go home." There was disappointment but not lack of understanding in his voice.

Just then I heard a scream, followed by a long moan from the far end of the ward. The morphine and chloroform had worn off, and the cry for help was what I needed to bring me out of shock and back to the need of the moment: the saving of Baptiste's life.

"What do you want me to do, Doctor?"

"Keep him clean and dry and quiet. We're low on morphine, but I'll give him all he requires. There's a ship expected through the bockade in a day or two which should restock our supplies. I'll show you how to change the dressings when they need it and I'm not around."

I followed Dr. Honoré through the ward and behind the screen set up to shield Baptiste from the other patients. He was quiet again, unconscious from pain rather than the restful sleep he needed if he were to recover. His face was still white, but now covered with sweat, so he had come out of shock. His black hair clung in tight, wet curls to his scalp and forehead. His breathing was shallow and labored, but stronger than when he was on the operating table.

It was some time before I learned how Baptiste had actually been wounded. After a number of violent spring storms all up and down the river, the men in the forts were hard put to protect their defenses against rapidly rising floodwater and to increase their strength with additional guns. Round the clock the crews labored, sandbagging the more vulnerable sections and building platforms for the extra guns.

On March 15, all of Farragut's flotilla sailed over the bar. Fog, squalls, and continued high wind kept hopes up that the ships would sink before they ever reached the forts. These were the same high winds that kept destroying the log rafts located beneath the forts to prevent passage of the Union ships.

The Mississippi continued to rise, swollen from more floods upriver and capricious storms around New Orleans. Gale winds churned the surface into increasingly higher waves that surged toward the embankment on which the forts stood. Baptiste was in charge of the crew sandbagging the weakest points. Across the river, a flatboat tied near the base of Fort Jackson strained at its mooring and broke loose under the onslaught, drifted over to Fort St. Philip, hit one of the explosives lining the bank, and blew up just below where Baptiste was checking his men's work.

Although the chances of his recovery were slight, Baptiste was given emergency care and then rushed upriver to the hospital in New Orleans.

So began my intensive care of Baptiste. I soon learned to change his bandages without cringing, to check for signs of infection, and to force liquids down his throat when he was barely conscious. In acute pain all of the time, Baptiste was under almost constant sedation. I bathed him, allowed no one else to change his linens, and sat with him by the hour to watch for any change in his breathing. A check of his eyes on the third day revealed irreparable damage to one from bits of flying shrapnel, and Dr. Honoré could only hope there was some sight in the other.

For over a week, Baptiste drifted in and out of consciousness, awake only often enough to take some nourishment. He seemed completely unaware of my presence beside him and merely responded automatically to all my attentions. Yet, every once in a while, when his hand was outside the sheet and I held it, he appeared to sleep more easily.

I never spoke to him when he was semiconscious, fearing that any emotional reaction on his part would set back the slow recovery he was making. Far from being out of danger, Baptiste could still die if the wounds did not heal properly or if infection set in. Nothing must be allowed to undo Dr. Honoré's careful, meticulous surgery. I did not know what his response would be to my nursing him. He might be pleased or he might be upset at what I was doing for him. He might be stirred by my nearness or he might be humiliated by my having to tend to his more personal, intimate needs. Either way, his peace would be disturbed. So I remained silent.

With the hospital short staffed, I resumed some of my former duties when I knew Baptiste was resting quietly. By the beginning of the second week, I was able to go home for a few hours' sleep each night rather than snatching short, irregular naps on the doctors' cot as I'd been doing.

By this time we had also learned the Union General Benjamin Butler and eighteen thousand troops had arrived at Ship Island on March 25. Still believing that the forts offered the surest defense against attack on New Orleans, the city's military officials continued to concentrate all energies on them and on the river itself. Only inconsequential inner defenses were constructed around the city. Colonel Edward Higgins, commander of both forts, sent word to New Orleans that Union ships were crossing the bars and heading upriver in force. In response, General Mansfield Lovell, in command of the city, sent an additional company of men to

St. Philip and dispatched two companies of sharpshooting swamphunters to harass the Yankee vessels.

Although most of New Orleans was blissfully unaware of it, the siege of the city had already begun.

As the Federals moved upriver, fire rafts were sent down to stop them, but they were sunk before they could inflict any real damage. In addition, the ships shelled the woods, killing many of the sharpshooters and destroying the telegraph lines.

Now the hospital became busier than ever, with wounded being brought in from all along the lower reaches of the river. My working day extended well into the evening and often past midnight, assisting in the operating room, talking with patients unable to sleep, or writing letters for those who could not hold pen and paper.

Returning one morning with clean sheets and towels to bathe Baptiste before changing his bed, I saw the first faint smile on his face. He seemed to be trying to focus his one undamaged eye, from which the bandages had been removed earlier, on something over his head. I stopped just short of the bed and watched as he stared intently at the ceiling. Once he had it, he smiled again. I hesitated to disturb his reverie, but I knew Dr. Honoré would be coming along in a few minutes to change the dressings and check the wounds, and I wanted to have Baptiste bathed and the bed changed by then. Baptiste continued to run a slight fever from infection, and the doctor was determined to bring it under control.

"Is that you, Cherie?"

I nearly dropped the sheets and towels. "How did you know?"

"You think I don't know your touch?" Baptiste's voice was weak but steady. "And the way you walk. I haven't been unconscious all the time."

"But you've never spoken."

"Neither have you. I had the feeling you didn't want me to know."

"I—I thought maybe you wouldn't want me taking care of you."

"After I took care of you when René was born?" There was humor in his voice now. "I figured you owe it to me. In fact, I like it so much I may let you keep on bathing me when we get home."

I knew Baptiste couldn't see clearly, but still I turned my head away so he wouldn't be aware of my crying. I couldn't bear it. If he'd shown any self-pity or had bemoaned the loss of his legs, I'd have understood and tried to help him, but I didn't know how to cope with his humor. Somehow I'd have to keep up the light banter if I weren't to break down completely.

"You lazy Creole. I should make you bathe yourself right now. I would, too, if Dr. Honoré said you could sit up. But I guess I'll take pity on you and do it for you."

"It's not Dr. Honoré who'll decide when I sit up," Baptiste fumed. "It's these damn legs. How the hell can I keep my balance? I'll fall over like a stuffed doll."

"No—no, Baptiste, there are . . ." I stopped. I'd almost given way and become serious. "No, your head's big enough to provide ballast."

"You've got it backwards, Cherie, but I appreciate the effort. Now bathe me quick. I think I'm ready to go back to sleep. For some reason what's not there hurts worse than what is."

Baptiste lay absolutely still, exhausted by his effort at talking, while I washed his body and prepared the dressings for Dr. Honoré to put on after he'd checked the incisions. I was confused by Baptiste's remark about something hurting that wasn't there, until the doctor explained. Certain nerves running from the lower half of his leg up through the thigh continued to carry sensations to the brain. Like other nerves damaged by the amputation, they were still painful, and Baptiste was feeling the sensations as a sore calf or throbbing foot muscle.

I watched Baptiste's face while Dr. Honoré palpated the area around each incision, and I winced when he bit his lips until they bled, but he made no sound. I shifted my gaze to the doctor. Try as hard as he could to maintain the stoic expression he wore when he examined a patient, he could not hide his thoughts from me. I looked for a raised eyebrow, an involuntary twitch of the mouth, or a closing of the eyes—all of which indicated a negative response. This time there was none of these. He peered closely at the stitches and the fine lines where the pieces of skin were joined. There was still more swelling then he liked to see, but he nodded his head in a positive way, and I released my breath. It was the first time since he'd been caring for Baptiste that Dr. Honoré had let himself show any optimism.

Baptiste slept the remainder of the day, rousing only to let me feed him, and except for a quiet "thank you" he remained oppressively silent after his earlier show of humor. Either that had taken more out of him emotionally than I realized or his body still needed a great deal of rest. I hoped it was the latter. It wouldn't be good for him to keep up a false façade of cheer when he really felt he would rather die than live helplessly crippled and completely dependent on others. I left for home with a nagging despair that Baptiste would never accept his condition.

In the morning I took time to speak to several of the men who were awake before preparing Baptiste's breakfast tray. Now that he could manage solid food, I would surprise him with ham and grits as well as good strong Creole coffee and thick cream. Being in no particular hurry, I went out and picked a dogwood blossom to brighten up the tray.

Baptiste was still asleep. Putting the tray down on the small bedside table, I smoothed the sheet and started to lift his head to make him more comfortable on the pillow. It might be, it just might be, that Dr. Honoré would release him to my care before too long.

I touched his cheek. It was hot. I put my hand on his forehead. The skin was dry and burning with fever. In panic, I realized his breathing was shallow and erratic. With no new wounded brought in during the night, Dr. Honoré wouldn't come to the hospital for another two hours. Nor were any other doctors around. It was up to me to do something to bring Baptiste's fever down.

I reached for the pitcher and poured the tepid water into the basin. Without stopping to think, I tore one sheet into strips, soaked them in the water and laid them across his forehead. I could hardly replace one before the second became hot. I did the same on his chest. One of the attendants walked by, and I asked him to get more water, as cool as possible. While waiting, I watched Baptiste closely and prayed for some sign that my efforts to help him were not in vain.

It was not the attendant who brought the water, but Dr. Honoré. He felt Baptiste's face, then ran his hand across his chest. Without a word, he immediately started cutting away the bandages on both legs. The stumps, now an ugly red, were swollen and puffy.

"Get me a scalpel!"

I lifted up my long skirts and ran to the operating room for his bag. I also grabbed a bottle of chloroform in case Baptiste awoke during the operation.

"Fold up that sheet and put it under his legs. Stand by his head and keep bathing it with water."

The instant Dr. Honoré placed the tip of the scalpel against the swelling on one leg, the edema burst open, spurting out a stream of bloody pus that soaked the padded sheet. He did the same with the other leg. For a few minutes he let them drain slowly. Then, with gentle but firm pressure, he steadily massaged the infected stumps. I was forced to change cloths often, at the same time wiping away the sweat running off Baptiste's face almost as fast as the infection gushed from his legs. He made no sound, but I knew he was suffering by his painful grimaces. Not until the last of the poisonous matter had spurted from the wounds did Baptiste's face relax and he breathed more normally.

"That's all for now," Dr. Honoré said, getting up slowly from his cramped, stooping position. "We're fortunate it's draining down his leg, not settling in another part of the body. As long as it doesn't start spreading through the bloodstream. If it continues to form around the incision, we may be able to keep it under control. But it will be touch and go for several days. We'll know how he's doing if his temperature remains elevated or if it begins to return to normal. Even if he continues to have some fever, I won't be too concerned once it begins to decrease. Can you stay with him?"

"You know I can."

"I'm going to keep the bandages off, at least until I check him again, so you can watch him closely. Since he was in a great deal of pain from the pressure of the swelling, you can get a hint of any new accumulation of infection by looking at his face. Keep him bathed and as comfortable as possible."

I carried the breakfast tray back to the kitchen. There would be no ham and grits for Baptiste this day. I made up a little broth, hoping I could get some down his throat from time to time.

Within two hours, the swelling appeared again, the skin gradually becoming more shiny and puffy. There was nothing I could do but give Baptiste water when he opened his mouth, and I kept bathing his face. Dr. Honoré returned and expressed more of the fluid.

"We've got to keep it draining," he said, more to himself than to me. "This constant opening will only induce more infection." He put clean dressings under the legs and left without saying another word, striding toward the operating room.

I resisted the urge to give way to panic. Baptiste's fever was still much too high, and he was moaning in his sleep. Why had Dr. Honoré left without any new orders? I needed to get fresh, cool water, but I dared not leave the bedside.

In another few minutes, however, the doctor came walking back between the other beds. In his hands he carried several short pieces of rubber tubing and strips of tape.

"I don't know how well this will work," he said, "but it's worth a try. I don't see how there can be any more danger of infection with these than by constantly opening the wounds."

I watched closely as Dr. Honoré made a short incision and slowly forced one end of the tubing in under the skin flaps as far as it would go. Then he waited. Nothing happened. The tube extended at an awkward angle about two inches beyond the opening.

Dr. Honoré nodded his head and brought out a pair of scissors. Holding the tube between two fingers, he cut it as close to the leg as he dared. A drop at a time, watery pus began exuding through the opening he'd created. I heard the quick release of breath and saw the doctor wipe his face with the back of his hand.

"It might work, Leah, but it hasn't solved all our problems. You're going to have to keep the opening clean and not let it get plugged. They've brought in four more wounded from the river, so I'll be in the operating room. Send for me if you need me, and when I can, I'll replace the tubing. We can't let the flesh begin to adhere to it."

The next thirty-six hours were harrowing ones. Luckily, I was too busy to give in to despair. When I wasn't checking the tubes, I was wiping Baptiste's face. The fever was not coming down. Hours went by with no change. Dr. Honoré replaced the tubing twice and the infection kept draining, but Baptiste's temperature remained elevated and he became delirious.

All I wanted to do was break down and have a good cry, but there was no time. I was losing Baptiste just as I'd lost René and my mother. It wasn't fair. I could have stood it better if he'd died on the operating table or within the first few hours when I thought he had no chance. But not after I'd gotten my hopes up and begun planning for the day I could take him home.

I pulled up a chair to ease the strain on my back, and I put my head on the bed, intending only to rest for a few minutes, but Dr. Honoré found me asleep, my hand across Baptiste's chest.

"Leah," he whispered, "wake up."

"Oh, Dr. Honoré, I'm sorry. I didn't mean to fall asleep."

"It's all right. I don't see how you kept awake as long as you did. You won't need to stay now. You can go home."

If I wasn't needed that meant only one thing; Baptiste had died while I was sleeping. For a moment I relived the terror I'd known when I lost René. I raised my head slowly, still keeping my hand across his body. It seemed as though he still breathed, so alive did he remain for me. I remembered how I'd held my son close to my breast, hoping somehow to imbue him with new life from my own body just as my body had originally given him life. But I had failed, and now for a second time I had to learn to let go.

"Leah, you did an excellent job." Dr. Honoré was speaking to me. "I'm proud of you. His fever has broken, and there's been no drainage for some time."

"He's still alive?"

"He's very much alive. And I think we've beaten the infection. But I'm not going to take the tubes out yet. I'll cover them lightly with bandages. We'll just have to wait and see, but you can go home and get some rest."

Baptiste was not out of danger yet, but at least there was hope once more. I walked slowly across Jackson Square, breathing in the fresh air, free from odors of sickness, mortified flesh, and chloroform. There were no screams of the wounded or moans of the dying. Here in the calm beauty one could almost imagine there was no war coming closer and closer to New Orleans. Once home, I undressed and filled the tub in my room with hot soapy water. Tired as I was, I lay back and let the water ease away the aches and tensions of the past weeks.

I slept for hours and awoke more refreshed than I'd felt for as long as I could remember. I had no idea what time it was, nor did I care. I dressed carefully, putting on one of my prettiest gowns. I could don a covering apron later.

Chapter Seventeen

ON APRIL 16, Union vessels fired on Fort Jackson, and by April 18, Good Friday, Farragut's mortar schooners came within the range of the fort's guns. By Easter Sunday, Fort Jackson was almost destroyed and the big guns were turned on Fort St. Philip. Both forts were under bombardment for six days, until on the morning of April 24, Farragut sailed past them and up the river to New Orleans.

At the beginning of the war, New Orleans had been converted into a shipbuilding center, and a number of ships were under construction at this time. Among them were the *Louisiana* and the *Mississippi,* ironclads which many thought could stand off the entire Union squadron. Unfortunately, they were just a few days from completion. Thus the Confederate naval forces— the last bastion of defense for New Orleans—consisted of a handful of converted tugs, river steamers, home-made rams, and the unfinished *Louisiana* that could only be tied against the bank and used as a stationary floating battery. Against the Federal ships steaming invincibly toward the city, the Confederates fought gallantly as they sailed downriver to their destruction.

Hour by hour New Orleans waited desperately for the miracle that would save the city from Federal capture, waited for the promised troops to converge on the city from the north and east.

Fortunately Baptiste had continued his slow recovery, and Dr. Honoré finally removed the tubes to allow the wounds to heal completely. Baptiste was still sleeping a good part of each day, and once again I felt no need to stay at his side. In fact, I found it restful to resume some of my earlier duties. By keeping my hands busy, I could forget for long moments at a time how close I had come to losing Baptiste and yet remind myself that in spite of his apparent improvement, there could be another relapse.

I was standing just inside the linen room when I heard the two voices.

"Dr. Honoré, Major Fontaine's wife has sent her coachman around with this note." The part-time clerk handed him a sheet of dainty paper, holding it as though it were a viper ready to strike. "Knowing how busy you are, I read it, thinking she was only asking when she could visit or if she could send us some supplies."

"But," the doctor said shortly, "I take it that's not what it says."

"No, she wants to know if her husband can be moved. She would like to get him out of New Orleans and take him to her grandfather's plantation near Natchez."

"Can I assume from your previous statement," Dr. Honoré said even more coldly, "she has not visited him? She does not know his condition?"

"That's right. This is the first word from her."

I knew I should not be listening to this conversation, but I would draw attention to myself even more if I stopped sorting the linens and moved away. It was more natural for me to go on. Methodically and automatically I continued checking the sheets, putting those that could still be used in one pile, others good enough only for rags or bandages in a second. My brain was numb. After all these years, why did Marie Louise suddenly want to have Baptiste with her? She'd made it perfectly clear from the beginning that the marriage was strictly one of convenience, of parental arrangement. She'd never objected to her husband's absence from the house as long as she was free to spend most of each year abroad in the company of the German baron or whoever her latest lover was. And now this concern about Baptiste.

"What do you think, Leah?" Dr. Honoré was speaking and I realized I'd missed the first part of what he'd said to me. I was sure he had no idea I was Baptiste's *placée*. He no doubt assumed that my concern was a natural one for a severely wounded patient. He spoke simply as doctor to nurse.

"The wounds are healing well," I said, trying to maintain the same professional attitude. "But as to his being moved—I don't know."

"The city will be under fire soon," he reminded me. I could tell he was talking to me merely to verbalize his hesitation. "If once the Federal ships get upriver—" He didn't finish the sentence. "And she is his wife. She has every right to request us to let her take him. She could give him better care, better food."

No! No! I screamed inside. Better food, maybe, but not better care. And I should be taking care of him. She won't know how. I've been nursing him through weeks of torture and agony. I know what hurts him when the dressings are changed and how to ease the pain. Will she know the most comfortable position when he sleeps?

"Tell the coachman Mrs. Fontaine may come to see him tomorrow morning," Dr. Honoré said with quiet misgivings. "We can decide then whether he should go. There's no time to write. I'm sure the man can deliver the message she's waiting to hear." Turning on his heels, he strode back to the operating room.

I found myself folding and refolding the same sheet. In less than twelve hours Baptiste would be gone, probably out of my life forever. Once Marie Louise took him north of Natchez, he might never return to New Orleans, certainly not as long as the war continued and the city was in danger of capture. Maybe with her money she could obtain the drugs now becoming harder and harder to get in the hospital. After Baptiste was nursed to recovery by his wife, I could not see him returning to me. A tender, loving wife would have a much stronger hold than a distant mistress.

But another fear was gnawing more painfully at my heart. Baptiste was not well enough or strong enough to leave the hospital and travel by carriage over the rough, dangerous roads to Natchez. There were already rumors of Yankee troops infiltrating the Natchez Trace along the river, sharpshooters hiding behind bushes or in trees to waylay travelers and snipe at Confederate troops. No, Baptiste was in no condition to survive such a trip even if the carriage were not attacked. His dressings needed changing frequently, and any jolting movement could send him into shock again or reopen the wounds.

I knew my words carried no weight, but I was the one who'd been handling the hour-by-hour care of Baptiste. If I dared talk to Dr. Honoré, maybe he would listen to my opinion—not as Baptiste's *placée* but as a nurse.

After carefully stacking the sheets in neat piles, and noticing how few unmended ones remained, I moved quietly between the rows of sleeping patients in the ward to the screened-off bed at the farther end. Baptiste was asleep, sedated by a massive dose of morphine to alleviate the intense pain in the raw stumps. Only one eye was covered by a bandage now, protecting the torn tissues around the area that would never see again. Slowly he was regaining more sight in his right eye, enough to distinguish forms and faces. Each day saw a little improvement, encouraging Dr. Honoré to predict that Baptiste would be able to see as well as ever within a few months.

I looked tenderly at his face, at the black hair curling around his forehead and against his cheek where it needed cutting. He had been in great pain again before his last dose of morphine. How much longer would he have to suffer until the wounds healed to the point where the skin toughened and became less sensitive to the slightest touch? I was already planning how I was going to work with him every day, restoring strength to his weakened legs and helping him learn to walk again with crutches and a wooden leg attached to the one cut off below the knee. Dr. Honoré had assured me it would take time and patience, but Baptiste should be able to move somewhat independently within a year.

Although I knew restoring Baptiste to good physical health would be an arduous and often seemingly futile task, I was ready to do anything to see him smiling once more, filled with pride in his own manly accomplishments. There was even a chance he might be able to ride again when his thigh muscle strengthened sufficiently. It was the internal suffering I worried most about. Baptiste was not a man who revealed his innermost thoughts easily. He was more apt to cover emotion or turmoil with an offhand compliment or witty remark. How would I know when he was trapped in a whirlpool of despair? He would go on as though everything were fine and he were feeling as well as ever. How did a man feel about losing his legs? Somehow I had to reach out to him, penetrate his mind. Time. I had to give myself time.

Baptiste moaned, shocking me back to the present. No, that's the way it would have been. Tomorrow Marie Louise would be taking him to Natchez. He would survive the trip and remain with her, or he would succumb from the shock of being moved. Either way, I knew I had lost him.

For the moment he was still under my care. Gently I lifted the sheet off his legs to check the bandages. There had been no bleeding since I last changed them nor any radiating red lines which would indicate incipient blood poisoning. Leaning over, I smelled the area round the dressings as Dr. Honoré had taught me to do. No odors of putrefaction. As long as the wounds continued to heal with no need of being reopened, the danger of Baptiste's not recovering lessened with each day that passed.

I pressed my hand lightly on his forehead. His face was drenched with sweat, but not from fever. For the first time since he was wounded, his skin felt cool—neither burning with fever from infection nor deathly cold with shock. I brushed his hair away from his eyes, and then finding the temptation too strong to resist, kissed his mouth and the dimples on either side. His skin had been ashen pale, but now I detected a faint flush of normal color.

Giving way to tears, I fell to my knees beside his bed and buried my head on my arms. Baptiste was going to live. For days I had watched dry-eyed while I thought he was slowly slipping away from me. I had fought with prayers and nursing and all my strength to keep him alive. Now, having kept him from falling into the great abyss, I should be the one sharing the joy of his recovery.

It wasn't fair! Marie Louise didn't love him. She must want him with her for some other reason. It might not even matter to her whether he were alive or dead. I froze with a new fear. Marie Louise might be a greater danger than either infection or marauding Yankees. It could well be it was not Baptiste she wanted but his money and property, and she had to appear to be a loving wife in order to insure she got her hands on them. Marie Louise could have everything Baptiste owned, if she would just leave him in New Orleans.

Moving to rest my head on Baptiste's chest, rising and falling with the even breathing of sleep, I felt a strong hand on my hair. Dr. Honoré must have seen me and come to urge me to leave for the day. I had no right to drop my professional attitude and let my feelings show in the presence of the patients, even when they were asleep. If I looked once more at Baptiste's face, I would not be able to leave, but as I tried to avert my gaze, I felt the hand turning my head slowly in his direction. I opened my eyes and found myself looking directly at Baptiste's smiling mouth.

"Crying, Cherie? Now that I'm getting well. You're going to make me think you don't like me anymore."

"Oh, Baptiste. Oh, my darling. Can you never be serious?"

"What's to be serious about? I'm alive and kicking—well, not exactly kicking, I guess." Baptiste tried to rise up in the bed, but fell back wearied from the effort.

"You're fine, you're doing fine, darling," I said. "I—I was just tired."

"So am I," Baptiste said with some effort. "Kiss me goodnight. I think I want to go back to sleep."

I leaned over, kissing him long and tenderly while Baptiste ran his fingers through my hair where it fell from under the white scarf.

"I love you, Baptiste."

"Why now, Leah?"

"Not just now. For a long time. But I couldn't say it. Afraid, I think, you'd laugh at me."

"Never, Cherie. You know I wanted to hear you say it."

"Then promise you'll never forget I said it tonight, because I'll always love you."

"Forget? I'll remind you every day for the rest of our lives. And every night, too. Not tonight, though. I'm not quite up to it yet."

"I—I'll hold you to that. Now it's time for you to sleep. Much more excitement and you'll be running a fever again."

I kissed him once more, feeling the warmth and tenderness of his lips against mine, stirring me more deeply than any of his passionate kisses ever had. Moving slowly until I rounded the shielding screen, I ran the length of the aisle between the other beds, seeking a place to be alone. Like a wounded animal, I needed the privacy of a secret lair where I could curl up inside myself and not be exposed to the chill winds of reality.

A single door opened into darkness, and I ran in, heedless of where I was going. Breathing deeply to keep from fainting, I pushed the door shut behind me before collapsing on the floor. I made no attempt now to control the sobs wracking my body or the tears streaming down my face. Holding my arms tightly across my chest, I rocked back and forth in an agony of despair from which I saw no relief.

As though in a dream, I felt myself being lifted up, and strong arms supporting me across the floor and onto the edge of a bed.

"Are you all right, Leah?" Dr. Honoré sat beside me, still keeping one arm around me.

"I—I'm just very tired. I didn't realize where I was. If I woke you up, I'm sorry."

"No," he said, "I wasn't asleep. Just resting and doing some hard thinking. The ship we were expecting didn't get through the blockade at Mobile. It was bringing chloroform and morphine as well as other supplies. If the war gets closer and we get more wounded, we'll be in trouble."

No point in speaking to him now about Baptiste. Dr. Honoré had enough on his mind without my problems, and Baptiste would be considered well enough to travel. His bed was needed for the new wounded coming in.

"Another ship will get through, I'm sure," I said encouragingly. "They can't stop all of them, even with the Federal boats working out of Ship Island. Or maybe overland from Savannah or Charleston." I stood up. "I'm all right now. I'll see you in the morning."

"Don't go, Leah. I need someone to talk to." Dr. Honoré stood up and put his arms around me. I felt his lips brush my cheek.

"You need your rest, sir, and so do I. I'd better go."

"Not sleep, Leah. I need you." His mouth had reached mine, and his hands were pressing me tightly against him. "I think you need me, too."

From the time I came to the hospital, Jules Honoré had been a doctor, not a man. Now I was aware of his gentle, compassionate face; his stocky, masculine body; and his blunt but strong fingers.

Maybe I did need him. Baptiste was no longer mine, and I was suddenly afraid of being alone. It had been so long since I'd felt desired, and unconsciously I let my body respond to his. His mouth was hard and demanding; his hands moved roughly across my breast and down the front of my dress. Jules Honoré was urging me back down on the bed, and I had no power to resist. I wanted him to make love to me, to ease the ache of desire and fill the emptiness created by the loss of Baptiste.

Drained of all emotion, my feelings for him were purely physical. He would satisfy one need without creating another. Tormented daily by the horrors of maimed bodies and the inability to save the lives of more than half who were carried into the hospital, I felt an even greater need to be reassured that at least the two of us were whole and physically able to act like normal men and women. Desperately I clung to him with one hand while with the other I unfastened my bodice and pushed down the top of my chemise. I hoped he would be rough.

When I closed my eyes, Baptiste's face smiled at me, but I willed it away. I would not be made to feel guilty.

I floated outside myself and stood to one side watching two unfamiliar figures lying on the bed and responding to a primitive urge devoid of all passion or sensitivity. The woman no less than the man moved with the haste of an animal to bring the act to a swift conclusion. Like an audience of one being forced to view a drama I did not want to see, I remained unmoved as the two actors continued to play out the wordless farce. The man lay still while the woman moved quickly out of the shadowless room and ran from the building.

Not until I was well away from the hospital and fleeing across Jackson Square did I become myself again. Gasping for air, I clung to the gnarled trunk of the sturdy dogwood I'd run into. I was crying uncontrollably now, my chest heaving with violent sobs and my body shaking from retching and vomiting up all the hate I felt for myself, for Baptiste's wounds, and for my inability to cope with what the war was doing to both of us.

Once home and repulsed at the thought of getting undressed and seeing the body that had betrayed me, I fell across the bed, dreading the thoughts I knew would haunt me all night. Instead I dropped immediately into a dreamless sleep, awaking only in time to change my clothes and eat a light breakfast before returning to the hospital.

It was a new day, a morning bright and clear with birds singing and the fragrance of spring all around me. Yesterday was past. Once gone, it no longer existed except in memory, and memory required thought. Therefore I would not think; I would only act. I would carry out those duties that had become so routine they needed no thought, and I would follow instructions.

Promptly at eight I went to the closet where I had so carefully sorted bed linens the evening before. No, I mustn't remember what I'd overheard while I'd been doing it. That belonged to the yesterday which could not hurt me now unless I allowed it to.

One by one, I changed the beds in the ward, stopping to talk to those who were conscious, bringing water to those who needed it. I'd always enjoyed this part of my work, knowing how much a freshly made bed eased bodies weary of lying immobile and how grateful the men were for my attentions. They waited for the chance to try to shock me with a new practical joke, like switching beds with each other to confuse me or lying in some grotesque position, pretending to be dead.

Most of the men in this ward were recovering from their wounds and would soon be returning to the war or going home for a brief leave. They were restless, and I had long since learned that one of the first signs of complete recovery was trying to make me blush by regaling me with the latest bawdy stories. Knowing they'd be disappointed if I didn't, I dutifully appeared shocked and then scolded them for repeating such things in my presence. The newcomers were cockily pleased with themselves, while those who had been there for some time recognized my charade and silently applauded me for it.

I had returned to the storage closet for a second supply of sheets when I heard a commotion at the far end of the ward near Baptiste's bed. The screen had been pushed aside so all of the small area was visible. Fearing Baptiste's condition had suddenly worsened and that Dr. Honoré would need me, I dropped the sheets and started to rush down the aisle. But almost immediately I turned and ran back.

Walking beside Dr. Honoré, dressed in an elaborately beruffled gown and jaunty little hat, was Marie Louise. I remained half hidden by the closet door where I could see and hear all that went on. So far Marie Louise was focusing her attention on the doctor, no doubt urging his permission to take Baptiste with her. His face remained stolidly calm and unexpressive. He was all physician now, completely in control of his emotions and concentrating solely on the needs of his patient.

I saw him shake his head once in answer to a question from Mrs. Fontaine, and it evidently was not the response she wanted, for she smiled a wide, beguiling smile as though she were flirting with a prospective lover. I saw her draw Dr. Honoré closer by grasping his arm more tightly. Once more she asked a question, and he nodded, agreeing reluctantly to something she'd suggested. Only then did Marie Louise approach the bed where her husband lay.

For the moment I remained hypnotized where I stood. Only later—and many, many times throughout my life—would I look back on this scene as the most nerve-shattering I'd ever witnessed. Marie Louise bent down to kiss Baptiste, then drew back convulsively, her hand over her mouth, when she saw the bandaged eye. Evidently no one had apprised her of Baptiste's injuries.

Without a word, Dr. Honoré pulled away the sheet, revealing all of Baptiste's maimed body. Marie Louise went white. The sight was not one a person could view unmoved even after weeks of seeing it day after day. But more shocking was the look on Marie Louise's face. There was no sign of pity or compassion or love. Only horror and revulsion and loathing. Her pretty face was now contorted into an ugly mask of hatred and disgust.

That was it, I thought. That was why Marie Louise wanted to take Baptiste with her. She hated him. All these years she'd despised him, for being her husband and at the same time being unfaithful to her. She must have thought she could get her revenge now by taking him away from New Orleans and his mistress, perhaps hoping he would die on the road or from lack of proper care.

She will not have him! I screamed to myself. Baptiste belonged to me. I loved him. I loved him with all my heart, I suddenly realized, and I wanted only to devote the rest of my life to his care. He was not going to die. He was going to live, and once again be the man who had three times come to my rescue.

I forced myself to look again at Marie Louise, whose chilling expression reminded me of a loathsome succubus intent on devouring the soul of the man lying on the bed in front of her. No more than a minute had passed since wife had looked at husband, but in that minute any ties still binding the two had been sundered forever. With a last single look of horror, Marie Louise signaled the final act of divorcement from Baptiste and turned her back on him.

Chapter Eighteen

Two HOURS AFTER Marie Louise fled the hospital, Farragut's fleet dropped anchor at New Orleans.

Unwilling and unable to face Baptiste after my degrading betrayal of him the night before and his nerve-shattering visit from Marie Louise, I fled from the building.

The terror of having the city captured by the Union was nothing compared to the horrors confronting all my senses when I walked out of the hospital. All over the city, alarm bells were ringing, and the entire waterfront was ablaze. As I walked toward the levee, the heat from the fires chafed my cheeks. In response to General Lovell's proclamation of martial law when he realized Farragut's approach could not be halted, a frenzied city had hauled thousands of bales of cotton from the warehouses to the levee and set them on fire. Others ignited the sugar and tobacco warehouses. When ships at the wharves already loaded with cotton had burned to the waterline, they were set adrift and floated downriver. Torches had been laid to steamboats in the middle of the river.

All around me New Orleans was a smoking inferno of cotton, sugar, tobacco, and other goods that singed the hair with flying sparks and filled the nostrils with acrid soot. The entire surface of the Mississippi was aflame. By stepping through a door, I had been transported to a living, manmade hell, created out of the fears and frustrations of a people betrayed to the enemy by the very forces sworn to defend them. I looked across the boiling river of blood and flames that for over two centuries had been the city's lifeline, that like an umbilical had connected New Orleans with the rest of the world.

In the lurid light of the ubiquitous fire, I watched a howling, enraged mob armed with knives and pistols advance on the levees. In one last act of desperation, this motley army of old men, women, and children—the only army left to defend the city—were showing their contempt for the invaders.

During her greatest hour of need, New Orleans had been stripped of the military forces needed to keep her out of the maw of the voracious Union behemoth. Nearly every Confederate soldier in Southern Louisiana and Mississippi had been sent to Virginia in March or to Beauregard's aid in the fight at Corinth. Knowing that once the Federal fleet sailed past the forts the city was doomed, General Lovell had been busy making plans to evacuate New Orleans. As the Union ships approached, he ordered hauled away light artillery, shells, clothing, blankets, medicine, commissary items, machinery, wagons, harness, and leather—almost everything except the heavy guns along the levee, useless without shot. The militia remaining under his command, about three thousand men, were sent to Camp Moore, some seventy-eight miles from the city.

Thus New Orleans was offered up as a sacrifice to overconfidence, inept military strategy, cowardice, Richmond's determination to protect Virginia, lack of preparation, and fear.

With tears streaming down my face, I rushed past the charred remains of Baptiste's warehouse and gutted office. Then I turned around and walked slowly back. I forced myself to look for several minutes at the ashes of his life's work, of everything he owned, of his whole future. With the Union in control of New Orleans and its environs, there was no way of foreseeing what would happen to the plantation.

Baptiste was going to live. Now I realized it was up to me to give him something to live for.

I walked to Baptiste's bed and waited for him to ask what was happening outside. The bells in every church tower were ringing; the alarm sirens went off sporadically; and as I reached the hospital steps, the armaments piled in front of the Customs House and Mint were blown up.

Baptiste lay impassive, as though nothing in the outside world had any meaning for him. His face was turned toward the wall, and his eyes were closed. Although he had never loved Marie Louise, the expression on her face when she saw him lying there—one eye blinded, both legs amputated—must have sent him into deep shock. To know that someone was as filled with loathing as she was would sear the soul of any man.

Understanding his need to be alone, I started to move away. There was much to be done to prepare for the casualties that would be coming in—civilian and military—as a result of the present conflagration and the fighting yet to come. I did not know then that the city, although never officially surrendered, would be turned over to the enemy with scarcely a shot being fired.

"Leah," Baptiste called softly.

"I'm right here." Now would come the questions, and I wondered how best to tell him that New Orleans had fallen; we would soon be at the mercy of the Union army.

"Leah, why did you tell me last night you loved me?"

It was the last question I expected, and I had no simple answer ready. How could I tell him I thought I was losing him to Marie Louise without reminding him of what he'd been through earlier? So I said the first thing that came to my lips.

"Because I do love you."

I looked for the smile in response to the words I knew he'd been waiting to hear since I first agreed to become his *placée*. There was no smile, only a grimace of pain.

"Please, Leah, don't treat me like a fool or a gullible child. I've been hurt enough today. Do you think I don't know the difference between love and pity? I once wanted the love, but I'll be damned if I'll accept the pity." He hunched his shoulder until he'd managed to turn his whole body away from me. I knew what pain the exertion caused him, and I wanted to cry. But it was not a time for tears.

"Baptiste," I said almost sternly, "turn back and look at me."

There was a long period of silence, and I knew that if I didn't reach him immediately, I never would. The one right moment would be lost forever.

"I can't," he finally mumbled. "My legs are twisted, and I can't move them." More silence. "I—I need your help."

I wanted to laugh. I wanted to cheer. But I did neither. Instead I gently rolled him over on his back and moved the still painful legs into a more comfortable position. Then I broke the first cardinal rule of a hospital—I sat on the bed and took both his hands in mine.

"Baptiste, I also know the difference between love and pity. I'd be lying if I didn't admit I have pitied your condition. I have also experienced other emotions—sickening horror during the operation, indignation that something like this could happen, fear when I thought you were dying. But I never confused them with love."

"But why now, Leah? Why not before, when—when I was whole and strong?"

"I don't know whether you'll understand, but I'll try to explain. Before you were wounded, there was not a day I didn't realize you could leave me any time you wanted to. If I did not give all of myself—if I held something back and did not allow myself to love you—then the hurt would be less when you left."

"So now that you think I need you, you're willing to love me. Is that so much different from pity?"

"No, no, Baptiste. That's not it. Need is part of it, yes, but not all. Last night I thought I'd lost you. After weeks of fighting to keep you alive, I was going to lose you to Marie Louise. I didn't just start loving you at that moment, but I did realize I had loved you for a very long time. And there was no longer any reason not to tell you."

"How can I believe you, Leah? How can I be sure you're not just trying to make it easier after what happened earlier today?"

"Look at me, Baptiste. I have never lied to you. From the beginning I've said I might go north the first chance I had. It would have been easy for me to say 'I love you', just to soothe your pride. I never did. And when I said it last night, it was not to ease any hurt. I thought you would be leaving. I knew Marie Louise was coming this morning. I had no idea I would ever see you again."

Baptiste remained very quiet for a moment. When he finally spoke it was to ask me to put up the screen, shutting off his bed from the rest of the ward.

"Now, Cherie, come lie down beside me."

"Here? Right now?"

"Right now! It's been far too long since I've held you close."

Feeling his warm tears against my cheek, I knew I had not been wrong in admitting my love for him. We were in our own world where there was no war, no burned city, no destruction of Baptiste's warehouse. Encircled by the invisible horizon of our own never-never land, nothing could touch us. Or so we thought.

Suddenly from the other side of the screen came a resounding cheer, followed by enthusiastic clapping. I had forgotten that the light beside Baptiste's bed, turned on earlier in the morning, threw our shadows in sharp detail against the linen screen. The men in the ward had watched every move we made, and I'm sure not even Edwin Booth had a more appreciative audience.

Embarrassed, I pulled the screen aside and was greeted with whistles and arms raised in victory salutes.

"Good for you, Leah."

"Good luck, Baptiste."

"More power to you, Major."

"You might've lost your legs, sir, but you haven't lost your——"

"Shut up, Jake, there's a lady present."

"I was going to say *arms,* you damned fool. Don't you think I know a lady when I see one?"

By this time Baptiste and I were laughing so hard I had a stomachache and he nearly rolled off the bed. I had to get him settled in again.

"All right, boys," I said, "the show's over. Quiet down or you'll all be running fevers, and I'll be running all afternoon bringing you water."

"We will, Leah, if you'll kiss him again right out in the open," called a grizzled old Cajun, one of the swamp sharpshooters who'd been hit at the base of his spine and would never again leave his bed to forage the bayous, be a husband to his wife, or carry one of his eleven grandchildren on his shoulders.

I bent over and kissed Baptiste firmly on the mouth. "I have to get to work now," I whispered, "but I'll be back before I leave."

Seeing Dr. Honoré at the far end of the ward, I didn't know how I was going to face him, let alone talk to him. Only by maintaining a severely professional attitude could I continue working at the hospital.

"Leah, I want to apologize for last night. I didn't mean it to happen that way."

"I prefer to think it never happened, Dr. Honoré. So I'd rather you didn't remind me of it."

"I meant it when I said I wanted you, but—but in a more permanent relationship."

"I'm sorry," I said, trying not to express the shock I felt. "That's impossible."

"Please, Leah. I saw you with Major Fontaine, but don't take him seriously. Many patients think they are in love with their nurses. He'll forget all about you when he leaves the hospital."

"I don't think you understand, Dr. Honoré. I have been Baptiste Fontaine's *placée* for four years."

"But—but last night—"

"—was a mistake I shall probably never be able to forget. I was out of my mind thinking I was losing him. I shall spend the rest of my life atoning for being unfaithful—and I shall do that by making him as comfortable and happy as I possibly can."

Dr. Honoré turned brusquely and walked away. Then he turned again. "There are two burn patients in the surgery."

"I'll be right there."

When officers from Farragut's flagship entered the city with a summons to surrender, Mayor Monroe refused to do so. On being asked to evacuate all women and children, so they would be safe from the fighting, Monroe asked that there be no shooting since there was no one left to fight except those women and children. Farragut's response was that he was preparing to enter the city, and if a single shot were fired against his men, he would level New Orleans to the ground. Thus was the city taken over, the only show of defense being the hoisting of the state flag over the city hall and the hauling down of the United States flag raised over the Mint by Federal officers.

The city was taken because it had no power to resist. From April 25 to May 1, when the final capitulation came and General Benjamin Butler arrived to take command of New Orleans, all was confusion. No one knew whether the mayor had surrendered or whether there was still a chance the promised reinforcements would join Lovell's troops and together repulse the invaders. There was an almost complete cessation of business, and people looked at one another in bewilderment.

Once in command, Butler wasted no time in letting us know what our lives would be like under his rule. The well-meaning but innocuous mayor and other city officials were immediately imprisoned in various forts, and over sixty prominent citizens were sent to Ship Island, shackled with ball and chain, and forced to labor at filling sandbags.

In any cataclysmic disaster, there is always one tragedy that stirs the blood more than any other.

A young man, William Mumford, had been the one to climb to the roof of the Mint and haul down the Union flag. Butler ordered his arrest and had him hanged on gallows ironically erected on the front lawn of the Mint. Everyone in the vicinity—I was on my way home from the Market—was rounded up, marched to the Mint, and forced to watch the young man's agony on the gallows. He was to be an example to all the people of New Orleans so they would know what to expect if they attempted to resist the Union occupation with firearms or any overt action.

The hospital was sent two important orders: they would now begin taking care of Federal as well as Confederate patients, and all Confederate officers were to be considered prisoners of war. For the time being they would remain in the hospital. Enlisted patients would be allowed out on parole to return to their homes after signing a pledge they would not again take up arms against the Union.

The words "for the time being" repeated themselves over and over again in my brain, and I thought of the seventy or more civilian leaders now incarcerated in various forts for no crime other than refusing to surrender.

There was no way to save all of the officers in the hospital, but I could do my damndest to keep Baptiste from going to a prison which would mean his death.

How, with all of the Union patrols, I would get him away from the hospital and through the streets to our house I had no idea. But if there were a way, I would find it.

I stood for a minute in front of the house I had often admired from a distance. Twin curved wrought-iron stairs led to a portico and double doors on the main floor. Between them an arched entranceway opened into a blue flagstoned passage some ten feet wide and forty feet long. Beyond was the courtyard, organized around a central plashing fountain and lush with palms, mimosas, oleanders, and camellias. Wrought-iron benches had been placed beside meticulously cared-for flower beds.

For the first time in my twenty-two years I climbed the familiar stairs. A liveried Negro servant answered the bell.

"I would like to see Monsieur Bonvivier."

"And who shall I say is calling?"

"I—I—just tell him, please, that Leah is here."

Since he held the door open for me, I assumed I was to follow him into the hall. Through a portiered archway I looked into the family dining room, and I saw the look of amazement on the face of my father's wife when my message was delivered.

"Send her away! Jean-Paul, I do not want that—that girl in my house."

"This is my house, too, madame." My father pushed himself back from the table and stood up. "Leah is my daughter. I will speak to her when and where I wish."

With no hesitation he gathered me into his arms. "Leah, my dear child, what brings you here?"

"I need your help, Papa."

"Let's go into the sitting room. Moses," he called to the servant, "bring wine and cakes."

The sitting room was large and comfortably furnished, chairs and couches already encased in their light-colored, summer slipcovers. In spite of its size it was charmingly informal and inviting. Three Palladian-style French doors were open to the courtyard, and the air was filled with the delicate fragrance of mimosa and lavender.

"Now, Leah," my father said as he poured the wine, "how can I help you?"

Quickly I told him about Baptiste's condition and the order from Butler that would send him to a Federal prison.

"I must get him away, Papa. He'll die without the right care."

My father listened intently until I finished. Then he asked the inevitable question. "And how do you propose to move him?"

"I don't know. I can't think."

Sipping slowly and staring off into space, my father finished his glass of wine before speaking again. "How are the patients who have died removed from the hospital?"

"Depends on the patient and his family. Hearse usually."

"If there's money," he nodded. "How about the indigent or those with no families?"

"There's a cart to take them for common burial."

"Who owns the cart? A hired scavenger or the hospital?"

"The hospital." I began to see what he had in mind.

"Is there anyone there you could trust to help you? To prepare Baptiste as if for burial and drive the cart for you?"

I thought of Dr. Honoré. Would he do this for me after he'd learned about my relationship with Baptiste? He was my only hope.

"I think so."

"Then don't wait. I've read Butler's orders, too, and he means to carry them out. Get Baptiste home. There'll be less danger of his being discovered in your house than anywhere else."

I knew what he meant. So far only the white citizens

of New Orleans were being harassed or threatened by the occupying troops. No free Negro or colored homes had been entered yet, and when the time came that they were, I would have a plausible story prepared.

"Papa, I'll do it tonight. You've been of real help."

"That wasn't such a problem, now, was it? Is there anything else I can do?"

"Yes, there is. Everything Baptiste had—his warehouse, his entire inventory of cotton—was destroyed in the fire. I need money, real money. The Confederate notes Baptiste left me when he went to war may soon be worthless. I have some jewelry I may be able to sell eventually, but I don't dare reveal I have them now; and I don't know who I'd sell them to."

"You have no Federal currency?"

"Some. Enough for a short time if I plan carefully. I have a small garden and a few chickens. It's not food I'm worried about right now as much as the drugs Baptiste may need for a long time. With even a small amount of gold I could save for emergencies, I'd feel a lot more secure. I have no idea what the situation is on the Fontaine plantation."

"I'll see what I can do, Leah," my father said. "Come back here tomorrow morning."

"Do you think your—Madame Bonvivier will like that?"

"Hang Madame Bonvivier. I'm sure you heard what I told her. You need help and I intend to do what I can for Clotilde's daughter. I loved your mother, Leah; please believe me."

"I do, Papa. I know that now."

"So come early in the morning. I want to know how you manage with getting Baptiste away from the hospital. I'll pray for your success."

Baptiste objected strenuously when I told him of the plan. "No, Leah, I'm not going. I can't run away like a coward and leave all these others to be imprisoned."

"I'm getting you out of here, Baptiste," I insisted

just as strongly, "if I have to chloroform you to do it."

"And I'll never forgive you if you do."

"Be sensible!" I was almost shouting now. "You'll die if you're sent to the encasement or one of the forts."

"Rather that than live as a coward."

"What're you trying to be, a hero or something? You're talking nonsense. No man *wants* to die. I always knew you were a stubborn Creole. Stubborn, bullheaded, stupid Creole!"

"No, no, Cherie. Not stupid. You're wounding my pride."

"Well, if that's all that was wounded I wouldn't worry myself about you at all. You've got such a surfeit of pride, you could lose half of it and still have more than anyone else I know."

"There, there, Cherie, calm down. It's that pride that's going to keep me alive. I'm not going to die in any damn Yankee prison."

"I know you're not," I said to myself, and I stalked off through the ward to look for Dr. Honoré. Much to my amazement, he agreed immediately to the idea my father'd proposed. He'd do everything possible to help me save Baptiste.

"Thank you, Jules. I wasn't sure how you'd feel about my asking you."

"Leah, when I said I wanted you, it was not just for the moment. My feelings go much deeper than that. Perhaps now you'll feel less harshly about me."

"I'd never think that, Jules. You didn't take me by force."

"No, but I took advantage of a desperate moment." He looked down the ward toward Baptiste's bed and then back at me. "Now," he said, "let's see if we can put your plan to work."

The cart was readied, and one of the orderlies alerted to assist us. Usually the deceased were placed in canvas bags—similar to those used on ships—for convenience in burial, but Dr. Honoré decided sheets would do just as well and would be easier for handling Baptiste in his condition.

Baptiste. He might prove to be the only stumbling block in effecting his own rescue.

"Everything's ready, Baptiste. Are you going to agree to leave?"

"You know my feelings."

"Have you given any thought to mine?"

"Not this time. If my city has fallen, I have to suffer with it. Would you want me to be like General Lovell? He'll be despised the rest of his life."

"General Lovell was not wounded." I wanted to scream at Baptiste, to shake him into the realization he was dooming himself to sure death.

Baptiste tried to sit up. "You act as though I'll be thrown on a heap of straw in a corner and left to rot. They'll give all of us the care we need. We'll be given treatment due our rank."

"No, you won't! That's what I'm trying to tell you. The city officials were promised accommodations commensurate with their rank. They were merely to be placed under guard and kept incommunicado. Everyone assumed they'd be held in the St. Charles Hotel or one of the bigger houses commandeered by the Union army. And where are they now? Sweltering in the sun on Ship Island and forced to spend twelve hours a day at hard labor. Those were men who had done nothing more than refuse to surrender the city immediately. So what do you think they will do to captured enemy officers who fought against them? You'll be lucky if there is a pile of straw."

"I'm sorry, Leah, my answer's the same. I can't go and leave all these others to the fate you think is ahead for us. If I go, it will only be under duress. By force."

Force, I knew, was out of the question. He would give himself away to the first patrol we met. He was still taking morphine, but he would know in a minute if I tried to give him a large enough dose to put him under.

I was almost ready to give up when I recalled my original threat.

"I'm going to get your lunch, Baptiste. I'll be back in a minute with warm water to bathe your face and hands."

I found Dr. Honoré washing up in the surgery and told him Baptiste would be ready in ten minutes. After filling a basin with water, I concealed a small bottle within the washing towel. Baptiste was lying propped on two pillows, grinning as he always did when he thought he'd won his point.

"You've got a good dinner today," I said casually, as though I'd given in to him. "Someone donated several chickens so they wouldn't fall into the hands of the Federals. Nobody's going to let those intruders have anything if they can help it."

"Bring it on, Cherie. I'm hungry. And from the way you talk, this may be the last good meal I eat."

"Let me wipe your face first. You've been sweating in this heat. Then I'll get your hands."

"Since when can't I wash myself?"

"Since you might not be here tomorrow. This is the last thing I might be able to do for you."

"If you insist. Wash away."

I wiped his forehead and then tipped the bottle against the wet towel. Before Baptiste knew what was happening to him, the chloroform put him under. I held it over his nose until I knew he had inhaled enough to keep him asleep until we had him wrapped in the sheets and laid in the cart.

The orderly, Étienne, was a big, strong Negro who had lost his beloved captain at Corinth. He had held his master's head in his lap while he died; and then—by dodging Federal and Confederate troops alike—had carried him from the northeastern corner of Mississippi. Traveling southwest and skirting Oxford, he had reached the Tallahatchie River. Following the river south by night, and during the day hiding from Union patrols that would have captured him and Rebel patrols that would have shackled him as a runaway slave, he finally reached Vicksburg. Traveling became more difficult as the Confederate river guard increased, but he continued southward, following the Mississippi but never getting close enough to encounter soldiers. Finally he crossed into Louisiana, and then he had to change direction southeast to reach his master's plantation just west of New Orleans. There, after days of rugged traveling, he delivered up the body of the captain.

In return for his devotion, the slave was freed. He then said all he wanted was to do what he could to thwart the enemy who had killed his master. Weakened by his journey, he was persuaded not to take up arms with the free Negro battalion. When it was suggested he help in the hospital, he merely nodded and walked into New Orleans to offer his services.

At first I was grateful for his strong arms as he carried Baptiste to the cart. Before long I was to be even more grateful for his presence of mind when it looked as though our plan of escape was going to collapse.

Sure that Dr. Honoré would accompany us, I was ready to call it all off when two emergencies were brought into surgery demanding his attention. 'Tienne, the former slave, looked at me intently and said very quietly, "Don't worry."

'Tienne drove and I assumed the role of a weeping mourner. The streets and banquettes were crowded with Union soldiers—slouched against buildings, lolling at street corners, or trying to look officially busy. There was a marked absence of civilians. We rode along slowly and without incident, our presence on the street arousing no comment or suspicion during this period of sudden and frequent deaths. Those on the street gave way, and a few of the soldiers doffed their caps, out of respect for the dead. At two corners, patrols stopped us as a matter of routine, but they accepted 'Tienne's explanation. Baptiste was still asleep, and there were enough sheets around him to prevent anyone's seeing the rise and fall of his chest.

Nearing the house, we met a third patrol. The leader was an arrogant young officer who seemed determined to exercise his authority.

"Halt," he ordered. "Where are you going?"

"To the graveyard," 'Tienne answered quietly.

"There's no cemetery in this direction," the soldier sneered.

"No, no," I said softly. "To the house first, then to the graveyard. My driver misunderstood you."

"Why are you driving this cart?" The officer turned on 'Tienne.

"Sir?" 'Tienne looked stunned at the question.

"No need to call me sir or drive the wagon for her. You're no longer a slave. You're free now."

"I know. I'se always been free."

I didn't know why 'Tienne had lied, but it took the officer back for a minute.

"Maybe you're telling the truth, but I think I'll just check the corpse to make sure."

Something had aroused the officer's suspicion. Maybe a slight movement I hadn't noticed or a faint odor of chloroform.

"I wouldn't do that if I was you," 'Tienne said in his usual placid, almost monotone voice.

"Are you threatening me?" He accented his question by raising his rifle.

"Naw, suh. Just warning you. He die from yellow fever."

There had already been a few cases reported, and Butler had issued warnings that he intended to keep the disease under control if he had to burn down the city. If the mention of yellow fever sent chills of fear down our spines, they aroused even greater terror in the Yankees who were unfamiliar with it.

I saw the officer, who was leaning over Baptiste, go white and drop his gun. He drew back so fast he stumbled over the edge of the banquette and fell in an ignominious heap at the feet of his men.

"Go—go on," he said, scrambling up and trying to recapture his dignity. "Get out of here and don't pass this way again."

'Tienne needed no second order to crack his whip over the mule's rump. His quick thinking had saved us. It had also given me an idea.

Having settled Baptiste in his bed, where I more than once thought I would never see him again, I asked 'Tienne to stay with him while I ran an errand that would take no more than an hour. Removing my shawl, cape, and hospital gown, I put on an old cotton dress and tignon. These would silence any doubt as to my status and allow me to move unmolested through the streets, a privilege not afforded to white civilians.

At the hospital I had a quick conference with Dr. Honoré.

"But where will we take them?" he asked.

"To the school. I'm sure Sister Angelique will approve, and she can persuade the Mother Superior."

"But she can't care for all of them, even if I could release some of the staff here, and I don't see how I can do that. And some will need care for weeks yet. Then where do they go?"

"To the homes of free Negroes and colored who are sympathetic. There are many such families, I know, and so far Federal troops aren't searching their houses the way they are the whites' in the city. Gradually we can move them into the bayous and then out to plantations or into Confederate-held territory."

"I don't see how it can possibly work, Leah."

"You've heard of the Underground Railroad, haven't you?" I asked, referring to the means by which many slaves were smuggled north.

"Certainly."

"We can work out our own. And we don't have so far to go. Once into the bayous and no Yankee could possibly find the men."

Baptiste had said he wouldn't escape capture if he had to leave other officers behind. Two words and the approval of Sister Angelique might just free them all.

I found Sister Angelique in the small house or convent attached to the school, which had ceased functioning as such the day Farragut landed.

"You're an answer to a prayer," she greeted me. "The sisters have heard dreadful rumors about what the Protestant Yankees will do to them if they go out of doors. But I've been frantic to know what's happening."

"It is almost as dreadful as the rumors, Sister. And we need your help. I haven't much time, so please listen carefully." Quickly I told her about the orders pertaining to captive Confederate officers and how we wanted to rescue those at the hospital.

"Certainly, my dear," she said without hesitation. "Bring them all here. I'll see what we can use for beds, but bring pallets if you can. Wrap the sheets around them and no one will know."

Kissing her impulsively on the cheek, I hurried out and back to the hospital.

"We'll never do it," Dr. Honoré said.

"Yes, we will." I insisted. "The soldiers are deathly afraid of yellow fever, and you know the officer and men we met will have passed on their experience to other patrols. By morning it won't matter if the truth leaks out, and there's no reason why it should."

"All right. But if you're caught—"

"Not a word about your part," I assured him.

"I didn't mean that."

"Or what hospital we're from."

"And if one of them is recognized as still being alive?"

"We'll say we thought he was dead. Or just that we're moving all cases to the school for quarantine."

Dr. Honoré laughed. "Go ahead. No one can argue with your logic."

How many times had Baptiste said the same thing? Maybe it was a good omen.

While Dr. Honoré went from bed to bed explaining what we were doing, I gathered all the sheets—soiled and clean—I could find. The former could be used for outer wrappings and would be a most convincing proof of our story. Another Negro orderly was dispatched to my house with orders to care for Baptiste and to send 'Tienne back with the cart.

We figured we could fit three men in a cart, and by moving out at irregular intervals throughout the night, we could save all but the few who were terminal cases. The men were so grateful for what we were doing, they vowed not to breathe from the time we left the hospital until we arrived at the school, some eight blocks distant.

As I'd surmised, word of the yellow fever peril had spread rapidly, and the patrols backed abruptly away when they saw us coming with the first two or three carts. The sisters had worked swiftly, and rooms were ready for us when we arrived with the first patients. Having worked at the hospital, Sister Angelique had been put in charge, and even Mother Montez was looking to her for orders.

That night the streets were emptied of most soldiers except those on duty, and they had begun their shift at twelve. At first I was concerned, but soon it was evident word had reached them, too. Three more carts—nine more men—arrived at the school. Eighteen were already settled in, and only seventeen remained to be transported.

We had begun to vary our route so as to minimize suspicion over the large number of deaths. But whatever road we drove along, we held our breaths with the sound of each footstep or the approach of a soldier. We never knew when one of them was going to challenge our presence after curfew. Two or three times we were questioned briefly, but the sight of the filthy, bloodied outer sheets repulsed even the most officious, and we were allowed to pass.

Sometime around three in the morning we were stopped by the captain of the night patrol making his rounds. The sneer on his face should have alerted me.

"And where do you think you're going?"

"To bury these dead."

"At the school?"

"They're—they're being kept under quarantine until a special Mass can be held tomorrow."

"Do you usually have so many deaths in one night?"

"They were severe cases." My hands were shaking, and I found myself clutching the sheet of the officer nearest me.

"Strange, too, that they should all be officers."

My head jerked up involuntarily. What had he found out?

"You speak very intelligently for a Negro," he said condescendingly, "so maybe you'll understand what I'm saying. After hearing all the reports about these yellow fever cases, I decided to investigate for myself. Only one hospital was evacuating patients throughout the night. By making a few judicious threats, I managed to persuade one of the staff at that hospital to talk. General Butler isn't going to like being denied the pleasure of punishing those enemy officers. So I think I'll just accompany you to your cleverly devised refuge."

One of the "corpses," a man with a chest wound, chose that moment to moan, and the Federal officer couldn't resist pulling back the sheets to mock him and let him know he'd been discovered. With no hesitation I poured some of the chloroform still in my hand over the rumpled sheet and forced it against the captain's face. 'Tienne, waiting for the most propitious moment to make a move, struck him over the head with the butt of his mule whip. Then he dragged the limp body to a recessed doorway nearby.

"What are we going to do now, 'Tienne? He's sure to be missed when he doesn't report in."

"We move faster. We got two more cartloads to deliver. So let's get going."

Rather than carry all three patients into the school, we turned them over to the nuns at the door and took right off again. A cart with three more was waiting at the hospital, and we left the one we'd driven up to be loaded while we were gone. Two more trips and we would have accomplished our mission. Knowing every minute was important, we followed the shortest, most direct route instead of the more circuitous one that we had hoped would deceive the patrols. We had no idea what the captain's routine was for checking with his men or which ones would be inquiring why he was overdue, so our chances were as good on one street as another.

We continued with as much confidence as we could muster under the circumstances. One more trip after this one, and I could return to Baptiste, satisfied that the first part of our mission had been successful. I thought how pleased he would be to learn he had not been the only one to thwart the plans of Butler to take captive all Confederate officers.

Within two blocks of the school, we found the street blocked by a five-man patrol, their rifles held at ready across their chests.

'Tienne didn't slow down a moment.

"Hold on, Miss Leah. They ain't gonna stop us now."

Once more he snapped his whip over the rump of the mule which had plodded without pause between school and hospital. The animal picked up its hoofs and moved as fast as is possible for a mule to move. Straight ahead 'Tienne drove, right toward the central man in the patrol, who cracked out a single order. Five rifles were aimed directly at us.

While I huddled between two of the patients, 'Tienne moved determinedly ahead. Not until the mule's muzzle was pushing against his chest did the middle soldier move. Whether stunned by our audacity or waiting for an order, the four other soldiers did not shoot immediately. As we drove between them, 'Tienne cracked his whip first to one side and then the other, and the men dropped to their knees.

We thought we were out of danger until a single shot startled us out of our complacency and a bullet struck the rear of the cart.

"Stop, 'Tienne! We'll all be killed."

"No, Miss Leah."

Another shot sent a bullet whistling alongside the cart. As they were still within close firing range, they could kill us if they wanted to, so I knew these first were only warning shots. How soon would one hit 'Tienne or me? With two more blocks to go, I didn't see how we could escape.

The soldiers were now on their feet and running to catch up with us. 'Tienne turned a corner to put us out of target range, but I knew they would soon close in unless a miracle occurred. Just as our pursuers also rounded the corner, 'Tienne turned the cart suddenly to the right and drove through an archway into a courtyard. I was sure we were now trapped in a *cul-de-sac,* but I had underestimated 'Tienne. Once more he saved us with his quick thinking: there was an opening in the opposite wall that led to the street adjacent to the school. In three more minutes we were behind its wall.

As I helped the sisters unload our patients, I thought about the two officers in the hospital who would now be captured. And I thought about the safety of those in the school, both the sisters and the patients, now that our refuge had been discovered.

"Go home now, Leah," Sister Angelique said.

"I can't. We're all in danger now. They know where we've brought the officers."

"Then go home and let us handle it. You've been seen. We haven't." She pulled off her habit. Underneath it she wore a tignon carefully wrapped around her shaved head and an old cotton dress. I looked around, astonished. All of the nuns had discarded their habits and were dressed in a variety of disguises.

"You see," Sister Angelique said, "we've been busy, too. Now—go home. If the authorities come here to search, they won't find a single officer. The families you suggested have been contacted, and enough agreed to take care of all of them until they can be gotten to the bayous."

"All right." I nodded. "I should be seeing how Baptiste is getting along. Where is 'Tienne?"

"He left as soon as you came in."

"I hope he gets through the streets safely. I was going to suggest he go undercover in the bayous himself. He could be executed for striking those Union soldiers." But 'Tienne was resourceful and clever. If there were a way to escape, he would find it.

When I arrived home just before dawn, Baptiste was sleeping naturally. The man I'd left with him said he'd roused twice, made no comment about where he was, and gone back to sleep. Suddenly I felt bone weary. I walked into the former nursery and fell across the bed.

The Bonvivier house was in an uproar when I arrived. Claudine was standing in the middle of the center hall screaming at the servants, some hauling out trunks and others carrying arms full of clothes. Two small children raced from room to room, chased by a harassed mammy who was puffing to keep up with them. In all the confusion, no one was aware of me standing in the doorway. This was hardly the time to ask for my father, but judging from what was going on around me, it would be my last chance. I would stay until I was told to leave. If I remained close by one of the pillars, Claudine might not see me.

"Leah, come with me." My father had walked up behind me. I followed him back down the stairs and through the passage to the garden.

"I'm sorry things are in such an uproar," he said, when we were seated on one of the iron benches. "When Claudine learned there was a ship bound for Le Havre and leaving in a few hours, she insisted that as a French national she had the right not to be prevented from leaving New Orleans."

"Is that true?"

"It is. The envoys of several European nations made it quite clear that their citizens could not be detained if they wished to leave. Butler realized that any attempt to stop them would meet with a decidedly negative reaction, and with England and France on a seesaw about aiding the Confederacy, he doesn't dare do anything to make them oppose the Union."

He put his head in his hands and sighed. "So Claudine is going and taking our daughters and their children with her. Their husbands and our sons are fighting somewhere in Virginia."

"And you?"

"I'll stay here and try to persuade Butler to release the city officials and other men they have imprisoned. I think I can exert a certain amount of influence."

"You think that's wise?"

"Maybe I can do some good, and I want to be here when your brothers come home."

I had never thought about the war in terms of having brothers fighting for the Confederacy. We were of the same blood. Through our veins flowed the courage and adventuresome spirit of the French, the beauty and pride of our Polynesian ancestors. Now that I had Baptiste safe under my care at home, I would pray for them.

"Leah, it's taken almost everything I could get my hands on to pay passage money, but I managed to put this aside for you."

He handed me a moroccan leather purse heavy with gold. When I'd asked for it, I didn't think the money would entail sacrifice on his part. Now I worried lest he be left in real need. His import house had been one of those burned.

"Thank you, Papa. Are you sure you can spare it?"

"I'm sure, Pet." It was the first time he'd used that name since I was a very little girl.

"I wish there were something I could do for you." I thought a minute. "Maybe there are some valuables I could keep for you. My house is in less danger of being searched, and I doubt they'd think I had anything of real worth to look for."

"You might be right, Leah. Come back in a couple of days. There are a few things I'd hate to lose, especially some paintings. I'll cut them from the frames and have them rolled and wrapped for safekeeping. Now, I'd better go give Madame Bonvivier a hand, or she'll be in a complete state of collapse before the ship sails."

Two days later I returned to the house. It had been commandeered by a high-ranking Union officer. My father had been given just enough warning to escape the city and flee into the Confederate territory. I never saw him again. I wished I had kissed him good-bye.

Chapter Nineteen

THROUGHOUT THE REST OF THE SOUTH, feeling ran high against New Orleans for allowing herself to be captured, as if the entire fate of the Confederacy depended on the invulnerability of the port city. Called traitor, her name was anathema.

As the war intensified in such widely separated areas as Virginia, Tennessee, and the Carolinas, New Orleans felt the weight of the Union's spurred boot bearing down heavier and heavier on her back. Our battles were not won with guns but with courage and ingenuity. The most virulent, debilitating enemies were shortages of food, lack of daily necessities, and above all, fear. Fear of being challenged when one appeared on the street and fear of humiliating searches when one stayed at home.

For a few days after our transfer of the officers, however, our spirits remained high. All of the men were evacuated successfully from the school and placed among free Negro families who promised to deliver them to the Cajun swamphunters in the bayous. From there they would be slipped into the Confederacy. I was even more elated when Sister Angelique told me about 'Tienne's heroism in carrying the last two officers in his arms, one at a time, from the hospital to individual homes, bypassing the school. He knew the streets would be carefully watched, but in spite of the hospital's being placed under close scrutiny, he was able to remove the men.

There were a few tense minutes at the hospital when one of Butler's officers came to investigate and verify the report made by the captain of the patrol who accompanied him. Dr. Honoré, however, was not to be caught off guard. Most of the beds were filled, not with men seriously wounded in battle, but with victims of too much cheap wine, a well-aimed blow during a bar fight, or a painful legacy from an infected prostitute. Normally, they would have been given emergency treatment and sent on their way; but, seeing them as God-given replacements for the departed officers, Dr. Honoré ordered twenty-four-hour surveillance. Since they were all Union soldiers, the investigating officer could scarcely complain about the treatment they were receiving. As an added precaution against retaliation for what we'd done, he had a predated release sheet for those officers specifically known to have been under his care.

Neither 'Tienne nor I had returned to the hospital; thus there was no one for the patrol captain to identify as his assailants. With Baptiste in my care at home, I had no intention of going back, and 'Tienne had disappeared into the bayous when his work was finished.

At the school, all was back in order. How the sisters managed, I will never know; but when the officer demanded to be allowed to search, they had once more donned their religious habits. All doors were cheerfully opened, and each room again looked like just what it was, a classroom.

Baptiste suffered almost no setback from his move, his recovery aided, I was sure, by the news about the other officers.

"I was furious, you know, when I woke up and found myself here," he grumbled.

"Why do you think I didn't stick around to see your reaction?" I asked.

"You did a terrific job, Cherie, getting them all to safety."

"Well, if I was going to stay away from the house

until you calmed down, I had to find something to do. I couldn't just wander the streets."

"Don't be modest. You did a fine thing, and you know it. Those men will be grateful to you for the rest of their lives, and so will I."

"They can be grateful to 'Tienne and the sisters, too. Without them, we could never have accomplished what we did."

"And the free Negroes and the Cajuns," he added.

"Right. I guess if we'd planned a long time in advance, it might not have worked. But on the spur of the moment like that, everyone pitched in without thinking about the consequences if we were caught."

Suddenly a new reign of terror began. Merchants refusing to sell goods to Union troops had their shops closed and all goods confiscated. Laborers, skilled and unskilled, who refused to work for the Union army were imprisoned. No one dared wear Confederate colors or emblems for fear of fine or imprisonment on Ship Island. None of this, however, touched me personally.

The women of New Orleans, unable to fight with guns and sabres at the side of their men, were nevertheless determined to do battle against the enemy invaders with what means they had. The more defiant continued to wear small Confederate flags in their hats or on their gowns, while the less aggressive pulled aside their skirts or stepped down into the gutter when a Union soldier passed in order to show contempt and avoid contamination. They left churches in the middle of the service or got off horsecars when Northern soldiers entered. They hummed Rebel songs as they walked down the streets or played them loudly on their pianos, with windows wide open, when troops marched by. More than one soldier was splattered by the contents of a carefully aimed slop jar. All this in the belief that Butler could not possibly imprison every woman in New Orleans.

Unfortunately, in their zeal they had underestimated Butler. His retaliation sent a shock wave of disgust and disbelief throughout North and South as well as across the ocean. Many Europeans, regardless of which cause they espoused, passed resolutions expressing their abhorrence of what he had done. He had issued the infamous General Order Number 28:

"As the officers and soldiers of the United States have been subjected to repeated insults from the women (calling themselves ladies) of New Orleans, in return for the most scrupulous non-interference and courtesy on our part, it is ordered, that hereafter, when any female shall, by word, gesture, or movement, insult or show contempt for any officer or soldier of the United States, she shall be regarded and held liable to be treated as a woman of the town plying her avocation."

Now a new fear had been released. How literally would Butler's soldiers interpret the order? Did it mean a woman would be safe if she merely walked along quickly, arousing no wrath, or did it mean she would be arrested if she refused to respond to any greeting, whether a brief nod of the head or a request to submit to a soldier's advances? Although I knew the order applied specifically to white women, I was as yet so unsure of my position as a light-skinned free woman of color that I chose to remain indoors rather than expose myself to risk. I sent Seena out to make whatever purchases we needed. By remaining behind the secure walls of the house, Baptiste and I were not too closely touched by the havoc affecting the lives of so many.

Then came Butler's order suspending the use of all Confederate currency. What money Baptiste left with me when he went to Virginia I had scrupulously hoarded, doling out small amounts only for necessities when I realized the war was not going to end in a few weeks. A very substantial amount remained, all in Confederate bills. With a single flourish of his pen, Butler had wiped out our entire savings, plus that of most of New Orleans. Now everyone would be forced to work for the Federal occupiers of the city at their price or starve to death.

True, I had the gold from my father, but I knew if I spent that, we would have nothing to fall back on. For several days we managed by eating the vegetables from our own garden and trading eggs from my generous hens for small amounts of fish and fruit.

Then I remembered again the jewelry Baptiste had given me. Many of the Union officers had sent for their wives once the city was secured, and the more beautiful homes of imprisoned city officials and businessmen were commandeered for their use. I'd seen these women driving around in "borrowed" carriages, flaunting their positions as leaders of New Orleans's new society. I was sure any of them would be delighted to own one or more of my fine pieces and would pay a good price for them, if I just knew a contact. It would not do for me to approach them myself.

While I was pondering how to accomplish such a sale, we learned what it meant to be the victims of an unannounced search. An obsequious young man came to the house, saying he was conducting a census of the city. Right away I knew he meant he was conducting a survey of properties to see which were valuable enough to be confiscated by the new government. As nice as my little house was, I thought I was safe on that score. But with every word he uttered, his arrogance became more contemptible.

He wanted to know how many people lived in the house.

"There is Seena, my Negro servant." I started with her first while I debated whether to mention Baptiste and then come up with an explanation for his presence.

"Okay," the man said, "two Negroes."

"No, just one," I corrected him. "Only my servant."

"And you," he said, staring directly into my face.

"No, I'm a free woman of color." I started to explain the difference, but he broke in rudely.

"Same thing. I have only two lists, Negro and white. And I never heard of a free Negro in the South, so I'll put you both down as slaves." He wrote something in his notebook. "Now, who owns this house?"

I decided if he were going to play games, I'd be better off humoring him. "Ma mastuh, mistah white man, suh. He done gone off to Virginnie and lef' me here."

"Well, we came South to free you, so maybe you'll be owning it pretty soon."

He glanced around the parlor. Thankfully I had closed the door to the bedroom. Maybe, just maybe, my little charade would keep him from discovering Baptiste. When he neither commented about the furnishings nor made any notes, I judged him as, fortunately, ignorant about fine antiques, and sighed with quiet relief when I closed the door behind him.

"By God, Leah, you did it again. You are a treasure," Baptiste said when I walked into his room, glad to be able to breathe again. "I thought I'd bust my seams to keep from laughing when you told him about your poor old master gone to war in Virginnie."

"Well, poor old master in New Orleans, you don't know how close I was to strangling him."

"Come here, my beautiful she-devil and tell me what you're fixing for my supper. And don't tell me collard greens and grits."

"Collard greens, grits, *and* an egg. Bessie and her friends were extra generous today."

"Well, thank them for me. But how about a good crawfish bisque or okra gumbo? Or has the Market gone out of business?"

Now I knew I had to sell some of the jewels. Baptiste's recovery had slowed down, and he would never get well without proper nourishment. And medicines. He was still in acute pain, and we had used the last of the morphine Dr. Honoré sent home with him. Baptiste never complained, but I knew how much he suffered when I saw his forehead covered with perspiration and his fingers clenching the bedcovers.

"Gumbo or a good stew tomorrow, I promise. I'll go to the Market myself." Above all, Baptiste must not know there was any lack of funds. I had not yet told him about the ban on Confederate money, nor had I mentioned the gold which I felt we should not start spending. Above all, he must not be allowed to worry.

I did not tell him either about the increasing length of time Seena was staying away from the house when I sent her out. To me she was still a child, but she had the figure and impulses of a woman. I must counsel with her the first chance I got, I thought, and then turned my mind to disposing of the jewels.

Numerous dealers, with well-established reputations, discreetly handled the sale of everything from single gold wedding bands to ornate chandeliers to complete suites of furniture for impoverished gentlewomen or inveterate gamblers of old Creole families. In a port city, I knew there was also a plethora of common pawnshops whose owners asked no questions of sailors or footpads who wanted quick money in exchange for goods of dubious ownership. These last, however, I would avoid if at all possible.

Summer had already come in with all its attendant heat and wilting humidity. Telling Baptiste I had to do a little shopping, I went out during the hottest part of the day, hoping in that way to find the streets fairly deserted. Southerners would be taking their usual afternoon rest behind draperies drawn against the sun; and the Yankees, unaccustomed to our climate, had quickly learned to take it easy during the middle of the day.

I had heard about the Oath of Loyalty to the United States, required of all officeholders, attorneys, and judges. Many in New Orleans had refused to take it and been forced to flee into the Confederacy, thus abandoning their property to the Federal government. I was not aware, until I passed shop after shop with shuttered windows and a notice posted prominently on the door, that no one could conduct business or ply his trade who had not also signed. This made my search for the right go-between all the more desperate.

It had rained for several days prior to my outing, increasing the dampness of the fetid atmosphere, and the gutters ran high along the banquettes. Suddenly, I felt something splash against my skirts at the same time a carriage with a single occupant passed close by. I recognized her as the wife of a Union officer I had seen driving along our street with her husband. She was just the kind of mark I'd been looking for: proud of her husband's position and arrogant about her own place in army society. I wished I had the nerve to approach her directly, but I was not yet destitute enough to withstand her withering looks or hated Northern accent.

I stopped and watched while she went into a jewelry store. I had thought about secondhand stores, but hadn't considered the possibility of dealing with a jeweler. I didn't have to wait long. She came out in such fury, I wondered who had been the victim of her ire. I saw who as soon as I stepped inside. The elderly man behind the counter was tenderly fingering a cheek that had obviously just been slapped—and slapped hard.

"She did that to you?" I couldn't keep my shock to myself.

"She did," he said, chagrined at my seeing him shaking with fright. "She'd left a necklace to have the clasp repaired, and I didn't have it ready. I suggested she come back later, and that's when she hit me. I'd have given it back to her as it was, she made me so mad, except I need the money. And Butler does insist his officers and men pay. It's about the only good thing I can say for him."

"You took the Oath of Loyalty?" I asked hesitantly.

"Had to. I have a family, children and grandchildren, to support now that the boys are gone. We might manage except for the children needing milk and decent food."

"Do you—do you get many calls for good jewelry, really fine gems, I mean?"

"Oh, yes, the women who come in here have money to spend. Stolen, I've no doubt, from safes in homes they've taken over, or from the sale of valuables they've confiscated. My inventory is low, though. Have to depend mostly on repair work. Not many items of jewelry were smuggled through the blockade."

"You could use some then? I mean, perhaps you could sell some fine pieces for a commission?"

"You have some?" He looked at me dubiously, wondering, I was sure, if I had stolen them from a former mistress.

"M'sieu—" I looked back toward the gilt lettering on the window for his name.

"M'sieu Thibedeau," he said.

"I am a free woman of color. Perhaps you recognize the names Bonvivier and Fontaine."

He nodded curtly.

"Monsieur Bonvivier is my father. I have been Monsieur Baptiste Fontaine's *placée* for several years."

He nodded slowly and began to smile.

"I have jewels given to me by M'sieu Fontaine, very fine and valuable pieces. He is now an invalid, wounded at Fort St. Philip, and there is much he needs in the way of drugs and comforts. I thought if you—"

"Say no more." Monsieur Thibedeau held up his hands. "I know the very pieces you're speaking about. I sold them all to M'sieu Fontaine, and I know their worth. You are right. They are extremely valuable, and every one genuinely unique. I'm sorry to hear he is not well."

"What do you think?" I asked.

"I can sell them immediately—within a few days— for less than they're worth, or I can wait for the right customer and get almost full value. How desperate are you for money?"

"I need some right away. Baptiste needs good food and medicine. Perhaps." I pulled out a small bundle, "perhaps you could sell these as soon as possible. I'll bring you more later which you can hold for a better price."

I spread the matched set of amethyst necklace and earrings on the counter.

"Ah, yes," Monsieur Thibedeau said, fingering each one delicately. "I remember these well. He said they matched your eyes."

"Within a few days, you said?"

"Within two hours, I think. The woman who was in here will see these and not be able to leave without them, if I'm any judge of feminine vanity. No one else in the city will have anything like them, and she will see to it they never do. Come back at five. Here," he handed me some Federal money, "go do your shopping and then come back. This is an advance." He then named the price he thought he could get. Even after he deducted his commission, it would have once been enough to last a year. Now, with the price of everything inflated, I would be lucky if it took care of us for three months.

In spite of my good intentions I splurged at the Market: shrimp, a few chunks of beef for a stew, fruit, and several fresh vegetables. Baptiste would not see collards and grits again for several weeks. I'd trade what came from the garden. Then to the apothecary for gauze and drugs. On my one visit to the hospital, Dr. Honoré had said he could supply no more morphine, so Baptiste must depend on laudanum to ease the pain. The smallest bottle took most of the money Monsieur Thibedeau had advanced me. It was back to tearing up sheets and laundering used bandages.

At five I returned. I scarcely dared hope the set had been sold, but as the jeweler said, he knew his women customers. She was delighted to learn he had uncovered some items in a long unused safe. He had named a high price, expecting her to bargain with him, but she had agreed immediately. So we each got a little more than we originally expected.

"Give my best to M'sieu Fontaine, and bring in what other pieces you want to sell."

"I will, and thank you. My best to your family."

We had successfully maneuvered our way through another crisis.

Baptiste was now improving steadily, and by late June was able to sit propped up in bed. The pain had lessened to such a degree he needed laudanum only at night for sleeping, and his legs were almost completely healed over. It would not be long before we could think about having an artificial leg attached to the one cut off below the knee. His main problem now was restlessness and boredom. He'd never been much of a reader, but when checkers began to pall, or I had to attend to things around the house, and he was finally convinced I could never learn chess, he agreed to explore my small but precious library.

"Here, try this one." I handed him a book of Poe's short stories.

"I hope he's more lively than the last. I'm not much for philosophy. Who was that man?"

"Emerson, a New England writer."

"A Yankee? No wonder I didn't like him."

"Well, Poe was a Southerner. So maybe you'll enjoy him more."

"What do you have to do now?" he asked petulantly. "Why can't Seena do it? Where is she anyhow?"

"Seena is gone. She has been gone for several days."

Before I could find time to talk with her, I caught sight of her chatting with a group of Yankee soldiers in the street. I didn't want Baptiste to know she had laughed at me when I tried to tell her what could happen to her. He would have skinned her alive when she came home. She began staying away nights, finally leaving for good. When next I saw her, she was sauntering down the street between two soldiers. Dressed in red satin and a feather boa, she was giggling shrilly and letting the men, really no older than boys, caress her as they walked along. Poor, pathetic Seena, I thought. So sure this new quasi-freedom would bring her riches and happiness. "We's all equal now," she said when I tried to explain things. "Them Yankees is our friends, and I'se just as good as they are."

"Where did she go?" Baptiste asked.

"With some Yankee soldiers."

"My God!" he exclaimed, "you know what that means. Why didn't you stop her?"

"Yes, I know, and yes, I tried. But she saw herself headed straight for the big rock candy mountain, and there was no turning her back."

"But she's still only a child."

"She knows what it is to be a woman now, and she must like what she's learned."

"You sound very callous, Leah. It's not like you."

"Butler has not made it easy to remain soft and stay alive at the same time."

"What if she gets into trouble, will you take her back?"

"Yes, my soft-hearted lover, I'll take her back. I'm not that heartless and cruel. Now let me go start that gumbo you've been hungry for."

Although I had not attended Mass in several weeks, I knew many priests and ministers were in trouble for either omitting prayers for the President of the United States or substituting the name of Jefferson Davis. On threat of having their churches closed, they were ordered to restore the prayer for the President and omit the one for Davis. When some tried to bypass the restriction against praying for Davis by instituting a moment of silent prayer, the clergy was threatened with imprisonment in military stockades. One minister defied the order, and when his church burned to the ground during the night, it was rumored Butler had personally issued the command to destroy it.

Thus it was that from day to day we did not know what new law or injunction would greet us when we awoke in the morning.

With midsummer came a new threat to the health

and safety of the city. More than ten thousand refugee
slaves who had fled plantations or deserted their masters arrived in the city. The Yankees had come to free
them, and now they were looking to their saviors for
food and lodging. Their privation was shocking, especially among the women and small children. While
their plight was not my immediate concern, I suffered
with them over their desire to be free and their need
for care. Many were the mornings I shared what little
we were having for breakfast with a mother and children who had found shelter during the night under one
of the trees in my garden. One by one all of Seena's
garments were doled out to those whose own coverings
were no more than rags. It was with a real wrench that
I distributed René's gowns, blankets, and small suits,
kept first as precious mementoes and then folded carefully away with prayers for a second child. The war
had made present needs more urgent than future
hopes.

It was well for me I did not know just how soon I
would be caught up in the refugees' problems. Jobs
were found for many of them, working for the city at
fifty cents a day. Still, there was constant fear of a general uprising as sporadic pitched battles broke out between Union troops and former slaves armed with
knives and clubs, who did not want to work and
thought they should be taken care of for nothing.

However, by the end of summer, Butler had solved
those problems as well as finding additional revenue for
his troops and, it was said, for himself.

In September he decided that all former citizens of
the United States who had not taken the Oath of Loyalty should now do so or be in immediate danger of
having to forfeit all their property. Having been regis-
tered as a Negro slave by the census taker, I felt I was
in no danger for the present. I realized how fortunate I
was that the young man had stubbornly ignored my attempt to explain my situation.

After all abandoned plantations and those belonging

to planters not signing the oath were seized by Butler, there began the rounding up of refugee slaves to work on them as well as on the fortifications of the city. There were constant rumors—cheered by the city's citizens and met with increased defenses by the Union—that Confederate troops were massing to rescue the city any day.

No distinction was made between Negroes who had lived in New Orleans all their lives and those who had recently entered the city. Worse than that, no attempt was made to determine whether they were free or slave. All alike—men, women, and children—were seized and carted out to plantations and were forbidden to return to the city. Women who had never done any work more arduous than caring for their mistresses' wardrobes or nursing children were forced to do the most strenuous work in the fields. Children and old men, prodded by soldiers with bayonets, were forced to dig fortification trenches. All who went out on the street were in danger of being hauled away at any time.

Yet with Seena gone, I had to go to the Market almost every day. But I did not dare let Baptiste know the risk I ran by appearing in public. I could wear a large bonnet that partially shielded my face and try to pass as white, in which case I might be stopped and asked to show the paper indicating I'd signed the loyalty oath. Without it the house could be searched, Baptiste discovered, and valuable property taken. Or I could be recognized as colored—Negro to them—and be immediately seized and transported to a plantation without being able to let Baptiste know what had happened to me.

By some miracle, by doing nothing to call attention to myself, I got through several months of 1862 without ever being approached by one of Butler's men. "Beast Butler" had not yet gotten his claws into me.

Chapter Twenty

Baptiste was deeply troubled. During the weeks he'd been in constant pain and completely dependent on me for all his needs, he was witty and uncomplaining. He laughed when he fell backwards on the bed the first time he tried to put on trousers; joked about the way they flapped below his stumps; referred to the laudanum as his Union-bourbon nightcap; mockingly scolded me for not scolding him when he wet the bed while trying to use the pan without assistance.

Fiercely independent, he forced himself to do for himself as quickly and expediently as possible. If he fell on his back, then he'd stay there while he pulled the trousers over his legs. One strong roll up onto his shoulders and he worked them over his hips to his waist. The extra length, tucked under the way one would a blanket, gave added warmth and protection to the still-tender areas. All adversity has advantages, and he avowed he slept better after laudanum than he ever did after bourbon.

If I'd put a night table beside his bed, he said, he could certainly bathe and care for himself now that he was sitting up. Would I mind still shaving him, though? I was ever so much more gentle than he. No whining, no "pity me" sighs because he could not yet focus well enough with one eye to see, when he looked in the mirror, that he was cutting too close.

"Almost lost half my mustache that time," he laughed.

"And with it half your charm. The hair on your

252

temples isn't even, either. One side's half an inch longer than the other."

"Here then." He handed me the razor and strop. "I'm all yours."

At his request I'd placed a chair at the side of the bed, and I knew he was practicing getting out of bed and onto it. I never asked how he managed, and I refrained from commenting on the bruises he sustained from time to time.

At the same time I was also preparing a surprise for him. I was having a rolling chair made by a carpenter. Two more pieces of jewelry had been sold at a far better price than the first set, and for the time being, I was free from financial strain.

"Look, Baptiste," I said, wheeling the rolling chair into his room. "Now you can move all around the house. We'll have a ramp made, too, so you can sit in the garden."

"Now, how do you expect me to get into that dad-blamed thing?" He sounded gruff, but I knew he was pleased.

"The same way you get into that dad-blamed chair beside the bed."

"Didn't fool you, huh?"

"No, you didn't. How're you doing?"

"Pretty well. Haven't fallen in two days. Have to hang onto the sides, though, or I go over on my face."

"Want to try this one?" I pushed the chair closer.

"Think I can manage it?"

"If you'll let me, I'll help you this time. See, it has this little lever down here for a brake, so it won't roll when you don't want it to. The carpenter said it's like the rolling chairs used at some European spas."

I'd bought a secondhand wicker chair with sturdy back and broad arms. Strong yet light, it would be comfortable for Baptiste to sit in for long periods of time, yet easy for me to push. Cushioned with padding, it gave him the much-needed support a hard, straight-backed chair would not provide.

So now he could be with me while I cooked, and we ate in the dining room or parlor rather than the bedroom. I had the ramp built, allowing us to enjoy the garden in the late afternoons and during the long summer evenings.

At the suggestion of Dr. Jourdin, who was now attending Baptiste, I also had the carpenter make and fit a wooden extension for the leg cut off below the knee. Baptiste was slowly learning to navigate within the house on crutches, but sometimes I wondered if his finally being able to walk was worth all the pain and frustration. Two or three steps and he was so exhausted he fell into the nearest chair. As usual, however, he refused to give up, insisting he could master anything. One wooden leg and two wooden sticks weren't going to prove more obdurate than he.

All would have been well except for one thing. Baptiste preferred sleeping alone. If I suggested rubbing his back, aching and cramped from sitting all day, he welcomed my ministrations; but if I showed any display of affection, he pulled away. He said he was not sleeping well and would only disturb me.

I thought I knew the problem. With part of both legs gone, he no longer considered himself a man. I was sure he was not physically impotent but simply fearful. I longed to tell him how I lay awake night after night in my own bed, my arms aching to hold him and my body hungry for the touch of his; but I could not speak of this when he rejected all attempts to get close to him. His rejection was a sharp knife tearing me apart.

I loved Baptiste. No injury, no mutilation would change that. If his wound had completely paralyzed him, I would have cared for him with every ounce of energy I possessed for the rest of my life. If the explosives had emasculated him, I would have accepted that and done what I could to make his life as complete and happy as possible. But I knew that he was still a man. He needed help to recognize this.

I didn't dare try to see Marie Laveau, the Voodoo priestess, nor did I know if she were still alive. I would evoke the help of Maîtresse Ézilée myself as well as make the charm necessary to restore Baptiste's desire.

After he was asleep, I snipped off one of his curls. With it I entwined a lock of my own. From a small supply of Voodoo ingredients I'd hidden in a cache in the garden, I took three hummingbird feathers and two dried mistletoe twigs. The hardest item to locate were two identical needles. No longer available in the stores, pins and needles were treasured like jewels. I had a large emery pincushion, and by feeling and probing, I managed to pry loose several long-embedded needles. Finally I found two the same size. One was rusted, but under the circumstances, I didn't think Maîtresse Ézilée would mind.

I reversed the needles so each point touched the eye of the other. By carefully bowing them slightly, I inserted the tips of the points into the opposite holes. All the while I sang the first part of the chant. Once secured, I positioned the needles between the two mistletoe twigs, wrapped the feathers and locks of hair around them, and tied it all with red string.

So far, so good. Now to slip the charm under Baptiste's pillow and let it remain there undiscovered until evening of the next day. Once, while I was repeating our names over and over in the second half of the chant, he stirred; but I had my hand under his pillow and out again before he was disturbed.

I had only one question: Was the charm for Baptiste, or did I make it to give me the courage to do what must be done? It was a potent talisman, but I had enough common sense to know a little human initiative was necessary to make any magic work.

Baptiste half sat up in bed. "What are you doing?"

"Brushing my hair."

"Why in here? Why not in your own room?" My own room was not my room; it was the nursery and

Mama's room and Seena's room. It was never *my* room.

"You used to like watching me," I said. "I thought it would give you pleasure."

"I'm tired. I want to go to sleep."

Ignoring his words, I got up from the bench and walked over to the bed. Sitting on the edge, I handed him the brush.

"Will you do the back? I can't reach it very well."

This had always been my signal. He would brush it for a few minutes, with long, even strokes, and then begin running his fingers through the strands until he pulled me down beside him. I remembered one time when he'd forgotten to drop the brush to the floor and rolled over on it while I was still locked in his arms. The way he screamed and leaped up, I thought he'd been stabbed. He nearly threw me out of bed in his frenzy to get off the stiff bristles. Baptiste didn't think it was funny, but I laughed until my sides hurt; and he threatened to spank me with the offending brush if I didn't stop.

I hoped he would remember some of this when I handed him the brush, but he only slid farther down under the covers and turned on his side.

"Please, Baptiste, haven't you room in your bed for me anymore?"

"Damn it to hell, Leah, don't you know that's all over for me! You trying to make me put a gun to my head? I'm not a man anymore, just a—a body with no legs."

"I'm sorry, Baptiste."

Once more he was shutting me out of a part of his world as surely as if I were a pariah guilty of the unmentionable sin. His silence was a warning not to penetrate his self-imposed isolation. Only he made one mistake. He took my matching silence for acquiescence.

Without a word I reached for the powdered starch I used when rubbing his back and legs, and he meekly turned on his stomach. He could never resist a gentle massage before going to sleep.

The leather cup and straps on his wooden leg, made from an old pair of boots, had cut into and irritated the stump to well above the knee. He must have endured excruciating pain each time he walked, yet I had been the one to insist he keep trying. Knowing how much his independence meant to him, I had pushed and prodded but had failed to recognize his resistance as more than exhaustion. The red streaks radiating from the scar reminded me of the signs of the blood poisoning we had fought to allay in the hospital, and I worried lest in my anxiety to have him use the leg, I had endangered his life.

Hoping Baptiste would not be aware of what I was doing, I gently palpated the flesh around the wound as I'd seen Dr. Honoré do so often. It seemed tender but not puffy. Perhaps the lines were due to the leather rubbing against the skin and not infection. A few days of not wearing the artificial leg would pinpoint the problem.

Meanwhile, to ease the pain. Once more I looked through my carefully garnered collection of herbs for one which when chewed or held between cheek and gum deadened the misery of toothache. Its efficacy had been proved when I cut each of my four wisdom teeth. A single leaf was harmless enough for teething babies, whereas several were strong enough for adult pain.

By crushing several leaves between the heels of my palms and mixing them with lard I'd rendered a few days earlier from fatback, I made an unguent I hoped would relieve Baptiste's pain.

Baptiste was still dozing, on the twilight edge of sleep but not completely out. Although he roused up when I began gently massaging the sore leg, he made no comment.

"This should make it feel better," I said quietly, as though to myself. "Maybe you ought to go without the leg for a few days."

Baptiste mumbled something into his pillow.

"What did you say?" I stopped smoothing the salve into his skin.

"I said, 'Whatever you say.'"

"You were doing it for me, weren't you?" I asked.

"Not entirely, but I felt so damned helpless, so dependent on the damned chair."

"Well, give it time. Now, relax and I'll put you back to sleep again."

I continued with long, smooth strokes up his thighs, along his sides, and finally across his shoulder blades and down his spine. I could feel the tension easing, the tight muscles relaxing. I thought he was asleep until I felt the bed shaking and saw him cover his face so I wouldn't see the tears.

It is not easy to watch a man cry. It is not a time for words. I was sure now what was troubling him. Baptiste had overcome almost insurmountable obstacles, had conquered numberless fears. He was a man of undaunted courage, yet now, when faced with the threat all men dread, that courage had been replaced with despair. At that moment his emotions were too vulnerable for me to scar them with a careless word or thoughtless action. But I knew that somehow I had to convince him he had not lost his manhood with the loss of his legs. He could still be the passionate, generous lover who was tender when I needed tenderness or almost brutal when I responded with a wild, animal hunger.

I lay down beside him. Now he lay in the curve of my body as I had so often nestled within his strong arms. I wanted him to know I needed him. Through all these weeks I had been the one on whom he could depend and to whom he'd been forced to turn for every need. Day by day, he'd become less—not more—of a man. While he'd been growing stronger physically, he'd been degenerating emotionally. Like a muscle atrophying through lack of use, his masculinity had been drying up steadily with each responsibility I assumed.

His complete dependency, his inability to fulfill normal functions, not his physical disability, had rendered him impotent. In turn he had used this as a rationale to protect himself from the humiliation of being an awkward or inept lover. Now I must find a way to restore what I had unconsciously robbed him of.

"Baptiste, please turn over and hold me close."

He did as I asked, but I got little comfort from his obvious reluctance to put his arms around me. He remained lying stiff.

"Baptiste," I whispered, "I want a baby."

His arm across my waist stiffened even more, and I could feel him trying to pull away.

"No! It's impossible and you know it."

I slowly moved his arm until one of his hands cupped my breast, and the painful longing to have him fill me once more with his love spread uncontrollably throughout my body. Baptiste offered no resistance when I turned toward him, drew his face close to mine, and kissed him first tenderly and then with increasing passion. In another minute, I knew his need was as great as mine. His arms crushed me against his chest, and his body was hard and demanding.

"Oh, God, Leah, help me," he whispered hoarsely. "Love me, please love me. I need you so much."

I didn't become pregnant as I'd really hoped I would, in spite of the folly of having a child during those desperate days of Union occupation, but I had guided Baptiste out of his self-destructive nightmare and toward full realization of his manhood.

Chapter Twenty-one

BAPTISTE AND I SAT before the fireplace on one of the first cool nights in November, I sewing and he waiting for the coals to need poking up. The only wood we could get was of very poor quality, giving off more smoke than heat. By sitting close to the fireplace, we could also keep from burning candles, now almost impossible to buy. Kerosene for lamps was nonexistent, and the gas was turned off almost every night. This also meant no streetlights, so no one dared venture out after dark.

I was afraid Baptiste would fall out of the chair when he leaned forward, but I stifled my impulse to jump each time he moved. Tending the fire gave him something to do. Finding things to keep him busy, to make him feel he was contributing to the running of the house, was a constant challenge. I couldn't seem to convince Baptiste I needed him for himself alone, that he was important to me for his own sake.

"What are you doing?" Baptiste looked over at the sewing in my lap.

"Turning a dress and putting on different trimming."

"I've never seen that one before."

"It's not mine," I answered quietly.

"You're accepting charity now in the form of clothes? I don't like that."

"No, no. I'm—I'm doing it as a favor. Madame Devereaux, right up the street, admired a dress I remade, and I said I would fix one of hers."

"How about the new shirts you promised to make

for me? Look at this one, so full of mends I'm ashamed to sit on the gallery for fear someone will see it."

"No one can see you on the gallery." Thank goodness, I thought, or at the least we'd be having the house searched. At the worst, Baptiste would be arrested as a prisoner of war, even though some disabled Confederate officers had been paroled to their homes.

I hadn't been able to bring myself to tell him that most of the Confederate men in New Orleans were wearing mended shirts, and some no shirts at all. With the money Madame Devereaux had insisted on paying me for altering her dress, I'd try to buy enough material to make him at least one new shirt. That is, if I were lucky enough to find the material at one of the stores allowed to do business. The black market price would be exorbitant.

I might have to go to the secondhand stores and try to find a shirt in good condition, given by a Union officer to one of his servants. The servants often preferred selling them for the money rather than wearing them. Then I would have to convince Baptiste it was one of his old ones which had been misplaced in a wardrobe. Either way I had to have money.

"Just as soon as I finish this dress," I assured him. "I've known the woman a long time, and she's had a great deal of unhappiness. Both her husband and son are in an Alabama hospital, and she's trying to get a pass to go into the Confederacy."

"What do you mean? This is the Confederacy."

"No, dear, New Orleans is a Union city, completely cut off in every way from the rest of the South. I told you about the Oath of Loyalty many have been forced to take or be turned out of their homes, exiled to the Confederacy or sent to prison."

"I need to get out and see what the hell's going on in the city. I'm like a prisoner in this house. Kept here by these damned legs. I want to show those bastards I'm not afraid of them and their damned oaths." He brought his hand down sharply on the arm of his chair.

"You want this house taken over?" I asked. "You want to be sent away? It could happen if you don't take the oath."

"Everyone still in town has taken the oath?"

"Well, no, but you never know who they'll choose to persecute."

"I'll take my chances. I want to go for a ride tomorrow. All over town and in my uniform. Where is it?" he demanded.

"It's gone. It was torn off you when you were wounded."

"Then get me a new one so I can ride out in my own colors."

"Let me finish this dress for Madame Devereaux. She has to see General Butler about getting the pass, and she wants to look her best. She has too much pride to let him see how poorly she's fared under his occupation."

The next day would be time enough to let Baptiste know it was impossible to get him a new uniform. There was no material to make one, all gray wool now contraband, and I'd heard that with the blockade, women in other states were making them out of blankets and any other heavy goods they could find. Certainly there were no uniforms in the secondhand stores now that they were forbidden to be worn.

Then I remembered Colonel LeConte. He had been furloughed home from Tennessee because of illness, and he had died from consumption aggravated by pneumonia as a result of exposure. If Madame LeConte still had his uniform—and I was sure she would have saved it—she might lend it to me when she learned why I wanted it. She and the Fontaines were close friends. Also, I had worked with her at the hospital where she was one of the few white volunteers to be pleasant to me.

I returned to my sewing feeling slightly relieved. I had not lied about the reason Madame Devereaux wanted her dress remade; I had merely not mentioned she was paying me.

Nothing more was said about riding out the next day, but Baptiste's cheerful conversation during the rest of the evening and his ardent lovemaking later told me he was really looking forward to escaping the confines of the house. I knew it was tiresome for him to sit on our gallery, his useless half-legs wrapped in a shawl. So little happened on our street during the day, which was well away from the center of Federal activity. It was no wonder Baptiste was restless.

Early the next morning I took the dress to Madame Devereaux. She was most appreciative of the work I'd done.

"Now I won't feel ashamed to see General Butler. That nasty man doesn't deserve all this extra attention, but I'll never let him know what he has reduced us to. If it weren't for my going to nurse Clare and Jean, I wouldn't give him the satisfaction of knowing I needed his help."

I worried about Madame Devereaux. She might get her pass and then not be allowed back into the city, and her home would be confiscated. Or if she were allowed to return, it would only be under the most brutal and humiliating conditions.

One very elderly woman who had been given permission to go out and care for a daughter during childbirth had been allowed to return. However, because she would not take the oath, she was put on parole and ordered to report to a Federal office every day in spite of the distance and the hardships she endured getting there. When she missed three days because of illness, two officers came and dragged her out of bed, forcing her to walk all the way in the rain. From then on a kindly neighbor transported her in a mule cart every day, but she suffered greatly from the humiliation of riding in the cart and from the excruciating pain of arthritis, which had worsened from the long trips in bad weather. Finally General Butler took pity on her and

said she need report only once a week as long as someone else took her place on the other six days.

Next I called on Madame LeConte. Still in deep
mourning, she seldom left the house. At first, she was
hesitant about lending me the colonel's uniform, as I
knew she would be. She had carefully folded it away in
a trunk which she had hidden in her attic.

"I kept it out for a long time as a memorial to him,"
she said. "I kept it pressed and hanging, ready for him
to wear, just as I did when he was alive. But when *they*
began searching homes for flags and other signs of loyalty to the Confederacy, I had to hide it. I cried the
whole time I packed it away."

I knew all about the searches. Any home suspected
of housing Rebel sympathizers—and most did—were
searched any time of day or night for such contraband
as uniforms, small flags, or anything with Confederate
colors, and even sheet music of Rebel songs. Those
who had not taken the Oath of Loyalty were natural
targets of these searches, and though nothing anti-
Union might be found, the occupants could be turned
out of the house or put on parole and forced to report
to a Federal officer every day.

Madame LeConte had bade me sit down while I told
her why I wanted the uniform.

"Oh, Leah, I just don't know. What would the
colonel want me to do? That's what I must consider
now. Baptiste was always like a little brother to me. I
had no other, just four girls in the family. I know how
much this means to him. Come, let's go up to the attic.
Maybe I'll know what to do when I see it."

I followed her up the beautiful winding stairway to
the second floor and then up a flight of rickety steps to
the attic. How this frail woman had gotten the trunk
up there herself I couldn't imagine.

"It took me all of one afternoon," she said, pausing
to rest on the step, "just to get the empty trunk up
here, stopping at each step to catch my breath. Then
more trips with the uniform and the things to put over

it. Even if they—" she never said the words *Union* or *Federal* "—looked in the trunk, they would see only old, discarded goods. Fortunately they've never asked to come up here. I guess they are looking for things displayed in the open. They did take some of my silver. Said the officers needed it for entertaining. I wish I could have melted it down and given it to them in one lump—on the side of their heads."

The thought made both of us laugh, and we sat on the steps to enjoy a good laughing-crying jag.

"Now," she said, "I feel better. Let's see about the uniform."

The trunk was hidden under an old rug, and we were both covered with dust by the time we pulled it off. Then we had to lift out all the odds and ends of clothes that filled two-thirds of it.

"Just throw them to one side, Leah. I'll never wear them again."

"But these are beautiful, Madame LeConte." I held up a rose silk ball gown and a deep green velvet tea gown. "Surely you're not going to discard these."

"The colonel is dead, Leah. There will be no more balls or formal teas for me. I'll tell you why I've decided to let you take the uniform. I've been given notice I can probably expect orders to leave for the Confederacy. They need my house for new officers coming in. I think they expect a Southern thrust to retake New Orleans and they're bringing in more troops."

The information about a potential Rebel attack was heartening, but not the talk of her leaving.

"They won't make you leave," I insisted. "They can't."

"Yes, they will. I've refused to take the oath. I would never be able to smuggle the uniform out with me. Only God knows if I'll ever be back or what will become of the house. One of my sisters is in Mississippi, so I do have some place to go."

She lifted the gray uniform out of the trunk. Nothing

was missing except his sabre. "They took that while he was still alive. Came to the house and took it right out of our bedroom. He never said a word. But I did. How did they think a dying man would use a sword against them? I told them they were cruel, but they only laughed."

Madame LeConte buried her face in the uniform, but not to cry. She wanted the feel of it against her cheeks one last time. Perhaps she remembered being held close to his chest each time he left or returned.

"Give this to Baptiste with my love," she said. "The colonel will like knowing he's wearing it."

"Thank you, Madame LeConte. Baptiste will feel honored knowing whom it belonged to."

She continued to hold the uniform in her lap.

"I'm worried, Leah, about giving this to Baptiste."

"Why?"

"You know he'll be in great danger if he's seen wearing it. But if he only wears it in the house. . . ."

She had forgotten why I wanted it, and I didn't remind her.

"I'll warn him. I think he just wants to feel what it's like to have one again. I—I won't need the boots, you know."

"Please take them anyway. Perhaps you know someone who can use them."

She looked at the two dresses I'd put to one side. "Take them along, too. It does seem a pity to have them stored away. They were so beautiful. I'm afraid those good times will never come again."

I gathered up the dresses, knowing there was always some use for good material. We returned to the first floor where Madame LeConte looked for something to wrap the uniform in so it would be well hidden. Finding nothing, we carefully tucked it inside the full skirts of the dresses. I quickly bade her good-bye and hurried the few blocks home. For the time being I put the dresses in the spare room wardrobe. Then I took the uniform to Baptiste, who had remained in bed while I was gone.

He held the uniform in his hands and looked it over slowly.

"This has been worn before. Why didn't you get me a new one?"

It was time to open Baptiste's eyes and prepare him for what he'd see when we drove out from the house.

"There are no new ones, Baptiste. There is no material to make them, and even if there were, there is no one here to wear them. They are contraband. You will be putting yourself in great danger when we go out. You don't know how things are in New Orleans. You need to get out and see how we're living."

Baptiste was more subdued. "Where did you get the uniform?"

"It was Colonel LeConte's. He came home ill on furlough and died. Madame LeConte had stored it away." Baptiste was getting enough shocks at one time. No need to tell him about her being threatened with exile.

"You asked her for it!"

"Yes. I knew she was a friend of your family. I didn't realize how close you were to her until she told me today. That is why she sent it to you. I told her you would feel honored to wear it."

"I am. I didn't know Colonel LeConte. He was from Vicksburg, and Émilée went with him into the army when they married. But we were like brother and sister."

"That's what she said. Now get dressed while I see about the carriage, and we'll go for a ride."

The rig Baptiste had given me was still in the carriage house and wouldn't take long to clean up. My horse was now being used by Dr. Jourdin. His had died soon after Baptiste was sent to Virginia, and I offered him the use of mine since I was no longer able to get feed and he couldn't continue making his rounds without transportation.

Before going to Madame LeConte's, I had checked with Dr. Jourdin, and he said he would be at the hospital all afternoon and could let us use both the horse and his buggy. No need for me to get the carriage ready. I thanked him, but said I thought Baptiste would like to ride in his own carriage.

Marcus, Dr. Jourdin's driver, not only brought over the horse but also hitched up the carriage for me and was waiting to assist Baptiste.

Baptiste demurred at first when he saw Marcus standing by the carriage, but the driver took no notice of his hesitation. He merely picked Baptiste up in his strong arms, carried him to the carriage, and put the reins in his hands. I tucked a robe over his legs, and we set off.

Baptiste said little during our ride. Too much had changed since he'd been wounded and brought to the New Orleans hospital to die. I saw several Federal officers glance our way, and I dreaded they might stop the carriage and arrest Baptiste for appearing in uniform. They could see he'd lost one eye, but they had no way of knowing he was also without legs. I was deathly afraid of what Baptiste would say if we were approached, but thankfully they left us alone.

The next few days were equally fine, and at two each afternoon, Marcus was waiting to start us on our way. Baptiste was slowly becoming cognizant of conditions in the city, but he was very tired when we returned home, and seldom spoke about what he had seen.

Then for nearly a week it rained, and we stayed home. When at last the weather cleared, I went out at our usual time, fully expecting to see Marcus standing by the carriage. He was there, but he was flanked by Union soldiers, and he looked scared to death.

"What is the meaning of this?" I asked the sergeant in charge. He was holding the horse's bridle.

"Colonel Bennett requests that you give him the

horse and carriage. His wife took a liking to them when you rode by her house the other day."

"You mean Madame Wolfe's house, don't you?"

"I'm not here to argue minor points. We're taking the horse and carriage."

"The horse is not mine," I said. "It belongs to Dr. Jourdin who merely lent it to me."

"No, we checked. The horse was yours." I was instantly aware of his use of the past tense. "I'm afraid the doctor will have to find some other means of transportation."

That's why we had not been stopped during our first rides. They were finding out exactly who owned the horse and carriage before confiscating them. Someone who knew the truth must have revealed the information. No doubt for a tidy sum. I was heartbroken. Not because it meant the end of our rides, although they had really perked Baptiste up, but because I had rewarded the generosity of a good friend by depriving him of something he desperately needed.

"By the way," the sergeant said, "General Butler would like to see you at his headquarters this afternoon to ask you some questions about the Confederate officer you've been seen driving with."

"I'm going with you," Baptiste said when I told him what had happened. "They can't take the horse away from Dr. Jourdin. And I won't have you trying to defend me."

"You can't possibly get down there, and you know it." I didn't want to hurt him, but he had to be made to see things realistically. "I'll have to walk and it's several blocks from here. There won't be any defending when I tell them you're a disabled veteran."

"What will they do to you?"

"Nothing. I'm listed on the census as a Negro, remember? All they'll do is try to persuade me they're my friends and you're my enemy. I've long since learned to walk the fine line between two cultures and not really belong to either one. I can do it again."

"Be careful, Cherie. I couldn't live without you."

"I will, I promise."

The interview went much as I expected. Many questions about Baptiste: who he was, when he was wounded, why he was with me. There was one frightening moment when they quizzed me about how he had gotten to my house and why he hadn't been listed in the census. I lied and said he'd left the hospital before New Orleans was occupied. I told them about trying to explain to the Union census taker the difference between Negro and free people of color, and in the confusion he had left before asking about white occupants of the house. I was verbally chastised for failing to report that information, but Butler was trying to convince the Negroes in New Orleans that the Union was their friend, so he didn't threaten imprisonment. He did give me a lecture on where my allegiance should be placed, but he said nothing about the uniform and that worried me. It could mean he would order a search of the house, and there were more things than the uniform I didn't want discovered. Butler said that as a disabled veteran Baptiste would not be disturbed—not for the time being at least, but it might be wise if he would sign the Oath of Loyalty. With that I was dismissed.

Our rides had one positive result. They put Baptiste in touch with many of his and his family's friends. To be sure, most were older men, but they gave him the masculine companionship he craved. One or two dropped by every afternoon, frequently staying for whatever I could rustle up for supper and then enjoying a game of chess before the fire.

I had envisioned Christmas as a particularly depressing time, but it proved to be anything but. Baptiste's friends decided we should have a good old-fashioned Christmas party. Since I could not be a guest in their homes, of course, and Baptiste would not go without me, they said they would bring the party to us.

No holiday celebration would be complete without candles and decorations and presents, so I got to work.

Candles, once imported from the North and particularly from New England, were no longer on store shelves, so people either had to make their own or do without. A variety of substitutes for candle wax were being used, most without success; but since some of them were readily available to me, I thought I'd try my hand at candle making. I gathered basket after basket of myrtle and bay berries, which could be boiled down for their wax. For wicks I braided together threads I'd pulled from scrap material, waxed them, and set them aside to dry. I knew I could tie the wicks around a long twig and dip them in the kettle of wax, but that would take hours, waiting while each layer dried. Remembering my mother once made her own candles, I wondered if any of the old molds were among her things I'd brought to the house after she died. So much of her stuff had seemed like useless junk at the time, I'd probably included the molds among the items I threw out. But it was worth an hour's going through what I'd stored in the carriage house loft if the molds were there.

I found them almost at once. Rusty and encrusted with dirt, two sets were badly broken, but one—with six molds—was intact. We would have fragrant candles on the table, at least, and maybe a few in the parlor.

The decorations were easier. Most of the garden stayed green year round, and there was holly, pyracantha, and nandina for red berries. From all these I made bouquets and garlands which I massed in every room. The house really began to take on a festive air. While Baptiste played chess or reminisced over the old days with his friends in the evening, I turned Madame LeConte's dark green velvet tea gown into a smoking jacket for him.

My ever-faithful hens laid enough eggs during the week before Christmas for me to save several and also have enough to trade for milk and cream from a mem-

ber of the Voodoo cult who'd managed to keep his cow
from being taken by hiding her in the swamp. Many of
the precious provisions we got came from these early
friends of mine who had long lived on the edge of the
bayous, a constant mystery to Union soldiers. When
Yankee patrols came around, these free Negroes van-
ished, as though swallowed up by the swamp itself. Yet
they need go only a few yards into the bayou to be
completely hidden, and no Yankee dared follow them.
A few had tried and become immediately lost or
sucked down into the morass. From my friends I got
herbs, dried leaves, and berries as substitutes for fla-
voring and spices no longer available and also as medicine and painkillers for Baptiste. These were the same
people who had helped the wounded Confederate officers escape from the hospital. Without them, our lives
would have been much more miserable.

With the eggs and the milk and some of the brandy
Baptiste had bought before the war, I surprised the
men with an eggnog-filled punch bowl. There were
even globs of whipped cream floating on top. One of
the men had used some of his precious shot to bag a
wild turkey, and others contributed yams, corn, and
dried fruit.

After the success of the party, Baptiste's friends said
they should get together more often as a group, maybe
go out to dinner at one of the restaurants still doing
business. All now had to cater to Union patrons, but
some kept private rooms where those with Confederate
loyalties could eat and drink undisturbed. After this
first supper they agreed to dine together every week,
meeting at a different restaurant each time.

Because of the warning to Baptiste about not wearing his uniform again, I sponged and pressed his old
dinner clothes, and one of the men came by to pick
him up. Four of them were wounded veterans, home
on furlough and trapped in New Orleans when the city
fell. So far they had been unable to get through the
Union picket lines and return to their companies; but

since learning of the help given me by the free Negroes, they were making plans to contact them. Unashamedly they and several of the other men had taken the Oath of Loyalty in order to avoid imprisonment or losing their businesses. To them it was a mock ceremony, having no more meaning than a child's promise not to raid the cookie jar again.

"They know we don't mean it," Monsieur Leblanc, owner of a small mercantile establishment, said, "but they can't prove it. You, Baptiste, have been spared any trouble so far, and the women of New Orleans, bless their hearts, have an idealistic sense of loyalty. That's great. I'm proud of them. But who's to gain if I'd refused? The Yankees would take over my business; my family and I would starve to death; and there'd be one less place where old patrons could do business at other than black market prices. My clientele know where my real loyalties lie."

The others nodded in agreement. The same was true for the officers. If they'd refused to take the oath, they would have been imprisoned with no hope of ever returning to the battlefield. The men did not fall in Baptiste's esteem; but unlike them, he considered oath-taking a serious matter. He would do nothing that could be construed as forswearing his allegiance to the Confederacy. I admired him for his convictions; I only hoped they wouldn't get him into trouble.

General Butler had issued an order forbidding meetings of any kind without his permission. Any group of more than three people gathering together would be classified as a meeting, unless all were immediate family members. In December, General Nathaniel Banks had replaced Butler as Commander of the Gulf Coast region, and he continued the proscription of such gatherings.

The morning after the fifth or sixth dinner meeting, two Federal Soldiers appeared at our door with orders for Baptiste to appear at General Banks's headquarters at two the same day. No reason was given. Within an hour, Monsieur Jacquart, one of Baptiste's friends, came to see us. The group now called themselves the D'Artagnan Club, after the French musketeer who went about righting wrongs in seventeenth-century France.

Monsieur Jacquart said all the men in the group had been ordered to appear, and he would come by to take Baptiste. I was worried, but I didn't see how a few friends eating dinner together could be construed as a seditious meeting. I was sure the worst thing that could happen was that Baptiste would be forced to take the oath.

New Orleans was deluged with torrential rains during January 1863, and whipped by tornadic winds. The temperature remained below normal for the entire month. The streets in the *Vieux Carré* were more like Venetian canals. Baptiste had caught a cold, and I dreaded seeing him go out in such weather. Pneumonia was always prevalent during periods of heavy rain in New Orleans, and few survived in this time of poorly heated homes and almost nonexistent medical care. The few doctors who had not gone with the Confederate army were elderly and semi-retired. They were forced to work a full day at the hospital to which only Union sympathizers or those having taken the oath were allowed to enter, and then only after the closest scrutiny of their needs. Union army physicians limited their practice to the military. Some civilian physicians, like Dr. Jourdin, tried to see as many of their older patients as possible after finishing at the hospital, increasing their workday to sixteen or eighteen hours. Baptiste must not get sick.

No matter how I tried to avoid the fact, the only really warm outfit Baptiste had was his uniform, yet he dared not wear it. I was going through his wardrobe, agonizing over what combination of coat and trousers would be the warmest, when the decision was made for me

"Will you press my uniform, Leah?"

"No, Baptiste."

"Yes. I'm not going to grovel before them. If I have to face the enemy, it will be as an officer in the Confederate Army."

"But if they just want to ask about the dinner parties, why antagonize them?"

"It's more than the dinners, Leah. You might as well know, because there's a chance I won't be returning home."

While I held my breath, he told me that the club was in touch with Confederate allies outside the city and plotting to work from inside New Orleans when the promised troops marched south to free the city. Each man had a designated area to ready for the entry of the troops by alerting people known to be sympathizers, planning ways to sabotage military equipment, and blocking the streets, particularly around Union-held buildings. Baptiste could not lend physical assistance but his name lent veracity to the plans of the group. When he'd finished, I was clutching the brass bed rail so hard my hand went numb.

"Oh, no, Baptiste. You couldn't be so foolish."

"If the troops come as promised, you'll have to have help from inside in order to regain the city. There'll be less bloodshed and a quicker victory."

"And you think General Banks knows about this? What good will all your work do now?"

"We're not the only ones. There are others to carry on. But obviously someone has overheard us talking, as careful as we've been."

"Or there's a traitor in your group."

"What do you mean?"

"I mean that one of your friends who claims he wasn't sincere when he took the oath is lying. Or he's become a paid informer."

"I don't think so, Cherie. They're all old friends." But I could see he was disturbed at the thought.

"You're too gullible, Baptiste."

"No matter. I'll know in a few hours."

Baptiste left a little before two, and I began pacing the floor. I tried sewing, but I made so many mistakes I had to rip all of it out. Then I unraveled three pairs of Baptiste's old woolen socks to get yarn for one good pair of gloves. So worn were the socks, the yarn kept breaking, and I took out my frustration by beating the poker against the wet, green wood in the fireplace. I pretended the stubborn pine knot was General Banks's head. The house was freezing, and I was miserable. I sat huddled in a quilt and had a good cry, after which I realized part of my misery came from being hungry.

All our dry twigs were saved for cooking, and I forced myself to fix a hot meal of baked cornbread, collards warmed over with a smoked streak-o-lean I'd gotten on my last trip to the bayou, and an egg. Except for the egg, I fixed enough for two, in an effort to convince myself Baptiste would be home soon. I also boiled some of our precious chicory. It wasn't coffee, but it wasn't dried acorns either, and it was hot.

We usually retired early to save fuel, but I couldn't possibly sleep. Gathering a second quilt around myself, I curled up in front of a sputtering fire. There were a few candle stubs left from Christmas, and I lighted one of them to keep me company. That damned Christmas party! It had brought Baptiste much-needed companionship, but it might also result in his imprisonment. I knew these had been his happiest weeks since being wounded, and he might think being caught was worth it. Much of his restlessness came from feeling unable to aid the Southern cause. Now he could play hero again. Damn masculine pride, I swore to myself.

Sometime during the night I dozed off and let the pitiful fire go out. The sudden chill woke me up, and I could either get more wood and start it up again, or go to bed. I took the easy way out and dragged the two quilts into the bedroom.

Baptiste was finally brought back the following afternoon, stripped of his uniform and wrapped in a long

Union cape. He was accompanied by two Union soldiers.

His story didn't take long to tell. All of the group had been placed in one room. The door was locked, and they were left alone for several hours, a torture well calculated to break them down. Although they suspected why they had been called in, they weren't given any information.

At first the men conversed as they would whenever together, avoiding only the subject of the dinner parties. Time went on with no one coming in to apprise them of their situation, bring them food, or allow them to seek physical relief. Gradually they became restless, and Baptiste was particularly uncomfortable on the hard, straight-backed chair. Two of his friends made a cushion from a coat, and he was able to rest on the floor. Baptiste said the hardest part was fighting down my suspicion that one of the men had betrayed them.

Sometime in the middle of the night, a guard came and led them to another office. The soldier refused to let the men carry Baptiste, who, at my suggestion, had left his wooden leg and crutches at home in order to appear more disabled. Thus he was forced to crawl along the uncarpeted floor under the scoffing eyes of other Union soldiers. After another hour had passed, General Banks strode in and ordered all the men to stand up.

Briefly, he knew about the dinner parties. The informer was a member of the group, a man whose brother was being held in a Northern prison as a spy. A waiter in the pay of Banks had first alerted the general to the weekly gatherings and aroused his suspicions. Still without mentioning a name, General Banks said he had called in a member of the club and confronted him with the information given by the waiter. In return for remitting the brother's death sentence, the general asked for names and specific information.

Baptiste and his friends were given no opportunity to deny or defend the accusation, nor were they given the name of the traitor. Each looked at every other member of the group, planting seeds of doubt and completely alienating former friends.

All of the businessmen were sent to Ship Island, and those who had taken the Oath of Loyalty were sentenced to hard labor for the infamy of being double traitors. The Confederate officers would be sent to a Northern military prison with the added stipulation that they were never to be among those exchanged for Union prisoners of war.

Then General Banks turned to Baptiste.

"I am not a vindictive or cruel man, Major. I can appreciate what you have suffered, but you are an enemy and a continued danger to us. You must be punished for your part in the plot. I am going to allow you to return home. However, you are not to leave the premises nor have any visitors. You will remain thus confined and incommunicado until the successful conclusion of the war. You will also relinquish your uniform as contraband and be liable to search at any time. Sergeant, escort Major Fontaine to his home."

Chapter Twenty-two

NOW THE MONTHS WERE MARKED OFF not by holidays or changes in weather but by new additions to the list of things in short supply. Seafood was available when the shrimpers and fishermen could get through the lines, but I could not remember when we had eaten beef or pork or veal. Even chicken was scarce. For a time, when feed was first hard to obtain, there were plenty for sale, with owners retaining a few for eggs. My hens were still laying well, in spite of their strange diet of whatever they could grub up in the garden. Chickens were the favorite forage of Union troops, and those who still had some kept them carefully locked up in sheds or carriage houses at night. Reluctantly I killed one from time to time to add variety to Baptiste's diet, but only after days of agonizing over the resultant loss of eggs to eat or barter.

Coffee, a staple in the Creole diet, disappeared from the shelves along with its cheaper substitute, chicory. When coffee first became scarce, we added more and more chicory, which many Louisianans were already accustomed to blending in, finding it gave coffee greater strength and a richer taste. Soon it was nothing but chicory, which by itself could be very bitter unless diluted with generous portions of sugar and cream. When even that was gone, we scrambled for substitutes, and much of the talk at the Market—when we dared go out—concerned which came closest to tasting like real coffee.

None did, of course, but some provided a hot, po-

tent, not unappetizing beverage once we got used to
the taste. Parched corn, when it was available, made a
weak brew; but if the corn were allowed to scorch during the parching process, the result was nauseating.
Among the favorite and more easily acquired substitutes in our area were acorns, and parched okra seeds,
peanuts, and beans. People who entered from other
parts of the South said rye was proving most popular,
but very little could be found in New Orleans. Some
who claimed to have found a palatable mixture offered
it for sale at prices higher than the original product
had ever brought.

Almost from the beginning of the occupation, we
were denied sugar. Louisana, the largest producer of
cane, was deprived of its own yield. Sorghum was
the most plentiful of all substitutes, but it had its
drawbacks. Honey was preferred when it was available;
and when in season, figs and watermelon could be
made into syrup and used for sweetening. Some,
laughingly, tried to imitate the bees and gather nectar
from certain flowers, particularly honeysuckle, but
hours of work brought only meager returns.

Why the shortage of sugar in the port city that had
made its wealth from distributing all over the world the
harvest of nearby cane plantations? When Butler had
to send his troop ships back to New England for more
recruits, he needed ballast. Filling sandbags, he said,
would take too long. So he loaded the ships with the
closest thing at hand: thousands and thousands of
pounds of sugar, which, it is said, he then sold at a
tremendous profit up North. When the confiscated
plantations were in operation again, they were worked
for the benefit of the Union occupiers. With one exception. Those planters who declared their allegiance to
the Union were allowed to sell their produce at exorbitant black market prices, far out of reach of all but
a few, usually those who ran their own black market
operations.

One day when I was fitting cardboard innersoles into my shoes, Baptiste watched with interest.

"Guess I'm lucky at that," he laughed. "That's one thing I don't have to worry about."

"Well, be careful and don't wear out your pegleg. There'll probably be a shortage of wood next."

He took one of my inadequately repaired shoes and inspected it carefully, turning it round and round in his hands. "Go get my old boots. These will never do for you."

"I can't wear your boots. I'd trip and fall with every step I took."

"Quit arguing, Cherie, and do as you're told."

Dutifully I obeyed. He picked up the knife he'd been whittling with as an antidote to boredom.

"Now you'll see how clever I am. The leather in this old boot is soft and pliable, thanks to my keeping it so with regular applications of saddle soap, and it's not too thick. Give me that piece of cardboard; I can use it for a pattern."

With deft strokes he fashioned a perfectly-fitting inner sole of good, stout leather. There was enough of the original sole to hold it in place, and I no longer had to dread getting my feet wet. By the time the shoes themselves wore out, he had devised a way to use them as a pattern for making new ones, which he put together by boring holes and stitching with old twine. They were somewhat oddly shaped, but they were comfortable, and at least I was more fortunate than those reduced to wearing canvas shoes or wrapping burlap around their feet.

With equanimity I drank okra-seed coffee, sweetened my food with sorghum, and made all-vegetable stews; but I became enraged when I saw the wives of Union officers parading in new shoes and unturned dresses. I had become adept at making one bonnet from the remains of three old ones, turning and retrimming dresses, and creating hats by braiding palmetto fronds, as had most of the women I saw. From old scraps of silk, I fashioned a pretty rainbow-hued parasol.

In the Market one day, I overheard two women discussing how impossible it was to find someone to remake dresses and hats. I thought about the dress I had remodeled for Madame Devereaux. Now I saw no reason not to use my ability and bring in some extra money. The women were delighted with my offer, and for several months I had as much work as I could handle, until my clients reached the end of their savings and had to use what little was left for necessities.

Two vastly different situations resulted from Baptiste's whittling and my remaking dresses: one fortunate and the other extremely frightening.

Baptiste often occupied his time by whittling, sometimes just wearing down a stick but often surprising me with a tiny carved animal or human caricature. He'd never been a pipe smoker, but when his favorite cigars were no longer available, he switched to a pipe. Complaining it was smoking hot, he asked me to get a new one. There were none in the stores, the majority having been imported before the war. The clerk laughed and said most men were trying to make their own. This gave me an idea.

Good, sharp knives of the right size and shape were hard to come by, so I called on my good friend Monsieur Thibedeau, the jeweler. Yes, he could get me a set of carver's tools, but they would be expensive. A sailor's widow, whose husband had carved at sea as a hobby, had been trying to sell them. Would Monsieur Thibedeau take a diamond stickpin for them? He would, and the value of the stickpin would easily cover his commission. After some research, I learned that pipes could be made from corncobs, but the best were carved from dogwood, cherry, and walnut. The first two I had in my own yard.

Back to the tobacconist. Yes, he knew several men who carved and who, he thought, would be willing to teach Baptiste.

Then came the problem of convincing Baptiste to turn a hobby into a source of income.

"I don't know, Cherie. I'm not that good. Maybe you wasted your money buying these tools." But already his fingers were handling them lovingly, balancing them proudly across his palm, and feeling the keen edges.

"Not if it gives you pleasure."

"What about those men you said would come here to teach me? How are we going to get around the prohibition against visitors?"

"There aren't many patrols on the street except after curfew, and we'll just have to take a chance we won't be searched during the daytime."

There had been two unannounced searches since the fateful dinner parties, but both late at night and more to harass than to confiscate.

"And you really think I could sell them?"

"The tobacconist said he will take all you make."

So began Baptiste's reentry into the world of business. After the first crude attempts he refused to sell, but which were placed proudly on the mantelpiece, he gradually learned to create pipes of great originality. He was never satisfied with making a plain, utilitarian pipe. His workmanship was of such quality, it was in demand as far north as Natchez, where some had been taken as gifts. When he learned that chess sets were at a premium, he began carving those too, delicate figures unlike any I'd ever seen.

The parlor became his studio, and on fair days, I moved the worktable into the garden. He was content to carve all day and often until late into the night to finish a special order, such as the one for President Jefferson Davis which a friend was smuggling out. Baptiste had a special knack for studying the woods with an artistic eye, cutting them with meticulous care, and then polishing for hours until the grain of the wood became an organic part of the design.

To see him happily busy gave me a peace of mind

I'd not known for a long time. More important, the money his carving brought in released him from complete dependency on me. It was the final assurance he was a whole man again.

With his carving and my sewing, our financial strain had lessened considerably in spite of the rapidly increasing inflation.

For one of my customers, a charming elderly widow, I was remaking an entire wardrobe. I think she had kept every dress she'd owned since she was married. With such a plentiful supply of materials and trims, it was a joy to create entirely new ensembles for her. Many of her dresses had been carefully packed away for years, but by cutting around weakened places and turning the faded sections, almost everything could be used.

One of General Banks's regulations required passes for all Negroes, signed by their masters who, in their turn, had taken the Oath of Loyalty. For a time, at the beginning of the occupation, all Negroes in New Orleans had been free. Then came the masses of slaves fleeing from surrounding plantations, their subsequent seizure by Federal troops, along with free Negroes and mulattoes, and their deportation to other plantations confiscated by the Union.

With Lincoln's signing of the Emancipation Proclamation, only Negroes in the Confederate-held sections of the country were freed. Thus, those in New Orleans and other Union-held areas were once again slaves, and they were required to carry passes with them at all times. Much to our horror, free people of color were also frequently stopped and asked to show their passes. I could have obtained one in either of two ways: as a free person I could take the Oath of Loyalty, which I refused to do; or, as Baptiste jokingly suggested, I could become his slave. However, this would have required his taking the oath, and I was as stubbornly opposed to this as he.

Thus, in many, many ways we who were free were

far worse off under Federal occupation than we'd ever been under Southern white law, and the slaves were certainly no better off. Negro males were frequently seized and conscripted for army duty. Homes were entered and fathers and sons dragged away and threatened with bodily harm if they did not "volunteer." One young man was brutally beaten and stabbed innumerable times when he refused, saying he had to support his crippled father.

I had to be extremely careful when I left the house, scheduling my trips for the hours when I knew the less stringent patrols were on duty. Through the months I had gotten to know some of them quite well. Many found the business of checking passes an onerous and humiliating duty.

But patrols change. I had finished two dresses for Madame Seignious, and I knew she wanted to wear one on this particular evening. I'd reached Madame Seignious's street, some three blocks from home, when I was rudely stopped and asked for my pass. Perhaps because I was carrying a bundle and looked like a servant, or perhaps because I was hurrying. In any event, I was stopped.

"I'm free," I insisted to the hard-faced sentry. "My mother was free and so was my grandmother!"

But he only jerked my arms around behind me and told me to shut up.

Then a cart drove up. To make the situation more untenable, I was out after the newly established curfew set at one half hour before sunset, which usually meant imprisonment or shipment to a plantation even if one had a pass. A few got off with a fine.

I was hauled roughly up into the cart. No way to get word to Baptiste, no chance to return for any of my own things. Once taken to a plantation, slaves were forbidden to send word to the city, and those attempting to escape were shot. The irony in all this was that as Yankee troops proceeded downriver, burning, looting, and confiscating plantations, they were encouraging the slaves to revolt and come to New Orleans, where they would be treated like royalty by their benevolent saviors.

This was not the first desperate situation I'd been in, nor would it be the last, but at the moment I felt completely helpless.

The cart was crowded with moaning, bewildered captives. There was no room to sit down, so I worked my way to the edge and stood by the waist-high wooden bar.

Suddenly from out of nowhere came a shout.

"Leah! What in blazes are you doing in that wagon? Driver, stop that cart. Stop it this instant, I tell you!"

Madame Seignious's voice was loud, and she spoke with authority. She had been standing on her front gallery waiting for me. After recovering from the shock of seeing me in the cart, she'd immediately called out.

"Sorry, lady, these slaves were out after curfew and without passes."

"Leah is no slave. I demand you release her immediately." She pounded the pavement with her cane.

"Can't do that. Against orders."

Without a word she began striking the arresting officer on the shoulder with her stick.

"Now, Leah," she said in a voice that brooked no argument, "get out of the cart. I have an extra pass. I got it for Emmaline, but the little fool ran away. Will you let me sign it over to you? You'll be my slave, you know, if you do," she added with a twinkle.

I would have agreed to be the devil's own slave at that moment.

"Young man, you will accept such a pass, won't you?"

One whacking had convinced him not to dispute her.

"Yes, ma'am. But what about the fine for being out after curfew? I gotta have that."

"I'll pay it, but it comes out of your money, Leah. That's to teach you not to be fool enough to go out after curfew. I could have waited until tomorrow for the dress. Where are my dresses, anyway? Don't want to lose them now. One was my second-day dress. That was the day Horatio finally got up the courage to make love to me. Can't lose that dress. Might need it again."

I pointed to the bundle still on the cart, and one of the less fortunate handed it down. All were laughing, in spite of their predicament, and no one would have denied Madame Seignious her second-day dress.

When I finally got back home, Baptiste and I were able to laugh, too, especially over my slave status.

"And you were the one who was going North to 'pass.' "

"It's ironic, isn't it, having to become a slave in order to be set free?"

In spite of pleasant autumn weather and a busy day in the garden, I was unable to sleep. I had still not become accustomed to the varied sounds in the night that were endemic in a city occupied by enemy troops: the hard footsteps of the patrols, the clinking of a sabre as the officer of the guard made his rounds, the clanging of alarm bells, the screams of people caught after curfew. Their errand might have been innocent or a dire emergency. No matter; they were taken into custody. Even the church bells, sounding out the hours and once soothing and reassuring, had now taken on an ominous tone, as if they too were controlled by the Union.

A drunk stumbled by on the banquette right outside my window. I listened to each of his halting movements. Twice he fell against the house. I dozed off a moment and then was awakened by the sound of someone fumbling at the gate. If he were after my chickens . . . or the second crop of beans just ready to pick! There was no way I could stop the thief if he were a soldier, but if he were one of the many strays in town, maybe I could scare him off.

I threw a robe around my shoulders and glanced out a side window overlooking the gallery before I opened the door. I couldn't see anyone, and the deep shadows seemed to move in a weird spectral dance of their own. Nonsense, I thought. Either there's someone out there or there isn't, and I'm not going to find out standing inside.

Opening the door, I nearly fell over something lying at my feet on the gallery. The damned drunk, I thought, had chosen my garden for a convenient place to pass out. Well, let him sleep it off, and maybe he'd leave in the morning. Heaven knows, there were plenty of reasons for trying to escape from the unpleasant realities around us; and if drinking did it for this man, who was I to condemn him?

As my eyes became accustomed to the dim light, I realized with a start that my comatose visitor was a woman, not a man, and a very small woman at that, not much bigger than a child. Drunken men I saw often and had learned to tolerate if not accept. A sodden woman, however, aroused both pity and abhorrence: pity for whatever had brought her to such a strait and abhorrence for allowing herself to become trapped in it.

Something more than pity or compassion moved me, perhaps a mystic tie with this young woman as she had been before she sought escape from an intolerable situation. Free or slave, she had undoubtedly suffered because of her color. Her face was partially covered by an upflung arm, but from the ravaged contours I could see, it must once have been fine and delicate. The night had turned chill, and I went in to get a quilt to cover her.

As I bent down to spread the quilt, I was shocked to see that the dark stains on her dress were dried blood, not dirt. Not only that, fresh blood was seeping from beneath her skirt. The girl was seriously hurt and needed immediate attention. Her frail body could not have weighed more than eighty pounds, no burden for me after months of helping Baptiste, but I almost dropped her when her arm fell away from her face. I was carrying Seena.

Placing her on the bed in the former nursery, I hastily gathered sheets and towels to absorb the blood now pouring from her. She was bleeding profusely from one or several wounds. Once I had her soiled dress off, I saw why. She was hemorrhaging from a self-induced abortion. God only knows what she had used—sticks, wire, knife—to bring it about. I saw, too, that her body and face were covered with swollen bruises.

I folded strips ripped from a sheet into small squares for packing, but it was no use. They immediately became saturated with blood. She had pierced at least one large blood vessel and ruptured one or more vital organs. She was bleeding to death, and there was nothing anyone could do to prevent it.

While I bathed her body and prepared to put a clean gown on her, she roused up and recognized me.

"I'se sorry, Miss Leah. Sorry to be such trouble."

"You're not trouble, Seena. I'm glad you came home. But you're very sick."

Too weak to say more, she gave me a wan smile. I wanted her to talk, to tell me what had happened, so I let her rest a few minutes. Her fever was dangerously high, and she had only a faint pulse. I watched her breathing the way Dr. Honoré had taught me to do when I was nursing Baptiste. I could barely see the rise and fall of her chest.

When she stirred uneasily on the bed, I raised her head and forced some wine down her throat. She fluttered her eyes, and I knew I had better ask my questions while she was still conscious. Slowly, a labored word at a time, she told me her sordid story.

The two soldiers I had seen her with had enticed her with promises of pretty things and a place of her own. At first the gifts were, for her, generous ones: clothes, cheap jewelry, and evenings in low-class bars. The place of her own turned out to be a shabbily furnished room, but she didn't have to take orders, and her two benefactors brought in her meals. The soldiers were crude, but they never hurt her.

Soon they began bringing their friends to the room, demanding she take care of them, too. Many were brutal, and some of the things they wanted her to do were abhorrent to her; but she was powerless to resist.

A few days earlier she had told her two original lovers she was pregnant. Their response was immediate. They beat her up and then threw her out, saying she was no good to them anymore. In spite of his mistreatment of her, she had fallen in love with one of the soldiers, and she thought he would take her back if she got rid of the baby.

Seena's face was bathed in sweat, and I knew she was suffering severe pain. She was whimpering now like a hurt child, not so much from the pain but from bewilderment that the world would allow this to happen to her. Now I'd heard her story, the best thing was to let her die in peace. If I could have saved her, I would have managed, in spite of the curfew, to get her to a hospital; but the bleeding had become more profuse, and I knew there was no way to repair the damage she had done to herself. About her was the odor of death I had learned to recognize so well while I was in the hospital. I gave her more wine mixed with a generous dose of laudanum. As I'd hoped, she passed away while asleep. No final agonies, no pleading for forgiveness, no fear of punishment awaiting her for what she'd done.

Poor, poor Seena. Her search for freedom and love had brought her this, a horrible, unnecessary death. I thought of taking her mutilated body directly to general headquarters and screaming at them, "Look! This is what your soldiers have done to someone you claim to have come down here to free." She was as much a casualty of the war as Baptiste or any of the Confederate soldiers lying in unmarked graves alongside a hundred battlefields. But I didn't. In the morning we arranged for a quiet funeral, and Baptiste carved a small wooden marker for her grave among her own people on the edge of the bayou.

Chapter Twenty-three

In 1863, MY JOURNAL, written by then on scraps of paper fastened together with heavy thread, included such entries as:

"Confederate prisoners are being kept in a house where a whole family recently died of smallpox. Several prisoners have also died."

"People are thrown into jail just on word of an enemy. Reminds me of the Inquisition. Wonder if they, too, get a share of the imprisoned person's property."

"Got approached by a soldier again today. Called me a 'Nigger whore' when I refused to go with him. Struck me as rather ironic."

"Many starving in the streets. People who can afford it being taxed to take care of them. Yankees bragging they are feeding the destitute of New Orleans. More fortunate taking in those who've been turned out of their homes, sometimes whole families."

"Passes to enter Confederacy and then return are no longer free but must be purchased at exorbitant prices. Some having to sell everything they own at a terrible sacrifice, so they really have nothing to come back to."

"Rumors coming in about homes along the river being burned. I know Baptiste is worried about the plantation."

"Men accused of sabotaging Federal cannon were stretched out on the ground with cannon balls attached to arms and feet. One died from lack of food and exposure to weather."

"More Yankee troops marching in. Never thought

I'd see so many. Must fear a Confederate attack from upriver. Wish it were true."

"Women returning to New Orleans tell about being stripped and searched for contraband. One had managed to find milk for her baby. Had to watch while it was poured out on the ground."

"Children now being arrested for singing Rebel songs."

"City is wild with the news that Louis Napoleon is going to recognize the Confederacy and will send troops. Probably another false hope."

"Major Prados buried today."

"Madame Pierre Beauregard buried today."

"General Sherman now living in Mrs. Pinkard's house. She was turned out when she would not lodge him."

"More servants of those not taking oath now ordered to work on fortifications at bayonet point."

"Three women arrested and thrown in with drunken soldiers for singing 'Bonnie Blue Flag' in their own homes. They failed to shut the windows."

"Orange trees now blooming. Honeysuckle and jessamine filling the air with sweet odors."

I read over these entries now and think about what people often say when things are going badly: "Someday we'll look back and laugh." I cannot laugh. They were tragic, desperate times. Those entries I have included here are ones that evoke particularly poignant and clear memories.

The unfortunate prisoners were Confederate enlisted men, captured near New Orleans and held for exchange with Union prisoners. Since the transfer was to take place within a few weeks and the local prison was full, it was decided to put them in a recently vacated house. Federal officials were not ignorant of the reason the house was empty. There had been several cases of smallpox in the city, brought in on a ship from Baltimore. Doctors in town protested the use of the house as a prison until it had been fumigated, but Union officials ignored their advice. Eventually over half the prisoners contracted the disease and many of them died for lack of proper care. Again Dr. Jourdin protested to the authorities that he should have been notified and allowed to treat the ill, but he was turned away before he could get to General Banks. Many who tried to plead a cause met with the same treatment. They were passed from official to official, each ruder than the previous one, and often never seeing the man who could answer their inquiry or approve a request.

On the streets no woman was safe from either the insults of Union wives and camp followers or the propositions of soldiers. Women sympathetic to the Union or family members of officers were easily distinguishable from Southern sympathizers. The former always rode in carriages, whereas the latter walked or rode horsecars. To ignore a soldier was to be branded a prostitute, according to Butler's infamous order, and more than one woman was imprisoned for supposedly insulting a Union wife. Now white women as well as Negroes and colored had to stand meekly back and wait while an arrogant officer's wife made her selections in a shop, or they had to step off into the gutter when wives walked three or four abreast on the banquettes. I should have been amused or considered it retribution for former injustices; and if I'd been the one on the banquette, I might have. But when Southern women were lowered to what had been my former status, I was raised to theirs, and no one knew it better than they.

One particular occurrence remains ingrained in my memory. I was waiting in line to enter a shop which had managed to get a few pounds of coffee. They were rationing it by the ounce—a dollar an ounce—but I knew how much it would cheer Baptiste, who was more lonely than ever after months of being forbidden to go out or see anyone.

A Yankee officer, lounging nearby with a group of

cronies, was bragging about his prowess with women, especially mulattoes who were hungry for the touch of a white man. Seeing me, he said he would show them right then how quickly I'd fall into his arms. Bets were placed and he walked over to me. When I refused him, he grabbed me by the arm, and without thinking, I jerked away. Before I knew what was happening, he'd fisted me several times across the face and knocked me to the ground. Certain I was going to be seized for resisting him, I just lay there. Then I heard a violent scuffle and looked up to see four of the white women, who had also been in line, beating and pummeling him with fists and shopping bags.

I thought we'd all be arrested, but for some reason the other men considered the whole incident hilarious and were laughing at their comrade for his ignominious defeat and loss of the bet. They told him to come along and forget it. Taking their advice, he flung his one last epithet at me—"nigger whore"—and stomped off. The women continued to aid me, assisting me to get up, brushing off my clothes, and wiping the blood from my face. They had relinquished their places in line to help me, but there wasn't a single murmur of regret. There was also a happy ending. We all got a share of the coffee, and Baptiste accepted my story that I'd tripped and fallen on a curb.

Funerals were no novelty during this period of bereavement, but two will never be forgotten by me or anyone in New Orleans at that time. A Major Prado had been murdered by a deserter, and his body brought back by his family. His funeral was attended by almost every Southern sympathizer in the city. Baptiste, of course, could not go, but I'd promised to bring him word of everything that went on, what each of the eulogists said. When word got to General Banks about the tremendous crowd congregating, he sent out troops to disperse it. The captain in charge of them said that only friends of the deceased would be allowed to remain.

"Tell General Banks," said one of the mourners, "that we are all his friends." And all the friends were allowed to remain.

The entry concerning the death of Caroline Beauregard actually came from my 1864 journals, but it seems fitting somehow to include it here. General Pierre Beauregard was New Orleans' best-loved son and greatest hero. The death of his wife in March 1864, while he was on duty in Florida, occasioned another large turnout. Fearful of a riot, General Banks stationed troops around the house on Esplanade, where she'd been living and which was filled with mourners, as well as along all the streets where her cortège passed on its way to the river down which the body was to be taken to her plantation. Out of respect for the wife of their hero, no incident marred the solemnity of the day, nor did the troops interfere with the mass movement of people toward the wharf as they accompanied the coffin like hundreds of honorary pallbearers.

One other funeral comes to mind. Father Mullen of the St. Louis Cathedral had already been in trouble with Union authorities for defying the order not to pray for Jefferson Davis. He replied that his soul and his body were his own, and he would pray for Confederates whenever he pleased. He was not exiled or incarcerated because General Banks was cognizant of the power of the Church, and he hoped to use it to his advantage to subdue its members. Called to the general's office and questioned at length about rumors that he had refused to bury a Federal officer, Father Mullen replied, "You are mistaken, sir. I would bury you all with pleasure."

"Do you know I can send you to Fort Jackson?" Banks said.

Father Mullen's answer ended the discussion. "And do you know I can send your soul to hell?"

Through it all the garden flourished. The shrubs bloomed in profusion in spite of death and deprivation outside their walled retreat. Birds sang as though in defiance of a proclamation not to be happy, and they challenged the sound of artillery upriver and gunboats patrolling the port.

Chapter Twenty-four

THE YEAR 1863 was one of rising and falling hopes. From celebrating the Confederate victory at Chancellorsville, the South went into mourning for the death of Stonewall Jackson on May 10. In New Orleans, Confederate sympathizers were arrested for wearing black armbands and hatbands. Few were fined or imprisoned, though, because most could name a relative for whom they were in mourning; and the Federals did have the grace to allow expressions of personal grief. During May we held out hope that, as long as the Mississippi remained open north of New Orleans, it was only a matter of time before the city would be relieved. It was not to be. After several Union assaults on Vicksburg had been repelled by Southern forces, more Federal troops were brought in, and the city surrendered on July 4. Lowering morale even more was the news of the cataclysmic defeat of the Confederate forces at Gettysburg.

Spirits soared once more with news of Southern victories at Manassas, Sabine Pass in Texas, and Chickamauga, as well as word that the South continued to control Charleston Harbor in South Carolina.

Until the close of the year, most Southerners were still looking ahead optimistically to foreign recognition and aid, followed by ultimate Confederate victory, in spite of an important Union win at Missionary Ridge, which opened the road to Georgia for their troops.

Victory or defeat, we would have remained abysmally ignorant of how the war was progressing if we had depended on the New Orleans papers, which could print nothing but news released by Federal headquarters. Our only valid sources of information were smuggled New York and Philadelphia papers. We were often cheering a Confederate victory on the same day Southern troops were being annihilated under Union guns.

The onset of a new year, 1864, saw the war stalemated, with a series of small skirmishes but no decisive battles. With Lincoln's administration facing an election, however, Union military conquest of the South was increased as the presidential nominations drew closer. Hopes for a decisive Confederate victory became more and more ephemeral. Dreams of foreign intervention faded, and the blockade of Gulf and Atlantic ports still in the hands of the Confederacy was drawn tighter and tighter, squeezing the very life out of the South.

Sherman's capture and burning of Atlanta and his subsequent march through Georgia to Savannah finally wrote finis to the expectations of even the most optimistic that the North was on the verge of military and political collapse.

By September, the last of the money from my jewelry had been spent; women were no longer able to pay me to have dresses and hats remodeled; austerity had made seamstresses of them all. Baptiste continued with his carving; but, as meticulous as he was about his work, it took days to complete a pipe and weeks for a chess set. Our lack of a steady income forced me to part reluctantly with a few of my precious gold coins. After Baptiste's brilliant success in establishing and running a cotton brokerage, I marveled at his naiveté about our day-to-day financial situation. I had kept him ignorant about the jewelry, fearing he would object and do something desperate to prevent my selling it; nor did I tell him about the gift from my father, intuitively certain there would come a time when it would be more urgently needed.

As part of Lincoln's reconstruction plans, Federal officials in occupied Confederate areas were urged to hire Negroes for work other than hard, physical labor on plantations, defense projects, and city improvements. Thus doors were literally opened and certain less strenuous jobs made available.

As I knew he would be, Baptiste was furious when I first suggested applying for such a position.

"No! Absolutely not. I will not have you so demean yourself working for Yankees."

"You'd rather commit suicide by slowly starving to death?"

"We've gotten along so far, haven't we? Why this sudden decision to work for the enemy?" he asked suspiciously.

"There's no more money. It's as simple as that."

"What about the women you were sewing for?"

"Have you seen me with any dresses lately? They have no money left either. Anyway, we weren't living entirely on that income." I had put it off as long as I could. Now he had to be apprised of what I'd been doing. "I've been selling the jewels you gave me."

"You've what!"

"We had to live, Baptiste, and Union women paid almost what each piece was worth. I sold them through the jeweler you bought them from, so he knew their value."

"I don't believe it. I didn't think you'd dispose of my gifts to you."

"Baptiste, believe me, it wasn't easy. I cherished every one of them as tokens of your love. But, I assure you, I appreciated them a whole lot more when they meant I could buy the food and medicine you needed. Each piece gave us a few more months of the necessities and comforts to make life bearable."

"All of them?"

"All but the pearls. I can't bring myself to part with them."

"You did it for me, Leah, don't deny it. You could

have left me and gone north any time you wanted. You would have been welcomed for fleeing the decadent, depraved South. Or as a white seeing the errors of the South's ways. Why did you stay?"

"Do you really need to ask, Baptiste? Don't you know my heart well enough by now to be sure I couldn't leave you?"

"What would you be doing if you did go to work for the Yankees?" He spat out the hated word.

"I don't know. I won't know until I apply."

"I don't like it. You'd be working for the same people who humiliate you on the street every day, who forced me to crawl like a deformed supplicant along their halls. No, we'll think of something else."

So for two more months we lived on what the garden produced, what my eggs could be bartered for, and gleanings from the fields and trees of my free Negro friends near the bayous. They insisted on my taking some of the meat when a hog was butchered and a share of the catch if shrimp or fish were brought in while I was there. My mother had been a Mamaloi, and I was assumed to be a priestess although I had never formally been elevated to that position.

"When the war is over," they said, "you'll come back to us. Meanwhile we give you what we can."

But trips to the bayous could not be made frequently, and thus we lived on the edge of starvation. Tops of carrots, roots of greens, all now went into the pot along with the parts usually cooked. Nothing edible was thrown away. No attempts at preparing savory, delectable dishes were made. Meals were no longer a delight but a means to stay alive.

In the mornings I searched for twigs and dried leaves to fuel our one fire that provided both heat and light in the evenings, and on which I cooked our single meal of the day. Daytimes we added extra layers of clothes to keep warm.

By late November the garden had been stripped bare of leaves, roots, and vines. A one-woman horde of scavengers, I greedily ripped out every particle of vegetation to meet the demands of our stomachs. When I saw a piece of fruit lying beneath someone's tree, I pounced on it as hungrily as if it were a rare jewel. Three half-rotten apples could be cooked up with a little sorghum for a tasty side dish.

During these trying weeks, I was often tempted to kill the last of my hens, but to do so would be like eating the seed rice, the last resort of the destitute and impoverished. It would mean all hope was gone. For half a week our diet consisted of an egg a day and some bread exchanged for other eggs.

"So it's come to this," Baptiste said meekly.

"It has."

"I'll have some money tomorrow for the pipe I've finished."

"It will feed us for two days, maybe four at the most," I said.

"Do you think you can get a job?"

"If there's anything available."

"No hard work," he insisted. "Nothing servile."

"The choice may not be mine, Baptiste. There is no disgrace in anything that will keep us alive. Do you think I felt degraded when I scrubbed floors at the hospital or emptied the slop jars? Many looked down on me, but I never looked down on myself. I learned long ago, it's what you think you are that counts, not how others see you. I'm a servant only if I think of myself as one. Life is too precious to view it through others' eyes."

"Do what you think you must then, Cherie."

Lieutenant-Colonel Blaise looked up with startled expression when I walked in. The only job open, as I'd expected, was as a cleaning woman for five officers. From five to eight in the morning I was to scrub, dust, and sweep. For the next two hours I would empty and polish—one at a time so the officers would not be inconvenienced—the brass spittoons. After that came the cleaning of the rooms designated as "latrines," emptying, scrubbing, filling pitchers with water. From then until six in the evening (in a fresh, clean apron) I was to keep pitchers and carafes filled, carry trays of food and wine, wash dishes and glasses used during the day, and run errands. A rather large assortment of jobs for one designated cleaning woman.

When I first applied, Colonel Blaise was reluctant to hire me. He obviously didn't expect his request for a Negro maid to be answered by one whose skin was almost as white as his. Whiter, actually, since he'd just come in off duty in the field. Once again I was confronted with the quizzical expression, the raised eyebrow of one unfamiliar with subtle variations in color. To him black was black and white was white, with no gradations in between. He was still recovering from the shock that not all nonwhites were former slaves.

Colonel Blaise spun his pen around on the blotter. "I—I don't think the work would suit you, Miss—"

"Leah. My father's name was Bonvivier, but I've never used it. Or do you mean I don't fit your image of a scrubwoman?"

"The work will be hard."

"Colonel Blaise, I have scrubbed hospital floors, emptied slop jars, nursed dying yellow fever patients, and for nearly three years been the sole support and companion of a man with no legs. I am not fragile and helpless. Nor do I shirk hard work. I need the money. Do I get the job?"

"You may start in the morning. This man you speak of. Is he—is he like yourself?"

"A free man of color? No, Colonel, he is a disabled Confederate veteran, wounded just prior to the capture of New Orleans."

"I'm surprised you would take care of a man like that, a white Southener."

"You needn't be. I've been his mistress since before the war. You should learn more about the customs of the city you have been sent to govern." I was amazed at my own audacity, and I waited for him to rebuke me.

"I see," he said quietly. "I'll expect you in the morning."

Baptiste was adamant about my not going back, but I was equally stubborn.

"The hours are too long, Leah, and the work beneath you."

"And the pay is good and we need every cent of it."

"The men will be rough and the language crude."

"I'm not naive, Baptiste. I've worked around soldiers before. They may try to shock or embarrass me at first, but ultimately their behavior will be a reflection of my attitude toward them."

"All right, but if one—just one—gets out of line, you're stopping. Promise?"

"I promise," but I was lying and I knew it.

The job was grueling. All five officers' suites had to be thoroughly scrubbed, dusted, swept, and everything put in order before any of the staff arrived at eight. Provided I wasn't needed for something else, the bathrooms could be done during the next hour, the doors kept open so there wouldn't be any embarrassing encounters. There were no inside facilities for me; merely a dilapidated privy overgrown with smilax.

Never a slow worker, I was sure I could handle the early-morning routine. If all went as anticipated. As usually happens, it did not. When I arrived the fourth morning, the place was a shambles. From the evidence on desks, tables, and floor, there had been a late-night conference. Papers were scattered everywhere. Empty glasses reeking of whiskey, overflowing ashtrays, cigar butts aimed at but missing the ashtrays and now scarring the wood, tobacco-spattered spittoons surrounded by halos of dirty brown spittle.

Where to begin? Getting a tray from the kitchen of the house now metamorphosized into offices, I cleared away glasses and ashtrays. The spittoons I emptied out the rear door and put under the pump. Later I would return and polish them. At the moment, I thought it would be more efficient to complete one particular task in all the rooms, rather than try to do everything in a single office. I realized my mistake when, at seven-thirty, while I was waxing the last of the desks and had only the floors to scrub, one of the officers walked in. I had been told a Lieutenant Pearson would soon be returning from leave, but I had not been informed about any of his habits.

"Why isn't my office ready?" he asked, coolly but not rudely.

"I'm sorry, sir. I understood I was to have them cleaned by eight o'clock."

"From now on, please have mine ready by seven-thirty. I prefer to begin work early."

"Yes, sir. If you'll sit in one of the other offices, I'll have your floor cleaned right up."

One of the more magnificent dwellings in the *Vieux Carré,* this house had been among the first commandeered and its owners evacuated after the Union captured the city. The broad hall ran the full depth to a rear gallery. Off it opened eight rooms: parlors, dining room, music room, library, bedrooms, and kitchen. When I first went there to work, the hall was used as a reception room; later desks were put in for subofficers.

Much of the original furniture, as well as carpets and draperies, remained; and I was horrified at the tears and scars and stains and burns on what had once been magnificent, treasured pieces.

Lieutenant Pearson occupied the small library near the rear of the house, so his office had borne less of the brunt from the previous night's rampage than the larger ones near the front. I had the high-pile oriental swept and the parquet border mopped within a few minutes.

Lieutenant Pearson was neither polite nor rude, just aloof. He showed me no more emotion than he would to a piece of furniture, neither raising his voice in anger to me when displeased nor smiling his thanks when his requests were granted. I filled the same function as his desk or chair, there to make his work more efficient, but not necessarily more pleasant.

"Where are the papers that were on my desk, Leah?" He forebore calling me Miss Bonvivier, although that was how I'd been introduced to the staff. Not because of my color, as a Southern white would do, but in acknowledgment of my position as servant. The former custom I had found debasing; the latter I accepted with equanimity as proper.

"I moved them while I dusted. They are here on a side table, still all in order."

"I prefer that they remain as I leave them."

"Yes, sir."

I finished the other offices, scrubbing tobacco stains out of the carpets with a stiff brush and mopping the wooden floors, by the time the rest of the staff came in. When I opened the door to the first bathroom, the odors and sights, more noisome revolting than anything I'd ecountered during my hospital work, forced me back into the corridor. I ran for the gallery and fresh air.

Slop jars had been pulled from the carved wooden commodes and left out in the room. Men, either drunk or careless, had missed, leaving puddles and stains on the floor. One jar had been knocked over, spilling its foul contents into a crumpled mass of towels, evidently put there in an attempt to clean up the mess. Small pools and spatters of vomit were drying to a hard crust in one corner and on the wall. Stale urine, stale vomit, stale feces. They were more formidable opponents to my determination not to quit than the superior, cavalier attitude of the officers who seemed unable to decide whether, having freed those whom they euphemistically called colored—to remove the taint of slavery—the saviors should consider the saved equals or a little less than human.

On the gallery I inhaled several deep breaths to clean my lungs of the nauseating odors. The sights I could not dismiss so easily. The decision was mine, and

I knew Baptiste would agree wholeheartedly if I chose to leave immediately with no advance notice. I knew also what remarks would follow me out the door. "Lazy slut." "Told ya nigras quit when there's any real work, would rather have a free handout." "Maybe thought she was too good for it. Mostly white, you know."

Pride of two heritages—no, three—pounded through my veins: African royalty doomed to slavery, light-hearted Polynesian spirit of freedom, and Creole strength of purpose. I would shame none of them by retreating before a situation soon remedied with hot, soapy water, a scrub brush, and strong muscles.

I tied a clean cloth across my nose and mouth, hitched up my skirts, started a fire in the stove, pumped several pots of water, and started in. I left the door wide open and took my time so the men could see just what I had to do. Colonel Blaise looked in once, his confused expression a mixture of sympathy and apology. The others passed by with averted faces. I worked without stopping, knowing if once I paused to rest, I could not return to it. By noon the two bathrooms were spotlessly clean, rid of all odors and stains. As a final fillip, perhaps of defiance, perhaps from a need to see beauty where there'd been ugliness, I put a large bouquet of fragrant December narcissus on a commode in each bathroom.

Many a morning I had to dust and straighten offices in which late-night conference had been held, but never again was I subjected to the onerous task of cleaning up foul, filth-bespattered floors or carpets. I assumed Colonel Blaise had made it patently clear what the terms "officer" and "gentleman" implied.

As Lieutenant Pearson had requested, I never touched the papers on his desk, but I often straightened and sorted those of the other officers. When Colonel Blaise saw my method of bringing order out of chaos by separating letters from orders, requests needing attention from those already handled, he asked if I would mind filing them rather than putting them in neat piles. Since it would relieve some of the tedium, I readily agreed and found it pleasant to be a part of the official routine. Soon I was doing the filing for several of the officers.

Frequently French and Spanish-speaking Creoles came to the office to request aid or in response to an order to appear. Many of them spoke no English, or at best understood only a few words. It made an already frightening situation more unnerving. They were already in deadly fear of a Yankee uniform and possible retaliation for an unknown infringement of a new law. Coming into the office during one such frustrating confrontation, I unconsciously began translating for the elderly Frenchman clutching and tearing at his hat. Once the situation had been resolved, I left and returned to what I had been doing earlier.

Within an hour, Colonel Blaise called me into his office.

"Stupid of me not to realize," he said, "that since you speak both French and English you could help us out with translating."

"Yes, sir, I could. I also speak some Spanish, although there aren't many who still use that language. I also understand the Cajun dialect; that is, the speech of those who live primarily in the bayous."

I enjoyed watching his expressive brows arch again in astonishment.

"It would appear you have a number of talents that would prove useful around here. Perhaps you should take off that apron and put them to work."

"Sir?"

"I'm going to put a desk in the center hall and install you as a receptionist. We need someone to sort the mail, decide which office the callers should be directed to, make appointments, and continue with the filing and translating when needed. I can't increase your wages because I'll have to get someone at least part-time to replace you as cleaning woman, but I think you'll find the work more enjoyable. Also you will not need to report until just a few minutes before eight."

Baptiste was as pleased as I with the elevation in status and became more amenable to my continuing. Already, the pay had considerably eased our financial strain, and the dinner table once more was replete with good food.

I put aside my cheap cotton dresses, and would have torn them up if I hadn't thought I might need them still. A simple, two-piece dark blue velveteen seemed suitable for the new position once I had substituted white linen collar and cuffs for the frayed lace originals.

"You look very nice, Miss Bonvivier," Colonel Blaise greeted me. His mode of address did not pass unnoticed by either the other men on the staff or me. It was an outward and visible sign of an inward and subtle hypocrisy.

"Thank you, sir," I smiled. The smile was my panache. The game was one I had played before.

PART III

The Decision

Chapter Twenty-five

GRANT RECEIVED LEE'S SURRENDER at Appomattox Court House on April 12, 1865.

Peace came and with it more uncertainties than ever. While the nation was at war, the citizens of New Orleans were the enemy and knew what to expect. At the same time, until the conflict was resolved, the Union conquerors subdued the individual Confederate sections with cruel and violent atrocities; but the South remained undaunted because there endured a very real if feeble flame of hope that eventually these dehumanizing acts would be avenged.

That flame was quenched forever when Lee relinquished his sabre. The Confederate States of America were ashes and rubble, torn-up documents, empty uniforms, gutted houses, and desolate fields. Worst of all at first was the bleak uncertainty about the future of the South. Would she continue to be occupied or would she be allowed to lick her physical and emotional wounds unhampered?

We waited, as one waits breathlessly for the rumble of thunder after the first flash of lightning, but nothing happened. Neither a violent upheaval nor a sudden return to normalcy. The streets continued to be crowded with Yankee troops who went right on playing their game of harassment with impunity. The political and economic life of the city remained under the control of army commanders. Hordes of Northerners, replete with money and the cunning talents of all scavengers, deluged the city. Like the mythological Harpies they came, sharpened claws outstretched, and began stuffing into their seemingly bottomless carpetbags whatever pleased their fancy. Businesses abandoned because of financial ruin, deserted by men going to war, or confiscated when the loyalty oath was not forthcoming were ready prey for these people. They sneered at the feeble attempts of the defeated to retain some pride, and blatantly declared they would soon own all of Louisiana. They came very close to being right.

When I saw the wives of these men parading the streets in their gaudy finery, I regretted I'd had to sell my jewels during the war. I could have received twice their value from these women eager to buy their way into New Orleans society. I probably should have used my father's gold and saved the jewelry, but there was no point in wasting my emotional energy on a *fait accompli*. Somehow my intuition still told me the gold was going to be invaluable to us in the future, that it was going to figure importantly in opening up a whole new way of life for us. Little did I know then just how dramatically it would affect our situation. Or how at times I would wish we had never possessed it.

Oh, there were changes, to be sure. It seemed as though, with all the comings and goings, the staff in our office was never the same from one day to the next. I learned one man's idiosyncrasies, only to find him gone and replaced with one whose quirks were vastly different but just as peculiar. One wanted coffee precisely at nine; another, tea at eleven. The office was busier than ever with the cases of lost businesses and other inequities multiplying each day. Abuses were rampant, and Colonel Blaise was hard-pressed to deal with all the injustices equitably and swiftly.

Then the day came when planters could apply to have their property restored to them. With the plantations under the control of Federal officials or usurped by freed slaves with the approval of those officials, former planters had feared the worst: the land would be confiscated as enemy property. Many of the owners had been lost during the war, either by death or exile. Others had their spirits broken, depleting the ranks of those available to argue their rights. I knew Colonel Blaise wondered why I, a free woman of color, should feel sympathy for whites who had kept me and others like myself—if not in slavery—beyond the pale of accepted society and under rigid restrictions. Did my white heritage influence my opinion in this area? I doubted it. The fact I was born in the South? No, it was a much more primitive emotion stirring in me during those trying years.

The only two men I had ever loved were white. I had learned of my father's death from a broken heart at being exiled and losing two of his sons, and Baptiste had been mutilated by his enemies. Therefore, they were my enemies, too. I had seen gentle people humiliated; innocent people, guilty of nothing more than loyalty to their own families, were imprisoned; and former slaves re-enslaved by what should have been freedom.

No, I had no reason to love the Yankees who had insulted me just as they did white Southerners. I had been called "nigger" and "whore," assaulted by soldiers who assumed that all women of color were used to being bedded by any white man lusting after a woman, and rounded up with former slaves to work on the fortifications. I had escaped the last terror only because one of the white women I was expected to despise interceded for me and made me her nominal slave so I could get a pass to walk the streets where from childhood I had walked in complete freedom.

Thus I knew the feelings of those who thought they would not be able to reclaim their land. Being allowed to do so was a first victory after so many defeats. It was the first step back—no, forward—to self-esteem for the many people dispossessed during the long, hard years of Federal occupation. Baptiste and I would be able to move out to the house which I knew was still standing although looted of its beautiful furnishings. Like a woman who has been violated, the exterior seemed curiously untouched if a little soiled, but the interior was scarred by the agonies of being raped again and again. While Baptiste supervised planting the fields of sugarcane, I could begin restoring the house. Not to its original grandeur, but as a comfortable home. I envisioned Baptiste sitting in the shade of an immense live oak while he directed the workers. More than enough former slaves were looking for work to supply the hands he would need.

There were several weeks before planting time in January, and by scrimping we could save enough to provide for the workers until the gardens they would cultivate began to produce. The old quarters could be fixed up for them to live in. And I still had the gold! This, I knew now, was what I had been hoarding it for.

I was impatient to leave my job, but I knew that each week I remained at it would add to the savings we would need to get over the rough months until our first harvest.

When I reached home after work, Baptiste was sitting asleep in his chair in the sunny courtyard. On his lap was a pipe he'd been carving; and beside him on the table, his tools. I paused a minute at the gate, noting the relaxed look on his face and the way he held the pipe gently in one hand. So different from the first weeks when his face was constantly lined with pain and anxiety, and his muscles remained tense even in sleep. A real inspiration getting him started on this hobby; it had kept him occupied, but more important, it had brought in a small income, enough to contribute to the household expenses. His hand-carved pipes, created to relieve a shortage during the war, had come to be valued pieces of real craftsmanship.

Baptiste worked most of each day. Soon after I left him at breakfast, he wheeled out to the gallery or rolled down the ramp, tools in his lap, to the table we had set up.

Tiptoeing over to him, I kissed his cheek.

"Wake up. I have special news."

"Good news?" he asked. "I could use some."

"Very, very good. Oh, Baptiste, you can go back to the plantation."

"Don't tease, Cherie."

"I'm not. It's true. You can apply to have it returned to you. Word was released today. Everyone's talking about it."

"How soon, Leah? How soon?"

"There will be papers to fill out to request reestablishment of ownership. They're going to post the hours tomorrow. I'll see if we have to sign up for an appointment. Surely it won't take long after that."

I thought Baptiste would be elated. Instead he answered glumly, "It's not that easy, Leah. I have no papers. No title, no deed. Not even a will."

"Are you sure?" I wasn't going to give up that easily. "Wouldn't they be somewhere in the house? Or with a lawyer?"

"The first two—the title and deed—were with our lawyer, but his office was burned just before he fled to Vicksburg. As to a will, I don't know whether there was one. I was the only heir."

"But surely there are parish records."

"Maybe so. We'll see." Baptiste turned in his chair as though to drop the whole subject, but I persisted.

"Cheer up. Just wait. We'll be moving out there before you know it. It'll be so much better for you than sitting here day after day."

"And how do we manage with no income?"

"Leave it to me. I have it all figured out."

"Do you, my beautiful financial wizard? Come here and sit on my lap. You're much more desirable than this pipe I've been working on. And a whole lot softer."

I knew that, deep inside, he was cheered by the news. He would be a planter again. Though he always disclaimed any interest in the land, saying he preferred the gay life of New Orleans, in his heart he cherished his family acres and was eager to put down his own roots. I could never be his wife, nor be accepted as mistress of the plantation; but after all we'd been through together, I cared little for what people would think about my living there. Changes of many kinds were already in the wind, and though those winds might blow slowly, one could already feel them bending long-established traditions.

Rereading the official announcement the next day, I learned Baptiste would need to make an appointment and take with him the very papers he said he didn't have. Others were in the same position, for a later paragraph recommended checking with the parish courthouse to have the titles and deeds investigated and certified copies made.

With written permission from Baptiste, I was allowed to make this request for him. Much to my disgust, the official I had to deal with subjected me to a thirty-minute inquisition, more to humiliate me with embarrassing questions than because he didn't believe me. When I informed the man of Baptiste's disability, the smirk on his face told me he was impatient to ask all the details of our personal life. By maintaining a haughty mien, I was able to intimidate him until he became more businesslike. Worse than the questioning, however, was the fact that having the title and deed checked took some of my precious gold. The claim had to be established through new surveys and a study of parish records.

Unknown to Baptiste, a will had been probated after the death of his parents in Virginia; and once the deed was cleared, he was told to appear at the headquarters set up to handle claims. I hired a buggy, which took more of the gold so carefully hoarded, but I would not have Baptiste exposed to curious glances on a public horsecar.

The attitude of those in charge was curt to the point of rudeness. Only reluctantly did they relinquish what control they maintained over Southern property. A red-faced, tobacco-chewing official, unshaven and wearing a grimy shirt, told us to sit down. He watched with obvious superiority as Baptiste struggled off his crutches and into the chair; then he made some crude remark I didn't catch but which set him laughing at his own wit.

Picking up the title and deed, the official rolled a tobacco cud around his tongue, pursed his lips, and spat a mouthful of dirty brown juice toward a brass spittoon at my feet. Whether by accident or design, he missed his target, and my skirt was spattered with the thick brown filth and spittle that splashed up from the floor. By concentrating on the desktop and squeezing Baptiste's shoulder, I kept myself from gagging and Baptiste from saying something that might have ended the interview immediately. I had long since learned, and Baptiste would have to learn, the secret of living within oneself and ignoring the ugliness now existing in the world around us.

Baptiste filled out the forms, answered many of the same humiliating questions put to me, and signed where he was told. A man who had never done anything he didn't want to, he was quickly learning to follow orders without argument. He was enduring all this humiliation with more pride than I had seen even when he was the most popular and eligible man in prewar New Orleans. His fine Creole heritage was evident in his soft-spoken manner and squarely set shoulders. Before the two of us left the office, the official recognized exactly who he was dealing with. He held the door open for us as Baptiste ignored his offer of help with the crutches. Baptiste would be informed how soon he could take possession of the family estate.

Once more a man of property, Baptiste became a different person. No longer would he be dependent on me for support, an intolerable situation for one brought up to revere and cherish women. No longer did he feel that the loss of his legs made him less a man.

Yet weeks went by with no official word about his claim, weeks which took us past first planting time in

January. We had until May to get the cane in, and already it was the first of March. If we were to feed our workers off the land, it was also imperative we get the hands hired and a garden planted. Baptiste got edgy again, and his depressed moods became more and more frequent. Every day I went by the land office, but was always told the same thing: the claims took time to investigate even when all the papers were in order. We would be notified as soon as possible.

To add to my difficulties, conditions where I worked became intolerable. Unfortunately for both himself and New Orleans, Colonel Blaise took the word "reconstruction" too literally for those Northern officials who thought it should be interpreted as revenge rather than rebuilding. He received orders to leave Louisiana.

I was in his office, helping him pack his books and papers.

"This is a very sad day for New Orleans, Colonel Blaise. I know you've been doing what you could to restore some sort of order and prosperity. You've been very fair."

"I took your advice. I listened and I watched. I've learned to love New Orleans, and I hoped I could help restore it to its former charm and greatness. At the same time, of course, that certain necessary changes were made."

I nodded. "Where will you be going?"

"Back to Connecticut, to a small farm. I'm not regular army so I'm resigning my commission. It's nothing like the plantations here. How is Mr. Fontaine's claim coming along?"

"Slowly, sir. We worry we won't get out there in time to plant the cane."

"I'll see if I can put in a word before I leave."

"Thank you, sir; we'd appreciate that. I'll miss working with you. There have been few Northerners like you."

"Perhaps more will come now the war is over, and there's no longer any need to consider the South an enemy. The major who is replacing me lived for a time in New Orleans, so we can hope he will be sympathetic to the city's needs. He's been attached to one of the other offices and is familiar with the conditions."

So had David Farragut—the Union admiral who captured New Orleans—been a Southerner, I thought. But that didn't prevent him from attacking the city and threatening to level it if his orders were ignored.

"I've enjoyed having you work with me, Miss Bonvivier, and I'm sure you'll get along well with Major Anderson."

"Thank you, sir. I can only hope he will keep me on."

Two days later I would have bitten my tongue before saying those words.

Charles Anderson was standing by Colonel Blaise's desk when I walked in. I wanted to turn and run, to get away from my former attacker as fast as I could and never return, but I was rooted to the spot. The thought of having to work with the man who had insulted me and tried to rape me at the quadroon ball years earlier made me physically ill. My only hope was that what had been a nightmare to me had been no more than a minor irritation to Anderson and he would not remember me. Almost eight years had passed since he'd seen me in a ball gown with hair piled up in curls and poufs. Now wearing a simple navy serge dress and my hair pulled back in a chignon, I should present quite a different appearance than I did that fateful night.

"Good morning, Major Anderson. I'm Miss Bonvivier, and I have been doing clerical work in the office while Colonel Blaise was in charge. Perhaps you would like me to continue in the same position."

Anderson turned around, and the sardonic smile on his face told me he knew exactly who I was.

"Good morning, Leah. This is really a most unexpected pleasure. You may indeed continue working in a position that should offer some additional benefits to both of us."

"How did you know?"

"I make it a point to learn about my subordinates. By knowing their weaknesses I can control them from the very first day. That makes it so much easier on all of us, with no differences of opinion to cloud the atmosphere. I may say I have looked forward to this meeting with genuine anticipation."

Every word he said had implications I did not like, but I could not leave or do anything to jeopardize my position until Baptiste and I were ready to move to the plantation.

"I think you will find my work satisfactory, Major Anderson. Colonel Blaise always seemed pleased."

"I'm sure I will, Leah. Just follow my orders and there will be no problems."

For the most part, Charles Anderson was all business in the office, and once evening came I could forget the ten hours I had just spent in his company. At first I waited tensely for some subtle advance or innuendo. I was not conceited enough to think he lusted after me every minute of the day, but I knew that somehow, some way he would avenge the humiliation he had suffered at Baptiste's hands the night of the ball. And what better way than to force his will on me now that he knew I was in the vulnerable position of having to work?

Soon enough I learned why he stayed aloof and superior in the office. Several times a day, Mrs. Anderson walked over from the home he had commandeered or rode up in her carriage after a morning of shopping. We had never been formally introduced, since it was beneath Mrs. Anderson's dignity to put one of my caste on an equal footing with herself. A bitter, dried-up woman in her early thirties, she made it immediately apparent she hated everything about the South. Her hate was intensified by the realization that her husband's lack of ability and influence had been the cause of his being given a minor position in what she considered the backwash city of New Orleans instead of an important post in Washington, D.C.

Mrs. Anderson's every action bespoke how little she trusted her husband. Although she seemed to ignore my presence, I was aware of her heavy-lidded, suspicious glances when she thought I wasn't looking. I overheard enough of their conversations, carried on behind the closed door of his office, to learn that Major Anderson was wont to return home late, very late, several nights a week. Each succeeding morning, she appeared at the office, first to upbraid him and then plead with him. If I hadn't hated her so much, I would have felt sorry for her. Not because she had a philandering husband, but because she married him in the first place.

Charles Anderson still reminded me of a lizard. If he were finding pleasure in places other than his own bed, it was not because women thought him irresistible but because he was paying for it.

Finally the official letter came apprising Baptiste that his claim was legitimate. There was also a second paragraph that threatened to be a much more formidable obstacle than any we'd encountered so far. Baptiste was carving a chess set for a man who'd bought a large piece of whale ivory from a sea captain. Baptiste had worked with more care on these delicate pieces than on any he'd attempted before, and he was justifiably proud of those already completed.

For a moment after he'd read the letter, I thought he was going to kill himself. With one of the knives, he stabbed and stabbed at the paper until he'd torn it to shreds. When he picked up a larger knife, I lunged for his hand, thinking he meant to harm himself; but he brought it down on an ivory king, completely destroying the beautiful, fragile piece. Then he collapsed on the table, sobbing uncontrollably.

The brief, happy interlude of hope and anticipation had been brought to an end with one word: *taxes*.

Baptiste was told he would have to pay taxes due on the land for all the years since 1861. The taxes and accrued interest had been figured at new rates, and they added up to an enormous sum. It was so far above what we could pay, it was ridiculous to think we could ever come up with that amount.

Baptiste had just two weeks to make the full payment or the government would repossess the land and it would be lost to him forever. It would be put up for sale at auction, and being productive land, it would bring bids much higher than the amount due.

"That's it, Leah," he said, scarcely raising his head from the table. "That's the end of all our dreams."

"No, it's not! We have two weeks."

"Don't be idiotic! Where the hell are we going to find that kind of money? We don't make that much together in a year, in five years."

"Don't call me idiotic!" I cried. "Maybe you're ready to give up. I'm not. By God, I've faced worse predicaments than this and come up smiling."

"Well, if you've faced anything like this, I don't know about it. If you have a magic formula for making money," he said almost sarcastically, "don't keep it a secret."

"All right, so I've never had to worry about this much money; but if I could learn to cope with shortages during the war, or—or not give up on life when I lost my only child, I'm not going to let this put me under."

"You're a dreamer."

"No, I'm not. I'm a realist, and that's my salvation. Let's look at what we have and what we need."

"Nothing. That's what we have." Baptiste slammed his fist down on the arm of the chair.

"Nonsense. Now help me add things up. Here, take this paper and begin putting down assets. First, this house. It's in good condition, should bring a good price. It's in a desirable location, too. Then the furnishings. They're all fine antiques. Our best bet is to sell them at auction, not to a store. Maybe to some of those Yankee wives who are enamored of anything that belonged to old Southern families."

"And where do we live when you put us out of the house?"

I began to sense a spark of admiration for my ability to get right to the point of the problem, although he was probably sure I was refusing to recognize the impossible.

"On the plantation, silly."

"And we sleep on the floor?"

"Yes, if we have to. Dammit, this is your land, your family's land we're talking about. Oh, hell, I don't know why I'm doing all this for you. My ancestors never owned land, just worked it for someone else."

"I'm sorry, Leah. It's just that it all seems so impossible."

"Well, it's not. How much do you think the house and furnishings will bring?"

"Less than half as much as we need."

"This chess set. Do you think Mr. Chastaine would pay in advance?"

"Perhaps. I'll ask him. It's almost finished, but that's still far short of what we need."

"There are the gold pieces," I said.

"No, we don't touch those."

"You're right. We need them to carry us the first few months.'"

"I didn't mean that. They're yours, and I'm not going to allow you to spend what is really your inheritance to help solve my financial problems. So we're still several hundred dollars short."

I said nothing for a few minutes. I had the solution, but I knew what Baptiste's response would be, and I wondered if I should suggest it. But we had gone this far, and there was to be no turning back. Baptiste had to trust my judgment.

"There is one way we can get the money," I said quietly.

"How?" The dull tone of voice showed his disbelief.

"The pearls. If I have something to sell, why hoard it?" I tried to speak in a light, bantering tone to hide my real feelings.

"No, Leah! They're all you have left." He'd been upset enough when he'd learned about my selling the other jewels, but he'd known why I did it. The pearls were his last gift before René was born, and he'd added an additional length the day our son was six months old. Baptiste slammed his fist down on the table, the completed chessmen flew in all directions.

I bent down to pick them up off the grass. "You saved my life twice, Baptiste, and I want to save yours now. I know what the land means to you. Once you have the plantation back, things will be different."

He, too, leaned over to recover the chess pieces and fell in an awkward heap on the ground. For one brief moment he forgot he had no legs.

He lay there moaning, but not from pain. He had become numb to physical discomfort, but under emotional duress he felt completely helpless. Although my arms ached to comfort him, I knew pity would only deepen his despair at his complete dependency on me.

"Are you hurt?" I asked as casually as possible.

"No. Just help me back into my damned chair."

Nothing more was said that night about taxes or the plantation.

Chapter Twenty-six

THE PRESSURE AT HOME was not eased any by a situation developing at work. Several times Major Anderson asked me to work late, and I agreed only because at least one junior officer was still around. Then came the night when the others had already left and he asked me to stay to finish some filing.

"I'm sorry, Major Anderson. This is the third evening in a row, and I really must get home." I started toward the door.

"Don't move away from me, Leah. I've asked you to call me Charles." He leered at me, and I saw the saliva trickling down his chin. "Remember, I know how you quadroons are brought up. Trained to please white men. That's all I want."

With each word he moved toward me, backing me into a corner. Instinctively I reached behind me and opened the foor into an adjoining room. That was a mistake. It was one of the bedrooms. The bed was made up, the sheets turned down.

"You see, Leah," he grinned, "it's all prepared. Just be as nice to me as you are to the other white men you give pleasure to."

"Let me out of here!" I screamed as loudly as I could, hoping my voice would carry to the banquette outside and frighten him into letting me go. "I'm not one of the whores you pay to service you."

"I know you're not, and I don't intend to pay you. You're going to become my mistress." He spoke calmly, but with an assurance even more frightening than his lust.

"Are you crazy? What makes you think I'd be your mistress? I find you hideous and revolting. Go home to your wife. She seems to find you desirable, though God knows why."

"Calm down, Leah. I want you for a mistress, and I think you'll agree I can be very persuasive. It's either that or go to prison for theft."

"Theft?" Now I was really beginning to panic. "I've never stolen anything in my life." But what would be my word against his, an officer in the United States Army, the victorious occupier of enemy territory?

"Yes, I believe you have a small, soft leather bag of twenty-dollar gold pieces."

"Given to me by my father, Jean-Paul Bonvivier, in 1862, right after New Orleans was captured. They are mine. I stole them from no one."

"But he is dead, isn't he? So who will believe you?"

Baptiste knew the gold had been a gift from my father; he knew exactly how much I had originally and how much had been spent. He would come to my defense immediately if I were accused and his first reaction would be to challenge Anderson to a duel, impossible in his condition. Even if Anderson had the grace to refuse—which with his satanic humor I doubted he would—he'd delight in humiliating the man who had frustrated his first attempt to take me. At the least Baptiste would insist on my quitting work.

"By the way," Anderson said, "if you are thinking of having your—your protector, I think you call him—verify your story, I will simply name him as accomplice, or at least a user of stolen property. I saw him pay for the title search with one of the gold pieces."

"You saw—"

"I was in an adjacent room. You didn't know I was there. That was really when I got the idea of making you my mistress. I was willing to wait when I learned that Colonel Blaise would be leaving and I would be taking his place. Very brilliant, I think. I knew you would only scorn my advances unless I had something to hold over you. So you see, I have a complete description of the red morocco bag and the approximate amount of money. After all, it can be assumed you've spent some of it. A search of your house would quickly turn up the stolen property. I can order the search right now, so don't be making plans in that pretty head of yours for hiding it."

"And if I let you make love to me tonight?" My mind was working ahead to the moment when either I would be in his power or he in mine.

"Oh, not just tonight, Leah. I said I wanted you as my mistress, for as long as I'm forced to remain in this uncivilized place. And it must be a cooperative venture. I shall expect to be the recipient of all the various techniques you—you quadroons are very adept at." He spoke the word "quadroon" in an unctuous tone, as one speaks of something that is both vile and fascinating.

He certainly knew I would hide the leather bag as soon as I got home, so there must be something else he could hold over my head that he wasn't revealing at the moment. I would have to be very, very cautious.

"I—I can't be away from home every night. I would have to explain my absence." I was fighting to work my way out of this nightmare, a nightmare from which I couldn't awaken. I might try to escape from him by fighting and clawing my way out, but aroused as he was, I knew he would be too strong for me. My best move might be to appear to give in to him, but by using delaying tactics, wait for an opportune moment to slip out of his grasp.

"Enough! I don't give a damn about your worries. I want you, and I want you now." His voice was no longer oily-smooth. His frustration was becoming deadly anger. I realized I had to be careful; he was not a man one could humor easily. I would have to take my cues from his actions.

Suddenly he grabbed me, covering my mouth and

face with slobbering kisses, all the while running his hands roughly up and down my body. He became more frantic, squeezing my breasts so hard I moaned in pain.

"That's it," he whispered huskily, "respond to me. You like it, don't you? Say you love me. Say it! Say it!" He bit my ear lobe, and I could no longer hold back the screams.

"Take off your dress," he urged. "Hurry! I can't wait much longer."

Thank God he didn't rip it off. As slowly as possible I undid the buttons and slipped the gown down over my hips. I had finally gained an insight into the workings of the man's unstable mind. In order to make love successfully, he had to attack suddenly, and the act must not be delayed. If I could succeed in putting him off a little longer, he might not lose his desire, but he could become impotent.

However, even as I finished removing my petticoat, he lunged and threw me down on the bed, panting with desperate lust. Repulsed by his bony, milk-white body, I buried my face in the pillow, all the while fighting when he forced me over onto my back. Then I realized my attempts to fight him off only aroused him all the more. It was just what he needed to keep him in readiness.

I changed tactics and lay limp on the bed, unresponsive but seemingly submissive. There was danger in defying him, but I would have to take that chance. It would probably mean my being accused of theft, as he'd threatened, and an end to all our dreams of going to the plantation, but pride more than fear of physical harm refused to let me be mastered by this man. I was not so foolish as to prefer death to dishonor, but if I could escape him this one time, I had a plan I was sure would put an end to his pursuit.

"Don't just lie there!" he screamed. "Fight me! Resist, damn you."

When I didn't obey, he bit one of my nipples until he drew blood; startled by the pain, I clawed his face until he stopped. It was all he needed to raise him to a peak of desire. I waited for the perfect moment. When he was most vulnerable, I raised my knee and aimed a single, swift jab directly at his scrotum.

Now it was his turn to scream and roll over helpless on the bed. Whether from pain or from shock that I would dare to attack him in such a way, he passed out. One arm and part of a leg dangled off the side of the bed, and he was breathing heavily into the pillow. I had to check an irresistible urge to smother him with the other pillow as he lay there. But I would follow my first idea, one that should end his advances and at the same time not put me in peril.

While he was still unconscious, I quickly put into a small packet, a piece of cloth dampened with his sweat, a small cutting from his hair, and two fingernail clippings from his left hand. I hurried home to Baptiste, hiding the articles until I could find time to work alone.

Just after midnight I went into the garden. The moon was almost full, and I recalled the Voodoo ceremonies I'd participated in on just such nights as this. A faint wisp of cloud blew across the face of the moon, and I heard a mockingbird stir on the branch above me. Then came the haunting sound of a mourning dove from somewhere deep in the bayou. I hoped I would remember the incantation I must recite. It had been a long time since I'd called on Damballa to come to my aid.

Afraid Baptiste would miss me beside him, I hurriedly dug into the cache hidden under an oleander bush. From it I took the other items I needed and slipped them into a bandana. Back in the kitchen, and working by candlelight, I laid the sweat-soaked cloth in a flat square. On it I placed the hair and nail cuttings. To these I added a narrow strip of snake skin, several grains of powdered brick, and a small amount of yellow ochre. Wailing in a low, monotonous tone, I sprinkled cayenne pepper over all this. I easily recalled the words of the chant once I'd begun the Voodoo ceremony.

Still repeating the required litany, I brought the four corners of the cloth up to make a small pouch, closing it with a red string twisted three times around the points. To fasten it securely, I sealed it with wax drippings from the candle I passed over the bag seven times. Just so the recipient would recognize the bag for what it was, I stuck four long pins through it in such a way that they touched and crossed exactly in the center.

Physically exhausted and emotionally drained after all I'd been through, I slid into bed beside Baptiste and immediately fell asleep.

Ironically, I had almost laid aside my plans about making the bag when I came home from the encounter with Anderson. Baptiste greeted me with the first good news we'd had in weeks. In spite of my being late again, he was waiting on the gallery with a big smile on his face. He was still a very handsome man, with his thick, wavy black hair, cheeks as rosy as a child's, bright eyes that never lost their sparkle, and a warm grin which always started my heart beating faster.

"Leah, I thought you'd never get here. But, Cherie, no more late nights for you. In fact, no more working for those damned Yankees. You're free! I mean really free now." He let loose with a Rebel yell that must have been heard clear to Congo Square.

"Why? Tell me before I go crazy."

"We have enough money for the taxes."

"Where? How?"

"Come in the kitchen. I've fixed supper, and I'll tell you all about it while we eat."

The news was surprising as it was welcome. Baptiste's father-in-law, who owned land next to the Fontaine plantation, had never lost his property or his wealth. Now he wanted to add to his holdings by buying some of Baptiste's land adjacent to his own. He had agreed to pay full value, but more important, he was willing to advance the money in time to pay the taxes on condition Baptiste deed the land to him as soon as the government released it.

"Why didn't he just wait and buy all the land for the amount of the taxes?" I asked. "He could have bid on it."

"I don't know." Baptiste shook his head. "I wondered the same thing. Maybe he feels guilty about the way Marie Louise treated me. Maybe he's trying to assuage a guilty conscience for some of the black marketing he did during the war. He made plenty out of his compatriots. Or maybe he was afraid someone else would bid higher than he wanted to go and then refuse to sell him the parcel of land he's getting from me. I didn't question him too closely, that's for sure."

"And it's enough?" I asked. "Really enough to make the payment on time?" I couldn't believe we were that close to saving the land.

"More than we needed. We'll still have to sell this house, but we won't have to worry about selling all the furniture. And we won't have to touch your gold. We'll have enough to get by until we harvest a crop."

At the mention of the gold, a chill went through me. All this still didn't release me from the threat of prison. I had to frighten Charles Anderson enough so he wouldn't dare to harm me. I would proceed with the Voodoo.

"Tell them tomorrow you're quitting." Baptiste interrupted my thoughts. "We'll ride out to the plantation on Saturday as soon as we've gone by the tax office." I swallowed my fears and smiled.

In the morning I arrived at work earlier than usual, and I was already busy at my desk before the junior officers arrived. As usual Anderson was the last to come in.

"What's this filthy thing on my desk?" Anderson yelled.

"It looks like a *gris-gris*, Major," Lieutenant Grimes said.

334 *Barbara Ferry Johnson*

"What the hell's a *gris-gris*?"

"Voodoo, Major. A Voodoo charm. Looks like somebody wants to do you in. That one there's the most dangerous kind."

Out of the corner of my eye I saw the lieutenant glance slyly over at me, but I continued working as though I hadn't heard any of their conversation.

"Nonsense," Anderson sputtered. "That kind of stupid Creole superstition died out years ago. Get this damned thing off my desk and out of sight. It's disgusting."

He didn't believe, but I noticed he didn't touch it himself, and for the remainder of the day he was more restless than usual. He jumped uneasily at every noise. He was frightened, not so much by the *gris-gris* which he didn't recognize for the potent charm it was—no Creole would have ignored it—but by not knowing what might come next. He didn't know he could seek out a Voodoo priestess or doctor to learn why someone was determined to harm him, or how to ward off danger. Certain he would ask about these things, I'd been prepared to enlighten him and then inform the priestess to whom I'd send him just what to tell him. That would be the end of his attacks on me. But in his ignorance, he didn't ask the right questions. I would have to find some way to propel him to do so.

Early in the afternoon, I walked into his office with papers I'd prepared for him to sign. "Do not ignore the *gris-gris*, Major," I said calmly. "It is strong Voodoo magic."

He looked up startled. "Don't be ridiculous, Leah. It's just a bag of trash."

"Oh, no, it is very powerful. Whoever put it there means you real harm." I should never have uttered the last sentence. I didn't know it, but it was going to lead directly to my own undoing and put my life in more serious jeopardy than it was already.

"Well," he growled, "I don't intend to be intimidated by the stupidity and ignorance of near savages." He looked directly at me.

"You are a brave man, Major. Not many would have the courage to ignore such a warning."

He puffed up like a frog, just as I knew he would, making easier my next request. I wasn't quite ready to say I was leaving permanently. That would take a little more time. Two junior officers were nearby when I spoke next, just as I wanted. I knew Anderson could not deny my request while they were listening.

"Major Anderson, because of previous plans, I won't be able to work late tonight. However, if the work piles up, I'll be able to next week. Also I would like tomorrow off."

I had never asked for time off, so I knew it would seem strange if he refused me.

"All right," he relented, glaring. "But if you're away tomorrow, you'll have to make up for it by staying late *every* night, and there will be no repetition of last night's folly. I'm sure you haven't forgotten so quickly the little surprise I have for you."

Once back from the ride to the plantation, I could contact other members of the Voodoo cult; and among them, they would work out a plan to send Anderson running for his life, not only from New Orleans but away from the South.

In the morning we set out in a rented buggy, going first to the tax office. With the amount from the land purchase covering more than half of what was owing, the official agreed to give Baptiste an extension on the balance due until he could sell the house. We'd never before met this man, who had kind eyes and a sympathetic understanding of Baptiste's disability. Relieved of the pressure of having to dispose of the house in the city at an unfair price, we rode through the country as gleefully as two children on a school holiday.

I had packed a picnic lunch, but Baptiste insisted on driving over as much of the land as we could take the buggy before stopping to eat.

"It's mine again, Leah. Do you have any idea what that means to me?"

"I don't remember your spending much time out here before the war," I teased.

"I was young and foolish. Time may not have healed my wounds, but it's certainly knocked some sense into my head. Father tried to tell me. He tried to make me learn all about cane production, but I wouldn't listen. So now I have to learn by trial and error. We might have a good crop, but we could just as easily have none at all. Ready to bear with me?"

"You know I am. How about the workers you're going to hire? They'll know enough to make a crop. They all worked the cane fields before."

"If they'll put forth the effort."

"Surely they will if they agree to work on shares as you propose. They'll be as eager for a good crop as you are."

"We'll see. Where's that lunch you fixed? I'm starved."

We pulled up in the shade of a mammoth live oak, just like the one I'd pictured Baptiste sitting under while he directed the work of the plantation. The sun was hot, but there was a cool breeze coming from the Mississippi, some two hundred yards beyond the house. The area between the house and the river was planted with lawn and towering shrubs of various kinds: camellias, azaleas, oleanders, pomegranate, gardenia, quince, lantana, and a dozen others. Most of them were still living but dreadfully in need of care. In addition there were towering peach, dogwood, pear, cherry, and bay trees that only needed a judicious pruning to bring them back to their once radiant glory. With Baptiste supervising the fields and my working in the gardens, I knew Belle Fontaine would be a showplace again in no time.

After lunch we explored the house. I had urged Baptiste to wait until there was a man to help him, but he insisted he could manage the winding stairway up to the main door, a good twelve feet above the ground or kitchen level. With one artificial leg and his crutches, he managed quite well on a level area, but even the four steps from the gallery to the courtyard in New Orleans were difficult for him. With each agonizing movement, the sweat poured off his face as he maneuvered up one step at a time. For many months I had known he was never completely free from pain in his nerve-damaged stumps, and I was afraid he would faint before reaching the wide piazza. The stone steps were slippery with moss, and I walked closely behind him, all the while resisting the temptation to place my hands on his back. This was one climb he was determined to make alone.

When Baptiste reached the top, he fell into a broken-down wicker chair that somehow had survived the onslaughts of weather and predators.

"Did you bring any wine, Leah?" he gasped. The Herculean effort had enlarged the veins in his neck and forehead, and his face was turning a deep scarlet from overexertion.

"No, but I have some brandy. I thought we might want to celebrate." I held the bottle to his lips, and forced him to take three or four good swallows before setting it down.

"Bon Dieu, Leah, you're going to drown me in that stuff. I just wanted a simple drink."

"That climb was almost too much for you. Stay in the chair for a few minutes. I'll sit here on the steps. We've plenty of time to explore the house and still get the buggy back when it's due.

I leaned gently against one of the wooden Ionic pillars, afraid for a minute it might collapse from decay, but it remained standing as one of the stalwart guardians of the magnificent fanlighted double doors, made of heavy cypress and little touched by time.

The interior of the house, however, looked old and forlorn, like an aged woman bereft of kin and despairing of ever seeing a loved one again. Denuded of most of the furnishings and filthy with dust and grime and the refuse of those who had used and then stripped her, she was a reminder of the desolation and indignity all New Orleans had suffered.

"Doesn't look too bad, does it?" Baptiste said. In his mind's eye he was seeing what he remembered, not what was actually there. "Pretty dirty, of course, and nothing to sit on, but I don't think it's hopeless."

"I see a couch in what must have been the parlor," I said. "We can go in there."

"Library," Baptiste corrected.

"What?"

"It was the library. Books and shelves are all gone, but we'll restore it. Let's look at some of the other rooms."

Most were empty of furnishings, and as I walked from one to the other, the hardwood floors were rough beneath my feet. The house had been ill-used, suffering the rough treatment of hob-nailed boots and, from evidence in some of the rooms, horses' hoofs. It was not the only house where the officers had quartered their mounts in the same rooms where they slept.

One small room, overlooking the garden and river, contained a narrow single bed still embellished with finely carved tester rails. Where once lace or fine gauze had been draped, there now were suspended cobwebs and strings of dust.

"This was my sister's room," Baptiste said quietly. "Lucy was an invalid most of her life. She died when she was only fourteen, but she loved this room. Said she could see everything she loved from these windows: the river and the garden. It was the center of the house, really, because we all came in here to tell her what was going on. I think it was when she died that I decided to live in the city. She was four years younger than I, and I couldn't bear to stay in the house after she was gone. She'd been the heart of it for me."

He ran his hand over the coverlet, spraying the room with dust.

"You're tired, Baptiste," I said gently. "I think we ought to start back."

"No, I want to lie here for a little while. I need to do some remembering. Turn back the spread for me. Maybe it's cleaner underneath."

There were sheets on the bed, and though somewhat grimy, they were considerably cleaner than the spread.

"I'll look upstairs while you rest," I suggested.

"There's time enough for that. I'd rather you'd lie here beside me."

"I don't think there's room for two of us."

"There will be if you lie real close. We've slept in narrower beds than this."

As soon as I lay down, Baptiste put his arms around me and began nibbling my ear.

"Not here, Baptiste. You don't know who might be around."

"There's no one anywhere near. The window is more than twelve feet above ground, and you can lock the door if it'll make you feel better."

In those strange surroundings we made love, more leisurely and more satisfyingly than in a long time. I didn't want to leave the serenity of Baptiste's arms, but I knew we'd have to start back soon if we were to get to town before dark.

"You know," I told Baptiste as we dressed, "I feel as though I've come home, too."

Chapter Twenty-seven

As WE DROVE into the *Vieux Carré* at dusk the sky glowed pink and the clouds hovered low over the horizon. We were pleasantly tired, ready to eat a light supper and retire early. I laid my head on Baptiste's shoulder while we rode along, and we held hands like young lovers. It was a good-feeling time; at long last we could see a bright future ahead.

While Baptiste was visualizing fields packed solid with long rows of sugarcane, I saw a house filled with love if not many furnishings. I knew we could have a comfortable parlor and bedroom on the first floor, which was all we would need for the time being, and there would be no need for Baptiste to climb stairs to the second floor. Instead of using the ground-floor kitchen area, I hoped to turn one of the first-floor rooms into a big kitchen—dining room, using its large brick fireplace for cooking until I could get a stove.

My original dream of going North and passing as white had long since been dispersed by the realities of life and become nothing more than a phantom of wishful thinking. This new life had substance which could be seen and touched.

We expected to be met by a boy from the livery stable where we rented the buggy. He was there in front of the house, cowering in the grip of two hefty sergeants whose looks dared him to move at the risk of severe punishment. His cheeks were streaked with dirt and tears. He was holding his legs tightly together to

4

prevent our seeing he had wet his trousers out of fear of the men in uniform.

Baptiste chaffed at remaining in the buggy while I got out to see what the problem was. Perhaps the men thought the boy was a loiterer or a young thief bent on entering the house. But it was not like the military to patrol the streets before the hour of curfew.

"May I ask what is wrong?" I requested of the senior of the two. "This boy was sent here to return the buggy to the livery stable. I'm sure he was doing nothing for which he should be arrested."

"We aren't concerned with the boy," he said sternly. "We merely wished to keep him from warning you."

"Warning me? About what?"

"You are Leah Bonvivier, aren't you?"

"Yes."

"You are under arrest. We have orders to conduct you immediately to prison."

So Charles Anderson had dared to do it. My early departure the night before and taking the day off made him furious enough to carry out his threat. And I was helpless to do anything about it, at least for the moment.

"And for what, may I ask?" I would force them to say it aloud so Baptiste would know and prepare to do what he could. He had friends, influential friends, and they would have me free before long. I would have thought of that sooner if Anderson had not frightened me so with his unexpected threat.

"You are under arrest for the murder of Major Charles Anderson."

"Murder!" As if from a distance, from someplace outside my conscious mind, I heard myself scream, and then I fell to the ground.

When I came to, I was still on the ground with my head in Baptiste's lap and he was smoothing the hair away from my face.

"What happened, Baptiste?"

"You fainted. The officers here say Major Anderson

has been found dead, and they want to take you in for some questions."

"But I thought they said 'murder'."

"So they seem to think."

"And I'm under arrest?"

"They've assured me they meant you are merely to be held until you've been questioned. I wouldn't let them take you otherwise."

I wasn't convinced. The men had said quite clearly that I was under arrest. Either they had lied to Baptiste or he was trying to comfort me and allay my fears. I didn't know why I was suspected, but I knew my position was tenuous. I would go with them not because I believed what Baptiste said but to keep him from worrying. If he really thought I was only going to be questioned, he wouldn't start an argument he couldn't possibly win. He might be hurt seriously if he put up any kind of struggle.

"I'm all right, Baptiste. Let me go with them now. But please do something if—if I'm not back home by tomorrow." I couldn't keep the desperation out of my voice.

"You'll be out in a few hours. After all, what can you tell them, Cherie, except that you worked for the major? I'll get in touch with Pierre Delisle, the attorney, right away, just in case we need him."

There was much more I could tell them, but I doubted I'd be asked. No one else knew about the threat over the gold pieces or why I had stayed late. Lieutenant Grimes might suspect I had placed the *gris-gris* on Anderson's desk, but that was a far cry from actually killing him.

Yet I couldn't get the word *arrest* out of my mind. They had some reason to suspect I had killed Charles Anderson, or at least knew something about his death. They might bring in everyone who knew him for questioning, but they would not arrest them. No doubt about it; they had already talked to someone, and that person had decided to throw suspicion on me. Perhaps that person was the actual murderer or someone who disliked me enough to want me found guilty. That raised more questions. Whoever he was, he either knew or had invented something the authorities believed was reason enough to put me under arrest. Which, I wondered, would prove the more dangerous for me: a truth I didn't see as incriminating, or a falsehood I could not prove was false?

The evening was growing chilly, but the officers were curt in their refusal to let me go in the house and get a wrap. I had intended getting a long cape to protect me in the open conveyance as we rode several blocks to headquarters, where I assumed we were going. I wanted it not so much for protection against the cold, because the weather was not that uncomfortable, but as a sort of refuge into which I could withdraw from what was happening. At that moment I was merely furious with their lack of consideration and their excuse that they had delayed long enough. During the next few days I would come to realize how really brutal and sadistic had been their refusal to grant that one request. Nothing could make tolerable the conditions I would have to endure, but the cape would have given me some comfort and mitigated to a great extent the misery I suffered.

"Don't worry, Cherie," Baptiste whispered. "I'll send word to Delisle right away, and you'll be home in a few hours, tomorrow at the very latest. I love you, and I know they'll have no reason to hold you."

Baptiste kissed me gently on the cheek, but his last words gave him away. He was afraid of the arrest, too, and he was trying to hold up and reassure me. Although more frightened of what might lie ahead than by anything I had experienced earlier, I left secure in the faith Baptiste would take care of me, as he had so often in the past.

Once around the first corner, and out of sight of Baptiste, the driver of the cart into which I had been most unceremoniously deposited and forced to sit on a wooden crossplank stopped long enough for the officers to fasten shackles around my ankles and wrists. Why, I wondered, had they not done that in front of Baptiste? Was there some fear that he, as a member of an old New Orleans family, still wielded some power in the city?

It was Baptiste's promise to call on Delisle that I kept uppermost in my mind as the iron bit painfully into my flesh. If I had to keep the shackles on for long, I would soon have raw, open wounds on my legs and arms. They had been attached with lewd sneers and obscene suggestions that they would be removed when the moment came I wanted my ankles free. I shuddered at the picture such words conjured up. Surely I would be guarded carefully against any physical danger during the few hours I was in custody.

The first alarm sounded in my brain when we passed the turnoff to the courthouse. The rest of the ride did not cover a great distance, but it was longer and more agonizing than any other I'd ever traveled. We were headed toward the stockade where Confederate prisoners had been kept.

Although I had never been inside the gates of the infamous prison, its horrors were well known to me. To it had been taken many Confederate sympathizers who had committed acts that aroused the wrath of the Federals. Among them were many owners of fine homes that Yankee officers wished to confiscate and occupy. The owners had done nothing but refuse to sign the Oath of Loyalty to the United States. Others were former city and parish officials whose acts ran counter to new laws. I had seen some of them when they were freed: frightened creatures who trembled at the sound of a friendly voice, emaciated caricatures of their former selves whose gaunt figures bespoke the starvation treatment they'd received. I knew that once through those gates, there was no telling when I'd return.

Baptiste and a Confederate attorney could be of little help to me now.

As I already suspected, there were no officials present to question me. I was not a material witness; I was a suspect. The iron shackles were removed from my ankles so I could walk unhindered. I was now shivering from cold as much as fear. My feet were numb from restricted circulation, and I fell when I tried to step down from the cart. Much to my embarrassment, I had to be helped across the pavement. My abductors became my aides. As much as I loathed their touch, I was grateful for their support.

A half-story staircase led up to the double doors opening into the main offices and, as I'd been told, interrogation rooms and small courtroom.

However, instead of climbing those stairs, the officers took me behind them to a door opening on the lower level. Our way led through a dark, silent anteroom to an even darker, narrow hall which sloped slightly downward as we moved toward the rear of the building. The floor was rough under my feet, the roughness of unleveled cement made coarser by heavy boots and many years' accumulation of filth.

All was deathly quiet, although beneath the silence I thought I heard faint sounds of breathing, muted by stone walls. I surmised we were passing cells occupied by other unfortunates.

My eyes gradually became accustomed to the dim light, and when the guards stopped, I saw we were standing before a heavy wooden door. So far neither had spoken to me, and after the door was unlocked and opened part way, they gave no orders but pushed me roughly inside.

As I heard the heavy door scrape against the floor and the iron bolt forced into place, I tripped over my skirt and fell to the floor. When I started to get up, my hands stung from being scraped across the cement. I lay there numbed by pain and despair, unable to move. The cell was below ground level, and in New Orleans that meant beneath the level of the river. Water had seeped through the porous walls, settling in small, stagnant pools on the floor and turning the filthy enclosure into a stinking cistern. I knew I had to get up and try to find a dry place or I would be sick. The dampness had quickly reached the skin under my thin clothes, chosen for an early-spring outing in the country, not a night behind thick stone walls.

A dim shaft of light came through a grating near the ceiling from a gas-lit street lamp. It illuminated an area just large enough to reveal the size of the cell and the accumulated filth on the floor where I had fallen. There was no sign of a cot or chair, and I shuddered at the thought of having to spend the night on the floor. Perhaps if I moved around, I could find a drier place to sit.

With my wrists still manacled, I found it hard to get my balance, and with my first step I fell over something that cracked against my shin and sent me sprawling again, this time with my face in water. I might have lain there, unmoving and succumbing to whatever fate had in store for me. My hands, when I put them out to break the fall, had touched something soft. Next to the stool which had tripped me up was a thin pallet covered with worn mattress ticking. I felt the holes where stuffing oozed through, and it was as filthy as the floor, but it would be some protection against the damp.

The mattress was almost as damp as the floor, and its nauseating odor of mildew and mold was overpowering. The air became colder with each passing minute.

The whole experience—the arrest, the cruel, sadistic treatment of the guards, the horror of the cell into which I'd been thrown, and above all, the desperate fear of what lay ahead—had numbed my whole body to such an extent I lay paralyzed for hours. I knew only that I was entombed as surely as if the cell were a crypt in a cemetery rather than a room in a prison.

When the iron-bound door was shut behind me, it was to separate me from life.

I knew morning had come when the steady light of the street lamp was replaced by the filtered rays of the sun. I saw the entire area of the cell; and in one shadowed corner, opposite from the pallet, was a single pail which served as the sanitary facility. From the foul odor, I knew why the last occupant had placed it as far from the pallet as possible. There was no basin or pitcher for water. I could only pray some would be brought to me. In the center of the room was the three-legged stool I'd tripped over.

When I moved uneasily across the floor to the pail, I was grateful for the privacy the solid door gave me. There was a small opening several feet from the floor, but high enough to keep passersby from looking in. It was well for my sanity that I didn't learn until many days later about the crack between the hinges through which the guards kept their eyes on their captives. However, by that time all courage and endurance had been so eroded by a series of vile experiences, I was immune to shame.

Chapter Twenty-eight

THE REGULAR ROUTINE I was to endure on each successive day began when I was brought a shallow basin of water which I was rudely told must take care of my needs during my entire stay. At first I hoped that meant I was to be there for just one day, but when the guard laughed as he spilled part of it on the floor, I knew I was the victim of another cruel joke. I learned later I could get more water, but many days of accumulated filth and almost unbearable torture would pass before I would consider paying the price.

With my wrists bound together, the jagged iron cutting into my flesh with every movement, it was extremely difficult to perform any necessary function. By placing the basin on the stool and bending over, I was able to splash some of the tepid water on my face and rinse off my hands, now covered with blood and dirt. In another few minutes the door opened again, and a tin plate was shoved through. In order to eat, I had to remove the basin from the stool, carefully so as not to spill any of the precious water, and place it on the floor. Moving the plate to the stool, I could sit beside it and eat like a dog lapping a pan.

Breakfast consisted of two hard, crusty rolls, which I gnawed at with animal hunger, and a cup of chicory. It was not the coffee for which Louisiana was famous, but it was hot, and holding the heavy pottery cup warmed me as much outside as the liquid did inside.

But I had to watch myself. If I were not to become an animal, degraded to the point of needing only food to stuff my stomach and a place to lie down and sleep, I had to remain mentally alert and physically active. This I managed to do, so when the time came for me to be in command of a situation, I would be neither mentally deranged nor physically debilitated.

But that first morning required every ounce of strength and endurance I possessed. I had barely finished eating when a burly guard, whom I'd not seen before, shoved open the door and indicated I hand him the plate and cup. Then he pointed to the utility pail and motioned for me to pick it up and follow him. I soon discovered he was a deaf-mute, and in another minute also realized why such a disability was a valuable asset to him. I picked up the pail, and with it banging against my knees at every step, lugged it into the hall. If I could have shifted it from one hand to the other the going would have been easier, but under the circumstances this was impossible. On that morning, the pail was not too heavy, but I wondered how often I would be forced to carry it out: once a day or once a week. From the stench in the cell, I feared it might be the latter.

Other cell doors were open, and I saw my fellow prisoners; but wrapped up as I was in my own tragedy, I paid them scant attention. Only one could not be ignored. Crouched in the corner of her cell, a gaunt old woman was screaming at her persecutors. Dirty, yellow-white hair fell in greasy strands over her face and across her shoulders. The ragged remains of what must have once been a dress covered her skeletal figure. Her filthy feet were bare, and her longnailed fingers were like talons.

The old woman's shouted imprecations sounded at first like a meaningless jumble of words from a creature long since driven mad by imprisonment. Or had she been insane before being brought in? Either way, I looked on her as an object of pity and horror. As the pathetic creature caught sight of me, she screeched louder and cackled with macabre humor. I caught some of the words when she pointed to me with obscene gestures and began ripping her clothes. Her language was the most vulgar, the most disgusting I'd ever heard; and when I tried to pass quickly by her door, the old woman lay down in a suggestive pose and beckoned to a second guard.

"Come on Granny," the guard shouted, "no time for that. Pick up your pail and come along. You don't want to feel the taste of the 'cat' do you?"

"You want the pail?" she screeched in her demoniac voice. "Here, take it."

Before the guard could jump to one side, the pail came flying through the air, and its entire contents of human waste hit him full in the face.

Although I gagged while the offal ran down his face and uniform, I wanted to laugh. I knew I did not dare, but even as I controlled myself, I knew I would be all right as long as I could find humor in such a situation.

All of us carrying pails were led to an open cesspool in the inner courtyard and told to empty them. Thankfully there was a pump at which we were told to rinse them out. Most took the opportunity to wash off their hands and faces, but they had to move quickly, for the guard continued to prod them along. Unfortunately, I was the first in line and not alert enough to see that I could wash and drink at the pump, saving the precious water in the basin.

Once back in the cell, the only other event in the long, weary day was the arrival of supper. Another cup of chicory, more hard rolls, and a plate of thin soup with a few pieces of mustard greens and several thick globs of rancid grease. I thought I couldn't possibly get it down; but as I heard the guard returning, I knew I had to keep up my strength and I forced myself to eat, swallowing quickly to keep from tasting it.

A few hours later my stomach revolted at what had been forced into it, and I barely reached the pail before I began retching and vomiting up the foul food. Even after I was spitting out nothing but green bile, I continued to gag. I thought I heard someone laughing outside the door, but in my misery, I didn't care.

Weakened from illness, my wrists raw and bleeding, I lay on the pallet and moaned, forgetful of my determination to remain stoic in the face of all adversity.

In the morning I didn't think I could move to pick up breakfast, and I wasn't sure I should eat anything. On the other hand, I decided maybe the bread and hot chicory would help settle my stomach. Like a whipped mongrel, I crawled across the rough concrete, tearing my skirt and scraping my legs. I didn't try to move when the deaf-mute came back, and he picked up the plate with only a single, pitiful glance. Was there a chance he was sympathetic to my plight? Was there any way he might be useful to me? When he didn't return to order me to carry out the pail, one of my questions was answered: we did not empty them every day.

Painfully I made my way back to the pallet and lay there unmoving. Thankfully the bread and chickory stayed down, so I was able to sleep through most of the day, with no nightmares to disturb my rest. Supper was the same as on the previous evening, but I took only the bread and chicory, pouring the soup into the pail. I was certain that if I returned the soup, my rations would be cut; and if I had the jailor's ugly humor figured correctly, it would be the bread that was eliminated, not the soup I'd refused to eat.

Day followed day with monotonous regularity. Breakfast and supper never varied in time or content. Gradually my stomach became accustomed to the revolting fare and while I never looked forward to the meals, I was glad for anything that forced me into action of some kind. With the others, I emptied the pail twice a week, and even that small amount of exercise, obnoxious as the reason for it might be, helped keep me physically active. In spite of being hampered by my manacled wrists, I worked out a regimen of exercise which I followed faithfully every day. I had always had a quick, retentive memory, and so for hours I lay on the pallet recalling pages of my favorite books. By concentrating intently, I found that each day I drew more and more from my memory.

I resisted giving in to panic until the morning I awoke not knowing which day of the week it was. or how many days I had been in prison. For once my memory failed when I tried to recall how many times I had emptied the pail. Since we did it twice a week, Sundays and Thursdays, that was my one clue. I had emptied the pail the day before, and I'd heard the bells of St. Louis Cathedral chiming for morning service while I was out. So it must have been Sunday. Once I began to think logically, the mist cleared and I knew I had been in prison for two weeks and one day. But I must not allow myself to forget again. I found a piece of broken stone and marked out a rough calendar on the wall, as I thought Edmond Dantès and thousands of other prisoners must have done.

Then it was two weeks and two days. Had Baptiste been able to do anything to obtain my release? Had he even been told why I was arrested? The murder of Charles Anderson was the reason given, but how did he die? And where? Or had Anderson himself ordered my arrest? Would I ever know or be given the chance to prove my innocence of whatever the charges were? These were the thoughts tormenting me throughout my waking hours.

The next morning when I awoke, I couldn't lift my head off the pallet. For several days I had not felt well, but I put it down to the poor food and loathsome conditions. In fact, I wondered if I would ever feel really well again. Now, however, I knew I was very ill and burning with fever. The raw wounds on my wrists never completely healed, the scabs rubbed off as soon as they formed. In addition, I was covered with sores from mattress vermin. I had no doubt the unsanitary conditions and lack of clean water had also contributed to my illness.

When the mute guard came in, I tried to indicate

what was wrong with me. His eyes had always looked at me with sympathy, and I hoped maybe he would have enough pity to help me.

Instead of simply putting the tin plate on the floor, he placed it on the stool and put his fingers over his lips in a signal of some kind. All I could do was wait to see what would happen next. In a few minutes, he was back, and to my surprise he carred a fresh basin of water and a clean cloth. Putting them beside me, he left but returned almost immediately with a bowl of clear, greaseless broth. Gently he washed my face and hands, put his fingers tenderly on my wrists, and sadly shook his head. Then while he rested my head on one of his arms, he spooned the hot broth into my mouth. My throat was so sore I wanted to cry out, but I tried to swallow the soup.

I didn't know how he managed it, but the mute stayed with me all that day and night, leaving only to carry out routine duties. Over and over he brought in pitchers of cool water to bathe my face and body. When he saw the sores, he brought pots of salves and with gentle fingers rubbed the medicine into my raw wrists and over the bites. Almost immediately the pain subsided, as though the salves contained an anesthetic of some kind. Next he crumpled dried leaves, herbs I recognized as the same kind I once collected with my mother, into hot water and spooned the concoction down my throat. In the dim light, I had assumed the man was white, and it was always another guard who took us outside. Now I looked more closely and realized he, too, was a person of color like myself. In a moment of inspiration, I formed my fingers into a sign recognizable to any member of the Voodoo cult. He nodded enthusiastically, pointed to me, and drew a circle around his head, indicating he knew I had been once designated as a future queen. That had all been years earlier, but he remembered. I would accept what he could offer, but I knew I could not put his life in jeopardy by asking him to help me escape.

Within twenty-four hours my fever began to subside, and in three days I was able to move off the pallet. How my utility pail had been emptied or what reason given for my not going outside, I did not know, but evidently the mute had managed somehow.

Or so I thought. I didn't know the real days of terror were about to begin.

One morning it was not the mute, but a foul-mouthed guard who brought breakfast. He let me know right away he wanted some of what the mute must have been getting for me to receive special treatment. Barter of that kind was not unusual within the prison, he said. The mute had been transferred so the goodies could be shared; but now that this second guard had seen me, he decided he'd keep them all for himself. I was tempted to imitate the old hag and throw the pail at him, but I desisted when he laughed and walked out. I would save that gambit for a time when I really needed it.

It was the nights I feared the most, and I scarcely slept during the next two, for each time the guard came around, his remarks were more lewd and obscene. On the third evening, when he took away supper, he said he would bring me a special dessert later. Something I had not had in a long time. That night I didn't close my eyes, but nothing happened.

Lulled into thinking the guard was taunting me with threats he wouldn't, or couldn't, carry out, I let myself fall asleep on the fourth night. So soundly did I sleep, I didn't hear the bolt slide slowly out of the lock or the creaking of the wooden door. I awoke only when I felt a fat, smothering hand over my mouth and nose. My skirt had already been pulled up, and the guard's other hand was exploring beneath it.

I couldn't scream, and with the weight of his obese body holding mine down, I couldn't move. Even if my illness had not sapped my strength, I could never have resisted his powerful arms and legs. He moved one hand to free my mouth so he could bring his own down over it. His foul breath made me gag, but when I bit his lip, he forced open my mouth. His hands were massaging me brutally. My only hope was that I could use the iron around my wrists as a weapon and jab with my knee as I had done with Anderson. But he was way ahead of me.

Without a word, he rolled me over on my stomach so that I was forced to lie on my manacles. Then he mounted me like an animal. Once he had gone, I wept as I hadn't done since the first night I was brought into that dreadful place.

How long could I go on, I wondered, before I too would go mad?

The nightmare continued: the days spent dreading the nights, and the nights filled with unmitigated horror. My persecutor delighted in such sadistic tortures as flogging me with chains, burning the tenderest parts of my flesh with lighted cigar tips, or biting and pinching until I was black and blue all over. No longer did I keep track of the days on the calendar or do my exercises or try to reconstruct my favorite books. I lay like one dead, and I moved like a zombie when I ate or went outside. I had long since given up hope of ever hearing from Baptiste or being given my freedom. Never again would I sit in my garden or smell the fragrance of bay blossoms and gardenias. And the plantation. That had been a dream from the beginning, something I had not known long enough to miss.

But I did not go mad. Instead I was awakened earlier than usual one morning by a strange guard who ordered me to follow him. Once he removed my shackles, he led me upstairs to an empty room and told me to wait. For the first time in a long while—actually only four weeks, but it seemed like an eternity—I began to hope again that I had not been completely forgotten.

In a few minutes a maid came in with pitchers of hot, soapy water, clean towels, and a light wrapper. I was to bathe and wash my hair. The maid would bring me fresh undergarments and a gown. There was no tub to bathe in, but I spent a long time lathering and rinsing off, over and over, to rid myself of the month's accumulation of filth and odor. My body had been soiled beyond the point of ever feeling clean again, but I could make my hair shine once more. Now washed and dried, it fell as long and full as before my ordeal began.

Next the maid came in with clothes, brand-new undergarments and a simple gray dress with white collar and cuffs. Someone wanted me to look as prim, proper, and innocent as possible. Once dressed, I sat waiting for another interminable period. It was probably no more than thirty minutes, but it seemed like hours. I had never been able to wait calmly for anything. As a child, I fidgeted when forced to sit in anticipation of anything.

When the guard returned, I was ushered into a second room containing a square table and two chairs. Seated in one of them was a man I judged to be a few years older than I. Relaxed and smoking a pipe, he arose when I entered and held the chair for me. His face was kindly and benign, and his smile friendly, but I had been fooled before. No gentle mien was going to break through my defenses.

"Please sit down, Miss Bonvivier. I'm James Andrews, and I've been given permission to defend you against the charge of murdering Charles Anderson. Don't be afraid. I'm not going to ask many questions today, just give you the chance to get to know me and learn to have confidence in me. Is there anything you need?"

My immediate response was to laugh hysterically and then collapse on the table in tears. This was some kind of a horrible new joke, to dress me up in clean clothes, build up my hopes, and then throw me back into the cell.

Chapter Twenty-nine

JAMES ANDREWS SAID NOTHING until I had sobbed out all my frustration. When I raised my head, he was sitting back in his chair, puffing as casually on his pipe as if he had not witnessed anything out of the ordinary.

"Leah, listen to me. I don't know what you've endured these past four weeks, but I can look at your face and see it hasn't been easy. I chose that dress carefully, but maybe I made a mistake. Turn back your cuffs."

I saw the first change of expression, from objective pity to disbelief and then horror, when he looked at my wrists.

"Oh, my God, no!" His voice was deep and resonant. "I had no idea. They told me to do all the background work before seeing you. I should have followed my instincts and come here first. I'm sorry. I'm terribly sorry."

I knew then I could trust him, trust him enough to tell him everything he would need to defend me. It wouldn't be easy, but I was ready to answer any question he asked if it meant I might go free.

"You asked me what I wanted, Mr. Andrews. If it's possible, I want to be moved from the cell where I've been kept. It's not fit for an animal. You've seen my wrists, but that is the least of my mistreatment. I—I'd rather not go into details, but I'm not sure I'll still be alive a week from now if I'm forced to return."

"No," Andrews said, "I won't ask for the details

now, but for the sake of other prisoners, I hope you will tell me during the next few days. A room on this floor has already been assigned to you, and you are to have anything you require, within reason of course."

"Thank you," I said quietly. "I already feel as though I've finally awakened from a nightmare. Now if you can tell me why I'm here and how soon I'll be free."

"Tomorrow I'll tell you all I can to answer your first question, but then I'll start asking the questions to see if we can find the answer to the second."

That night I enjoyed my first really comfortable and worry-free sleep in many a week, undisturbed by physical abuse or frightening noises. The bed was soft and covered with clean linen and a light quilt. At my request, the maid brought a large metal tub, and I was able to have a long, relaxing bath before I retired. As I washed my body, I looked at it closely. After all the torture it had endured, it seemed little changed. The sores had healed, and my skin was as smooth as ever. But it masked the part of me where the real damage had been done. I wondered if I would ever feel like a real, whole woman again, able to respond to Baptiste with all the love I still felt for him. Would he sense a change in me? If he suspected I'd been raped, would he love me any less? However, none of these questions bothered me for long after the maid brought in a palatable meal complete with real coffee. I was asleep as soon as my head touched the soft feather pillow.

James Andrews arrived promptly at ten the next morning. He wasted no time in filling me in on all that had occurred. Charles Anderson had been found dead on that fateful Saturday morning by two of his aides. Collapsed across the bed, he had died from a stab wound in the chest. It seemed he had been dead for several hours.

"And," I said, "now for the big question. Why was I arrested?"

"From statements given by the two aides," Andrews

informed me, "the evidence was pretty strong, but I consider it all purely circumstantial. That's why, when I heard people talking about the case, I asked if I could defend you."

"You heard people talking?"

"Another lawyer had already been contacted by a friend of yours, and I overheard them talking while having my morning coffee at the *Café du Monde*. It's not important now, but sometime I'll tell you why I happened to come south to New Orleans. Anyway, they were concerned that this other lawyer, being a Southerner, would do more to jeopardize your case than to win it. I couldn't resist joining in their conversation. It seemed, from what they said, so brutally unfair for you to be in danger from prejudice. So Mr. Delisle, the lawyer, is working behind the scenes to gather information, but I'll be present in court."

I smiled inwardly. Baptiste had been trying all this time to set me free.

"Now," Andrews continued, "convince me you're innocent, and we'll be off and running. Even if you're guilty, I'll do my best to defend you."

"I'm innocent."

"By reason of self-defense?"

"By reason of not killing him at all. What did the aides say that made me a suspect?" Outwardly I remained calm, but inwardly I was churning.

"Did you ever spend the night with Major Anderson?"

"No."

"Did you ever stay later than usual—than normal working hours?"

I looked at Andrews leaning casually back in his chair, the smoke from his pipe curling around his rusty hair and mustache. His ruddy cheeks set off clear, honest blue eyes. What he was asking me was strictly professional. Only with the truth could he set me free. I had to be honest with him as he was with me.

"Yes, I did work late several nights. I—I think I'd better tell you the whole story from the beginning."

"That would be best. Don't leave anything out, no matter how incidental it may seem."

"All right." I took three deep breaths. "In the spring of 1862, about the time the—the Union captured New Orleans, my father gave me a generous allowance of money, real money, I mean. Gold coins, not Confederate money.

"Your father?"

"I see I'll have to go back even farther. As you know, I'm an octoroon. My mother was my father's mistress. He was Jean-Paul Bonvivier, a wealthy exporter and merchant. You may not be familiar with New Orleans customs, but Creole marriages are usually arranged, and the men often have mulatto or quadroon mistresses. Sometimes these arrangements, called *plaçages,* end with the man's marriage to another Creole; sometimes they continue for a lifetime. My mother and father's did. My mother died of yellow fever in 1860, but I stayed in touch with my father."

"Were you . . ." Andrews asked, "are you also mistress to a Creole gentleman? The one talking with the lawyer?"

"Yes, but I prefer to leave him out of it—for personal reasons."

"Leah, I said I needed to know everything if I'm to help you. I meant *everything.* That doesn't mean it will all go past this room, only what I absolutely need if you are to go free."

"I met Baptiste Fontaine in 1858 and become his *placée* or mistress a few months later. In the spring of 1862, just prior to the capture of New Orleans, Baptiste was very seriously wounded. He lost both legs and one eye. I was nursing in the hospital, and I watched his wife when she came in. I—I can't begin to describe the look on her face when she saw him. There was no love, not even a touch of pity, just horror and loathing. She said she had to leave the city with her family. But he knew the truth: she could not bear the thought of ever living with him again. I might add he has never heard from her since.

"I took Baptiste home to nurse him, to prevent his being captured as a Confederate prisoner of war. I won't go into details, but life was not easy for us during the war, Mr. Andrews. As Baptiste had supported me the first years, I in turn took care of him."

"You have always been free, Leah?"

"Yes. My mother was freed as a child by her father, her mother's master."

"In these relationships, this custom of—"

"*Plaçage* is the Creole term you're looking for."

"In this *plaçage* custom, are all the males white and the women Negro?"

"Colored, not Negro. Negroes have no white blood, colored do. The greater percentages of colored were free here in Louisiana while most Negroes were slaves."

"I see," Andrews nodded, "thank you."

"As I said earlier," I continued, "I received a generous amount of gold from my father. We used the gold sparingly for medicine and food when I was not earning money, but we saved most of it for emergencies. I would have been better off if I'd spent it."

"How do you mean?"

"When Baptiste was given the opportunity to regain his plantation, we used some of the gold to have the title researched and the deed certified. The taxes due almost ended our dreams, but we managed to scrape up some money, and by a stroke of luck, a neighbor bought several acres of adjoining land."

Andrews nodded again as he refilled his pipe.

"Is all this information necessary?" I asked.

"It is. Go on."

"As I said, we used some of the gold. It seems that while we were there, Major Anderson was in another office and saw us. I had met him many years ago, before the war, at a quadroon ball. In fact, I was shocked when I learned he had been assigned to the office where I worked. I knew from his remarks and actions he still found me attractive, but I ignored his more blatant suggestions. One day he asked me, or rather ordered me, to stay late. I worked late several times, and then one night he coolly informed me that unless I became his mistress he would accuse me of stealing the gold from him. He could describe the leather purse in detail and guess the amount pretty accurately, saying, of course, I had spent some."

"But surely you knew Baptiste could explain it was yours."

"I thought so, too, but Anderson had that figured out as well. He was very shrewd. He said he would accuse Baptiste of being my accomplice, or at least a user of stolen goods. Remember, Baptiste is a Confederate veteran, a declared enemy of the United States. His word would be worth no more than mine."

"And your father is dead?"

"Yes."

"How about your father's wife? Would she have known?"

"She knew, I think, but she has never returned to New Orleans from France, where she fled soon after the city was taken. She claimed to be still a French citizen and was allowed to leave, as were many nationals of other countries."

"So there were no reliable witnesses?"

"None. It would have been my word against his."

"And you agreed to his terms?"

"Not exactly. That is, I stayed late that night, and he forced me into the bedroom. Once we were—we were on the bed and he began to attack, I defended myself in such a way he was completely helpless."

Andrews nodded again, knowingly. "You could have reported Major Anderson to his superior officer. He would have been dealt with severely. And I'm sure your friend Baptiste would have been believed."

"I don't think so. How long have you been in New Orlean, Mr. Andrews?"

"About six months."

"And where are you from?"

"Indiana. A small town in Indiana."

"Then you cannot conceive," I said strongly, "of the fear of Federal officers people have had ingrained into them here. Years of occupation by the enemy makes one do anything—anything—to keep from getting into trouble that could mean prison or further deprivation. You are the enemy, too, and yet I trust you, although I'm not sure why."

"We were never the enemy of the Negroes or the colored, as you refer to yourself, although I'll admit I thought they were one and the same. We came South to set you free and make you equal."

"Mr. Andrews, it didn't matter whether one was a Negro slave, a free person of color, or a Southern white. All were treated shamefully. Slaves, once set free, were rounded up and forced to work at hard labor on fortifications, street repairs, or on the plantations. You are not alone in thinking all people of color were the same. I, too, suffered such indignities as being herded with other conscripted workers until I was rescued by a white woman. I've been called vile names, accosted by men who assumed that because I was colored I was fair game for any man who wanted me, and had wives of Yankee officers suggest that, for the same reason, I was only good enough to be a maid. Would it surprise you to know I own my own home? Or shock you to learn I had a slave?"

"Surprise me, yes. But I'm suddenly finding myself shockproof."

"A number of the large plantation owners, with many slaves, were free men of color. Do not assume all felt allegiance to our Northern liberators. The free colored of New Orleans had their own distinct society, quite apart from either the Negroes or whites, and we had pride. Oh, don't misunderstand me, it was not an ideal situation. I hated it, and I planned to go North and 'pass' the first chance I got. There were definite rules we had to follow. All of them to remind us to remain in our place. But I was never mistreated or humiliated as I have been by many of your Yankee compatriots."

"Was it—was it difficult?" Mr. Andrews spoke hesitantly, searching for the right words. "Belonging to that unique stratum of society? Being neither Negro nor white?"

"Neither fish nor fowl, you mean? In many ways, yes. I was as well educated, in a convent school, and as closely guarded as any white daughter of the South. Yet the only white person I was ever expected to know well would be my protector, if I were fortunate enough to become a *placée* to a wealthy Creole. Most Negroes hated and envied us at the same time they scorned us. If we had been set free, we must not have been considered valuable enough to keep. You must realize that many slaves, while avidly desiring their freedom, took great pride in who their masters were and the position they themselves held in the household."

"Leah, this is all most interesting, but we need to get back to your problem. We'll talk about this another day. You fended off Major Anderson's attack, rather forcibly, I gather. Was there a second night?"

"No, just the one, and I was there for less than an hour."

"He didn't ask you to stay again?"

"No, the next day, the night of his murder, I asked to leave early, and also for the next day off. He was mad, I knew, about what I'd done to him, and he indicated quite clearly he would be asking me to stay again and there had better not be a repetition of the night before. I made the request in front of Lieutenants Taylor and Grimes, on purpose so he couldn't refuse. They were both there when I left."

"Both there?"

"Yes. Lieutenant Grimes in the reception hall and

Lieutenant Taylor in the next room. I said good night to them. Only Lieutenant Grimes answered, however."

"If they heard you ask for the day off and permission to leave early, they might also have heard his reference to the night before."

"I doubt it. He spoke very low."

"We'll leave that for now, but it could be a motive for your killing him. To avoid a repetition of his advances. Now, Grimes says you were there when he left, and Taylor says he did not see you either go or stay."

"They are lying. At least Grimes is."

"Would he have any reason to lie? He says he knows why you stayed. He stated he came back the night before and heard you and the major in the bedroom."

"I know of no reason," I said, "unless it's jealousy. He, too, suggested he would like to sleep with me. No, that's not true. He called me a whore, said he knew all colored women like white men. That's what I mean about being shamed and reviled. But I simply ignored him."

"Hm. Jealousy or maybe something else. It raises the thought he might have killed Anderson. Because of you, because of a desired promotion. There are many possibilities."

"You think that's true?"

"I don't know. But it's worth keeping in the back of my mind. If he did hear what Major Anderson said about another night with you, he could have thought it would be easy to place the blame on you. Is there anything else you want to add, any little detail?"

"No." I was very definite.

"Are you certain?" Andrews urged. "What about Voodoo?"

"Voodoo!"

"Yes, didn't you try to frighten Anderson off with something called a *gris-gris*?"

"That has nothing to do with the matter."

"I told you everything that happened or was said

could be of vital importance. Now, what did Lieutenant Grimes mean when he mentioned the *gris-gris*? What is it?"

"It's pronounced 'gree-gree,' and it is a Voodoo charm to ward off danger. I learned it from my mother."

"To ward off danger or to bring danger?"

"Well, to frighten someone, yes, but certainly no danger can come from the charm itself, unless the person decided to eat some of the material it contained. That might give him indigestion."

"Don't be flippant, Leah. Your own life is in danger now, and the fact you practiced Voodoo against Anderson indicated you wanted to harm him in some way. Grimes says you even told Anderson he was in danger from whoever left it."

"To frighten him, Mr. Andrews, to frighten. Any sensible Creole would have recognized the *gris-gris* and known what it meant. Anderson had lived for some time in New Orleans, and I was certain he was familiar with most Creole customs. At any rate, if I'd intended to kill him, I wouldn't have warned him first."

"But you will not be tried in a Creole court, Leah. To Northerners, Voodoo is witchcraft, and that conjures up memories of Satanism and New England witch trials."

With that, the conversation ended for the day. Subsequent meetings were spent going back over the same territory—again and again until I thought I would scream, but James Andrews insisted I might think of something new. Something I'd forgotten. He said that a seemingly innocuous word or action could make all the difference.

Although I was not being tried for witchcraft, Andrews was worried that my being a member of a Voodoo cult would prejudice the case against me. When I tried to explain that Voodoo was a religion, not witchcraft, he said it made no difference. Either way, I was a heretic.

"I'm not a heretic!" I screamed. "I'm a Christian, a good Catholic who attends mass regularly at the St. Louis Cathedral."

"To staunch New England and Midwestern Protestants, they're the same thing. They fear Catholics as much as they do witches. They think they're both in league with the devil. They look with suspicion on a service where English isn't spoken. They think the mass is a lot of mumbo-jumbo, not fit for American ears. Why else would it be in Latin?"

So there I was, damned as a heretic or damned as a Catholic. Andrews implied several times that my French accent wasn't going to work to my advantage either. Anyone who had lived in the United States all her life and spoke with a foreign accent was sure to be suspect.

My one hope lay in the fact I was to have a semi-private, pretrial hearing before a board of officers chosen by the adjutant-general's office. There would be no public spectators; only those directly connected with the case would be present because Anderson was an officer killed on military property. Although I was a civilian, my working for the military put me under its jurisdiction. I felt I would have the courage to tell my story before a board of professional, impartial judges but never before a motley crowd of leering faces, their mouths drooling in anticipation of hearing a sordid story. Enemies though they were, I had to have faith and trust the panel to be fair and objective, or I might as well resign myself to prison or hanging.

My feelings about James Andrews were more ambivalent. On the one hand, as kind and concerned as he was for my welfare, I felt he had reservations about my innocence. He wanted me free, but I was sure he believed me guilty. Several times, when we came to an impasse, he suggested I plead self-defense. I knew he had only my best interests at heart; I knew we could probably win with that defense, but I would not agree to being branded for life as a murderer. I could not do that to Baptiste. It would be better to die proclaiming my innocence. Baptiste must never know what I had gone through with Anderson, and for that reason I refused to let Andrews talk to him about it. In accordance with my wishes, Baptiste had been told only that I was alive and being ably defended.

On the other hand, I was strongly attracted to James Andrews, and I felt myself succumbing to his tender, compassionate strength. For too long I had been leaned on by a man; I had carried a heavy burden of responsibility, and now I was ready to pass it on to someone else. I had been through hell in the prison, and Andrews was offering me salvation. It was my turn to be sheltered and protected, and I wanted to give myself completely into his care. There were times when I wondered if I were falling in love with him, in the way women were said to fall in love with their ministers or priests.

If I were of two minds about James Andrews, he was a man of consummate equilibrium: he listened patiently as I told my story but demanded immediate investigation of the abuses I related; he was tender with me when I was distressed by what I was forced to tell him but harsh with those who had caused that distress or who would postpone setting the date for my hearing.

I had conquered the twin tyrants of physical abuse and emotional distress. Now I was tired. I was not sure I could hold up much longer, but I placed all my faith in James Andrews.

During all of the days we were seated together at the table in the small inquiry room, I gradually came to know a great deal about him. At thirty-seven, he was older than I'd first thought. Not quite as tall as Baptiste, he was broader in the chest and shoulders, with the rugged look of the frontier about him. His clothes had been chosen for comfort rather than fit, and usually his tie was cocked to one side under a slightly rumpled collar. His hair looked as though it had been combed with his fingers. About him was an aura of pungent pipe smoke, while his jacket and shirt front were seldom free from shreds of tobacco.

James Andrews had not served in the war for two reasons. He was a circuit-riding, country lawyer who felt he couldn't deprive the small communities he served of needed legal services. Also his wife was an invalid with no other family. Torn with guilt after her death because he'd been away when she died, he'd been urged by friends to travel. Having always wanted to see the South and New Orleans in particular, he chose to sail leisurely down the Mississippi. He had enjoyed the visit, and now he was ready to go back.

When he brought the news that the hearing had been set for the next day, we sat at the table for a long time without saying anything. We both knew we had done all we could in the way of working up a defense, and now it would be up to the panel of three officers to decide if I were telling the truth.

Andrews reached across the table and took both my hands in his, grasping them gently but firmly enough so I could not pull them away.

"You're going to go free, Leah; just keep thinking that and you'll be all right."

"How can you be so sure? And I will not plead self-defense, you know."

"There is no real evidence against you. Every bit of it is circumstantial. Even if the panel believes you left after the subordinate officers, there is always the possibility someone came along later that night. There is only one thing we need to do: make our defense one of reasonable doubt. And that is what I'm going to press for. Remember, this is just a hearing, not a trial."

He continued to hold my hands, willing his strength and determination to flow from his fingers to mine, as though he were already friend, confidant, and lover. His nearness became disturbing, but I knew I must not be swayed by the emotions of the moment. He was lonely for his wife just as I was lonely for Baptiste's love. In another few days James Andrews would be gone, become only a memory of a time I must learn to forget.

Chapter Thirty

PROMPTLY AT TEN in the morning, James Andrews arrived to walk with me to the hearing. Once again I was wearing the gray dress with the white collar and cuffs. Although Baptiste had not been able to visit me, he had sent over a few of my own clothes for me to wear during the days James and I were preparing my defense. My only communication with the outside world had been a few notes carried by Andrews to Mr. Delisle and then to Baptiste. His, in turn, came to me by the same route. As much as my situation improved, they were the only things that really kept my spirits up when it seemed impossible to hope I would be found innocent.

"My Darling Leah,
    Thank God I can now get word to you even if Andrews says I must not try to see you. These past weeks have been torture. First not really knowing why you had been arrested and then being kept in ignorance about what was happening to you. No one at headquarters would tell me anything though I hounded them every day. Andrews assures me you are now being well taken care of. He says nothing about how you were before he was able to see you. Please send a note back by him. I love you. B."

"Dear Baptiste,
    The weeks were torture for me, too. (But never

would he know what I meant by that word.) I think Andrews is doubtful about my innocence, but in spite of that he seems hopeful of an acquittal. Thank you for the clothes you sent through him. He is waiting to leave, so I close with my love. L."

"Darling,
Your note was so short, but Andrews said his time was about up when you wrote it. He also said you seem to feel that nothing was being done for you until he came along. Please believe me, I contacted my friend Delisle, the attorney, the night you were arrested. The next day I went around the city to everyone I knew—veterans, brokers, merchants, and former city officials— anyone I thought could be of help. All said the same thing. There was little they could do. After all the years of Yankee occupation, many are broken men, completely humbled and intimidated by blue uniforms and scalawags. They may be right, though; any cause they aspired to would be lost. Have faith in Andrews. I hear he is a very good lawyer, and he assures us, too, that you will be acquitted. I wait anxiously for more word from you, and from him the date of the trial. I love you. B."

"Dearest,
I never really doubted for a minute that you were not trying to get me set free. But the days and nights were so long and conditions so intolerable, I had to struggle to keep my faith. I love you and long for the day when I will be out of here, a free woman. L."

"My Darling Leah,
Andrews assures me the trial will be soon. I know you will be free and am making very special

plans toward that day when I can bring you home. I yearn to have you with me, and to feel my arms once more around you. I haven't had a decent shave or haircut since you've been gone. All my love. B."

"Dearest,

Do be careful when you shave. I wouldn't want you to ruin that handsome mustache. And take care with the temples. I understand they are calling them 'sideburns' now, after that dreadful Yankee General Burnside. You know how you are inclined to chop them off too short. Yes, I think the trial will be soon. But I dread it as much as I wait anxiously for it. I'm terribly, terribly frightened in spite of Andrews's calm reassurances. Tell me what the special plans are so I will have something to look forward to besides my 'day in court' as Andrews puts it. I love you. L."

"Darling,

The time is getting closer. Andrews says they will have to set a date in a few days. No, I will not tell you about the special plans. They are to be a surprise, and I think you will be pleased. Let me just say they have kept me from going insane these past weeks. I want to see your face when you find out. Do not be frightened of the trial. I understand the judges will be fair and impartial. This may be the last note I will have to write. Until I can hold you in my arms again, I send you all my love. B."

I was not nearly so concerned about the judges as I was about the testimony we had to present.

Was it as weak and unsubstantial as I suspected it was, or would it prove strong enough to set me free?

The hearing was held in an office rather than a large courtroom, and its very size seemed to assure an informality which would make more bearable the testimony to be offered during the course of the morning. There was a large desk around which the presiding panel of officers would sit, and an irregular arrangement of chairs for witnesses, legal counsel, and the few visitors permitted to attend, all of whom were connected in some way with the case.

We were among the first to arrive and took chairs near the front of the room. I was relieved that James Andrews had honored my request not to have Baptiste present. Soon after, Lieutenants Grimes and Taylor walked in, followed by Mrs. Anderson in widow's weeds. With her sallow complexion, black was a most unbecoming color. All of them studiously avoided looking at me. There were a few others: officers who had served with Anderson, clerks, two lawyers from the adjutant general's office, and of course the guards. Mrs. Anderson and I were the only women in the room.

The door opened once more, and I saw a man I thought to be Delisle, Baptiste's friend and lawyer. He was there only if we needed him to provide information. He remained by the door, and I wondered why he did not come in and sit down. Through a side door I had seen the three senior officers I presumed to be the panel for the hearing, and I sensed they were waiting for everyone in the room to settle down. Soon my question was answered when I saw Delisle helping Baptiste maneuver to a chair. He smiled at me, and although I was upset at seeing him, I felt maybe everything was going to be all right.

"You promised," I whispered crossly to Andrews. "I didn't want him here."

"I'm sorry. Delisle and I thought it best. We might need him to corroborate your testimony that you didn't return to the office that night."

Two young majors and a colonel, whom I judged to

be about forty-five or fifty, walked in and took their places at the desk. As presiding officer, Colonel Scofield directed the hearing with a calm, no-nonsense approach. He listened carefully to everything that was said, asking only the most pertinent questions, and interrupting only when a point needed clarification. The two majors remained silent throughout most of the proceedings, deferring to their superior at all times.

Lieutenants Grimes and Taylor repeated how they had found the major's body. No, there had been no weapon at the scene, but it was obvious he had been stabbed several times. They listed the places where the weapon entered the body: neck, chest, and stomach. Each told how they had immediately notified headquarters.

Lieutenant Grimes repeated his earlier statement that I was still there when he left. Lieutenant Taylor said he did not see me leave. Grimes also told about returning to the office the night before the murder and hearing someone who sounded like me with the major in the bedroom, and he repeated word for word what Anderson had said to me about staying late all the following week. Under further questioning, Grimes mentioned the Voodoo *gris-gris* and why he thought I had placed it on the major's desk.

After an army doctor testified that Lieutenant Grimes's statement about the wounds was essentially correct and that they were probably made with a knife rather than a conventional army weapon, the hearing was recessed for an hour. James Andrews and I ate a quiet lunch brought to an adjoining room for us.

"Who do you think will be asked to testify next, Mr. Andrews?"

"I don't know, Leah. Unless there is some information we don't know about, some witness who has been called at the last minute, I rather expect Colonel Scofield will want to ask you some questions."

"I don't know if I can answer them—with Baptiste sitting there, I mean. How can I possibly talk about what

Anderson tried to do to me? What will Baptiste think of me?"

"He will think just as I do, that you're a very strong, proud woman. And don't you think we've known each other long enough now for you to call me 'James' rather than 'Mr. Andrews'?"

"Thank you, James. I do think of you as a friend. So, knowing both you and Baptiste believe in me, I guess I can get through it all right."

"Good girl. Now let's go back and convince them you're innocent."

In spite of James's encouraging words, I thought it would be impossible for me to speak after Lieutenant Grimes's testimony. Baptiste now knew why I had stayed late those nights, and I was afraid he was thinking the worst. Fortunately the witness chair was turned so that it faced toward the desk where the panel sat and away from Baptiste. I found Colonel Scoffield's calm manner and quiet voice more reassuring than frightening, so perhaps James had been right. We need only establish doubt to persuade them no trial was necessary.

"Only a few questions, Miss Bonvivier. Did you often work late for Major Anderson?"

"Five, maybe six times."

"And what did you do on those nights?"

"Filing, taking notes. Whatever Major Anderson required."

"How late did you usually stay?"

"Never later than eight o'clock."

"Could that work have been done during normal working hours?" Colonel Scoffield leaned forward in his chair.

"Yes, sir, most of it could have."

"Was Major Anderson your lover?"

The question took me completely by surprise after the way he had guided me so easily through the first ones. I'm sure that was just what he intended. I knew everyone in the room was waiting for my answer.

"No, sir, he was not."

"Yet, Lieutenant Grimes says he heard you in the bedroom. Were you in the bedroom with Major Anderson?"

"Yes, sir, on that one night only."

"But you say he was not your lover. Would you please explain?"

How much should I tell? How much would he believe? The whole truth, James had said. I looked over at him, and he nodded.

So I repeated again what I had told the lawyer so many times: about the gold, Anderson's threats, and his insistence I become his mistress. Without going into detail, I merely said I had managed to defend myself against his attack and then fled the house.

"Miss Bonvivier," Colonel Scoffield began, "you admit to being threatened with prison if you did not submit, to having defended yourself—by some sort of physical force, I assume—and to getting away. Lieutenant Grimes has told us about the Voodoo charm and conversation he overheard in which Major Anderson insisted you stay late the following week, but with no repetition of what happened the previous night. Can I assume that what he said was correct?"

I nodded.

"So, if we believe Major Anderson was not your lover, and you admit to what Lieutenant Grimes said about the Voodoo and Anderson's further requests, we can only assume you were still intimidated by his threat to accuse you of theft unless you became his mistress. Yet you say you did not kill him."

"No, sir, I did not murder Major Anderson."

"Lieutenant Grimes said you were still there when he left that night."

"He—he is lying, sir."

"Perjury is a very serious offense, Miss Bonvivier. Do you think an officer in the United States Army would run the risk of the punishment such an offense would incur?"

"Nor would I, Colonel Scoffield."

"Not even to save your life? I know this is a delicate matter, but if you admit to being subdued by force—to being raped—on the night of the murder, you can plead self-defense."

"I did not kill Major Anderson. I left soon after five o'clock and I did not return. I was not the last one to leave."

Baptiste could be called to corroborate my story that I had not returned but not that others were still there when I left. So now I knew. It was on my word alone my future would be decided. I turned to look at Baptiste, his face drawn in pity and compassion. How would it have looked if I had lied and said what I knew both James and Colonel Scoffield wanted me to say. One word—*rape*—stood between me and freedom.

There was a sudden, ear-shattering interruption. Perhaps it was only an overly loud knock at the door, but to me it came like a thunderclap on an oppressively still day. After a brief dialogue between the guard and the panel of officers, the door was opened.

I stared in amazement as the most enormous woman I'd ever seen walked into the room. She must have weighed well over three hundred pounds. I had no idea of the woman's age, dressed as she was in ruffles and flounces and with either dyed hair or a wig, but I guessed somewhere between fifty-five and sixty. How the woman maneuvered across the room, I don't know, but she was an impressive figure. She neither panted nor heaved her way as so many obese women do, but churned steadily ahead like an overloaded steamboat.

The presiding officer addressed her. "You are Madame Broulé and you requested permission to appear?"

"Yes, sir. I think I have some important information in this case." Her voice was surprisingly low and well modulated, far from the hoarse, wheezing tones I had expected to emerge from such a huge bosom.

"We'll be glad to hear whatever you have to say. Please sit in the witness chair."

Madame Broulé's deep, jovial laugh started her huge body shaking, from her feet up to her dimpled cheeks. Every ruffle and flounce was set astir, and she held her incongruously tiny hands over her bulging stomach as though in that way she could stop the quaking.

"Sir, if you will look at me and then at the chair, you will see you are asking the impossible. Thank you, but I will stand."

Colonel Scoffield motioned to two of the soldiers on guard duty, requesting they bring in a wooden bench with a slatted back. While this was being done, there were a few minutes of subdued conversation.

James leaned toward me. "Do you know her?"

I shook my head. I turned to look at Baptiste. He was grinning, but whether because of the absurd figure she cut, because he knew her, or because he thought she could help, I had no way of knowing.

"I believe you will find this more comfortable," Colonel Scoffield said, with no change in expression.

Madame Broulé sat down, spreading her enormous girth and ample skirts the width of the bench.

"Now, Madame, if you will, please detail to this panel your information. I may interject a few questions, but we'll hold any cross-examination until you have finished. Please tell us first why you did not come forward sooner."

"I have been in Natchez—on business. I left the day after Major Anderson's death and only returned late last night. It was then I learned from one of my employees about the case, and I realized I had vital information."

"As I understand it," the colonel hesitated a moment, looking for the right words, "you operate a place of—of entertainment."

There was a hint of subdued laughter in the room.

"Yes, sir, I own the finest, most exclusive 'house' in the *Vieux Carré*, in all of New Orleans or Louisiana for that matter. My girls are all carefully handpicked by me."

The half-concealed titters now became genuine laughter, and the colonel sat back smiling, undoubtedly glad for some relief from what had become an almost unbearably oppressive atmosphere. In another minute everyone quieted down enough for him to speak.

"Please go on. I trust there will be no more interruptions."

"As you can see by my size," Madame Broulé smiled, "it's difficult for me to move easily. In the evenings, when business really gets underway, I sit in a chair—especially made for me—by the front window on the second floor. I can see everyone who enters or leaves my place, and also greet every guest as he passes the parlor door on his way to the hospitality room across from it. I never move from that chair from before five until after midnight. You can take my word or ask my doorman who brings up all the guests."

The presiding officer nodded.

"My house is directly across the street from the one commandeered by Federal officers. And oh, what a beautiful house, such a shame when the Leblancs were forced to move out. But I digress. I saw everyone who entered or left the evening of Major Anderson's death."

"And," Colonel Scoffield leaned forward, "I apologize for interrupting, but you are quite certain about that, and about the order of their going and coming?"

"Yes, sir, and I'll explain as I go along."

"Fine. Proceed."

"Beginning with early evening, which I think you are most concerned with, a number of young officers— maybe five or six—came out alone or in pairs. They began leaving about five-thirty. Then Miss Bonvivier left, close to six o'clock, I would judge. I know she left then because it was still daylight, and I admired her beautiful dress and bonnet which I saw very clearly. She walked away at a normal pace, very proud and sure of herself as always. Remember, I was quite familiar with those who were there every day. That is, I didn't know their names, but of course I know hers now."

"But you are certain it was this particular day you are remembering."

"Yes, because I was thinking how beautiful the color she was wearing would look on one of my girls who—who was going with me to Natchez. No one else came out for some time. The lamplighter came by, and I tapped on the window and waved to him. Then these two officers came out." She pointed to Grimes and Taylor, who were sitting at the front of the room. "First one"—she pointed to Taylor "—and then the other—" and she pointed to Grimes. "I saw their faces under the street lamp."

There was again an undercurrent of commentary. This disagreed completely with the testimony they had given.

"Maybe an hour later—I could get the exact time from the appointment book—Major Anderson came out and hurried across the street to my place. He merely nodded as he went by my door. He never came in to speak to me, as the others did, just rushed by very rudely. Came in two or three times a week but never spoke. Stayed less than half an hour. Queer man. Could tell you strange stories."

Like a well-trained chorus, all heads moved forward a few inches, anticipating the details, but Madame Broulé continued her account of the night Anderson met his death.

"But that's neither here nor there. He returned to his office. A light went on in the front room, then out, followed by a light in a back room which stayed on as long as I was by the window. Within another hour it began to rain, just a drizzle, but enough to call it rain. Some time around nine-thirty or ten, a public hansom drove up. A woman stepped out, paid the driver, and indicated for him to go on. I couldn't see her face, but she walked into the house opposite as though she knew exactly where she was going."

There was a hum of conversation which ceased only when Colonel Scoffield frowned.

"She was in there," Madame Broulé continued, "for forty-five minutes to an hour. She came running out, seemingly unaware of the rain—heavier now—but she stopped when she got to the street lamp. She clung to the post. I could see her face clearly, and she was crying hysterically. I started to send someone over to her to see if she needed help, but she got herself under control and started running again until out of my sight. From then on nothing else happened that I could see. I was there until nearly three in the morning because we had a particularly busy night."

"Before I ask either of the lawyers for questions," Colonel Scoffield said, "I wish to pose a few myself. Lieutenant Grimes, please stand up."

Lieutenant Grimes rose and began to speak, but the presiding officer put up a hand. "I'll direct the course of this investigation, if you don't mind. You stated under oath that the defendant was still in the office when you left. Do you wish to change your testimony?"

"Yes, sir. I lied. She left first."

"Just why did you perjure yourself?"

"I was afraid, sir. Afraid I'd be accused if it was learned I had been the last one in the office that night. I knew I hadn't killed Major Anderson."

"So you put this young woman in danger of prosecution for murder to save yourself."

"Well, I figured if she wasn't guilty, there'd be no harm. And she might've come back and done it. I knew she hated Major Anderson, and anyway she's only a—"

"That's enough!" Colonel Scoffield brought his hand down on the table. "You are already guilty of perjury. Don't add contempt of court to the charges. Sit down. I'll sentence you later. Lieutenant Taylor."

"Yes, sir."

"You also said the defendant remained after you left."

"No, sir. I said I did not see her leave. I was in another room. I did not see her leave nor did I see her there when I left."

"I stand corrected. No charges."

During all this, Madame Broulé had been looking calmly around the room. I watched her, wondering just how far the woman's testimony would go toward freeing me. Part of my story had been proved true, but was it enough? Who was the woman who had come later and run away in hysterics? If she were not found or not proved to be the murderer, I knew I could still be accused if it were thought I had come back later. Would Baptiste's word I had not left the house be accepted?

Colonel Scoffield turned once more to Madame Broulé. "Would you recognize the woman who you say came later and left the house if you saw her again?"

"Yes, sir. I don't know who she is, but she'd been to that house several times, so once I saw her face, I knew she was one of the women who visited it frequently."

"You don't know who she is. That makes it difficult. She may already have left town if she is the murderer, or be afraid to come forward if she discovered Major Anderson's body."

"No, sir," Madame Broulé interjected. "She's sitting here in this room."

All eyes followed those of Madame Broulé to Mrs. Anderson. Her face had gone white, in startling contrast to her black dress and widow's veil.

"Are you quite certain of what you are saying, Madame Broulé? That is Major Anderson's widow."

"I didn't know. But she's the woman."

Mrs. Anderson stood up, gripping the back of the chair in front of her, her face still white but contorted with fury. "A whore! You'd believe a whore, accusing me, the widow of an officer in the United States Army."

"Please, Mrs. Anderson," Colonel Scoffield said calmly, "no one is accusing you of anything more than visiting your husband. Certainly there is nothing about that to get you so upset."

"She's implying I killed my husband!" Mrs. Anderson was screaming now. "Trying to save that other whore—that—that woman who calls herself a 'mistress,' who says my husband attacked her. They're all whores, all of them."

Mrs. Anderson had become so hysterical, Colonel Scoffield requested two of his men to hold her before she hurt herself.

"All of them, night after night. He never came home. He laughed at me."

"Mrs. Anderson," Colonel Scoffield asked, in a cajoling but firm tone, "would you like to sit down and tell us all about it?"

Calmer now and seemingly relieved at the opportunity to pour out her frustrations, Mrs. Anderson told the story of that fateful night.

"I went to the office to plead with my husband to come home. I—I wanted to be the wife he desired. He bragged about all his conquests. I didn't know he was paying or forcing them. I went in quietly. The front room was dark, but he was lying asleep, naked, in the bedroom. I begged—yes, I begged—and I pleaded with him to make love to me. But he only laughed, as he always did, and said he'd already had his pleasure for the evening. 'Get out,' he yelled, 'go home and leave me alone. Can't you see you just bother me?'

"I left the room, but went into the kitchen. And I waited until I knew he was asleep again. I stabbed him while he was sleeping. I'm only sorry he didn't know."

Mrs. Anderson fell back in the chair. She was no longer crying, only waiting passively for what would come next.

Poor woman, I thought, maybe if she'd threatened

him sooner, instead of pleading with him, her husband would have found her more desirable. He liked his women to fight him, he'd said, to resist him.

"Miss Bonvivier," Colonel Scoffield addressed me. "You are free to go, and we apologize for all you've been through."

Suddenly the whole room was crowding around me, and I was laughing and crying at the same time. Baptiste remained seated, waiting for me to come to him.

"Hey, Baptiste!" Madame Broulé's voice rang out when she saw him still sitting on the bench. "Haven't seen you in many years. Why you stay away so long?"

Baptiste first looked embarrassed, then threw back his head and laughed. "You can look at Leah and still ask that question? You crazy or something?"

Chapter Thirty-one

I STEELED MYSELF TO EXPECT . . . I didn't know what when Baptiste and I were alone later that night. Rejection because of what he'd learned that day? To reject him unwillingly myself because of what I'd been through in prison?

James and Mr. Delisle had insisted on taking us to dinner to celebrate. Knowing the murder of Anderson and the subsequent hearing were receiving an inordinate amount of notoriety, they reserved a private upstairs room at one of the city's finest restaurants. I appreciated their consideration. I was not ready to come out of complete isolation into a crowded world of people.

The dinner was more elegant than any I'd seen since before the war. Bouillabaisse, crayfish bisque, lobster and shrimp casserole, delicately broiled birds, spiced fruit compote, fresh vegetables, and tiny almond cakes. All accompanied by the finest wines and hot *café au lait*. With the first sip of the bouillabaisse, my stomach began to churn, and I had to swallow hard to keep down the sickening waves of nausea. It was my first meal in the cell all over again. Having learned to tolerate scant, greasy prison fare, now I could not swallow the highly seasoned or delicately flavored dishes set before me. I would be better off with our bland wartime diet as an interim regimen.

Knowing James and Mr. Delisle had meant the evening to be one of gaiety and celebration, I did my best to eat a little of everything served. By the end of the meal, the nausea had subsided somewhat with help from the wine and coffee.

Baptiste sat close and kept my hand in his, but refrained from asking the questions I dreaded. Neither of us said much; just being together was all we required for the time being, but the two lawyers kept the evening light with easy banter and a never-ending store of tales about humorous courtroom incidents. As close as I was to tears of relief, it was good to be able to laugh. The wrong word, any expression of sympathy, and I would have started crying.

"You look tired, Leah," James said. "I think we ought to bring the celebration to an end."

"I am tired. I feel as though I could fall asleep right here if I put my head down on the table. Thank you for a wonderful evening. I really appreciate it."

"You say you're going back to Indiana soon, James?" Baptiste asked.

"In a few days. I have reservations on a paddle-wheeler up the Mississippi to the Ohio and to Louisville, then overland to Indiana. It's a beautiful, leisurely trip. I took it down, and I don't know when I've felt so relaxed."

"Leah's always dreamed of going by steamboat up the Mississippi," Baptiste said. "I've been several times, and I once promised her we'd make the trip."

"Well, then, you must come on up the Ohio, too, and visit me. My home is only a hundred miles from Louisville, and there are good train connections. I'd love to show you our part of the country." He spoke to Baptiste, but he looked directly at me the whole time. "I want you to know that not all Northerners are damn Yankees."

"No, we've learned that already, thanks to you," Baptiste said. "In a year or two, when things are finally underway on the plantation, we'll accept your invitation."

I was tired, but I dreaded the moment when Baptiste and I would be alone. My nerves were too raw to be exposed to the touch of words or flesh. They needed a protective gauze of silence and distance.

Baptiste was sitting on the edge of the bed. He had already removed his shirt and trousers. I had not yet begun to undress.

"Leah, would you prefer sleeping in the other room tonight? I'd understand if you did."

"I don't know. I feel so terribly lonely, and yet I've grown used to being alone. I seem to want to find another cell and crawl in. I don't suppose you can really understand what I mean."

"No, but I know what it's like being afraid of getting too close to someone you love. You're afraid of revealing too much of yourself, of letting loose something you should keep hidden inside and then not being able to get it back. The wounds are still too new, aren't they? They'll heal, but it'll take time."

"Thank you, Baptiste. No, I don't want to sleep alone. But I don't want—I mean, can you just hold me close without asking any more?"

"I'll put my sabre between us."

"What?"

"It's an old custom, a guarantee I won't betray your honor. Ah, you're smiling. That's what I wanted to see."

Baptiste reached up and pulled me down to sit beside him on the bed. His gentle touch began to disintegrate slowly the protective cocoon I had spun around myself.

"Cherie, I know you suffered the tortures of the damned in that prison, but I will never ask you any questions about it. All that matters now is you are home."

With that I broke down completely. With Baptiste's comforting arms around me, I wept without shame and then sobbed out much of what I had endured during those weeks. The worst, the brutal violations by the guard, would remain my secret. The memory of those nights would forever haunt me, but as long as I never saw its specter reflected in Baptiste's eyes, I could live with it.

Baptiste's healing love flowed around and through me like a refreshing stream cleansing the internal wounds and soothing the external fatigue. Not until the next day did we talk about such concerns as the plantation and the plans that had so engrossed us before my arrest.

"I have a surprise for you, Cherie," Baptiste said at breakfast.

"A good one from the smile on your face."

"I was very busy during these past weeks. Once Delisle and Andrews insisted they would take care of everything, I had to find something to do to keep from going crazy. Of course, if I'd known—if we'd known —what you were going through! It was days before we could even learn why you had been arrested. And over and over the officials assured us you were being well cared for but could not be seen. Oh, God, Leah, I would have burned down the prison or forced my way in."

"Please, Baptiste, it's over. We said we'd never speak of it again."

"I'm sorry. Anyway, I thought the one thing I could do was go ahead with with getting the plantation ready for us to move out as soon as you were free. No matter how long it went on, I never doubted for an instant they'd find you innocent."

"You had more faith than I."

"Well, I knew you were innocent, so I felt sure the evidence would prove it."

"The evidence came mighty close to doing just the opposite," I sighed. "We might have shown reasonable doubt, as James said, but if it hadn't been for Madame Broulé—" I shuddered. "I think I should go round and thank her."

"If you like. I'd like to go myself and see her again."

"Again? Oh, that's right; she said she hadn't seen

you in a long time. You must have been a frequent visitor." I tried to frown my disapproval, but could only smile at the chagrined look on Baptiste's face.

"I and every other young Creole blade. It's another old French custom, my dear, for fathers to initiate their sons by enlisting the aid of an older, experienced woman. It makes things much more pleasant and less embarrassing on the wedding night. It is also supposed to keep intact the honor of young Creole ladies who might otherwise be seduced by a too ardent swain. When an evening of close contact with charming females in low-cut dresses begins to get to him, he can always relieve the pressure at Madame Broulé's. Such a custom has many advantages."

"And ones you were not averse to appreciating, I gather."

"Nor you, my dear. You must admit, I am more than just an adequate lover."

"So," I said, "I have much to thank Madame Broulé for."

"Saving your life will be sufficient."

"Now, since I've received my lesson for the day in French customs, what about the surprise?"

"The plantation is already under cultivation. More than enough former slaves applied when I advertised. The cane buildings have been restored, the fields planted, and the gardens as well."

"Oh, Baptiste, that's wonderful news."

"But there's more. The house is ready for us to move in."

"How? How did you manage it all? Has this house been sold? Where did you get the furniture? And the money for all of it? And how were you able to pay Andrews?"

"Whoa, one at a time. First, James Andrews refused to take any money. He said he didn't need it, and he was glad to get back into harness after months away from his office. He told you about his wife's death?"

I nodded.

"Well, he said the case was the kind of challenge he likes. And he absolutely wouldn't hear of being paid. Neither this house nor the furniture has been sold. We can keep it for a town house, which could later be very handy, or sell it, just as you wish. We can decide that later. But it brings me to the second surprise. I received a very considerable inheritance from my maternal grandmother in Virginia, where, as you know, my mother and father went during the war. Actually, she outlived them both, was over ninety when she died. There were only two heirs, a cousin I haven't seen in years and myself. Her estate—a house, several buildings, and hundreds of acres—was sold. Unfortunately to a Yankee, but they're the only ones with money now, and it brought a substantial sum. So financially we are now very well off."

"I can't believe it. After all our worrying and plotting to scrape together a bit here and a bit there."

"But without that plotting we might not have held on long enough for the inheritance to benefit us, not with the plantation, anyway. And you did that, Leah."

"Not alone. You say the house is all furnished?"

"That was Catherine's idea."

"Catherine?"

"Pierre Delisle's sister. A widow. Her husband, David Fouché, was killed at Shiloh. We grew up together on nearby plantations, so she knew the house well. She carried out all the ideas we had: the parlor and bedroom on the first floor; even the kitchen you wanted there. Except you do have a stove and won't have to cook in the fireplace. She found just the right furniture, and drove out almost every day to make sure it was arranged properly. I could never have done it without her."

"It sounds wonderful, Baptiste." But inside I was crying. Someone else had selected what I had looked forward to choosing, had arranged them to her liking. Would Baptiste be displeased or think me ungrateful if I wanted to make some changes?

"Just as soon as you feel up to it, Cherie, we'll drive out there and make plans for moving. Leah, I never go in there now without seeing you in every room as you were the day we were there. If it weren't for you, I wouldn't have the plantation, and you're going to grace it like a queen. I wanted it to be perfect for you."

I was wrong to be ungrateful. Like any man, he'd turned to a woman to help in ways only a woman could. After all, he'd known Catherine Fouché all his life. I must not begin to imagine ghosts that did not exist.

Later that morning I sent a note around to Madame Broulé asking if we might visit her sometime during the day, and received the reply that she would be delighted to see us at five o'clock.

Once we were well away from the hearing and seated at dinner, both Pierre Delisle and James admitted that without Madame Broulé's unexpected appearance, the chances of my being found innocent were almost nil. In spite of Colonel Scoffield's obvious sympathy for my cause, the evidence was too damning for him not to order a trial. From the trial, the least I could have expected was life imprisonment, and more likely I would be hanged. Having experienced prison life, death would have been preferable. I would have sought it at first opportunity.

So our call was to thank Madame Broulé for literally saving my life, but I was also titillated at the prospect of seeing the inside of a high-class bordello. Her house was one of the most elegant on a street of imposing three- and four-story homes that once belonged to the élite of *Vieux Carré* society. From the outside no one would have recognized it for anything but a private home. Its French-style façade and intricate wrought-iron balconies bespoke conservative wealth.

An elderly, liveried Negro opened the double doors for us, said the madame was waiting, and indicated we should follow him up the free-standing circular staircase. Seeing the large, beautifully appointed rooms opening off the hall, I wondered at her choice of an upstairs room for herself. Surely it must be difficult for her to climb those stairs every day. Then I remembered that she spoke of constantly watching the street, and I realized she was a woman whose greatest pleasure was satisfying her curiosity about what went on in the streets outside. I owed my life to that insatiable curiosity. At the top of the stairs we were ushered through a wide, velvet-portiered archway into Madame Broulé's room. She was seated, as I'd pictured her, by the front window in the oversized chair she'd had especially made for her. Her afternoon tea gown of lavender velvet was simplicity itself, much more becoming than the gaudy dress she'd worn to the hearing. I wondered if she'd cunningly chosen the latter for the effect it would create when she walked in.

The remainder of the room was in startling contrast to her and the chair she sat in. A delicately carved Empire couch and two chairs were upholstered in hand-worked petit point. Gilt and white side chairs with cut velvet seats and backs flanked a pink marble fireplace. A magnificent Aubusson rug covered most of the parquet floor. Watteau and Fragonard prints along with Sèvres accessories carried out the fragile pastel motif of the room. From where I stood, I looked into an adjoining bedroom, dominated by a huge, oversized tester bed with hangings of fine lace.

Across the wide hall was a drawing room which was undoubtedly the hospitality room she had referred to. Unlike her personal suite, it was a profusion of red velvet hangings, huge gilt mirrors, plush couches—no single-occupant chairs—and crystal chandeliers. In one corner was a carved mahogany bar. In every room, there were bouquets of fresh flowers.

Madame Broulé asked us to sit down and pull our chairs closer to hers. We had no sooner gotten settled than the liveried servant brought a tray with a selection of liqueurs, and our hostess served us herself.

"Now," she said with no polite preamble, "what brings you here?"

"To say thank you, Madame Broulé. Without your testimony there was no way I could prove my innocence."

Unlike most obese women whose eyes are obscured by swollen lids and puffy cheeks, hers were large and of a deep, brilliant green. They twinkled with secret glee as she looked at me.

"Or to take the opportunity to see what a bawdy house looks like?" she asked.

She knew immediately from my reddening cheeks she had hit the mark.

"Well," she laughed, "Does it look like what you imagined?"

"It's—it's a very beautiful home."

Baptiste was grinning at my discomfort but said nothing to help me out. Just wait, I thought, 'til we return home. You'll get yours then.

"And I worked damn hard for it. I put in my apprenticeship on a pleasure boat moored at Natchez. You ever been to Natchez?"

I shook my head.

"It has the best and the worst, and the worst is really the dregs. I wouldn't think of telling you what goes on in some of those places. I was sold by my parents when I was twelve. Does that shock you?" She had seen the startled expression I couldn't hide. "It shouldn't, honey. It's done all the time. There were eight younger than me at home, and a nubile virgin brought in good money. I thought I was going to be the madame's personal maid; so I'd been told. I was as ignorant as a baby about life. You any idea what happened the first night?"

Again I shook my head, too bewildered to say a word. I had thought the quadroon balls were cruel affairs.

"I was strapped to the bed so I couldn't try to escape or resist and given a whiff of chloroform to ease the pain and subdue my screams. Not all girls are even that fortunate. To assure I wouldn't upset the man by crying out, a cloth was available for him to stuff in my mouth once he'd finished working himself up and was ready to get down to business. He had paid plenty for the privilege of deflowering a virgin, and he had the right to use me as he desired for an entire night. Believe me, he got his money's worth. But he also taught me a lot.

"I stayed on that boat three years. My share of the proceeds were meager, but I saved every cent. During that time I learned two things that changed the whole course of my life: how to be the most expensive girl in the establishment, and that I was determined to have a house of my own. It would be the finest, most exclusive place in Louisiana.

"When I was fifteen, I ran away. Knowing I would be reported to the police and there'd be a search, I fled to Europe. Steerage in that direction was far less crowded and more pleasant than for those coming over here. I had taken my whole wardrobe with me, and before long I was getting invitations to entertain fine gentlemen in the first-class section. They often amused themselves by watching us when we were allowed on deck for air and exercise. And believe me, I took advantage of their watching me. So I landed in England with a larger bankroll than I'd had before I bought my passage.

"For a year I did just what I had originally thought I would be doing—I worked as a personal maid to a wealthy American widow in England who was out to capture an impoverished duke or lord. She was hoping for the first, but finally settled for the second. Again I began saving my money. More important, I learned what I needed to know about being an elegant hostess and running a large house. How to furnish it, what to eat, the etiquette of serving meals. Also I traded my gutter speech for proper English.

"At sixteen I opened my own house in London, recruiting girls from the poorest level' of the working classes. It was not the fine establishment I'd envisioned, but it was a beginning, and it allowed me to build up my bank account.

"From then on I moved steadily upward, and finally came to New Orleans. Along the way I purchased fine pieces of furniture whenever I saw something I liked, and I married M'sieu Broulé. I was young and beautiful then, though you might not believe it now. It was a true marriage of love. When he died, I assuaged my grief with food."

She laughed and her eyes twinkled again. "Some women fade away when they go into mourning. I just began to get fatter and fatter, but my years of needing an appealing figure were behind me, so food became my substitute for love."

She refilled her glass and reached for a benne cake.

"Yes, I need beauty around me, and my girls deserve the best I can give them. I'm a demanding mistress, and they work hard for me. They are also well paid. No stingy ten percent for them. You won't see them, though. They're resting, and I don't parade them like monkeys in a zoo. If they're invited for a ride or to the opera, they're free to go, but I don't advertise by sending them out in carriages to attract customers.

"Now," she said bluntly, "has your curiosity been satisfied?"

"Please, Madame Broulé," I insisted, "we really did come here to thank you."

Her face wrinkled with smiles. "I know you did, honey. I was just teasing. I appreciate it. You probably shouldn't have come here. There'll be all sorts of gossip."

"We owe you too great a debt," Baptiste said, "to care what people think. It's a debt we can never repay."

"I'm sure," I added, "you put yourself in danger of prosecution by coming to my defense. Aren't there new laws?"

She started laughing again as she had at the hearing when Colonel Scoffield suggested she sit in the chair.

"Honey, those laws don't worry me. I know enough officials well, too well, for them to harm me. I keep records, and they know it. No, I was perfectly safe. I wasn't going to let an innocent young woman be punished for killing a man I knew to be more evil than the devil himself. Now, I'll tell you a secret but if you ever repeat it, I'll deny it. However, I don't think you will.

"I lied, Leah, about seeing you come out of the house across the way. I didn't, but I had watched you often enough to feel I knew the kind of person you are. If you said you'd left before the two officers, you were telling the truth. Now, I did see them as the last ones to leave—of the men I mean—but you could have been still in the house, for all I knew."

I gasped. She had perjured herself to save me.

"As I said, I saw the men leave, and I saw Mrs. Anderson. But if I'd figured it wrong, if she'd said she went in and found her husband already dead, the fat would've been in the fire."

"Bon Dieu!" Baptiste said. "You cut it pretty close."

"Don't think I wasn't holding my breath when I saw her sitting in the room. But I knew then it had to be her or one of the officers, and all we needed was to have one of them break down."

"There's no way I can thank you for such faith in me."

"Honey, if I'd figured you wrong, after all these years of appraising young women and trusting my judgment, I'd have been ready to close up anyway."

We refused her offer of another drink, and she rang the bell for her servant.

"Time for you to go," she said. "Can't have you here when the customers begin to arrive. My reputation rests on my being able to protect their good names."

"What do you mean protect their names," Baptiste

challenged, "after what you said to me after the hearing?"

"You're an exception, Baptiste. But then, you're an exception to everything. Now go along. It was good of you to come, but I won't invite you back."

The next morning I went shopping at the Market for the first time in weeks. My purse was full, and I could buy whatever struck my fancy. I would cook Baptiste's favorites all afternoon, and we'd dine lavishly that night. When I returned home, Baptiste said a messenger had come from James Andrews asking if I would meet him for lunch at one o'clock.

"What do you suppose he wants? Asking just me, I mean."

"Probably wants to say good-bye. After all, he did spend a lot of time with you. He scarcely knows me."

"You wouldn't mind?"

"Not at all, Cherie. You owe him that much."

Chapter Thirty-two

JAMES STOOD UP as I walked through the gate into the garden restaurant. Above the small table he'd chosen for us, the swaying branches of a dogwood formed a sheltering canopy. There were no more than a dozen tables in the flagstoned court.

"Thank you for coming, Leah."

"I'm glad for the chance to see you once more before you leave."

"I can't get over how rested you look."

"It must be the new dress. Baptiste insisted I buy the prettiest one I could find."

"You should wear pastels. I see I made a mistake in buying gray." He rested his pipe on the table.

"No, it was right for the time. I looked just like I felt—a mouse in a trap."

"I waited to order," James said. "So tell me. What's the best New Orleans offers?"

"They're famous here for crawfish bisque, delicately flavored with sherry. Then perhaps shrimp with herb dressing and hot croissants."

"So be it. That's what we'll have." He signaled to the waiter.

Once he'd ordered, a strained silence enveloped us. We would probably never see each other again, in spite of his invitation to visit Indiana, and there seemed to be nothing left to say.

"Are you still leaving tomorrow?" I asked. A stupid question, but I had to dispel the embarrassing silence.

"No, I've postponed going for a week."

"Oh, really? Any particular reason?"

"Yes, a very important one."

The waiter brought the soup, and we busied ourselves talking about how it was made and how good it tasted. Once the shrimp was served, I felt more at ease, but completely unprepared for James's next words.

"I love you, Leah."

"Oh, no."

"I want you to marry me and go back to Indiana with me."

"Please, James, I wish you hadn't said that."

"Why not?"

"Because as much as I admire and respect you, I don't love you." Why was I haunted by a ghostly voice from the past reminding me I had once wanted to live as wife to a man I could respect?

"I know that," James said quietly. "I'm not asking you to love me. But I promise I'll do everything in my power to make you happy. I know about your dream of going North to pass."

"But—"

"As my wife, Leah, your past would never be questioned. You'd be accepted as you've always wanted to be."

"Have you forgotten I belong to Baptiste?"

"As a mistress, Leah, not wife."

"No, you don't understand. He loves me."

"I know he loves you. For that reason he'll understand if you choose to go with me. I love you, too."

"He needs me, James. You know how dependent he is on me." I was groping for words, any words, to cover my confusion.

"Are you sure? Or have you encouraged that dependency?"

I paused to think. Perhaps I had unconsciously kept Baptiste dependent on me to assure he didn't leave. Considering our circumstances, however, it didn't really matter.

"There's something you need to know," I said. "I'm pregnant. I'm carrying Baptiste's child."

"I see."

Yes, I thought, that does make a difference. You want me, but not another man's child.

"Does he know?" James asked.

"No. I was going to tell him the night I was arrested. Somehow, I haven't been able to since I came home."

"You know why, don't you?"

"No."

"Because you knew I'd fallen in love with you."

"No, that's not true," I insisted.

"And you feel something for me, too."

"It was the trial and what I'd gone through. Nothing more."

"You said Baptiste loves you. You didn't say you love him."

"But I do, I truly do. And now I'm going to have his child."

"If you marry me, Leah, the child will be mine. No one need know when we were married."

"You're kind, James, but I wonder if the time mightn't come when you'd be sorry. You'll always know whose child he is."

"He's yours, Leah. That's all that matters to me. What do I have to say to convince you I love you—and persuade you to come with me?"

"I would never fit your way of life. I—I've lived in the *Vieux Carré* too long."

"But you've always wanted to go north. Now I'm giving you that chance. You have more than half your life ahead of you, and it can be the life you've dreamed about. Don't give that up. If you don't love me, at least let me make that dream come true."

"You sound as though you're offering me the world on a silver platter, James."

"I wish I could, Leah. I love saying your name. It's a beautiful name." He reached over and took both my hands. "All I'm offering you is a small house on about four acres of land. Just outside a town less than half the size of the *Vieux Carré*. Two churches, a town square where cows still graze sometimes." James laughed. "Maybe I'm painting too bucolic a scene for you."

"It sounds beautiful. Very peaceful." I didn't resist when he lifted my hands to his lips. "But what would your friends think? Your marrying a—a Southerner?"

"They'd think I'm the luckiest man in the world to have you."

James said nothing when I slipped my hands out of his and picked up my coffee. As I knew he would, he pulled out his pipe and tobacco pouch, spilled several shreds on his shirtfront, used three matches to light up, and finally sat back puffing energetically. His knuckles were white as they gripped the bowl. I was not alone in feeling tense at that moment.

"No, James. I have to remain in New Orleans. My roots go too deep. My son was born here and is buried here. It's true I once longed to go north, but some dreams are not meant to come true. You think you love me. Maybe you really do. But there is too much about us that is different. I don't mean color; that's least important. I was not reared to be a small-town wife, to attend teas and church socials, organize charity bazaars. I would be unhappy, and soon we'd both be miserable. Remember me kindly, James, because I'll never forget you."

"Leah, give yourself time. Think it over. I startled you. I'm sorry. I was sure you knew how I felt. Don't give me your final answer now. I'll be at the hotel until the end of the week."

"I'll promise you this, James. I—I'll be in touch before you leave."

"Until you do, I'll keep hoping. I love you, and I don't want to leave without you."

As I look back on the five days following that luncheon, I'm amazed at the serenity with which I moved through them, considering I was facing the most important decision of my life.

When I left James, I had no thought but that the decision had been made, and I had no intention of carrying out my promise to see him again before he left. Although not in love with him, I was fond of him and found him very attractive; but I knew my feelings sprang from the situation I was in prior to the trial. Time would loosen those ties. Time, Baptiste's love, and the new life within me. James would soon be only a memory.

Baptiste and I began sorting through all the things we planned to carry to the plantation or leave behind.

"Leah, do you want to decide on any of the furniture now or wait until you see what we'll need?"

"Let's wait. There are some pieces I'd like to have with me, but no point in taking others we'd only bring back. If we do keep the house here, we don't want to strip it."

"Thought the same thing. How about these old clothes of mine?"

"Throw them out! Or give them away. I'm glad Pierre Delisle talked you into going to the tailor for new ones."

"Not Pierre, Catherine."

"Oh!"

"Her taste is better than Pierre's. Drove me over for each fitting. I could never have done it without her."

"She certainly devoted a lot of her time to you while I was in prison."

"Catherine is an old and dear friend."

I did not tell Baptiste about the baby.

Two days after the luncheon I was shopping at the Market when I saw James. He was not there by accident.

"I knew you'd be here, Leah. I had to see you again. Can't we have some coffee?"

For the next three days I met him every morning at

the *Café du Monde*, and gradually I learned more and more about the man who wanted to marry me.

"I'm a simple man, Leah. After riding the circuit, I like to come home to a hearty meal, then take off my shoes and relax with a pipe in front of the fire. Or in the summer, putter about the garden. Small vegetable garden. A few flowers. Also a cat and several dogs. Such a life isn't very exciting, is it?"

"No, but no one wants excitement all the time." Somehow I knew he would have dogs.

"We do have chautauqua. Orators and musical groups. Sometimes even a troupe of players. They come to a bigger town, only ten miles away."

"I've never heard a famous speaker."

"Heard Stephen Douglas once. Not in one of his famous debates with Lincoln, but he was powerful. Also the Booths in Shakespeare. Too bad Edwin has to stay off the stage because of what his brother did."

"Yes, I saw them, too." I smiled, remembering the night Baptiste gave me the pearls.

Another morning, in spite of my protests, he insisted on telling me about his marriage to a woman who had been an invalid most of their years together.

"I was never unfaithful to her, Leah, but now I want a real marriage with—with love and children. I want you."

James was handsome in a distinctive, rough-hewn way, masculine and authoritative, honest and ingenuous. It was hard not to love him. With the years of mourning over, many war widows were carefully putting away their black veils. He would not be a widower long.

Later the same day, Baptiste and I rode to the plantation in our own buggy. All was ready for us to move in whenever I wanted. I walked from room to room. Baptiste had been right; Catherine had excellent taste. I could not help but wonder if, as she selected and arranged each piece, she had seen herself in the parlor, the kitchen, and the bedroom in the role of Baptiste's wife. With its large open rooms and broad verandahs, the house was built for entertaining. Baptiste had reveled in a gay social life before the war, but there could be no Christmas house parties or three-day hunting parties if I lived there as his mistress.

Looking across the sweep of lawn to the Mississippi, I envisioned children playing and watching the once-more busy river. Would Baptiste want children of our love or legitimate sons to bear his name? His was a proud old New Orleans family. Dare I be the one to write finis to the family name?

"Leah!"

I turned and went inside. Baptiste was standing by the window in the bedroom. "Lock the door," he commanded gently. "Remember," he asked, "the day we came out here just a few short months ago?"

"I remember."

"And you said you felt as though you were coming home? You are home now. This is where we belong, Cherie. We'll have those babies you want and when they're grown up, we'll let them take over while we rock on the verandah and watch the boats on the river. You're not sorry you let me plan your life for you?"

"No, Baptiste, never."

"We've had rough days, Cherie, but they're behind us now. I meant it that night when I drank to us. There may not be diamonds and amethysts for a while, but it looks like a good cane crop, and we'll do more than survive."

His arms reached out for me, and he kissed me as he had the night I became his *placée*. As I lay beside him, I knew that, no matter what, I would always love him. But was love enough for either of us?

I walked over to Jackson Square. All around me were sounds from the levees, children playing in the park, people on their way to market, worshipers leaving the cathedral, horses clattering on the cobbled streets, sellers on the banquettes hawking their wares, the bells pealing in the cathedral tower. This was the *Vieux Carré*. I had always thought of it as my home, but was it where I really belonged?

I had procrastinated long enough. James was leaving in two days, and I could not in good conscience make him wait any longer for his answer.

I picked a bouquet of late-spring flowers, walked the paths where I had often run as a child, and sat on a favorite bench.

I looked past the cathedral toward the theatre where I'd attended quadroon balls. There I first met both Baptiste and Charles Anderson who, with the vagaries of fate, had put me on a collision course with death and brought James Andrews into my life.

Although I did not love James, I knew marriage to him would be the fulfillment of a dream I had long since thought to be forever denied me. Life with him would be pleasant and comfortable, if not exciting, and I knew I could be happy. He wanted a normal marriage, with love and children, all of which had a certain attraction for me. I had no reason to doubt his sincerity when he declared he loved me and asked me to be his wife. On the other hand, I was just as certain many women would be attracted to him, and he could meet someone else who would love him and make him a good wife. Once on the steamboat, he would soon forget about me. Nor would he ever be haunted by the secret fear that someone might reveal my heritage and color.

And Baptiste. Our love, born of rapture and nourished by mutual need, had survived the travails of death, war's turmoils, and privations. He would be hurt if I married James, but if I left, he would be free to marry someone like Catherine Delisle Fouché and have sons to carry on his name. Marie Louise had escaped from Natchez prior to its capture by the Union, and she had fled to Richmond. For some reason, she had then made her way to Washington and was often seen in the company of a colonel on Lincoln's staff. It was there she had died of diphtheria. Perhaps the knowledge that Baptiste could now marry someone who really loved him would make my decision easier.

I must not remember our days and nights together, the way his lips brushed against my hair before he gathered me into his arms, the long, lonely times when we were apart, or the child I was carrying.

The child. In New Orleans, he or she—maybe a little girl with Baptiste's dimples and my eyes—would grow up free to run through the cane fields, play on the grassy lawn, lie on the river bank, and in imagination sail up and down the great Mississippi. He would be educated in France, and perhaps inherit the plantation. He would be adored by his father, but he would be illegitimate.

In Indiana, he would live in a small town, play on a village green where cows occasionally grazed, and perhaps dream of being a lawyer or doctor. He could go east to one of the best universities as James had done and return to establish his own business or profession. He would be loved by a foster father, and he would be legitimate.

Suddenly I knew why I'd been unable to reach a conclusion: I had been concerned with the needs of everyone but myself. I had left myself out—not as prospective wife, mother, or mistress, but as me, a person.

I had been responsive to the needs and desires of others for so long, I had scarcely considered my own. This time I would, and the problem was simplified. Did I want to be mistress to the man I loved or wife to a man I could learn to love? I was aware that whatever my decision, there would be moments of wondering about what might have been, but I would never let myself be destroyed by regrets.

The cathedral bells chimed the hour, and a steamboat, with two blasts from its twin stacks, announced it was ready to start churning upriver. It was less than three hours until sunset, little enough time to choose the man I wanted to spend the rest of my life with.